An American Soldier

Dreams of a Child

Warren Reiten

Copyright © 2005 by Warren Reiten

All rights reserved. No part of this book shall be reproduced or transmitted in any form or by any means, electronic, mechanical, magnetic, photographic including photocopying, recording or by any information storage and retrieval system, without prior written permission of the publisher. No patent liability is assumed with respect to the use of the information contained herein. Although every precaution has been taken in the preparation of this book, the publisher and author assume no responsibility for errors or omissions. Neither is any liability assumed for damages resulting from the use of the information contained herein.

This is a work of fiction. Names, characters, places, and incidents either are the product of the author's imagination or are used fictitiously. Any resemblance to actual events or locales or persons, living or dead, is entirely coincidental.

ISBN 0-7414-2809-1

Published by:

INFI∞ITY
PUBLISHING.COM

1094 New DeHaven Street, Suite 100
West Conshohocken, PA 19428-2713
Info@buybooksontheweb.com
www.buybooksontheweb.com
Toll-free (877) BUY BOOK
Local Phone (610) 941-9999
Fax (610) 941-9959

Printed in the United States of America
Printed on Recycled Paper
Published December 2005

This book is dedicated to my mother and father for their guidance in my life;

to Tom and Laura Joyner for their fifteen years of encouragement in developing this story;

to Steve Smirnoff for his belief in the value of this story;

and to Nancy for her tenacity in getting this story published.

Warren Reiten

AN AMERICAN SOLDIER
(Novel chapters)

Chapter One	Dreams of a Child	1
Chapter Two	A "New" Soldier Emerges	9
Chapter Three	The Junior Officer Corps	17
Chapter Four	Hooten Plantation Massacre	28
Chapter Five	A New Era Begins	37
Chapter Six	Destiny Calls	65
Chapter Seven	Out West – A New War Brews (Lone Wolf's Saga)	73
Chapter Eight	Merging with Destiny (What Price, My Son, Do You Pay for Glory?)	85
Chapter Nine	The Strong Young Men	110
Chapter Ten	An Officer and a Gentleman (A Code of Conduct)	124
Chapter Eleven	"Shorty" – A Young Recruit	159
Chapter Twelve	Mud on Face	168
Chapter Thirteen	The Dream Continues	175
Chapter Fourteen	Head'n West	183
Chapter Fifteen	Patrol Detail	194
Chapter Sixteen	The Death Dance	210
Chapter Seventeen	A New Patrol Concept	216
Chapter Eighteen	Ambush at the Arikara	236
	Day one…	238
	Day two…	247
	Day three…	250
	Day four…	251
	Day five…	253
	Day six…	257
	Day seven…	259
	Day eight…	264

	Day nine…	267
	Day ten…	274
Chapter Nineteen	A Sad Goodbye	286
Chapter Twenty	Wallace City Saloon	297
Chapter Twenty-one	The Bonding	301
Chapter Twenty-two	A Night to Remember	313
Chapter Twenty-three	American Justice	324
Chapter Twenty-four	Mexico – A New Life	341
Chapter Twenty-five	Caught in a Revolution	357
Chapter Twenty-six	El Presidente's Commitment	381
Chapter Twenty-seven	Mortal Consciousness	388

CHAPTER ONE
DREAMS OF A CHILD

In the eyes of a child there is hope and faith in the future: Hope that his dreams will come true and faith in those who will guide him. Such is the case of Henry Washington.

THE BEGINNING

The year is 1860. A dark political cloud hangs over America.ABraham Lincoln is elected President of the United States, and the South secedes from the Union. Paramount to this internal strife is slavery in the new territories and the abolitionist movement.

Lincoln's inaugural address emphasizes his determination to save the Union. To emphasize this point he states emphatically, "Physically speaking, we as a country cannot separate."

With regard to the South's seceding, a most pressing problem for the President is what to do about the Federal property in the Confederacy. The answer comes quickly as Confederate artillery bombards Fort Sumter in Charleston, South Carolina. Lincoln then declares war on the South. This is the beginning of five bloody years of war with brother against brother.

But these issues are of no concern to young Henry Washington as he hides in the tall grass behind his parent's slave shack. He is dealing with major issues of his own. At six years old, he and several other children are playing a serious game called "the Blue and the Gray."

Each child carries his own weapon made out of tree branches or a piece of scrap wood. There isn't much to their uniforms other than a pair of old pants, but they have enthusiasm and there is no doubt in Henry's mind whose side he is on.

"Bam! Bam! You's dead, Johnny Reb!" Henry exclaims, as he runs from the grass to hide behind an old, run-down log cabin. Shouting as he runs gives him both the offensive and defensive military maneuvering he wants. The battle is getting intense now as the children begin firing at each other from different vantage points. "Shots" are flying in all directions and the noise is deafening…Bam! Bam! Bam!

But as in all battles there comes a time to cease fire and as usual it is directed from a higher authority.

"You chillun stop dat now, and Henry, you git in here," yells Henry's mother, Laura, an attractive, slim, Black woman in her early twenties. It is obvious to the children that she is upset as she stands on the porch of the slave shack with her hands on her hips. Her voice carries strong and firm and she has that look on her face that Henry has seen more than once. Henry and his friends are used to minding grownups as they see "minding" take place on the plantation every day. But on this day there is a streak of defiance in Henry's soul that even his mother will never understand.

"I's a com'n, Ma," he yells as he gives a farewell look to his friends and slowly walks to the cabin kicking up dirt puffs on the way. This was the first time Henry immersed himself into the deep thoughts of a child. "What would it be like to be a real soldier," he wonders? But his thought process is suddenly interrupted by the reality of the situation.

"Don't you be play'n dat game, ya' hear? I's gonna tell yo' Pa," his mother scolds.

"But, Ma," Henry begins, only to be immediately interrupted by his angry mother.

"Know yo' place, boy! We's slaves! Massah Hooten won't take kindly to young'uns play'n Union soldiers!"

Henry looks to his mother, his eyes wide with determination and purpose. His child-like, high-pitched voice responds immediately with conviction, "I's gonna be a Union soldier when I gets big!"

THE REALITY CONCEPT

Far from the mind of a child there is another game taking place, an adult version of "the Blue and the Gray." Their rifles are real, as are the bullets they fire. The dead are not playing, and they do not come back to life to have a sandwich and a glass of milk. The red color on their shirt and pants is not catsup or red berries. There is no bed to crawl into at night and dream dreams of glory ... "when I get big."

There is only the reality of the experience of war. And the memories of those who have died live in the memories of those who have survived. Many families will never see their loved ones again, or at least not see them as they once were before the gruesome experience of battle. This adult game called the Civil War, will forever affect the lives of millions of men, women, and children. Henry Washington's life was no exception.

SETTING THE STAGE

The first two years of the Civil War are generally disastrous for the Union. Although neither side originally anticipated much of a conflict, the battlefields are already strewn with tens of thousands of dead soldiers, a hundred thousand or more maimed and wounded, mentally as well as physically.

The Confederate victory at the first Battle of Bull Run outside of Richmond, Virginia, in the summer of 1861, leaves the Union Army in total disarray and threatens the nation's capital. The battle strikes fear into the residents of Washington, D.C. as they feel complete disappointment in the Union Army leadership and fear Confederate overrun of their own city.

For those citizens who drive their horses and carriages out to watch the battle and have a picnic, the scene is horrific and they too get caught up in the Union Army's retreat. The sounds of gunfire and artillery barrages are deafening. Even above the noise of weaponry, the yells and screams of men wounded and dying are distinctly heard. The eerie, high-pitched screams of wounded horses curdle a person's stomach.

Not far from the main battle lies a young Union soldier. Severely wounded, he attempts to hide among the trees and brushes down by a small stream in the thicket. Exhausted and bleeding badly he washes off his wounds as best he can. Rest for a bit, he reasons, and then try to make it back to my unit. I don't want to be considered a deserter. The sounds of the battle can be clearly heard in the distance, and his conscience tells him he must make it back to his comrades. "I will," he tells himself.

Suddenly a bullet rips into his side. He falls on his stomach, motionless, blood running profusely out of the wound. A young, fourteen-year-old Confederate soldier walks cautiously toward the fatally wounded Union soldier, his bayonet fixed. As the young soldier approaches to within four feet of his enemy, his body begins to shake uncontrollably. His hands are trembling so badly that he can't steady his bayonet for a thrust. The tears in his eyes are so heavy that he is unable to focus on what he was taught to do: "Kill all Yankees. Don't take any prisoners."

The internal conflict between what he was told to do and what he doesn't want to do is tearing him apart. In a fit of anger and frustration, he thrusts his bayonet into the wounded soldier and drops to his knees crying. He stares endlessly at the soldier lying before him, his heart pounding with rapid beats. "Who is this man," he wonders? Where's he from? Stunned at what he has done to another man, he looks to the sky. "God, please help me. I can't do this anymore. This war is insane. Dear God, please, let me go home. I just want to go home!"

THE POLITICS OF MORALITY

President Lincoln is seriously concerned about the threat of losing the war after the fiasco at Bull Run. He knows he has to change military commanders, consider the political demands of Congress for a victory, and deal with his own personal compassion for soldiers on both sides of the conflict.

By temperament and character, Lincoln is well fitted for the terrible ordeal of being President, probably more than any other man of his time. By most assessments he is honest, flexible, and understanding, but he also is firm in what he sees as the moral right of all Americans ... their freedom.

A tall, lanky man, his suit hangs on him loosely, giving him the appearance of a careless dresser. But his rugged, yet sensitive face seems to warm all who met him. This day, however, he shows concern and worry that is unprecedented.

Lincoln paces the floor in his office saying nothing for a good ten minutes. Finally he stops in front of the large picture window overlooking the Washington Monument. He gazes steadily at it for a moment, and then turns to his Cabinet advisors. His voice is clear and firm, "Gentlemen, we must preserve this Union. I am committed to the preservation of the United States. A nation divided against itself cannot stand."

Lincoln walks to his desk, picks up several reports from his Secretary of War and scans them briefly. With a solemn look on his face, he looks to each of his cabinet members. "Gentlemen," he begins in a firm, yet compassionate voice, "we need more men!"

The response from Simon Cameron is immediate, if not somewhat defensive. "Mr. President, as Secretary of War, I have ordered the recruitment of as many men as possible to the regular army. I can't control the desertion rate or the casualties. I have also appealed to all state governors for increased enlistments on the Volunteer Army. We have simply exhausted our manpower."

Lincoln listens intently, and then looks at each of his staff. "I know what you are saying, Mr. Secretary, and that is why we must bring Negro males of good health into the regular army. They have reason to fight. Their freedom is at stake here ... as well as their families."

Shocked at this statement, the Secretary of State, Mr. Steward, exclaims with disdain, "Impossible!" His hostility is apparent as he continues, "Who will lead these illiterates? There are no Negro officers, much less any Negro who is trained in army leadership."

Lincoln shows obvious irritation at the attitude of his Secretary and reacts strongly. "That's not the issue! It is my intention to free all slaves, and although this is a moral issue, I believe it will give all Negroes a reason to fight ... in the North as well as in the South."

The room is deathly quiet as Lincoln walks over to the table where the cabinet members are sitting. He puts his large hands on the table as he bends over and looks each member in the eyes. "As far as the officer question, all colored soldiers will be led by experienced white officers."

Still astounded by this proposal, the cabinet members glance at each other briefly before Mr. Steward begins to comment. "Mr. President, I don't think ..."

Lincoln interrupts him immediately. "I will draw up such a decree immediately. It will give us the additional troops we need and will strike directly at the social structure of the South which will, in all probability, do more damage to the Confederacy than battle itself."

The cabinet members listen intently as Lincoln emphatically continues. "Gentlemen, I shall call this document the Emancipation Proclamation. I intend to present it to Congress in one week."

The members stand silent as Lincoln continues. "If there are no other issues, I suggest we retire for the evening. Tomorrow we will continue to pursue the serious business of this country. Good night, gentlemen."

Without a word, all cabinet members nod a "good night" and silently leave the room.

On the day of the joint meeting of the House and Senate, Lincoln enters the Senate Chamber to a standing ovation from his supporters, but his adversaries are loud and unruly. The name calling and cat calls are so intent that it takes the President Pro Tem of the Senate more than twenty minutes of pounding his gavel to get the Congress to become quiet. The tension is so strong with opposing factions that Lincoln views them with disbelief. Finally, as Lincoln begins to speak, the room grows silent.

"Gentlemen," he begins. "It is our duty to preserve the United States at all costs! We have little choice on that ... other than the destruction of our beliefs as a nation and the failure of the Constitution as our forefathers envisioned."

Lincoln clears his throat. "Our nation cannot stand divided. The fundamental principle upon which our nation was founded is freedom."

A cheer arises from the pro Union congressmen and Lincoln supporters. Lincoln halts his speech briefly, and then continues, "And that brings me to the issue at hand. That I as President of the people of this country believe that no man shall be a slave to another!"

The Congressmen erupt in their seats. The noise is so great that it is difficult to tell who is for his position or who is against it. Again, the President Pro Tem pounds his gavel as Lincoln waits for the members to quiet, then continues, "Therefore, under the emergency that currently exists in this land, I hereby proclaim an Emancipation Proclamation, that all slaves are to be free men and all men to be free of any bondage."

The eruption resumes with some members calling for Lincoln's resignation, as well as his being applauded by the majority present. As the Senate chamber calms again, Lincoln makes it clear that he will tolerate no further interruptions. If so, he will simply curtail his speech, citing to the Congressmen that they can read about it in the newspapers. Even the members of the opposition party, probably out of curiosity, quell their harassment on the President.

Lincoln continues on with vigor and confidence. "This Proclamation will strike at the morale and very heart of the Confederacy. It will assist us in meeting the troop strength we need to win this war. In that regard, I am ordering the formation of ten regiments of colored troops. They will be trained and led by experienced white Union officers."

A Congressman yells from the floor, "Negroes won't fight their own masters!" Another yells, "No white officer worth his salt will lead Negroes into battle. You're insane!"

Lincoln continues on. Again the members become quiet, as if everyone has been bitten by the President's statement but wants to know more. "Gentlemen, I take full responsibility for this action. I firmly believe that if we hope to win this war, that this is the correct course of action to take, for ourselves, our children, and our grandchildren. History will be our judge."

CHAPTER TWO
A "NEW" SOLDIER EMERGES

Major newspapers in both the North and the South headline Lincoln's plan. The *Washington Daily* runs a special edition that same night.

PRESIDENT LINCOLN PASSES EMANCIPATION
PROCLAMATION!!
FREES ALL SLAVES!

Black regiments to be formed in Union army!!

Emotions on the issue are intensified, but no rage is more apparent than at the Headquarters of the Confederacy in Richmond, Virginia.

The office of the President of the Confederate States of America is in turmoil. Jefferson Davis is having a fit. "Damn, that son-of-a-bitch!" he mumbles to himself as he finishes reading the Richmond newspaper.

President Davis, a competent man and a graduate of the United States military Academy at West Point, distinguished himself as an officer in the United States Army during the Mexican War and was Secretary of War for the United States under President Franklin Pierce.

Upset at Lincoln's declaration, he hastily walks out of his office to confer with the Confederate Secretary of War. It is agreed that a meeting of the Confederate Congress is imperative and that drastic measures have to be taken concerning the black soldier issue.

The Confederate Congress meets one week later with an unprecedented eighty-five percent of the South's Representatives present. The Convention Hall is buzzing with activity and vocal interchange as the delegates anxiously await

President Davis. The atmosphere of anger and frustration towards President Lincoln is vocally vicious and emotional.

As President Davis walks to the podium there is a loud cheer of support. But, once at the speaker's stand, the Congressmen become respectfully quiet. Davis, himself, displays his anger and speaks with emotional rage. "Gentlemen, I strongly protest this so-called Emancipation Proclamation!" He waves a copy of the *Richmond Gazette* as the Congressmen cheer, taunt, pound on tables, and scream obscenities about the North in general. Davis raises his hand and asks for quiet. The members respond immediately and amicably to his request. "I have sent a telegram protesting this Proclamation to Abraham Lincoln! Now I want your opinions!"

Again members of the Confederate Congress erupt into a frenzy, swearing at Lincoln in effigy. Immediately the Senior Senator from Georgia demands recognition for the floor and receives it. "Mr. Davis, in all due respect, we must do more than protest! If these Negroes rise up against us and are not severely punished, nothing will stop them from rebellion or running north to join the Union Army! We need a strong deterrent!"

The cheers of the Congressmen are immediate, to the point of a mandate, as the Representative from South Carolina demands to be recognized. Full of emotion, he begins in a loud, stern voice, "I also propose that we take strong measures against any Negro who thinks he is free to fight against the South. I move we pass a law, here and now, that any Negro who fights against the South, and is captured, should not be considered a prisoner of war but should be shot immediately. Is there a second?"

The "seconds" are yelled by hundreds as all members unanimously agree. But the South Carolina Representative continues, "Let me make an amendment to the motion, if I may. I also move that any white Union officer leading Negro soldiers will likewise be executed!"

The screaming and yelling that instantly erupts is deafening. The Congressmen overwhelmingly approve both motions and go wild with enthusiasm. Instantaneously they all join in a loud chorus and sing "Dixie."

Newspaper headlines in all major cities carry the new Southern declaration the following morning:

Confederate Congress passes new law!

"ANY NEGRO SOLDIERS, OR ANY WHITE OFFICER LEADING A NEGRO UNIT AGAINST THE CONFEDERATE STATES OF AMERICA, IF CAPTURED, WILL NOT BE CONSIDERED A PRISONER OF WAR BUT WILL BE IMMEDIATELY EXECUTED!"

As Lincoln predicts, the Emancipation Proclamation affects all Southerners. It especially creates a concern among southern plantation owners never before anticipated. Surely, the Southern land gentry begin to think, if a slave is able to pick up a hoe, he will also have the ability to pick up a rifle, once the idea of becoming a free man enters his mind. It creates a fear in the slave-holders that Negroes might get the wrong idea of their alleged freedom proposed by the North and consequently instills even stricter measures of control and bondage on slaves.

THE HOOTEN PLANTATION

It is the summer of 1862. The Union army has not been able to penetrate the South, and the war up North seems so remote to most slaves that it seems to be but a symbol of idealism.

On the Hooten Plantation, where Henry's father works, more than one-hundred slaves are picking cotton as five white slave guards on horseback look on. The slaves, both men and women, are very cautious about fraternizing with one another since talking while working is strictly forbidden. The punishment for any violation of this rule is ten whip lashes and ten days in a stone shed no larger than a typical outhouse.

The guards openly display their rifles as they patrol casually around the perimeter of the cotton field. The slaves, meanwhile, discreetly observe their every movement. When the opportunity to talk is available, they talk in low whispers, but never look at one another.

It is noon when Joshua comes to field number ten from field number two. A strong, rugged-looking man at twenty-nine years, he has a reputation of being gentle, yet doing the work of ten men. This reputation and his gentle personality, earn him respect not only among fellow slaves, but also the plantation overseers. The going price for the average male slave in 1862 was one-thousand dollars, but Joshua was purchased for more than two-thousand dollars when he was nineteen.

As Joshua intermingles with the workers and establishes his territory to pick cotton in the field, another cotton hand named Jeremiah "picks" his way near Joshua. Jeremiah works diligently and eventually moves close enough to Joshua to talk to him in a low voice. "What yo know 'bout dis here 'Mancipation, Josh?"

Joshua hesitates, and then scans the field to get a bearing on the location of the guards. "We'se free now, Jeremiah."

Somewhat frustrated by Joshua's answer and not fully aware of the law as it applies to the South, Jeremiah replies in a defiant manner. "Den why's we still pick'n cotton? Tell me dat?"

Joshua thinks for a moment then responds. "Cause dey ain't no is'capin" ... and 'sides, I got me a wife 'n a boy."

Jeremiah is thinking as he looks up to the place where the guards might be riding. It is obvious to Joshua that Jeremiah is acting a bit abnormal and the tone of his voice is more defiant than it has ever been in the past. Jeremiah keeps looking at the ground and continues picking. "Well, Josh, I ain't got me no kin, an I be goin' north ta join the Union army. I hear up north dey got us coloreds fight'n 'gainst de South, cause we spos' to be free."

"When you be leav'n?" inquires Joshua.

Jeremiah replies quietly, "I's be leav'n com night ... two days."

Both men continue to work and say no more until they hear the guards' call to formation for the march back to the plantation.

Jeremiah still puzzled by this new law, whispers to Joshua. "Tell me mor', Josh. I's gotta know mor'."

Joshua continues to look forward, as is required by the guards, but he addresses Jeremiah firmly. "You hush, Jeremiah. Ya' know we cain't talk on dis here march ... and 'sides, I don't know no mor' an' don't wanna talk 'bout it, ya' hear?"

Later that evening Henry's father and mother are sitting at the table inside their one-room slave shack. The lantern is low and they are preparing for their evening meal. Henry notices the secretive tone of voice in which his parents are talking. As a result he pretends to be preoccupied, but is listening intently.

"Ya' know we be free now," Joshua says to Laura. "You be want'n to go north?"

Her response is direct. "No! You crazy? Cain't go! We got dis boy to worry 'bout. Best we stay where we is. See what goin hap'n here. Dis ain't our war!"

Henry sits quietly but alertly at the table playing with his food. He is trying hard to hear what his parents are talking about, but he can only pickup bits and pieces of what they are saying. In his mind he is aware of a war, and that the reason the North is fighting against the South has something to do with slavery. As his parents continue talking, Henry suddenly looks up, smiles, and boldly interrupts. "I wonts to be a Union soldier, Ma. I wonts to free you!"

Shocked at this statement, Henry's mother scolds him. "Hush now! You ain't no soldier! You be a six-year-old boy. Eat yo' food, ya' hear! An you don't need to be listn'n to big folks talk!"

Feeling dejected, Henry looks down at his plate, the smile gone. But he knows in his mind that he is going to be a soldier someday, and nobody, not even his mother, is going to tell him he can't be. Suddenly, he runs to the door and stops and screams at his parents, "I'm not hungry, an I don't like eat'n slave food."

Joshua slowly gets up from the table. "Com'on, son. Let's take a walk."

Henry is proud of his father. He knows his father is strong and that everyone respects him. But most of all Henry likes just being around him, listening to everything he has to say.

As they walk outside, Joshua puts his hand on Henry's head and rubs his hair lightly. "Let's go down to the pond, son. It be quiet there."

Neither of them talk during the brief walk. Both are thinking their own thoughts as they settle on the grass and begin tossing pebbles into the water.

"Tell me, son," Joshua begins compassionately, "'bout this dream you have, 'bout being a soldier."

Henry thinks seriously as he picks up another small rock to throw. "Don't know, Pa. Just wanna be one. Wanna be a officer."

Joshua smiles slightly, and then puts his hand on Henry's shoulder. "That's big ambition, son. Takes educat'n and 'termination." Joshua realizes this is a child's dream, but doesn't want to discourage his son from his fantasies. At the same time, he feels he has to tell him about the realities of his situation.

"I wont the best for you, son, and I wont you to remember somt'n ... you'se a person, and you must live with you'self.

Many times you be struggling with that. Be honest 'n do what you think right good, no matter what you be."

Henry thinks quickly about his father's words. A smile grows on his face as he turns to his father. "I will, Pa! Ya' know that!"

Four days later, Henry and several other children are playing near the horse barn when Henry notices the plantation owner and several slave guards coming down the back road. He takes a second look and steadies his gaze on the men as he notices something unusual draped over a guard's saddle. Alerting the other children, they stop playing and run to hide behind several old wagons near the barn.

The plantation owner is leading a group of six men and yelling orders to other men on the ground near the main buildings where the cotton is stored. Henry watches as they stop under the big oak tree in the center square. One of the horsemen throws a rope over a long, low hung branch about twelve feet above the ground. Henry looks at the other children with a surprised look on his face.

"Who's that?" Henry inquires. The other children just shrug their shoulders. "Do'n know."

They watch as a guard puts a rope over the head of Jeremiah. The rope is brought taut around his neck to stabilize him from falling off the horse. Another guard steadies the horse in position. Yelling loudly, the plantation owner orders his men to assemble all the slaves, including women and children, to the location at the big tree. In less than thirty minutes all slaves are hustled in from the fields at the Hooten plantation and assembled at the center square.

Upon arriving at the site, everyone is horrified, especially those who know Jeremiah. Joshua is stunned to see him and stands quietly, staring defiantly at the guards. Henry and his mother stand directly behind Joshua shocked at what is taking place before their very eyes.

Jeremiah's body is badly mutilated and blood drips from the wounds to his face and torso. It is impossible to determine if he is dead or unconscious. Everyone is silent. Even the guards are silently obeying their orders until the quiet is broken by the plantation owner's voice. "Crack that horse!"

As the horse speeds out from under Jeremiah, there is the clear sound of a snap, like that of a twig breaking. Jeremiah, his feet dangling only two feet from the ground, looks like a rag doll hanging from the tree limb.

Henry, frightened by this scene, instantly grabs his father's legs from behind and peers out from between them. The sun shining through the tree branches directly on Jeremiah's body gives it an eerie, silhouette appearance. Henry feels an emotion in himself that he has never felt before. It is hard for him to grasp the sight of a dead man, the first he has ever seen. His fear and the sight of Jeremiah's body unleash many questions he has never contemplated before. "What is it like to be dead," he thinks?

The plantation owner is furious and is screaming loudly as he rides back and forth in front of the assembled slaves. He cracks his whip several times at Jeremiah's body, and then spins his horse around to face the slaves. "Let this be a lesson to you!" he screams. "This is what will happen to you if any of you niggers think you're gonna be free men!" He then turns to his guards. "Get these bastards back to work!"

Henry follows his father to the field this particular day, mostly out of fear of being alone. Tears come to his eyes, and he begins shaking. Confused as to what has just happened, he grabs his father's hand tightly and looks up to him. "Why'd they do that, Pa?"

Joshua does not know how to respond to his child's question.

CHAPTER THREE
THE JUNIOR OFFICER CORPS

Away from life on the plantation exists another way of life that is equally harsh and horrifying. The war between he states is intensifying and at this point neither side has any sign of victory in sight. In 1863, the Union army exceeds more than a million men, but the South has reached its peak of conscriptions between the ages of eighteen and forty-five at just over a half million men. The balance of manpower has shifted to the Union army.

Being a junior officer in the Union army in 1863 is not much different then being a lower ranked enlisted man. Normally they eat the same food, live under the same adverse conditions, and are in front of the men they lead into battle. Generally, it is lonely, dangerous, tedious, and unglamorous. The amenities are few, except possibly the title given when commissioned: "You are hereby pronounced an officer and a gentleman by an act of Congress."

The formation of black units in the United States Army creates a problem for most soldiers of officer status, especially of the junior rank such as lieutenants. The thought of leading blacks into combat is new and perceived as dangerous by most white officers. They simply feel that blacks can't be trusted under combat conditions. "What if they bolt and flee under fire? Can I trust them with my life?"

As a consequence of this thought, it is difficult to find officers who will commit to such duty. This role is usually assigned to young, idealistic volunteers, and most of these officers are strict abolitionists.

On November 25, 1863, Generals Grant, Olson, and Sheridan of the Union forces drive their attack into Chattanooga, Tennessee. This is a massive onslaught for both sides, but ends in a major victory for the Union army, thus setting the stage for the eventual final blow into the deep South.

In order to prepare for penetration into southern territory, General Grant orders probing patrols sent into Confederate-held areas. These eight-to-twelve-man units are mainly used for intelligence gathering. Normally these enlisted men are led by a junior officer and are considered expendable.

Jon Peterson, a twenty-three-year-old Norwegian immigrant, had been in the United States for five years when he joined the Minnesota Volunteers. When the Civil War broke out, he established himself in the Abolitionist Movement and felt a deep, moral conviction against slavery. He is a compassionate, religious man whose goal is to be a farmer and teacher. Having some education, he takes officers training under state militia conditions, which is brief and informal, unlike the four years of vigorous military training Regular Army officers receive at West Point. However, Jon Peterson has an uncanny ability to understand the elements of leadership and under normal conditions seems to show common sense. Thus, he is commissioned as a Lieutenant in the Minnesota Volunteers, and then assigned to General Grant's command in the Tennessee River Valley.

When orders come down from Grant's Headquarters to conduct probing patrols into the Confederate territory south of Chattanooga, Lieutenant Peterson eagerly volunteers for the duty. His orders follow that he will lead a patrol of eight black soldiers, disguised as slaves, into Confederate held territory, gather information on enemy positions and food supplies, avoid any contact with the enemy, and report back to his commander.

"Are there any questions?" Lieutenant Peterson asks, after briefing his reconnaissance patrol. The eight black soldiers shake their heads slightly indicating they understand their mission. "Okay, men, let's move out! Sergeant Johnson, you take point. The rest of you men spread out about fifteen feet apart but always keep eye contact with the man in front of you. Let's go!"

Lieutenant Peterson watches diligently as the first four men move cautiously in the direction of their objective following Sergeant Johnson, a nineteen-year-old from southern Indiana. He then assumes his position of control or sixth man in the middle of the unit.

The men move steadily and quietly through the night avoiding any roads or trails that might alert the Confederates. It is day-break when they stop to reassess their situation and position. The tree line and thick brush give them adequate cover and the men are becoming exhausted by the fast paced, long night's walk.

"Okay, men, let's rest here through the day and we'll begin again this evening. Eat your rations as you see fit and try to get some sleep. Make sure you cover yourselves well with branches."

Sergeant Johnson approaches Lieutenant Peterson quietly. "Sir, don't ya' think we should put out a sentry or something?"

"Not necessary, Sergeant. We'll be well covered and we all need to get some rest for tonight's patrol."

Sergeant Johnson looks at the Lieutenant puzzled, shakes his head, and replies, "Okay, Lieutenant."

The men sleep peacefully through most of the day but are awakened in the late afternoon by a Confederate artillery column moving down the road and across the river. Lieutenant Peterson hurriedly calls his men to his side. "It looks like we're where we should be. Those artillery columns mean we're in the center of a huge Confederate buildup. Cripes! There must be thousands of infantry and cavalry all around us." Turning to Sergeant Johnson, Lieutenant Peterson seems unsure of what to do. "What do you make of it, Serg? Should we try to get outta here now or wait til dark?"

Sergeant Johnson shakes his head and speaks quietly. "It all be the same, Sir. We's gonna have trouble day or night. They look to be as thick as flies all o'er the place."

Lieutenant Peterson ponders the situation for a moment. "You're right, Sergeant. Okay, men, cover yourselves well. Looks like we're going to be here for a few more hours. We'll move out at dark."

The thought of being so close to the enemy shudders Lieutenant Peterson's emotions. On one hand he feels scared stiff, and on the other, there is a slight feeling of excitement. Either way, he realizes that he must not show either of these emotions in front of his men. He knows he has a mission to accomplish and as a professional soldier he must act accordingly.

By ten o' clock that evening it is dark enough to travel. The conditions are good for night patrol as it is just starting to rain and there is a low cloud cover as opposed to a bright moon. The pace is steady as they quietly maneuver through the trees to avoid any contact with the heavily saturated Confederate forces.

It is five-thirty in the morning as the first light of day begins to appear. The patrol has just moved into a thick tree line at the bottom of a hill.

Blam! The distinctly clear sound of a muzzle loader interrupts the quiet morning air. Lieutenant Peterson instinctively drops to his stomach, reacting quickly to the sound of the rifle. Unsure of where the shot came from, he cautiously looks over the blades of grass where he is lying. It is a matter of seconds before he sees Sergeant Johnson lying on his back, blood running out of a hole in his chest.

"Ambush! Stay down!" Lieutenant Peterson yells to his men as they cower down and seek the best cover they can find.

"Where'd that shot come from?" Lieutenant Peterson asks in an excited whisper. Neither he nor any of his men can determine from where the shot has been fired. It was all so quick. Shaken and scared he knows that his mission has now been exposed, that there is no way out of this situation without conflict.

Raising his right hand with an open palm, Lieutenant Peterson signals to his men to stay where they are. He then quietly and carefully crawls to Sergeant Johnson. A deep rage of anger fills his body as he realizes Johnson is dead. Trying to regain some composure he turns to his men. "Do ya see anything out there?" he whispers. All seven men shake their heads silently replying to the negative. Suddenly a loud voice calls out from Lieutenant Peterson's left flank. "Surrender or we'll kill ya' all where ya' are! Ya' hear that, Yankee?"

Lieutenant Peterson looks to his men and raises his index finger to his mouth. "Damn it!" he says in a low voice, his mind reeling in fear and confusion. Blaming himself for the situation, he starts to question his own leadership. How the hell did I get us into this situation, he thinks to himself. But his thoughts are quickly interrupted by the unseen voice.

"Ya' don't have a chance in there, Yank! Save yourself and your men! I'll give ya' five minutes to come out or we'll tear that brush to the ground with gun fire!"

Lieutenant Peterson ponders seriously what to do ... fight it out and risk his men's lives as well as his own or should he surrender, even though it means a Confederate prison camp for the duration of the war. He realizes it is his decision and his alone.

"Ya got one minute in there, Blue-belly, and then wer'a blast'n!" comes the voice.

Scared and feeling helpless, Lieutenant Peterson sees the same fear in the eyes of his men. He realizes that his response must be quick and that it must be a moral and humanitarian one. "Hold your fire! We're coming out!"

Lieutenant Peterson looks to his men and in a voice that is almost apologetic, attempts to give reason for surrendering to the enemy. "Men, this is the best I can do ... otherwise it's be killed or wounded. This way we've a chance for life ... even if it means being a prisoner of war. I'm sorry!"

His men look at him in disbelief. "Sir! You sure 'bout this," questions one of the men?

Lieutenant Peterson gazes at him for a second then responds briefly. "No, no I'm not."

"Hurry up, Yank! Your time is up! Ar' ya' com'n out?" yells the voice.

Lieutenant Peterson replies again, "Hold your fire ... we're coming out!"

"No tricks now, Yankee. We got a bead on all ya' blue-bellies! An keep ya're hands up?" the voice yells.

Lieutenant Peterson and his men walk, one by one, in the direction of the calling voice. As they enter a small clearing, he notices that the voice is that of a Confederate Lieutenant of slim build, scraggly hair, and torn uniform.

"Hey! Looky what we've here!" shouts the Confederate Lieutenant to his Sergeant. "A damn Yankee officer leading a bunch of niggers ... Sheeeit!" The Confederate Lieutenant chuckles and smiles as he looks around to his men and back to the prize captives who are walking toward him.

"Keep ya're hands up now!" yells the Confederate Lieutenant as he then calls to his Sergeant. "Sergeant! Line these prisoners up and have someone check the brush for any stragglers ... and, Sergeant, be careful of these black blue-bellies. I hear they bite!" The Southern officer laughs at his own comment with a sick, hee-haw, sucking nasal sound.

As Lieutenant Peterson and his men are lined up in loose formation, he attempts to inform the Confederate Lieutenant that Sergeant Johnson is lying back in the bushes, dead.

Ignoring these comments, the Confederate officer, his pistol drawn, walks up to Lieutenant Peterson and talks in a slow, cocky drawl. "Leading these niggers, huh? Got news for ya', Yank. By the laws of the Confederacy you and ya're men here aren't to be prisoners of war." The Confederate Lieutenant pokes his pistol barrel into the throat of Lieutenant Peterson, looks him in the eyes, winks, and laughs loudly. "Know what? Ya're to be executed. Yup, that's right! And right here on this very spot!"

The Confederate Lieutenant scrawls a menacing grin. Lieutenant Peterson, the gun barrel still pointed under his chin, tries to speak with some authority. "We're Union soldiers! The Code of Conduct states that all prisoners of war are to be treated as such! I demand ..."

The Confederate Lieutenant instantly interrupts. "Shut up, ya nigger lovin', blue-belly!" then hits Lieutenant Peterson in the face with the pistol barrel. Peterson staggers down in pain, blood gushes out the side of his ear.

The Confederate soldiers reactions are instinctive ... all guns cocked and aimed directly at the prisoners, trigger fingers ready to squeeze at the slightest provocation or order.

Now out of control, the Confederate officer yells at his Sergeant. "Sergeant! Get over here!"

The Sergeant, a bull of a man, struggles at quick time over to the Lieutenant. "Yes, Sir! What is your orders, Sir?"

The Confederate Lieutenant whispers in the Sergeant's ear. The Sergeant steps back, salutes, and hustles over to his men and yells loudly and distinctly. "Troops! Aim your weapons ... Fire!"

The gunfire is voluminous. Immediately, Lieutenant Peterson drops to the ground as do the seven black soldiers next to him. One black soldier lies moaning in a pool of blood.

The Confederate Lieutenant, his pistol still drawn, walks casually over to him, puts the pistol to the soldier's head and pulls the trigger. He then looks over to the body of Lieutenant Peterson with cold and piercing eyes. The animosity boils inside him that a white officer would actually lead Negroes into combat. He cocks his pistol, walks slowly over to Lieutenant Peterson's dead body, places the barrel to the Union Lieutenant's head and pulls the trigger. Blam! "That one's from me!" yells the Confederate Lieutenant defiantly.

After gazing at the Union Lieutenant's body for more than a minute, the Confederate Lieutenant orders his men to pack up and get ready to leave the area. "Leave the bodies in place," he commands. "Let the sons-a-bitches rot!"

After six days of intense battle, the Union forces begin to push the Confederates back more than fifty miles. Unaware of Lieutenant Peterson's small patrol in once held Confederate territory, a Union scout under the command of Major John Carr's light cavalry accidentally comes across Lieutenant Peterson's body and the bodies of the dead black soldiers. Shocked at what he sees, he quickly rides back to his unit to report the incident.

Major Carr knows only too well the atrocities of war, having been wounded seriously at the first battle of Bull Run. But even so, he knows this incident is different. Never before has he seen the whole-sale execution of soldiers taken as prisoners. He is stunned and angry as he mutters to himself. "Those bastard Rebel cowards … sons-a-bitches!"

Pulling a bandana from his jacket, he covers his nose and mouth as he walks to Lieutenant Peterson's body, which is decomposing, his face all but recognizable.

Emotions running high, Major Carr calls for his junior officer. "Lieutenant! Get a detail over here! Bury these men. Mark the graves and record this location. Pull off their I.D.'s if they have any."

As he watches the men, Major Carr takes out his notebook and begins to write. He stops for a moment and waves a corporal to his side. "Corporal, take this message to General Grant personally. Tell him it's of utmost importance! Quickly now, move!"

The Corporal takes the message, salutes, mounts his horse, and rides out at a gallop. Major Carr stands silently, watching his men dig makeshift graves. He sighs deeply, looks to the sky, and turns to his Lieutenant. "God help us!"

WASHINGTON D.C.

President Lincoln is in the middle of conferring with his Chief of Staff and other Aides when there is a knock on the door. Lincoln looks to his secretary and asks her to inform security that he is not to be disturbed the rest of the morning.

After doing as instructed, the secretary hastily returns moments later. "Mr. President, you have an urgent telegram from General Grant!"

Lincoln quickly opens the telegram and after reading it, solemnly looks to his staff. Without saying a word he begins writing on his notepad. In a matter of minutes he hands the paper to his secretary. "Send this message to General Grant immediately. Send the same message to President Jefferson Davis!"

Curious as to what the message is about, his staff members look to each other with puzzled expressions. Lincoln then asks them to be seated around his conference table and hands the telegram to his Secretary of War, Mr. Cameron, who reads it and passes it on to the other members. Lincoln begins to speak in a quiet, serious tone of voice. "Gentlemen, this war has taken a new turn."

Lincoln, who in the past has consistently tried to make decisions without letting his personal feelings get involved, suddenly appears sad and melancholy. "Gentlemen, I want to inform you that I have just strongly protested to Jefferson Davis, the execution style killing of Lieutenant Peterson and eight black soldiers. That's all for this morning. We'll resume our meetings this afternoon. Thank you."

Lincoln then returns to his desk, sits down, and seriously ponders, how would I react to this telegram if I were Mr. Davis?

The war is not going well for the South and Jefferson Davis is frustrated by the major defeats Southern troops are taking in all sectors of Tennessee, Alabama, and Virginia. General Olson's Union Army now controls all of the Mississippi River and has three armies pushing toward Atlanta, Georgia. The Confederacy is running out of men and the desertion rate is at a staggering twenty-five percent. More so, economic conditions are barely tolerable and the social and political structure has become sectionalized between each of the southern states.

These are but a few of the problems President Davis is wresting with when his Senior Aide knocks on his door. "Come in!" Davis quips.

His Aide, who is obviously excited, enters with the telegram in his hand. "Sir, a message for you ... marked top priority. It's from President Lincoln, Sir!"

Preoccupied with his other problems, Davis nonchalantly responds. "Damn! What's his problem?"

"Don't know, Sir, haven't read it."

Davis reacts in a sarcastic voice. "Well, open the damn thing and read it to me, Lieutenant!"

"Sir," the Lieutenant begins, after stumbling to open the message, "it reads like this ... 'Dear President Jefferson

Davis; I strongly protest the field execution of Union prisoners! I refer to the killing of a white officer by the name of Lieutenant Jon Peterson and eight enlisted colored soldiers. I consider this type of atrocity to be a war crime of the highest degree. You, as Commander of all southern soldiers, will be held personally accountable for such acts against humanity! Signed, Abraham Lincoln, President, United States of America.'"

The Aide stands at attention waiting for a response from President Davis. After more than two minutes, the Aide interrupts the silence in the room. "Mr. Davis, Sir ... do you ... do you want to respond to this, Sir?" Davis shows no reaction to the Aides question. "Excuse me, Sir. I can wait in the outer office if that's okay with you, Sir."

President Davis continues to look at the War Board hanging on the wall to the left of his desk. He says nothing, but nods his head in apparent approval of the Aide's suggestion. The Aide salutes, does an about face, and quietly starts to walk out of the room. President Davis slowly turns in his chair, takes a deep breath, and calls the Aide, "Just a minute, Lieutenant! Tell me something ..." Davis hesitates for a moment, and then continues, "What kind of moral values do men retain in a time of war?"

The Aide, surprised by the question, replies, "Well, Sir ... I, well, I just ..."

President Davis immediately interrupts him. "You don't have to answer that, Lieutenant! Carry on. You're dismissed!" President Davis turns back to the War Board, and then shifts his eyes slightly to the right. There, on the wall, hangs a large Confederate Flag. He gets up out of his chair, walks over and puts his hand on the flag and says in a low voice, "What price, man's inhumanity to man?

CHAPTER FOUR
HOOTEN PLANTATION MASSACRE

One thing seemed paramount in the minds of both southern soldiers and civilians since Lincoln issued the Emancipation Proclamation; will the slaves rise up against their own masters and other whites? As a result of this thought, the Confederate soldiers are especially distrustful of any black, male or female. It is also the general point of view that the horrific social and economic conditions are at least partially caused by the blacks themselves. This frame of mind is evident on July 20, 1864, when a column of one-hundred-five Confederate soldiers raid the Hooten plantation, originally for desperately needed food and supplies.

It is eight-o-clock in the evening when Henry and his parents finish eating. Henry is doing his assigned chores and his mother and father have just sat down to read from the red Bible that was given to them by the plantation owner's wife, Pearl Hooten. For a moment the scene seems perfectly peaceful and routine. Suddenly they hear the yelling of soldiers and the screaming of men, women, and children. Joshua instinctively cautions Laura and Henry to remain silent as he jumps to the door to look outside.

"Confederate soldiers! Raid'n the place!" he yells back to Laura. "They too close to 'scape now!" he says fearfully as he turns to Henry. "Henry, get in de hid'n place, now!" Joshua quickly picks up the end of a twelve-inch wide lank flooring. "Get in there, and be still. Don't say not'n, no matter what happens, ya' hear? Laura, get de light out!"

Henry obeys his father as he always does and scrambles into the small crevice. His father replaces the plank, and then turns to his wife who is shaking and frantic. "Josh, shat is it, what's they want?"

"Do'n know," he replies as he cracks the door open a quarter inch and peers outside. Reluctant to tell Laura what he is seeing, he begins to react to what might happen when the soldiers get to their cabin. "Jus stay quiet," he says in a hushed voice. 'We cain't go outside now. Jus stay calm. I's think'n!"

The soldiers are all around the slave housing area randomly forcing all black men, women, and children out of their cabins. Joshua firmly tries to quiet Laura as she is shaking with fear. The terrifying screams and gunshots are making her lose control of herself.

"Be quiet, woman!" Joshua yells as he peeks through a crack in the door. Joshua watches as five Confederate soldiers enter the cabin across the path from his. "Too late to run," he mumbles to himself as he contemplates his next actions.

Outside, three confederate soldiers force a black man out of his cabin as he screams helplessly. "Leave my woman alone … leave her be! We dun not'n to ya'!" His wife's screams can be heard inside the cabin as he struggles violently with the soldiers outside.

Bam! Suddenly the struggling slave lies motionless on the ground. The cabin interior is also quiet as a confederate soldier appears in the doorway laughing. "See ya' got yourself one," he jokes loudly to the three soldiers standing at the base of the cabin steps.

"Ya, not much for trophy tho," replies the confederate soldier standing with his pistol in his hand.

"Ya, same inside. Com'on, best get the others 'fore it gets too dark."

The soldiers join the others in what has become a contagion of the killing frenzy that has driven them totally out of control. The beatings and shootings are now affecting all the slaves on the Hooten plantation. Mr. Hooten, himself, was shot in the beginning of the violence, protesting the invasion.

Even the Confederate Captain has given up trying to restrain his soldiers.

As the violence continues just outside, Joshua realizes that it is only a matter of minutes before the soldiers are likely to break into his cabin and then what? What choice does he have when they come to his door? He grabs a knife off the table and positions himself against the wall near the door. He then instructs Laura firmly. "Laura, you run outside and try to hide the minute de soldiers come in, ya' hear?"

Laura, tears in her eyes and her hands over her mouth trying to contain her fright, nods okay.

"And you's gotta stay alive, woman. You's gotta take care of de boy!" orders Joshua.

Suddenly the sound of boots is heard on the porch steps. Joshua and Laura wait in dead silence. A big, burly, unshaven Sergeant stands on the small porch yelling at his men. "This one here," he yells as he waves over four men carrying a plank used as a battering ram. "Door's bolted!"

As the men position themselves on the porch with the plank, the Sergeant orders, "Hit the door!"

Crack! One hit and the door flies open, hanging on one hinge. Initially it is quiet and dark inside. One of the soldiers confidently peers inside and within a matter of a second or two falls backward out the door screaming in pain and bleeding from the throat.

"Son of a bitch!" yells the Sergeant, "Get that nigga!"

The other men rush in, rifle bayonets fixed, the Sergeant immediately behind them with his pistol. Joshua grabs the barrel end of the rifle and struggles with the soldiers desperately but it is only a matter of a minute before the other soldier is able to stab him in the stomach.

Laura screams as she tries to make it out the door but is immediately shot in the back by the pistol carrying Sergeant.

Joshua, hearing Laura scream, attempts to crawl outside to her, but is stabbed once again in the back.

The Confederate Sergeant stands in the doorway quickly surveying the situation and feeling his mission accomplished, seems anxious to continue his gruesome venture. "Leave these," he orders. "Get the ones in that cabin under the trees."

The soldiers leave Henry's parents lying on the porch of their cabin where they have fallen.

Henry followed his father's orders but instinctively leaves his hiding place as the soldiers leave the cabin. He does not dare go outside yet, and is too shocked and frightened to cry. He sits motionless in the shadow of the doorway looking at his parents. The yelling and screaming still going on in the distance falls deaf on his ears. He just sits staring at his parents' motionless bodies.

It is early morning, but still dark, when Henry wakes up. For an instant he thinks that he has had a bad dream, but the reality of the situation is quickly apparent as he focuses on his parents dead bodies. A strange fear instantly strikes him. He cowers behind the door and peers outside. It is quiet now, very quiet.

"Have the soldiers left, or are they just sleeping?" he asks himself. But that doesn't seem to matter as some force deep within compels him to pull the bodies of his mother and father inside. As he cautiously peers outside he can see the bodies of other slaves: men, women, and some children, lying on the dirt path in front of the cabin.

The full moon makes the sight even more gruesome and frightening. Emotionally and physically exhausted, he wipes the tears from his eyes. His strength seems to be reinforced by his brave determination to drag his lifeless parents back into the cabin. He struggles desperately to first bring his mother inside, then his father. It is a gruesome task and Henry is reacting more than acting at the sight of his dead parents. Once he has both bodies inside the cabin he slowly closes the door. He positions his mother and father close together in a semblance of an embrace. Having done this he simply lies down between them, puts his arms around each of them, and quietly cries himself to sleep.

It is late morning of the following day that word has spread of the massacre at the Hooten plantation. The first to arrive is a group of clergy and members of the African Episcopal Church. Appalled at the scene, they immediately set to moving the dead onto wooden planks, lining each of them up for identification and burial.

"God, have Mercy!" exclaims Bishop Jon Jackson, a six-foot tall, heavy set, forty-eight-year-old black minister, as he observes the hideous sight. "How many have you found so far?" he asks Jay Hampton, a church member and teacher at the Episcopal Orphanage in charge of the detail.

"Fifty-two, Jon, including the ones we found burned in the horse barn," replies Jay quickly as he places a blanket on the most recently laid body.

"Are there any survivors?" inquires the Bishop.

"Not to my knowledge. I hope some escaped. Haven't checked those far shacks though," replies Jay Hampton.

Bishop Jackson looks down the dirt walkway towards the cabin in which Henry's parents lived. "I'll check that end one myself," says the Bishop. He hesitates, and then motions over to Jay Hampton. "Jay, come with me, let's check that end cabin."

Jay has never witnessed such a grisly sight and is noticeably upset. "I think I'm going to throw up, Jon," he garbles as he puts his hand to his mouth.

"I know how you're feeling, Jay. In all my years, I've seen a lot of death but this has to be the most senseless and despicable act I have ever witnessed ... and possibly God will bear witness with me."

Bishop Jackson walks over to Jay, puts his hand on his shoulder and calmly says, "Stay here, Jay. I'll look in that last cabin myself."

Jay shakes his head. "No, I'll go with you. I'm alright now."

As the two men approach the cabin, Jay notices something red on the steps of the porch. He instantly grabs the Bishop's arm. "My God, Jon, look at the blood on that porch! Look at those bloody drag marks going back inside!"

Both men hurry their pace and carefully race up the porch steps trying to avoid the thick, drying puddles of blood. Stopping abruptly before entering the cabin, Bishop Jackson cautiously and quietly opens the broken door. He slowly peers inside. "My God!" declares Bishop Jackson in a low, emotional tone of voice. "Jay, come here!"

There on the floor lies young Henry between his mother and father. 'Are they all dead?" inquires Jay.

The Bishop does not reply but instead quietly steps to the bodies and kneels down. He reaches out to touch Henry. Weak from crying and emotional trauma, Henry responds only slightly to the touch as his eyes open slightly and then close. It is as if life has almost drained itself from him and he has no energy to care what happens.

"Jon, give me your coat," requests Bishop Jackson as he carefully put his hands under Henry and begins to slowly raise him to a sitting position. "Here, son, let me put this coat around you," the Bishop says quietly. Henry, his eyes red from crying is numb and listless. The Bishop carefully helps Henry to his feet and lifts him over the bodies of his parents to a chair in the corner of the room. "Sit here for a moment, son. You'll be okay."

As Henry becomes more alert he begins to shake violently. Then in an instant he stops shaking and focuses his eyes on his parents.

Bishop Jackson puts his arms around Henry, slowly picks him up and sits down on a chair with Henry on his lap.

Henry's response is immediate as he grabs tightly to the Bishop's arm and begins to cry profusely. "My, Pa! My, Ma!" Henry cries in a half sniffling tone.

"Easy, son," says Bishop Jackson softly. "You'll be fine. Just rest easy for now."

Jay, in shock, has tears in his eyes as he stands helplessly by watching Bishop Jackson trying to comfort Henry. "What can I do, Jon?"

"Nothing for now. Best go get some help with these bodies. I'll take care of the boy," says the Bishop.

As Jay rushes out the door, Bishop Jackson quietly rocks Henry back and forth trying to calm him. Suddenly Henry begins to mumble in a low, quivering voice. "Dem Reb soldiers come in an kill my Ma and Pa." Continuing, Henry blurts out angrily, "I hates dem Reb soldiers. I hates Johnny Reb!"

"Shusss," says Bishop Jackson compassionately. "Come with me, son, we'll take care of you now." Slowly Bishop Jackson puts his hand on Henry's chin and turns his face toward him. "What's you name, son?"

Henry looks silently and hesitantly at Bishop Jackson. "Henry," he murmurs in a low voice, as Bishop Jackson raises and carries Henry outside to the carriage.

After a day of sleeping and quiet crying at the Episcopal Orphanage outside Atlanta, Georgia, Henry is still coming to grips with the trauma of witnessing his parents' death. His sobs are periodically heard through the door of his room as Bishop Jackson closely monitors Henry's welfare. The Bishop's concern for the young boy is apparent as he discusses the situation with Jay and Bo Reed, the Orphanage Assistant Director. "What's your opinion, Bo?"

Bo, a short, stocky, black man of thirty, had been well educated through the orphanage school when he was a boy and now holds a certificate in education.

"I don't see any choice under the circumstances," Bo replies. "The Confederacy will soon be finished and I have no idea what the Northern Federals will do as far as reconstruction, especially in a school setting. I think we should make all the necessary preparations to have the boy remain here. At least we can guarantee him an education. What to do about the loss of his parents is another matter. We'll have to try and guide him through this time in his life as best we can. We can't leave him on his own."

The Bishop ponders the course of action open to them, and then speaks with empathy. "Best bring the boy in here so we can talk with him. Why don't you go get him, Bo? We'll do the best we can to ease his pain and offer him some security."

"I'll do that," says Bo as he gets out of his chair and leaves the room.

It is about ten minutes before Bo and young Henry enter the Bishop's office. Henry, scared and shy, looks around at the office and then at the three men.

"Henry, please sit down," says the Bishop as he moves a chair in the direction of Henry. "We would like to talk to you. We know this is a hard time for you."

Henry cautiously takes a seat. His eyes are wide as he again briefly scans the office. Then suddenly emotionless, Henry casts his eyes down at the floor; both hands firmly grasp the arms of the chair.

"Henry, I can only imagine the feelings you carry inside, but I want you to know that we are here to help you in anyway we can," say Bishop Jackson in a calm, sincere tone.

Henry's eyes continue to lock on the floor as he shifts into an even more rigid position in the chair. The feelings of anger and hate coupled with the thought of revenge, race through his mind as he tries desperately to hold back the tears. He thinks of his parents and how hard they had worked in the fields on the Hooten Plantation. It was his only security, the knowledge that he would at least see his mother and father daily. That was all gone now. He wonders what his future will be ... and if he even wants a future.

"I hates Johnny Reb!" Henry exclaims suddenly. "I wonts to be a Union soldier. I wonts to kill all dem Johnny Rebs!"

Bishop Jackson is taken aback as he looks quickly to the other men and then back to Henry. "Calm down, son. You mustn't think like that. For now you must think of your future ... your education. You can stay here and we will try to help you work through this. You must be strong now, Henry. We can't turn back the clock on these tragic events, but we can continue on. You can carry on for your parents. You can make them proud of you. I believe they would want you to do that."

Henry continues to stare at the floor, periodically wiping tears from his eyes. Without looking up, he speaks in a low, but serious voice. "I still wonts to be a Union soldier."

Bo, as compassionately and understanding as he can, replies, "Henry, this war will soon be over. We coloreds can look to a new America. One day maybe you too will be a proud American."

CHAPTER FIVE
A NEW ERA BEGINS

Throughout the Civil War much of the Union's manpower comes from the constant flow of immigrants to the United States from Europe and other countries. The expansion westward has been an ongoing movement since the discovery of gold in California in 1849, but travel west becomes an integral part of the development of the United States after the Civil War. People are moving west for many reasons, but for most it is simply a chance to begin a new life.

Civil War veterans, as well as civilians, are told by the United States government that they could have free land under the Homestead Act. One-hundred-sixty acres on which to build homes and communities. Even southern blacks, finding little change in the south after the war, feel they can better their lives in the western territories.

It is not an easy life for the "settlers" as they are called. It is a strange land for all newcomers no matter who they are or what their background. Language and customs are a major barrier and the hustlers and rustlers take advantage of the settlers at every opportunity. The naiveté of the immigrants creates danger for not only themselves but those around them. Their innocent travels also creates animosity among the native tribes. It is just a matter of time before the settlers will be clamoring for the United States Army to send troops to protect them and retain some semblance of law and order.

The regular army has been reduced to less than twenty-five-thousand men after the end of the Civil War, barely enough men to man the Eastern garrisons, much less provide protection for settlers moving west. But the conflict is growing and it mostly involves rights to territory. The general consequences creates more than twenty years of warfare with the Indian populations in the West. Even the United States Government cannot curtail the westward explosion.

THE IMMIGRANTS

In March of 1862, Hartvig and Inga Larson arrive in America; both are only sixteen years of age. Sweden is under severe economic and social turmoil, and the young pioneers think they can better their lives in the United States. They left Europe with the little bit of money they have saved, with loads of hope and inspiration and a fair knowledge of English.

Inga is excited about the stories she has heard about the free land for homesteading in America, but more so anticipates a new found freedom in a new land.

The excitement of entering the harbor of New York brings intense joy to Inga. Her heart is beating fast in anticipation of the things to come in this new land. Hartvig on the other hand is cautious, reserved, and barely displays any emotion.

The trip from New York to Chicago is uneventful, but tedious. It isn't until they head south to St. Louis, Missouri, when Hartvig begins to have second thoughts. "Are you sure you want to go all the way west, Inga?" Hartvig inquires as they sit in the passenger car pulled by an old steam locomotive.

"Ya, I do!" Inga replies. "We didn't come this far for no reason, husband."

"Ya then, so when we get to St. Louis we buy a wagon and two horses, maybe a plow. We have only enough money for important things," Hartvig ponders as he calculates in his head the finances of the trip.

"We get what we need, husband and that be it," Inga agrees firmly.

Hartvig, a big strong man who stands six-foot-four-inches tall, and weighs two-hundred-forty-five-pounds, is capable of doing almost anything physical. However, at sixteen years old and not being able to speak good English, he is having trouble deciding what to buy in preparation for the trip west.

Together Hartvig and Inga make a list of things they think they will need: two horses, a covered wagon, harnesses, some pots and pans, food staples, a rifle, a pistol, and ammunition among other miscellaneous items. The plow has to wait.

St. Louis is a bustling town. The excitement of the immigrants preparing for one of the "trains" west is especially stimulating to Inga.

The first thing they buy is a wagon to sleep in. It is a matter of three days before Hartvig is able to find the necessary horses and equipment to get his rig complete. Inga seems happy sitting in the back of their newly purchased wagon and Hartvig feels content working with the harnesses and horses of which he has had much experience back in Sweden.

It is in the evening of the day before the wagon train is to move out when Inga turns to Hartvig and says, "Husband, I have something to tell you."

"Ya?" Hartvig responds nonchalantly.

"Ya," Inga teases. "I'm pregnant!"

Acting numb and shocked, Hartvig looks at Inga in total surprise. "Ya' gotta be wrong! he replies with cautious emotion. "No, I'm not wrong," Inga relates with a smile.

"Well, that is goot, Inga, but do you think that maybe now we should stay here until the baby is born?"

Inga laughs. "I'm only two months pregnant. The baby will be due in late October and we are not waiting here for seven months to have baby. We go now!"

Hartvig, suddenly concerned, doesn't crack a smile. He is serious. Now that there is a baby coming he is more serious than ever.

Inga is full of life this particular day, much more so than her husband. At sixteen, she is strong and agile. She has been use to hard working conditions at her home in Sweden, and feels confident about her ability to continue on the trip to their new home. At five-foot-five-inches tall, she has a slim figure and blond hair down to the middle of her back. Her deep blue eyes sparkle and as her skin darkens from exposure to the sun, her appearance takes on a rugged, attractive look.

At five a.m. the next morning Hartvig is up earlier than usual. He makes coffee and quietly thinks to himself that sleeping in the new covered wagon isn't bad. In fact, it is quite different than he had anticipated. A home on wheels, he thinks to himself as he brings the harnesses out for cleaning. The tarp keeps the rain out and there is ample place to sleep, but this is nothing like the home he envisions he will build for Inga. A home with three rooms and a fireplace. A home on their own land.

Inga wakes up at six a.m., peeks out the back of the wagon and feels a sense of joy as she watches the other immigrants rush to and fro getting their wagons and gear ready. "What an exciting day," she exclaims as she begins dressing.

Moments later Hartvig knocks on the side of the wagon with his rifle butt, an old single shot Remington he bought two days earlier. "Time to get up, Inga," he bellows in his slow, but loud voice.

"Ya, I'm almost ready," Inga shouts in her distinct Scandinavian accent.

"Ya, hurry then. The wagon master says we leave soon," Hartvig replies as he begins to check the horses, wagon, and equipment.

Inga climbs onto the buckboard style seat at the wagon's front, fixes her new dust bonnet, and gleefully states, "I'm ready to go to our new home." She then smiles at Hartvig and starts to wave to everyone who walks by. As Hartvig crawls up on the wagon to sit next to her, Inga grabs his right arm and leans over and kisses him on the cheek. "Let's go!" she says confidently, neither of them mentioning her pregnancy.

It is the second day on the trail and the weather soars to ninety-five degrees. When Inga isn't walking along side the wagon she sits in the back of it trying to avoid the hot sun and the dust from the wagon wheels and horses. The glamour seems to be wearing off as Inga spends more of her time in the rear of the wagon swatting flies and trying to find some way to cushion the bumps and jolts that seem to take place every minute or so. "Where are we, husband?" she yells from the back of the wagon as she tries to brace herself against the sideboard.

"Ya, I don't know, Inga. I'll ask."

Dennis Young, a wagon drover on horseback, is yelling instructions to another wagon driver as Hartvig draws near.

"Is there a problem, Mr. Young?" Hartvig inquires.

The drover turns to Hartvig, smiles, then chuckles. "Problem? You think I have a problem?" the drover yells back as he shakes his head in wonderment. "Say, Pilgrim, where you headed? Oregon?"

"Ya, I guess so ... to homestead," Hartvig replies slowly.

The wagon drover breaks into a loud laugh. "Well then, if you think I'm having a problem here, just ya wait. We ain't seen no Injuns yet. Haven't had to cross the big rivers yet. By golly, we haven't had a rainstorm yet! Oh, or a snowstorm or cholera. How's that for starters?"

Hartvig doesn't respond. He just looks at the drover with an expressionless sense of bewilderment.

The drover spins his horse around to look at another wagon that has pulled out of line with a broken axle, then makes another one-hundred-eighty degree turn back facing Hartvig. "See that wagon over there with the brok'n axle?"

Hartvig looks in the direction the drover points and nods.

"That's just a small delay. Ya'll wait for the big'ns. This be my fifth time on this run an I've see sickness ... mostly cholera, dead animals galore, gunfights over not'n, a lot of dead people, an I ain't even mentioned the Diggers yet. Problems? We ain't got none so far. Now you be gitt'n your wagon caught up yourself, ya hear?"

Hartvig nods his head affirmatively, flips the reins, and the horses jar the wagon forward. In a quick reflection to the drover's words, he asks himself, what's a Digger? But his full attention reverts back to Inga.

"Did ya' hear that, Inga? Inga, did ya hear what he said?" Hartvig waits for a reply, but Inga doesn't answer. "Inga, you okay?" Hartvig yells back into the wagon as he tries to steer the horses back into the wagon column.

There is still no response from Inga and Hartvig starts to feel a strange sensation in his body as if something is not right. He quickly pulls the team to a halt just outside the main body of moving wagons. He pulls back the secondary curtain Inga had hung up earlier. Not being able to see in back of the wagon clearly, he jumps off and runs to the rear, frantically he pulls back the flap. His eyes scan every detail and blanket of the interior, but there is no Inga. Upset and scared, he starts screaming her name in wild abandon. Acting disorientated, he runs to the head of his horses yelling frantically for Inga, and then runs back to the rear of the wagon yelling at the top of his voice, "Inga! Inga! Where are you?"

The passing wagons pay little attention to Hartvig's behavior as many have seen men go mad on the trail already. But Hartvig is adamant and begins running and screaming to each wagon that moves past him. "Have you seen my Inga?"

No one knows what Hartvig is referring to. They just shake their heads no and continue on. Hartvig is becoming not only frantic, but totally incoherent.

INGA'S PLIGHT

The wagons file by as Hartvig continues to run to each approaching wagon asking the same question and receiving the same answer. No one has seen her. How could this happen? Hartvig thinks to himself. How could Inga disappear so quickly? Hartvig's worry continues to intensify.

On a routine check of the train's progress, drover Young sees that Hartvig's wagon is pulled out of line. As he rides up to it, he notices that the undercarriage, wheels, and horses all appear to be functional and in good shape. He pulls his horse to a stop, looks around, and sees Hartvig running up and down the trail. Quickly Young rides over to Hartvig. "Got a problem there, Pilgrim?" he yells out to Hartvig sarcastically.

Hartvig, distraught with emotion runs to the drover and begs for help. "My Inga, she's gone! I can't find her nowhere! You gotta help me find her!"

Hartvig grabs at the drover's coat in desperation. "Whoa, down, boy!" exclaims the drover. "Get a handle on yourself, son!"

Hartvig releases the coat from his grasp and looks apologetic. "I'm sorry, Mr. Young," he says in a heavy Swedish accent. "I need help, I gotta find my Inga!"

Drover Young, realizing Hartvig's concerned and frightened state of mind, dismounts and looks Hartvig in the eyes. "Okay, Mr. Larson, calm down and tell me what's go'in on."

Hartvig tries to explain the situation. How after he and another drover last talked, Inga had disappeared. That he has been asking everyone in the passing wagons if they have seen her.

"Well," says the drover, "she must be around here somewhere," as he looks to the far hills. "There's not too many places for a woman on foot to hide. If she is wandering away from the wagons alone, one of my men would have spotted her or even another wagon would have reported her."

The drover puts his hand on Hartvig's shoulder in a show of compassion. "If it's any comfort to you, son, she must be around here somewhere. Just don't you fret. We'll find her."

Hartvig looks to the sky, tears running down his cheeks. "Please help me find my Inga," he begs.

"Tell you what, Mr. Larson, you just try'n relax. Get yourself back on your wagon and get it in line. I'll ride to the wagon master and report this problem. See what he knows. Ya' just calm down and do what I say, ya' hear?"

Hartvig nods his head and starts to walk back to his wagon.

"I'll put word out on the train. Be back in a bit!" yells drover Young as he gallops away.

Drover Young hasn't returned by the time the order is given to encircle the wagons for the night camp. Hartvig's heart is pounding and his mind is racing with thoughts of every magnitude. His emotions are leaping from deep worry to outright anger and frustration. "Damn her!" he blurts out loud. "What has happened to her?"

All the time that he is unhitching the horses he keeps mumbling to himself. "I can't wait for the drover to come to me. I go find him myself." Hartvig starts walking over to the main encampment. The sun is beginning to set in the west but the heat of the day is taking its toll on his temperament. Most of the drovers pay little attention to him approaching as they sit by the fire drinking coffee. "Where is Mr. Mulligan?" Hartvig demands as he stops short of the drovers' circle.

"O'er in the lead wagon," one of the drovers responds nonchalantly. "O'er thar do'n paper work."

Hartvig briefly looks for the drover he had talked to that afternoon, but failing to see him, starts to walk toward Mr. Mulligan's wagon.

"Looks like one ornery sons-a-bitch," quips a drover.

Upon arriving at the lead wagon, Hartvig forcefully pulls back the tarp and sees Mr. Mulligan sitting at a makeshift desk. "What has happened to my wife?" Hartvig yells.

Mr. Mulligan surprised and startled, reacts instantly. "Who the hell are you?"

"My name is Hartvig Larson, and my wife is missing! You know where she is?"

Catching some grasp of what is taking place and seeing the frightening look in Hartvig's eyes, Mr. Mulligan takes his bifocals off and responds directly. "So you're the one. I've had my drovers looking for your wife since the middle of the afternoon. She's not in camp and not on the back trail."

"Then where in tarnation is she?" demands Hartvig.

The wagon master shakes his head and tries to remain calm. "Look, Mr. Larson, if I had to baby-sit every man, woman, and child on this train I wouldn't have time to get my pants on in the morning. All I know is what has recently been brought to my attention. I don't make it a policy to get involved in family matters."

Hartvig is to the point of rage. "Involved in family matters? What you mean? My Inga is missing!"

Mr. Mulligan senses Hartvig's pent up anger and adjusts himself accordingly next to his revolver in the wagon. "Well, Mr. Larson, I don't know if it's my position to tell you this or not, but I guess someone should say som'tin to you. Possibly for your own good."

"Tell me what?" Hartvig screams as he squeezes the rear gate of the wagon with such intensity the knuckles on his enormous hands start turning white. "What you talking about?" Hartvig again demands.

Trying to defuse a volatile situation, Mr. Mulligan takes off his hat, places it on top of his pistol and leaves his hand resting there. "Well, Mr. Larson, sometimes what people do on this train is their own business, if you know what I mean. I'm not a man to get involved with the problems of others, unless, of course, it involves the overall mission of this train or some other serious disturbance."

Hartvig's frustration is at a boiling point. "You tell me where my Inga is now or I ..."

"You'll what?" yells back Mr. Mulligan, hand on his covered pistol. "You best calm down, my friend b'fore your anger gets the best of you. We've got enough problems on these trips without put'n up with a man 'n wife dispute."

Hartvig, not sure of what he has just heard, thinks for a moment before responding. "Man and wife dispute? Me and Inga never have disputes!"

The wagon master, trying to avoid any further conflict, attempts to console Hartvig. "Look, Mr. Larson, you just go back to your wagon, get something to eat and relax. You can discuss all this with your wife when she gets back. Now let me be before I have to call my sentinels."

Hartvig responds angrily and makes a threatening gesture. "When she gets back! Then where is she?"

"Mr. Larson ... back down! I have a gun pointed at your chest and I don't want no trouble with you. Your wife should be back in the morning. Until then, you deal with it. Now get your angry ass out of here! Ya' hear?"

Hartvig slams his palms down onto the back of the tail gate with such force that it splinters in several pieces and shakes the entire wagon. Alarmed, the wagon master fires a shot in the air to signal the sentinels. Hartvig, realizing that he can't fight all these men, quickly back steps away from the wagon and walks back to his own hitch, now more confused and emotionally upset than before.

"What the hell is the matter with the dumb son-of-a-bitch?" asks Mr. Mulligan as he and the drovers watch Hartvig walk away.

"Shit! Cain't keep track of his wife, I reckon," laughs one of the drovers as he picks up the broken tailgate. "That woman being in a heap of trouble if she come back here."

"What about that new sentinel she took off with on horseback, Capt'n?" inquires another drover.

"Don't know," replies Mr. Mulligan. "Might have to let him go. Just know I'd hate to be the man that tangles with that sun stunned Swedish lunatic."

It is after midnight, and although tired, Hartvig just can't seem to settle down to sleep. Thoughts about Inga and why the wagon master talked about things like "family problems" and "when she gets back," twirl in his mind.

At five o'clock the next morning, Hartvig has his horses hitched and ready to go. Having had no sleep that night, he is exhausted. He thinks to himself about turning back and looking for Inga on the trail, but finally concludes that he best stay with the train. It is evident to him that the wagon master has some kind of knowledge where Inga might be, but for some reason wouldn't tell him. In his mind he is preparing for the worst. As he patiently waits for the others to ready their wagons he sticks his loaded piston in his pants and then loads his rifle.

Just as the wagons begin moving out, one of the drovers rides by and pulls up to Hartvig's wagon. "How's it go'in today, Mr. Larson?"

Hartvig, not in the mood to talk, simply nods his head.

"I see your wife hasn't returned yet, that right? the drover jests.

Hartvig's look is cold and hard. His patience is waning, but he doesn't dare push his luck with the sentinels.

"Well, adios, Amigo. Maybe you'll see your wife this afternoon ... at the Cannon Water Hole. We should be stop'n there to fill the barrels 'n water the livestock." The drover laughs a loud hee-haw, neck reins his horse around, and gallops off toward the lead wagon.

Hartvig's frustration and emotional state is making him think he is going insane. Why would she be at the Cannon Water Hole? How did she get there? Why did she leave without telling me?

THE CANNON WATER HOLE INCIDENT

Inga is laughing and trying to pin up her long blond hair when Cajun throws his lariat around her. "Now I drag you to my place if you not go willingly," Cajun growls in a serious tone of voice.

"Ya," says Inga jokingly as she quickly removes the rope. "Where is that?"

Cajun, who has only been a sentinel for the wagon train since they left St. Louis, is a rough and coarse man. His life consisted mostly of being a trapper and part-time scout for the army until he joined the train. Standing six-feet tall, he wears a full beard, which seems to somehow fit his heavy frame of two-hundred pounds. His attire compliments his role as a sentinel; a black, four-inch leather brim hat, dark brown cow-hide coat and pants. The only part of his attire that doesn't seem to match are his black civil war boots, and he will never tell anyone how he obtained those.

Cajun's personality is the only admirable part of his personage, if that could even be considered an asset. His mannerisms and uncleanliness are overlooked by the few friends he has, mainly because of his hearty laugh and sometimes good natured way. Even when drunk he would sometimes be friendly and courteous. In fact, the other sentinels would talk about the time he gave a poor old lady twenty-five dollars. Half his pay for a month as an army scout, but as he stated at the time, "That lady needs the money more than I do. It may keep her from starving."

Although Inga initially was enjoying Cajun's company and the scouting they did to find water, she is beginning to feel uneasy about her situation. So far Cajun has been polite and quite accommodating. But now she senses his personality is changing and this is beginning to scare her.

"I have many places to take you," Cajun responds as he begins retrieving his rope. "You will like all of them."

Inga looks at him seriously. "But surely you are joshing me, Cajun. You know that I'm a married woman carrying a child."

Cajun reflects on her statement. "You need man like me to help you raise kid out here. The boy you claim as husband is too young to protect you."

Inga is but a child herself in many ways, but in this case she knows now that she has made a serious mistake accepting a ride from a man she doesn't know, even though he is an employee of the train.

"It'll be maybe another hour before the wagons get here. Maybe you and me can get to know each other better, no?" suggests Cajun.

Startled by Cajun's innuendoes, Inga becomes even more uncomfortable. The first time she met Cajun was back in St. Louis and she felt then that she could trust him. He has a rugged air of the American frontiersman about him. This initially intrigued her, plus he seemed sincere. In fact, that is her rationale in accepting the impromptu ride with him. He promised to show her sights off the beaten path and it was only to take a few hours rather than almost a day and half. Anyway, it seemed in her mind that it would be more enjoyable than riding in a bumpy, dusty old wagon.

"But now, who is this man, really?" Inga thinks to herself. "I don't know what you mean by getting to know each other better, Cajun. Besides, I don't know what I am going to tell my husband about staying out all night, especially being with you like this."

Cajun laughs. "Hey! He will say nothing as long as I'm around. He may not like it, but he is a boy and I am a man. You stay with Cajun here and I make you proud of me. I protect you."

Cajun dismounts from his horse and walks to Inga. Inga's smile disappears and her eyes search for a place to run, just in case.

"Okay, Inga, tell me. What your man do if you come with me?" Cajun then stoops over to look Inga in the eyes. "He will do nothing, no?"

Inga looks at Cajun with disbelief. This can't be, she thinks, although faintly believing that he would never touch her against her will. But, her thoughts reel ... what do I do if he does? Inga is well aware that the wagon train is still miles away, and that she really has no means to protect herself from this large man. Suddenly Cajun grabs her arm, pulls her to her feet. As her eyes meet his she sees a glare of rage that she has never seen in any man before.

"Cajun, let go of my arm, you're hurting me!" Inga's brief scream is quickly interrupted by her tears as she begins to cry profusely. "Please don't hurt me, Cajun!"

Cajun forcibly swings her around as if throwing a saddle from a horse. Inga stumbles to the ground and immediately struggles to regain enough balance to stand. Cajun is enraged. "Why you tease me?" he yells. "No woman goes for ride with man overnight unless she interested in him!"

Inga is in terror. Her body shakes as she stutters out her words. "No! I did not tease you! I went ... I went with you because I thought it would be fun. I ... I trusted you. I didn't know you wanted this."

Inga's tears drip off her cheeks as she tries to wipe her face with her hands. "Please, Cajun. Don't do this to me. Please let me be. I ... I'm going to have a baby! Please! Please!"

Cajun grabs her arm, pulls her close to him, and puts his other hand on her shoulder firmly. "Inga, Inga, my sweet flower. Cajun not here to hurt you, just show you what real man is like. Come now, don't be afraid. I will teach you many things about the west."

Cajun slowly massages Inga's shoulders as he draws her even closer to him. Inga instinctively knows that if she resists she will lose and the violence will escalate. But on the other hand she knows that to be passive will also invite his sexual aggression. Holding her forcefully close, Cajun begins kissing her neck and moving his free hand down her side.

Inga's emotions become frantic, but she knows she can't lose self-control now. It is only a matter of time before the lead scouts from the wagons will arrive. "Cajun! Cajun, stop!" Inga says as calmly as she can. "Okay. I'll give you what you want ... but not just now. We must wait. The train scouts will be here soon, you know that. We wouldn't have time to do this the way I know you would like it."

"What do you mean, the way I like it?" Cajun retorts instantly, his passion overruling his reason.

"You know, where … where we both can enjoy it. Where we have time to be together peacefully … before, during and after, and with no interruptions. We can make love as many times as you want."

"What? Are you lying to me?" Cajun grabs her with all the force his strong muscles can generate. "If you lying to me, woman, I kill you."

"Please, Cajun, believe me! It would be better for both of us. For me because of my husband and you because of your wagon master. Please, Cajun, you're hurting me."

Cajun thinks quickly, maybe she is right. Maybe now is not the time to have sex; that should have been last night. She'll be on the train for many weeks yet and there will be other times. His hands lighten their grasp on her arm and shoulder. "How do I know you speak truth … that you won't tell the others … that you mean what you say?" Cajun asks forcibly.

Inga looks Cajun in the eyes and tries to speak convincingly. "Because, it would be too embarrassing for both of us, especially for me."

Inga, still fearing for her welfare, thinks in terms of delay and biding time as long as she can. I must tell him anything he wants to hear until someone arrives. God, I will never do anything like this again, she pledges to herself as she contemplates her next move. I must for now try to pacify him.

"Cajun, you know how good it would be if we were alone and we knew that no one would disturb us, don't you? It would just seem so … so right."

Cajun's hands slowly move up and down her arms and waist, his thumbs maneuvering around her breasts. His eyes scan her body as he thinks about the situation and the possibility of a time like she describes.

"Okay, maybe you be right," surmises Cajun as he steps back to arms length, his hands still on her upper arm and his eyes fixed on hers. "You and I wait for a better time ... and a long time together, yes?"

Inga breathes a sigh of relief but knows she can't stop the act now. "Yes, Cajun, we will be together for a long time and it will be good for you. I will do anything to please you. I promise you that."

Cajun smiles, seemingly satisfied that his wishes and desires will be fulfilled, if not at the moment, soon enough. He instantly grabs Inga, pulls her close, forces a kiss, then pulls back. "See, Cajun will show you how a man can make a woman go wild."

Inga, repulsed by this very thought, continues her ploy. "Yes, Cajun, I see what you mean. Just don't forget to treat me like a lady, okay?"

Cajun becomes passionate and boastful. "I will treat you like queen and take you to many nice places."

Taking the opportunity to pacify him with some feminine display she slowly removes his hands from her arms and says calmly, "Cajun, let me wash my skirt down at the water hole? You can watch out for me if you wish."

Quite pleased by this suggestion, Cajun agrees. "But of course, my queen. I will watch you from a distance ... so I can get used to looking at you. I protect you." Cajun then smiles at Inga, releases his hands, and waves in the direction of the water hole. "You go, I will adjust saddle on horse and sit here on rock till you finish."

"Thank you, God!" Inga whispers under her breath as she walks to the water hole. Now, if I can just keep him entertained until the scouts get here. How long I wonder?

Inga enters the water, turns to look at Cajun, and gives him a brief smile and wave.

It seems like hours before the scouts arrive, when in fact, it is only twenty minutes. Inga's heart pounds with relief as she sees the two men ride up to Cajun. "They're here. Thank you, Lord. They're here!" she says out loud to herself as she takes a deep breath, puts on her skirt, and runs toward the men.

The two scouts are in a heated argument with Cajun as Inga reaches them. The last words she hears upon her approach is, "Somehow you'll have to answer for this, Cajun."

"I'm so glad you're here," Inga screams to the scouts as she stops a few feet away from their horses, avoiding any contact with Cajun. "How far back is the train?"

"Good to see ya', Ma'am," says the lead scout. "They should be here in about a half hour or so. You can see the dust cloud right over the horizon."

The scout then directs his attention back to Cajun. "Com'on over here for a minute, Cajun. We best talk a bit."

Inga's nerves are twisted in knots. "What am I going to tell Hartvig? What am I going to tell him?" she repeats to herself in a low voice. "I must think of something …"

It is late in the afternoon when the first wagon appears at the top of the hill. Inga immediately starts running toward the oncoming wagons. As she runs against the flow of the wagon train, no one speaks to her or even acknowledges her presence. More than forty wagons have passed and she hasn't seen Hartvig.

He didn't turn back did he? she thinks to herself in fear.

Exhausted and tired, Inga finally sits down and watches each wagon as they pass by, trying to avoid the horses, cattle, and dogs that are being herded at the side. After more than an hour of diligent scanning, Inga feels a sense of panic overtake her emotions. What if he turned back and left me?

What am I to do then? Distraught at this thought, she puts her hands over her face and begins to cry.

It is just a few minutes later that she hears her name being called. "Inga! Inga! Inga!"

Surprised, she looks up to see Hartvig standing on the seat of their wagon waving his arms frantically. Shocked and excited to see her husband, Inga scrambles to her feet, lifts up her long skirt, and starts to run toward him faster than she has ever run in her life. Her heart is throbbing with joy and relief.

Hartvig has pulled the horses out of line and is galloping them toward Inga as fast as they can pull a wagon. Once they are within one-hundred feet of each other Hartvig pulls the horses to a stop, ties the reins, and jumps off the wagon at a run.

"Husband! Husband! I'm so glad to see you!" Inga yells as they approach each other. "Oh, I missed you!"

Even though Hartvig seems eager to see her, she feels a cold chill as he does not embrace her, but stops short of her at two feet. Hartvig's eyes have a strange look to them as Inga stands, pleadingly, looking into them. "Hartvig, please don't do this to me. I'm sorry. I'll explain all this to you. Please, just hold me."

Hartvig stands silent, like a stone pillar. Inga gazes into his eyes. They're so cold and unforgiving, she thinks to herself fearfully.

"Get into the wagon, woman," Hartvig demands.

Without hesitating, Inga climbs onto the wagon wheel and pulls herself up onto the seat. Hartvig follows behind her, grabs the reins, and pushes the horses cruelly at a hard gallop toward the water hole. He says nothing and Inga dares not interrupt his silence.

Once at the water hole the horses became difficult to control. Their need for water is obvious, but the sweat on their bodies and foam in their mouths plainly display that giving them water now will certainly founder them.

"Let the horses cool down for awhile, 'bout half an hour, then give them something to drink and fill the barrels. I've got something to do." Hartvig hands Inga the reins, jumps off the wagon, and begins walking toward Mr. Mulligan's stop site.

"Husband, where are you going? Stay here!" yells Inga.

"Never you mind, woman. Just wait here and water the horses!" retorts Hartvig.

Inga has never seen Hartvig show anger before, not even when he was teased by ruffians in New York City. His behavior frightens her. 'I caused all this," she mumbles to herself. "Oh, God, what have I done? What is he going to do? Dear Lord, don't let anything happen to him!"

THE LAW OF THE TRAIN

"Wagon Master!" Hartvig yells, as he approaches Mr. Mulligan's lead wagon.
Several of the scouts and sentinels are talking when they hear Hartvig's voice. "Damn!" the lead scout utters to the others. "Here he comes again!"

"Where is the Wagon Master? I want to talk to him! Now!" Hartvig demands boldly, as he comes to a stop in front of the men. The look on his face and the glare in his eyes clearly shows his frustration and anger. Hartvig's large hands open and close like two pumping pistons.

"Just a moment, son," says one of the scouts. "He's tend'n to another wagon at the present, but I reckon I can get him for you."

It is a matter of a few minutes before Mr. Mulligan and the scout return from behind the wagons.

"What is it that you want, Mr. Larson?" queries Mr. Mulligan in an irritated tone of voice.

"Me and you talk private, okay?" Hartvig demands loudly.

Mr. Mulligan thinks briefly of the confrontation the night before and knows what is on Hartvig's mind. "Alright, Mr. Larson, let's step over by my wagon. We can talk there."

The two men begin to walk to an area of privacy as the scouts stand alert and observe. It is obvious to the scouts that Hartvig is irate as they see him waving his hands in the air and occasionally raising his voice. Hartvig and Mr. Mulligan confer for less than five minutes before the wagon master walks back to his scouts.

"Which of you scouts first saw the sentinel, Cajun, this afternoon?"

"We did," answers the two scouts who had first arrived at the water hole.

"Was Mrs. Larson with him?" asks the wagon master. "Well ... yes," came the answer as the wagon master interrupts and turns to his lead scout. "Go get Cajun! Tell him I want to speak with him immediately!"

"Ya betcha, Capt'n," replies the scout as he begins to mount his horse.

The wagon master and Hartvig continue their discussion under the watchful eyes of the scouts. It is only four to five minutes before the scout returns. "Cajun says he'll be here right pronto, Capt'n."

"Mr. Larson, wait here for a moment." Concerned about a possible confrontation, the wagon master pulls his lead scout to the side. "Take two men with you and move those first five wagons down the way. I don't know what might happen here, but it doesn't look pleasant. Just don't want those families witnessing an argument. Do it quickly!"

"Gotcha, Capt'n."

Hartvig takes his wide brimmed hat off to wipe his brow and squints as the low setting sun hits his eyes. He can barely make out the silhouette of Inga in the distance as she is putting the water pails in the back of the wagon. As Hartvig waits he continues to look at Inga.

The wagon master walks to his wagon to get his hat and revolver. He is walking back to where Hartvig is waiting when he sees Cajun in the distance. "Here he comes now. You let me do the talk'n; do you understand that, Mr. Larson?"

Hartvig nods his head maintaining a silent demure.

Cajun rides in at a full gallop, reins in his horse, and jumps off. "You want to see me, boss?" Cajun jowls in a nonchalant manner as he quickly glances in Hartvig's direction.

"Ya, Cajun. Matter of fact, I do. It seems like we may have a serious problem with one of our train members here and for some reason you seem to be squarely involved in it."

"Me?" cajoles Cajun. "Com'on, Capt'n, I don't get involved in no problems."

Hartvig's emotions are barely containable as he listens to Cajun's denial of any misconduct.

"I'll get to the point here, Cajun. I want to know what happened with you and Mrs. Larson?"

Cajun chuckles, then laughs a nervous laugh. "Capt'n, nothing happened. I don't know what you're talking about. There's no problem."

Hartvig, against the previous advice of the wagon master, cannot help himself as he steps toward Cajun and interrupts. "You, Liar! You will pay for what you did! I see to that!" Cajun smirks as the wagon master puts out his arm to halt Hartvig from getting any closer to Cajun.

"Get this boy off my back, Capt'n, or I'll have to do something I don't like!"

"You hold it, Cajun! Back off before I have to so something I don't like!" retorts the wagon master. "You got that?"

Both Cajun and Hartvig stand silent for the moment as it is obvious that Mr. Mulligan is in no mood to play dialogues. "Okay, now you two listen to me! By the agreed laws and rules of conduct on this wagon train, I'm compelled to take a complete written statement on any alleged violation." The wagon master hesitates and looks to Cajun, who is staring at Hartvig.

"Cajun! Cajun, listen! Mr. Larson here has accused you of ..."

Cajun interrupts abruptly. "Accused me of what, Capt'n? That bitch wife of his begged to come with me and I ..."

Hartvig, unable to control his anger any longer, lunges forward at Cajun and grabs his leather coat with both hands. Cajun, reacts instantly, pulls out his skinning knife and slices Hartvig across the stomach. "Back off, boy! You just let this be. I've killed more men than you have years ... and I don't think you want me to add your dumb ass to my count!"

"Put that knife down, Cajun!" yells the wagon master.

"You stay out of this, Capt'n. It's not your concern now. You know the law out here!"

Hartvig slowly runs his hand across his stomach and is more surprised at the blood oozing out of his wound than of being seriously injured. His eyes immediately return to Cajun, who is holding the knife ready.

"Just back off, kid!" Cajun yells, as he holds his position for a fight and waves the knife menacingly at Hartvig.

"You see that, Capt'n!" Cajun screams. "You see that! That kid tried to choke me! That big, dumb bastard tried to choke me!"

The words, "big, dumb bastard" infuriate Hartvig. He has always hated it when someone called him big and dumb as a little kid ... and he is not a bastard. Triggered by this statement and his emotions over the situation with Cajun and his wife, Hartvig instinctively reacts by lunging at Cajun again.

Cajun jumps back, waves the large ten inch knife at Hartvig's face and taunts him mercilessly. "Com'on! Com'on, you big, dumb lux! You stupid bastard! Com'on!"

Cajun slowly circles around Hartvig, sneering and flicking the knife at his face, then his stomach. Hartvig turns with him, arms stretched out wide, looking for an opportunity to get the knife. "Com'on, boy!" yells Cajun. "I'd like to cut you up. Your little woman and me don't want you 'round no more anyway!"

"Put that knife down, Cajun!" yells the wagon master.

"You stay out of this, Capt'n. This is personal! It be settled between me and him!" Cajun retorts.

Mr. Mulligan knows he cannot get involved and realizes that the situation is out of control. But he tried again. "Put the knife down, Cajun. The boy is unarmed!"

Cajun just laughs as he continues to circle and jab at Hartvig. "Come on, boy! You afraid? Your wife isn't. Me and her have big plans, boy, and they don't include you!"

Hartvig's rage is beyond control. He makes a quick lunge for Cajun and immediately pulls back as Cajun's knife swishes by his face. Again Cajun slashes at Hartvig but this time Hartvig's left hand makes firm contact with Cajun's wrist just above the knife, pulling Cajun off balance. In a split second Hartvig's right arm is around Cajun's neck. CRACK!! The sound of bones breaking can be heard clearly by the wagon master and scouts as Hartvig holds Cajun's lifeless body dangling inches above the ground.

"For God's sake, son, you've killed him! Drop him! Drop him, now!" screams the wagon master, but Hartvig continues to twist Cajun's neck again and again.

"Stop it! Stop it! Damn it!" the wagon master yells frantically. Hartvig finally looks over to the wagon master, stares him momentarily in the eyes, then drops Cajun to the ground. "For Christ sake, kid, you've killed him! I've got to make a report on this now. Damn it!"

The wagon master is beside himself; both frustrated and angry at having to deal with a matter like this on his train. "Go to your wagon, Mr. Larson! Go now! You know I have to make a report on this, damn it! There'll be a train council meeting tomorrow on this. You know that don't you?"

Hartvig says nothing, just momentarily looks at Cajun's body lying on the ground, then turns away and starts walking toward his wagon.

As Hartvig approaches his wagon, Inga runs out to meet him. It is dusk now, but she recognizes Hartvig's frame even at a distance. "What happened?" Inga asks excitedly. "You okay?"

"We go to sleep now, Inga. We find out tomorrow."

Inga didn't sleep much during the night and is up before sunrise. She is confused by Hartvig's lack of questioning on the water hole incident and what transpired down at Mr. Mulligan's wagon.

Once Hartvig arises he spends the time sitting on the wagon hitch cleaning harnesses and remains totally silent. Inga dares not interrupt this.

At ten o'clock that morning a scout rides up to Hartvig with a message from the wagon master. "The train council requests that you present yourself, Mr. Larson," the scout relays in a sober tone. "They would like you to be at the main tent within an hour. What should I report?"

Hartvig gets up slowly, stands silently for a moment, then replies, "Tell them I be there at that time."

Inga's stomach is churning as she cleans the wagon. Her emotions are so mixed that she doesn't' know what to do or to say to Hartvig. She senses that something is drastically wrong, but doesn't know what. She watches as Hartvig saddles one of the horses. Finally she breaks through her fear and runs to Hartvig. "What is wrong, husband? Tell me! I must know what you are thinking. Please!"

"I tell you later," Hartvig responds as he mounts his horse. "You get the wagon ready."

Inga, with tears in her eyes, watches as Hartvig rides toward the Council tent.

The Council, an elected body of train members, including the wagon master, Mr. Mulligan, are sitting behind a make shift table as Hartvig enters the tent. Appearing larger than life, Hartvig walks quietly and erectly to the front of the Council.

"Mr. Larson," the Council chairman begins. "I presume you know why we have requested your presence here?"

Hartvig remains silent, but nods his head affirmatively.

"Let me start by saying that we are not a court of law in the eyes of the United States Government or this Territory. You are not being tried here for any legal crime by us. Do you understand that, Mr. Larson?"

Again Hartvig simply nods his head.

"However, this Council does represent the laws of the wagon train and its Code of Conduct. I want you to know that we enforce these regulations. The same ones you signed upon joining us on this trip." The chairman shows Hartvig a copy of the contract. "Do you understand what this agreement says, Mr. Larson?"

Again, Hartvig nods affirmatively.

"Mr. Larson, let me review last nights incident as it was related to me by Mr. Mulligan."

Hartvig listens intently as the chairman reads the report. When finished, he looks up at Hartvig. "Is what I have read an accurate account of the incident between yourself and the sentinel, Cajun?"

This time Hartvig states affirmatively, "Ya, it is."

"In that case, Mr. Larson, here is our view of what must be done." The chairman looks to the other members and each nods a sign of approval of the statement they prepared earlier that morning.

"We all agree that the emotional turmoil you have gone through is tremendous. However, it appears that you threatened the deceased, Cajun, causing him to defend himself initially. We understand that he drew a knife and slashed you in the stomach. We all agree that at that point the issue of defense shifted. That in fact, scout Cajun then became the aggressor, using deadly force. But our problem lies in the realm of who committed the more excessive force since you did kill him by breaking his neck."

Hartvig continues to stand silently and emotionless, listening as the chairman breaks momentarily to look up at him.

"Let me continue, Mr. Larson. As I say, we are not a court of law, but we do rule over ourselves and this committee has a moral obligation to enforce those rules we have all previously agreed upon. You understand that, don't you, Mr. Larson?"

Hartvig nods his head yes.

The chairman looks up to Hartvig, clears his throat, and reads from a prepared document. "Mr. Larson, it is the unanimous decision of this Council that you and your wife are to be banished from this wagon train."

Hartvig reacts only slightly and starts to turn to leave.

"Wait one minute, Mr. Larson, if you would, please," the chairman asks. "Please let me continue. However, in a gesture or humanitarianism, and for the protection of you and your wife, we will allow you to continue on with us until we reach Fort Hayes. If, at that time, you are still with us, it becomes our responsibility to turn you over to the army authorities. We, then, will let them determine your fate. This is our decision."

Hartvig, showing no emotion, turns and leaves without saying a word.

Inga, who has been waiting outside, rushes to him as he leaves the tent. In a sudden burst of emotion she throws her arms around him and begins to cry.

"I'm sorry, husband. I'm so sorry. I love you! I will go with you! Please forgive me." Tears are running down Inga's cheeks as she clings to Hartvig. "We will raise our baby together! We will always be together! I never want to be away from you ever again!"

Hartvig looks at Inga, puts his hand on her chin lightly, gently tilting her head up toward him. "I know you love me, Inga. I love you too. That's why I am not mad at you. I know that you love me."

Inga smiles and hugs Hartvig even closer.

"We will settle someplace in this territory," continues Hartvig. "Maybe near one of the settlements up the road." Hartvig puts his arms around Inga and lifts her up to kiss her as the tears spill from her eyes. "Ya, soon I will build you a beautiful home. For you and baby and maybe more babies. We see. We give our babies a good American education, huh?"

Inga then hugs Hartvig even tighter as she agrees with him between sobs. "Yes, husband! Yes! Yes!"

CHAPTER SIX
DESTINY CALLS

It's two o'clock in the morning when Leon is awakened by Henry's screams. Leon, in the next bunk, is terrified. For a moment he just sits on the edge of his bed watching Henry, trying to figure out what to do. "Henry, what's wrong?" Leon yells.

Henry doesn't respond to Leon's question. His whole body is trembling and hundreds of small sweat beads dot his forehead. Leon stares silently, scared as he watches Henry toss and turn in his sleep.

"Henry! Henry!" Leon yells frantically. "It's just a dream. It's a dream, Henry! You're okay!"

Henry starts to rub his eyes. Confused, he slowly rubs his arm across his eyebrows as he peeks over toward Leon. He takes a deep breath and shakes his head as he looks down at his shaking hands. "God! It all seemed so real." Henry takes another deep breath. "I thought it was happening all over again."

Leon and Henry, who are both age eight, have been roommates now for almost two years. Leon has witnessed Henry's talking and screaming in his sleep before, but has never seen a display of such intensity as this night. "What is happening, Henry?" Leon inquires softly.

Henry doesn't respond, only continues to wipe his eyes as he tries to calm himself.

"It was really bad this time, Henry. I've seen you do this before, but not this bad. I think I should go get Bishop Jackson, don't you?" says Leon in a very concerned voice.

Henry doesn't respond immediately as his recollection of the dream is so intense that he is still almost in shock. "No, I'll be alright. Just give me a few minutes to wake up. I'll try not to dream like that again, Leon."

"Just the same. If you don't tell Bishop Jackson I'm go' in' to," Leon states in a firm manner, "'cause you're starting to scare me."

Henry lies back down on his side and pulls the covers up over himself. "You go to sleep, Leon. I'll talk to the Bishop in the morning. I promise."

Leon lies back down in his bed hesitantly as he keeps his eyes on Henry. "You keep that promise, now. Cause I think there's something wrong with you."

Henry takes a deep sigh. "Just go to sleep, Leon."

Bishop Jackson is sitting at his desk when Henry walks into his office. "Good morning, Henry," the Bishop says cheerfully, "How's your day thus far?"

"Fine, Sir," responds Henry as he walks to the chair he usually sits in when in the Bishop's office.

"Well, mine too, son." The Bishop leans back in his chair and looks Henry in the eyes. "What can I do for you today, young man? You look like you have something on your mind."

Noticing the look on the Bishop's face, Henry avoids bringing up the issue of his dream, smiles, and instead asks an unrelated question. "Oh, nothing, Sir. I just wanted to know if I was going to pitch in the game on Saturday?"

Without responding to Henry's question, Bishop Jackson gets up out of his chair and walks to a chair next to him. "How do you like it here so far?" the Bishop asks as he pulls the chair closer to Henry and sits down.

Taken somewhat by surprise at this question, Henry responds quickly. "You know I like it here, Sir. I've told you that before."

Bishop Jackson hesitates, thinks momentarily and looks at Henry. "Well, let me put it another way. If you could wish for someplace to be right now, where would you like that to be?"

Henry, confused by this question, ponders for a moment. "You mean other than here, Sir?" Bishop Jackson nods his head affirmatively. "Well," continues Henry, "I guess I would like to be at the Military Academy, Sir."

Bishop Jackson is taken off guard by this answer. Having been a minister for almost nineteen years and director of the orphanage for ten of those years he has never heard a response from an eight-year-old like this one. "Hmm, that's interesting. I wasn't expecting an answer like that from you. Tell me, how long have you had this idea?"

"Ever since I can remember," retorts Henry.

Henry's answer concerns Bishop Jackson in the sense that he well remembers the day he first found the boy lying next to his parents' bodies, and his statement about wanting to "kill Johnny Reb." After observing Henry in the orphanage school he knows there is something about this youngster that is special; his mannerism, his personality, his excellent grades. The faculty even makes occasional comments on how precocious he is.

Bishop Jackson has been aware of Henry's nightmares for several months. And now this boy is thinking of a military school. The combination of the two suddenly strike the Bishop's concern.

"Henry, you know that I'll support you in whatever goals you decide on, but I think it is a little soon to be thinking about being a soldier, isn't it?" The Bishop gets up and walks behind his desk, seriously concerned by Henry's desire to be a soldier, and at such a young age.

"Well, Sir ..." Henry begins, but Bishop Jackson quickly interrupts him.

"How do you feel about your education?" asks the Bishop in a serious tone of voice. Henry recognizes the Bishop's change of mood and hesitates to answer. He just sits in the chair looking at the floor.

"I can't tell you," the Bishop continues, "how important it is for a young man to get a good education ... especially with the reconstruction of the south and the development of the United States into the western territories. Certainly you realize that you have the talent to be someone special, someone who will someday make good things happen here in Georgia."

The Bishop, feeling a special bond towards Henry, reasons in his mind that now is the time to start guiding this young boy into some form of professional training. "How can I convince this talented young man to develop his natural talents?" he thinks to himself. Maybe a doctor, lawyer, or even a teacher ... anything but a soldier. That is not what Black America needs.

Suddenly the Bishop catches himself trying to formulate this boy's life. "Henry, I'm sorry. I'm not here to tell you what you should do with your life. But there is something else that we should talk about and I know you are hesitant to bring it up."

Henry looks at the Bishop with a blank expression on his face. "What's that, Sir?"

"I want to talk with you about those terrible nightmares. They've been going on for some time now and are getting worse."

Henry is immediately alert and takes a defensive posture in the chair by folding his arms and looking away from Bishop Jackson.

"Can we talk about them?" the Bishop inquires.

Henry does not answer and continues to look at the floor. Bishop Jackson approaches him and puts his hand on his shoulder. "Listen, son," he begins, "I can only attempt to understand the emotions you hold inside of you. But as time goes on all wounds will heal ... but when not dealt with, they can leave deep, long lasting scars, physically and emotionally." The Bishop hesitates, looking for a response from Henry, who shows no emotion or response.

"Henry, let's keep this talk of ours between us and possibly you can think on it for awhile. In the meantime, I want you to know that if you ever feel the need to just sit down and talk I will be more than happy to do so ... and about anything you like. I just want you to be aware of that."

Henry says nothing for well over a minute. It's apparent to Bishop Jackson that he is still troubled over the deaths of his parents and that these recurring dreams are of a post traumatic emotional response. He has seen that occur in other children and some of the soldiers after combat. But for the moment, he figures, it is just as well to let him sit there and think.

The Bishop sits down at his desk, pulls open the drawer, and brings out paper and a pen. He hands them across the desk to Henry. "Here, take this with you and maybe you will write down some of your ideas and feelings as they come to you. It's a wonderful way to express yourself."

Henry looks up at the Bishop. His eyes show a certain relief that the Bishop has brought this issue out in the open, but in his heart there is a churning, a desire to understand that term, feelings.

"Uh, thank you, Sir, uh ... is that all then?"

"Yes, that's all," says Bishop Jackson, "just try that paper stuff. It may surprise you how you really feel about things."

"I'll see, Sir," says Henry as he hesitantly walks out of the Bishop's office.

Thinking that he may have broken down some emotional barriers, the Bishop ponders the situation deeper. Possibly it is best now to just let Henry think about his feelings by himself and see what develops. Other than the nightmares, there doesn't seem to be any other behavior or emotional problems. Now is the time to let the boy work on his own emotional development. It will be to his benefit when he gets older and has to deal with the real world. "Yes, we will give this boy extra guidance and attention," the Bishop says to himself in a low voice. "He is unique."

After leaving the Bishop's office, Henry walks to his class in the adjacent building. On his way an overwhelming feeling of despair makes him stop dead in his tracks. His body breaks into a cold sweat and the dizziness is so bad that he has to sit down on the wood floor. He puts his head down between his knees and wraps his arms around his ankles. "This can't be," he mumbles to himself. "I'm hearing my mother's voice." Henry sits silently for several minutes trying to clear his mind.

"Hey, Henry!" a voice from above sounds. Henry looks up and sees Leon standing over him. "What's wrong? Are you having that dream again?"

Henry shakes his head no and motions his hand to invite Leon to sit down. Leon struggles to sit, finding it difficult to maneuver his five-foot-two, one-hundred-fifty pound body onto the floor. Plop goes Leon's butt as it makes contact with the floor. Henry, although still reacting to his sudden experience, can't help but chuckle as Leon gets himself floor orientated. "You don't have to make a big production out of it, Leon," Henry jokes.

Leon, in his normal jovial candor, laughs also. "Ya, I know. You're just lucky you don't have to carry all this weight around. That would be just something else for you to worry about."

"I'm sorry," says Henry as his mood changes. 'I didn't mean it to tease you."

Leon makes his final wriggle into a comfortable position and adds his point of view. "I know, but I hope we intend to stay here for a bit, cause I think we both need the rest. Say, did you go see the Bishop today like you said you were going to do?"

Henry hesitates for a moment acting somewhat irritated at Leon's straight-forwardness. "Ya, I did."

"What did he say? Are they going to send you to an asylum?"

"No!" Henry retorts quickly.

"What then?" Leon queries humorously. "Damn, Henry, you're a lunatic case if ever there was one."

"Spit on you, too, Leon. If anyone needs help in that department it's you." Both laugh briefly and are temporarily at ease until Leon brings the issue up again.

"Seriously, Henry, what did the Bishop say?"

Henry looks away for a second and wonders whether he should mention anything to Leon, but then recalls what the Bishop said about talking about feelings. "Leon," Henry begins, "can I trust you?"

Leon looks to Henry in a frowning, quizzical way. "Of course you can. Don't you know that? We've been friends and roommates since the day you got to this place. We can talk about anything and keep it between us."

"Okay, then," Henry begins with quiet enthusiasm. "What if I told you that the Bishop believes that someday I could become a doctor or a teacher?" Henry hesitates to say what is really on his mind, but thinks about two things that have been said to him this morning: One, that he should talk about his feelings, and two, that Leon is his best friend and he can talk to him.

"Leon, I'll tell you something if you promise not to say anything about this to anybody for the rest of your life ... promise?"

Leon looks at Henry seriously and says, "I promise, ol' buddy. Only you and I will know."

Leon then looks around as does Henry to make sure no one else is within hearing distance. When all seems clear to talk privately, Leon bursts out with anticipation. "Com'on. Tell me, Henry. I'll keep it a secret. Promise!"

Henry takes a deep breath and begins talking with the confidence and sincerity that only one would convey to a trusted friend. "You know those dreams I've been having?"

Leon nods his head as he listens intensely.

"Well, they're dreams about my Ma and Pa. Back when we were slaves. I remember my Ma being afraid of the Confederate soldiers, that's why she and my Pa never went north. And I remember telling my Ma that I was going to be a soldier someday. But before the war was over Confederate soldiers came into our cabin and killed them."

Leon's eyes open wide as he listens to Henry. But when he learns of the death of Henry's parents he can't help but interject. "They killed both of your parents? I mean … the Confederate soldiers killed both of your parents?"

Henry's mood becomes melancholy. His eyes show a sadness that reflects the pain and hurt that is deep in his soul. He begins to answer Leon's question, but tears start to run down his cheeks. Leon is unsure of what to do, but his heart is filled with as much compassion as a young boy can contain. "Gee, I'm sorry. I don't know what to say except I'm glad that you told me. I'll keep it a secret, cause I'm your best friend and I keep my promises."

Henry looks to Leon. His eyes show a trust and faithfulness that he has never experienced before. He reaches his hand out to Leon who grabs it tightly with his and then whispers to Henry, "Be a soldier someday, my friend."

CHAPTER SEVEN
OUT WEST - A NEW WAR BREWS
LONE WOLF'S SAGA

Three years before the Civil War ends a new war against the United States Government is beginning. From North Dakota to Texas and from southern Minnesota to the Southwest, settlers are streaming across the Great Plains. The railroads are developing as fast as spikes can be laid and ground is being broken wherever even a most meager sustenance can be made.

During the Civil War, the bulk of American fighting power is concentrated on the preservation of the Union. As a consequence, most settlers moving west must rely on the law of the gun and band together in small settlements for their own protection against raiding Indians and outlaws. Homesteaders living two miles or more outside these small communities are at the mercy of both natural and unnatural elements.

August 17, 1862, starts out as a peaceful Sunday for the Stevensons. They are taking a Sabbath rest as they have worked hard all week to get the fall harvest of grain in.

It is like most days this time of year in southern Minnesota. There is a blue early morning haze in the horizon and the smell of dry sweet grass is in the air. Gladys Stevenson and her two daughters are preparing for an outside afternoon dinner. She has invited their neighbors who live on an adjacent homestead. This is the only day of the week her family takes time to socialize and it is important to her that everything is prepared just right.

Dan Stevenson is raking the horseshoe pit as the Emerson family arrive. Being a friendly, hospitable man and anxious for company, Dan drops his rake and walks over to the buggy to help the Emerson's with their food baskets.

"Good morning, Dan," says Gary Emerson as he jumps out of his buggy and shakes hands with him. "Good morning to you, Gary, and you too, Mrs. Emerson. Hello, kids!" greets Dan Stevenson with a smile.

They all exchange informal greetings as the Emerson family mix with the Stevensons around the large picnic table set up in the front yard. Dan and Gary walk back to the horseshoe pit and start playing a game of "shoes" while the women and children occupy themselves with the dinner preparations.

"How's the crop this year, Dan?" questions Gary Emerson.

"Not too bad. I think by the time it is all in, it will be a bit above thirty bushels an acre. Probably the best since I broke the land four years ago. How about yours?"

Gary looks a bit glum as he explains that he is having problems with the rocks that keep rising to the surface every year from frost. "Not as good as yours, Dan. I don't know how much longer I can last on this land. It just seems to be the worst land in this township." The two continue to talk about farming and throw horseshoes as they wait for the big feast.

Two miles down the road a small band of Sioux hunters sit by a small pond watering their horses. The Buffalo hunting in Dakota Territory has been unsuccessful as most of the animals were moving farther west toward the Missouri River. Disgruntled at the poor hunting and upset that the Lower Sioux agency, which is operated by the United States Government, is months behind in the Indian annuity payments, their mood is snappish.

Lone Wolf, at nineteen, is by all accounts a good hunter and although young, thought highly of by his elders. At six-feet-one-inch tall, he is strong and wiry of build. His biggest defect of character is his quick temper. If things go his way, he is outgoing and courteous. If not, his mood swing will cause him problems even with his closest friends. At the age of fifteen he killed his best friend over an argument concerning who killed a deer. The Tribal council allowed the incident to be adjudicated by the dead man's family. Lone Wolf, in retribution, gave the dead man's family five horses. The incident is then settled.

Today is not a good day for Lone Wolf as he discovers a nest of eggs laid by one of Dan Stevenson's hens. "Look at this!" yells Lone Wolf, as he picks up two eggs from the nest. Raising them above his head he yells to the others in the hunting party. "See! See this! This what I think of White Man's Agency!" He then squeezes the eggs together in his hand. "A man must eat, but not scrounge for food like a dog!"

The other members of the hunting party view Lone Wolf's action with mixed emotions. "Come, let's visit a short hair's farm. They give us good meat!" demands Lone Wolf.

"You go to short hair's farm, Lone Wolf. I'm going home. I don't want trouble with white man," says Swift Fox.

Lone Wolf looks at Swift Fox with disdain. "You! You go back! You not a brave or warrior. You go home, sit in women's tent ... eat government dung."

The confrontation between the two is close to a fight and individuals are lining up on sides.

"Which of you warriors are brave enough to go with me?" Lone Wolf yells.

"I will,' is the decision of four of the men.

"We go then. And you, Swift Fox, you tell Little Crow that I am a man not afraid." Lone Wolf spits on the ground toward Swift Fox in defiance.

Following the dirt road to the Stevenson's farmstead, Lone Wolf's eyes catch site of the homesteaders outside, milling around the large table. He motions to his followers to stop. "See!" he says as he points in the direction of the settlers.

"They have plenty food. They give us food or we take it. It no matter. I hungry! I die as a warrior than be fed like a dog. I have a plan. Let's go!"

The five men, dressed in their buckskin hunting gear and carrying rifles, surprise the settlers, although they are not unusually alarmed. They have seen many Indian hunting parties pass by their homesteads in the last two years and there have never been any problems.

Lone Wolf, is forward and direct as he walks up to the table. First he looks at all the food laying before him and then at each of the settlers, including the children. "How!" he says in a seemingly friendly manner, reaching his hand out to shake.

"How!" says Dan as he walks up to reciprocate.

"You share this food with your Indian friends, yes?" implies Lone Wolf.

As the women and children stand in silence, Dan smiles and thinks for a moment. "Certainly. We will give you what you need, but then you must be on your way. We have company today and …"

Lone Wolf interjects, pointing to his rifle. "No! We have a shooting contest for food. Whoever wins gets food, yes?"

Surprised by this intruding offer, Dan looks to Gary, then to his wife who is shaking her head negatively.

"Well, I don't know … what's your name again?" Dan asks, biding for time to assess what is going on.

"My name Lone Wolf … we have contest?"

"Well, Lone Wolf, tell me, exactly what is this contest?"

"You have weapons. Repeating rifles. You shoot repeating rifles against Indian single shot." Lone Wolf smiles as his accomplices look on.

Gary, as well as the women and children, are now more apprehensive about what is taking place. This is not the usual contact with the Indians they are accustomed to. They silently and secretly look at one another through the corners of their eyes.

"What are we to shoot at and what distance?" Gary replies as he becomes drawn into Lone Wolf's ploy.

Lone Wolf looks around and sees a group of pumpkins on the ground about fifty yards from where they are standing. "See, we shoot pumpkins and one who breaks most, wins, yes?"

Dan is apprehensive, but feels he doesn't want to be antagonistic. "You say we shoot our rifles, me and Gary," says Dan as he points to his friend, "and you shoot your rifles, is that right?"

Lone Wolf winks at his companions and replies, "Yes, we take ones over there and you take ones over there," as he points to the left.

"Honey! Come over here a minute will you, please?" yells Gladys as she meets Dan at the point half way between the table and where the Indians are standing. "This is getting scary. What is going on?"

Dan tries to calm her concern. "Don't worry, dear. They're just making a game out of getting something to eat. I'll handle it ... we'll play their game, then give them some food and they'll be gone, okay?"

Gladys gives Dan a concerned look as she turns to walk back to where Mrs. Emerson is standing.

"Okay. Let's make a game out of this, Lone Wolf," Dan says with confidence. "We'll get our rifles and shoot from behind that fallen twig over there," as he points to a long, thin branch lying on the ground about twenty feet from where they stand.

Dan and Gary pick up their seven shot Springfields and walk to where the firing line has been established. Lone Wolf and his five companions walk over and stand to their left.

"Go ahead, Lone Wolf," says Dan. "Let's see what you can do."

Lone Wolf steps up to the firing line, aims and fires. Crack goes the sound of his rifle as the bullet smashes a pumpkin into hundreds of pieces. He then steps back and begins to reload.

"You next," motions Lone Wolf to Gary.

Gary looks back at his wife and daughters, then steps up to the twig. He notices that he is a bit anxious and his bracing arm is shaking. He puts his rifle down, takes a deep breath and raises it to aim a second time. Crack! The shot goes just a hairline to the left. Gary looks to Dan, shrugs his shoulders and tries again. This time he is on his mark. Satisfied he did his part, he steps back and motions to one of the Indians that it is their turn. As the shooting continues turn after turn, the Indians keep their weapons reloaded and watch as Dan and Gary expend their cartridges.

Dan fires his last shell, shooting the last of the pumpkins. With a smile on his face he turns to look at his wife and friends and waves a victory sign. Putting the rifle over his shoulder he walks up to Lone Wolf. "It was a good match, Lone Wolf, but before you leave we'll give you some food and provisions for your trip to the agency."

Lone Wolf does not respond. He looks back at his followers and raises his right hand, a signal to begin the attack.

Immediately Lone Wolf points his rifle at Dan and fires, wounding him in the left side. Dan spins around as if he were hit by a steel piston. Realizing that he has no ammunition left, he tries to get up and run to his wife and children. "Into the house!" he yells as another bullet tears through his side and kidneys.

Reloading quickly after each shot, the Indians begin firing at the women and children as they run toward the house and barn.

It is a race between Lone Wolf and Gary now. Gary reacts as fast as he can to inject a shell in the chamber of his rifle, but a bullet from Lone Wolf's pistol tears through his chest like it did the pumpkins they shot earlier. He falls to the ground, dead. Lone Wolf smiles as he reloads his rifle and says out loud as if talking to Gary, "I won!"

A bullet blasts Gladys Stevenson in the back as she tries to get her two daughters into the house. She falls immediately and is lying in a pool of blood on the porch steps, her daughters screaming, "Mom! Mom!" Two more shots crack though the still afternoon air and both young girls join their mother lying in a macabre type embrace on the ground.

Mrs. Emerson makes it to the barn with her five-year-old son. Screaming loudly she tries to get her son under a pile of hay. "Get in there and hide. Don't make a peep!" she screams frantically, tears running down her cheeks, and a look of terror on her face.

"Mommy! Mommy!" her young son cries as she runs to divert the raiding Indians away from the barn and into the woods by the river. Another "Crack" sounds from a rifle as Mrs. Emerson falls dead in her tracks.

Lone Wolf walks over to where Mrs. Emerson lies motionless, looks out of the side of his eyes to his companions and comments, "This easier than shooting buffalo!" He laughs and heads toward the barn. "Go find boy. He only witness."

Lone Wolf and one of his companions cautiously enter the barn, while the three other Indians begin removing jewelry items and watches from the dead settlers.

"Be careful!" says Lone Wolf. "He may have weapon." The three enter the barn, stalking quietly and looking for possible hiding places. They look in the box stalls as they pass and into each manger of the tie stalls. After searching all the stalls they focus on the straw pile. "This only place left," says Lone Wolf, motioning one of his companions to start poking it with a pitchfork.

Swhoosh, swhoosh. The sound of the pitchfork hitting the straw is in itself threatening. After five vicious stabs, the sounds of crying are easily heard.

"He on that side," says Lone Wolf as he motions to the left side of the hay pile. "Drag little buck out. Take him back of barn and kill him!" Lone Wolf turns to walk back outside to the others.

"Please don't kill me!" screams the boy as the Indian struggles to carry him to the back of the barn.

"Yiyiiiee!" yells the Indian as the crying boy bites his wrist.

Quickly there is a loud, dull thud sound as the Indian hits the boy in the head with a hammer he picked up in the barn. The boy falls motionless to the dirt barn floor and then another "thud" sounds as the Indian hits him one more time to insure death.

The farmstead is quiet now with the exception of sounds created as the Indians ravage through the house picking up as many lightweight items of interest as is possible to carry.

"Get horses out of corral," yells Lone Wolf to two of his companions in an authoritive and commanding voice. "Get bridles and saddles out of barn. I butcher cow over there and we go!"

"Hey, you Inkas," Lone Wolf yells to the other two men in the house, "bring me blankets to put meat in ... and pack horses!"

Quickly and efficiently the five men strap everything they can carry with them onto four pack horses. Lone Wolf claims the only good saddle as his. Finally, the five men mount their new found horses and start the forty mile trip north toward the Red Cloud Indian Agency and Reservation.

News of the massacre travels fast throughout the area as the bodies of the seven white settlers are discovered the following morning.

Back at the Agency, Little Crow calls a council meeting among the Indians concerning the events that have transpired with Lone Wolf and his followers. The council meeting is heated with argument and debate. The members are essentially split down the middle as to what to do; declare war on the whites or turn Lone Wolf and his companions over to the white authorities.

Little Crow has assumed leadership and respect in his later years as opposed to his dissipated youth. He initially leans in favor of turning the recalcitrant members of his reservation over to the authorities, but the arguments on both sides of the issue are strong.

"Now is the time to rise up against the false promises of the Great White Father and forked tongue half-breed traders and agents," argues Full Moon, a man still bitter from the early wars between the Sioux and the Chippewa, the latter, who are aided by the French Government and traders in Northern Minnesota and Canada.

"The White Father is fighting a great war in the East and has no soldiers to fight us now. It is time." Full Moon continues, "The white man comes from a place across ocean and has no understanding of the Indian way. He forces us to live on a reservation, promises money, yet gives us no money. What they say is false and we must survive. I say we take back what is ours."

Little Crow interjects, "Yes, that true, but we cannot think that there will be no war. Even now White Eyes are from volunteer armies to come after those who have killed the white settlers."

Little Crow looks to all the council members, then continues. "We have no chance to win. We must think in terms of our women and children. What is their future?"

The Council members continue to argue both sides of the issue throughout the night with no agreement on either side. Indians from the Lower Agency pour into the Red Cloud Agency that evening and group according to which side of the issue they sanction. Those who want war are outspoken and rebellious, dancing and drinking throughout the night. By morning their anger and frustrations are further wetted by the thoughts of freedom and perceived injustice.

As Chief of the reservation, Little Crow thinks long hours about what he will do to retain control of his people. However, in the final analysis he opts to lead those warriors who sought battle. In his mind set, it is either do that, or lose his political power and prestige among his tribe. He thinks to himself and rationalizes his decision on the fact that power and politics go hand in hand. He also thinks to himself that if this doesn't work, he will lead his people into the Dakotas far away from the white man and his laws.

Early that morning a fight breaks out in the Agency store. The owner and his wife are killed by the raging elements of the Mdewakanton/Whapekute tribes of the Sioux Nation. Little Crow is committed now or will be ostracized from the leadership of his own tribe. His destiny is set.

In August, 1862, Little Crow assembles a force of close to nine-hundred Indians outside the town of New Ulm, Minnesota, in Blue Earth County. The white settlers hang on desperately to the peripheral houses at the edge of the small town as Little Crow attacks. The battle rages through out the night and into the next day. By noon, thirty-two whites are dead and sixty-three wounded. Two hundred houses are burned to the ground and only twenty-one remain. But making no progress after that, Little Crow eventually gives the order to abandon the action.

Other raiding parties continue to roam the prairies to the west. In eastern Dakota Territory an isolated settlement of Norwegians is all but wiped out of its forty members; thirty killed, some taken as prisoners, and a few escaping by whatever means possible. The battles rage as far north as Fort Abercrombie in present day North Dakota where the Sioux factions there kept that fort under siege for six weeks.

Panic has spread across southern Minnesota. Thousands of settlers pack up and flee to eastern sanctuaries in Wisconsin and Illinois. Many make narrow escapes from Indian attacks and have witnessed the killings and atrocities. Some hide in sloughs and survive by eating wild berries.

In all, twenty-three counties are depopulated in a region 50 by 250 miles. Nineteen-thousand people flee their homes and farmsteads. The number of citizens killed by Little Crow and his followers are over one thousand men, women, and children.

After organizing the Minnesota all Volunteer Army, General Sibley pursues Little Crow with a vengeance. First, following him all the way to Devils Lake, North Dakota and then further west to the Missouri River. Little Crow, who seeks refuge with a few die hardened, loyal followers, is refused lodging by the Sisseton/Whapeton Tribes of the Sioux Nation at Devils Lake.

Believing that the Canadian Government will give him protection under a treaty established in 1812, Little Crow leaves for Canada. But the Canadian Government ultimately forces Little Crow to go back to the United States under threat of arrest. It is in Northern Minnesota where he is finally killed, trying to steal a horse from a farmer.

Lone Wolf, scared of being apprehended by the Volunteer Army under Generals Sibley and Sully, discretely travels his way through Northern Dakota Territory and on toward the Badlands. From there he cuts south to join existing hostile tribes of the Lakota Sioux, in particular those of Crazy Horse and his Cheyenne allies. His merciless attitude and rebellious nature is exactly the type of brave that Crazy Horse, leader of the Oglala band of the Teton Sioux Tribe, can use in his conflict with the Crow Indians, and later, the U.S. Army.

The consequences of Little Crow's actions further divide the Sioux Indian nation tribes into what the whites call "hostiles" and "friendlies." General Sibley rounds up two-thousand Sioux males of which three-hundred are considered directly hostile and tried. Thirty-seven are hanged. The majority of the Sioux have left Minnesota for the Dakotas by the winter of 1864. The Sioux migration westward is now under full throttle.

The beginning of the Sioux war on the plains also sets the destiny of those to follow. The Sioux Nation spreads and strengthens their hold on territory throughout the Dakotas and eastern Montana, where they encounter the alienation of the Mandan, Airikara, Idatsas, Assinibon, and Crow Indian Tribes.

Lone Wolf's mentality is geared for war with the whites. Within the next several years his name will be held in high esteem among the Lakota Sioux of the western Dakotas, Wyoming, and Nebraska and held in contempt by his adversaries.

CHAPTER EIGHT
MERGING WITH DESTINY
WHAT PRICE, MY SON, DO YOU PAY FOR GLORY?

The years after the Civil War bring a new focus on the West in general. The Union army is reduced to less than 25,000 men. Territorial settlers are demanding statehood and the protection that will provide some form of law in what they consider a lawless country.

In the mid 1860's, Immigrants are continuing west by the hundreds of thousands with fewer of the casualties their forebears entailed. In general, the idea in Washington power circles is to include all land from the Canadian border to Mexico and from the Atlantic to the Pacific in one Great Nation. This idea is further enhanced by the Homestead Act, which allows title to one-hundred-sixty acres of land free to anyone who will farm it for three years. This act eventually creates a movement to almost every available livable space n what is considered the American Frontier.

The problems relative to his are many. Greed, corruption, and swindle are but a few of the elements in the Great Land Rush of the 1860's and 70's.

The movement west creates additional problems on the plains, especially for the Native American Tribes. For the most part immigrant travel is peaceful, but problems develop in the Dakotas, Northern Nebraska, Wyoming, and Montana.

The great Sioux nation, in their plight to find new hunting land and avoid the volunteer armies of General Sibley and Sully, move westward disrupting the territory and lives of the Mandan, Idatsa, and Arikara Tribes on the upper Missouri River in present day North Dakota.

As the Sioux move on to new hunting grounds on the Dakota/Montana border they also become bitter enemies of the Crow Indians in Montana.

The conflict is well intermingled between Indian tribes, the settlers, and the army. Each pursuing their own interests, yet conflicting with one another. Efficient transportation and communication systems are initially nonexistent, with the exception of the developing railroad and the stringing of telegraph lines; both systems being dependent on the army for protection from Indian raids.

By 1868, the contest for land rights among all the different factions is reaching a boiling point. The clamor for protection from "hostiles" by all new territorial citizens forces Territorial Governors to demand of Washington more soldiers. The problem is where will these soldiers be found. The sparse frontier army of the 1860's, has a reputation of being inept. Living under intolerable conditions, their attitudes are anything but that of professional soldiers.

THE LARSONS – OSTRACIZED AND ALONE

Since leaving the wagon train, Hartvig and Inga travel aimlessly. Neither one of them know the territory and both assume that they will be able to find a small settlement on the trail south of the Platte River. As they figure it, Fort Hayes is twenty-five miles to the southwest and if they continue in this direction they will surely meet other pioneers or at least some army troops. But Hartvig also fears that the wagon master may have reported him, thus he thinks to avoid any close contact with soldiers. In any event, Hartvig and Inga have decided to homestead in the area once they locate a town with a Recorder.

Inga and Hartvig are tired as they step down from their wagon. It is dusk and a steady wind is blowing in from the west. A strong gust of wind causes Inga to grab her bonnet. She has been quiet all day and has a strained expression as her eyes now fix on the black clouds on the horizon.

'What we do now, husband?" she asks sheepishly in an exhausted tone of voice, as she holds her bonnet on with both hands.

"We stay here for the night," Hartvig replies calmly. "The storm will move on, and tomorrow we will continue to our land. It should only be two more days according to this survey map. Then we can stake our claim. I'll unhitch the horses and hobble them. You tighten the canvas ropes on the wagon. Looks like a bad one."

Inga moves to the rear of the wagon, hesitates for a moment and suddenly grabs for the rim of the wheel to steady her balance. "Hartvig!" she yells, "Help, I feel dizzy! I can't see!"

Hartvig drops the reins of the horses and runs to Inga's side. He steadies her and gently sits her down on the ground. "What is wrong, Inga?" his voice deep with concern.

"My side, it hurts. Life a knife ..." Her voice fades as her head drops to her shoulder.

"Inga! Inga!" Hartvig yells as he tries to make her regain consciousness. Inga's eyes remain closed and she doesn't respond to Hartvig's constant attempts to revive her. "God!" Hartvig says to himself. "What I do now?"

He looks at the storm moving closer and realizes that they cannot stay where they are. He knows he can turn back a mile and get shelter from a grove of trees, especially if he gets on the downwind side. He gently picks up Inga and places her in the rear of the wagon, quickly making her as comfortable as he can. Excited and not knowing what is wrong with Inga, he runs to the front of the horses, grabs the reins, climbs on the wagon, and hurriedly starts them at a gallop.

"If she's seriously ill, where can I take her?" he thinks, his mind racing with frustration and anxiety. "What is wrong with her? Is the baby alright? I must find help, but where?" he thinks to himself.

The unbroken, rough ground causes the wagon to bounce and jar constantly. Becoming immediately aware of this he pulls the horses back to a walk. His emotions are frantic. What can I do? Where can I take her? Damn this forsaken country! Why did I bring her along? I should've come by myself first. Gotten things settled, then gone back to get her.

Hartvig hasn't gone half a mile when the rain and wind hit hard. The strong winds and pelting rain rip the canvas off the wagon and expose Inga to the pouring down rain. Hartvig pulls the horses to a stop and retrieves the canvas to put over Inga. In his rush to protect her, he forgets to tie the reins. A crack of lightening bolts the horses into a head on gallop down a small hillside. In total desperation Hartvig crawls to the front of the wagon but the reins are dangling at the feet of the frightened horses. Looking back for a brief moment at Inga's bouncing, unconscious body, Hartvig is stricken with panic. He has to stop the horses.

In a moment of quick thinking Hartvig grabs on the break handle and uses all his strength to slow the movement of the horses. The wheels just skid on the rain soaked grass and do nothing at all to slow their speed. Everything is out of control. In a last desperate attempt to get control of the reins, Hartvig readies himself to jump on the horses back.

Suddenly, another crack of lightening strikes in front of the horses sending them hard to the left. The quick turn embeds the right wheel in the ground. The wagon flips up and to the side throwing Hartvig to the ground. This only scares the horses more and in a few seconds the wagon flips over onto its side. Inga and all the belongings are thrown out in one uniform thrust.

Still dazed, Hartvig struggles to his feet. He sees the wagon on its side about four-hundred feet away. The horses, exhausted from pulling the upturned wagon, are standing still, breathing hard. "Inga!" he screams at the top of his voice. Looking around he notices her lying half way between himself and the horses. His fear is real. "Inga!

Inga!" he yells. His mind is racing with thoughts of the possible injury to Inga and the baby. The fear of losing her is drilling him into shock.

The intense rain has caused the ground to become slippery and muddy. In his mind it is taking forever to get to her. "Inga! Inga!" he keeps screaming as he approaches her lifeless looking body.

Lying down beside her he puts his left hand over her face as he tries to wipe the mud and water away from her closed eyes. "God, help me!" he cries. "Please, help me!"

The tears in his eyes are indistinguishable from the rain dripping down his face. Both he and Inga are soaked with rain and mud. "Do something!" he says to himself as he quickly looks around.

He focuses his eyes on the torn canvas of the wagon. Slipping as he gets up, he runs over to the wagon, tears the canvas off, and runs back to Inga. His experience as a boy fishing in the seas off the coast of Sweden, has taught him how important it is to keep dry in the cold and wetness of the boats. That experience is making up for some of his ignorance on the plains. His father had taught him well how to dry himself if sprayed by waves ... a crucial act of survival.

After building a lean-to for cover, Hartvig lays the remaining canvas on the ground, then carefully lays Inga on top and covers her. He thinks about carrying her over to the wagon, but figures that he might do some injury to the baby. After protecting her from the elements as best he can, he changes her into some dry clothes he has found in the wooden travel trunk. Once this is done he unhitches the exhausted horses and hobbles them to prevent them from running away again.

"Now, what to do?" Hartvig says under his breath.

Exhausted, wet, physically and emotionally drained, he contemplates thought after thought on what he should do next. Inga is alive, he can feel her heart still beating, but she is unconscious, and what about the baby. Are there internal injuries? There is no place to go tonight.

If I'm going to die, I want to die in Inga's arms, he thinks and proceeds to gather the remaining canvas to build a more permanent lean-to on the overturned wagon.

Upon completing the shelter, Hartvig builds a fire and gathers what blankets are left in the trunk. "We'll rest here tonight. Tomorrow I'll get some help," he keeps whispering to Inga as he lies down close to her, putting his arms around her to give additional warmth.

Finally the rain stops and the morning sun is just beginning to create enough daylight to distinguish human form. Hartvig tries hard to focus on the silhouettes on the distant hill. He rubs his eyes and squints to make sure he isn't seeing things.

"My God!" he says in a whispering voice. "It can't be!" He quickly scrambles for his rifle, checks that there are enough shells in his ammo belt. He lies still, gazing out at the eight men on horseback.

"Are they "friendlies" or "hostiles"?" he thinks to himself as his concern over his situation makes him alert with fear. Although he has never seen an Indian, he has heard that some are friendly to whites, but those that aren't, are ruthless. "Which are they?" he wonders in a state of fear and panic.

The strange silence during the next ten minutes is overwhelming. Hartvig looks at Inga who is still lying unconscious just ten feet away. Suddenly he feels the thrust of pain. THUD!! An arrow pierces his left side. THUD! THUD!! Two more arrows penetrate his middle and lower back. THUD! THUD! Two more find their mark.

Shocked and in intense pain, Hartvig struggles to crawl to Inga, leaving a macabre trail of blood and dirt. "Inga! Inga!" he moans in a low guttural voice, as if Inga could hear him. "Inga, I love you!"

His hands grab and claw at the ground in a vain attempt to reach Inga. The protruding arrows create excruciating pain with each movement. In a last desperate attempt to clasp Inga's hand Hartvig breathes hard and collapses dead, just ten inches from his beloved wife.

Lone Wolf, his bow drawn, walks cautiously toward the two unconscious bodies, watching for any sign of movement. As the other braves approach, Lone Wolf lets out with an excruciating yell. "Haiiyee!!" He then turns to his braves and screams. "Two more white eyes meet death!"

Lone Wolf kneels down to pick up Hartvig's rifle, hesitates, then puts his ear next to Hartvig's chest, listening for a moment to Hartvig's heart.

"This one dead," he declares. "I check woman."

Lone Wolf listens intently to Inga's heart beat and looks up to his fellow warriors with a strange and confused look. Again he puts his ear to Inga's chest, then feels her stomach. "Woman alive," he says mild mannerly. "And she carry baby!"

After a moments hesitation he looks to the other braves. "Get lodge poles. We make travois. Take woman to Spotted Deer."

The presence of Inga being alive diverts the attention away from mutilating Hartvig's body. The Indians take Hartvig's horses off the hobbles, place Inga on the travois, and begin the trek back to the village. The wolves keenly eye the situation from a distance. It is only a matter of time now that they too will enjoy the taste of the spoils of war … and it is only a matter of years before two different warriors clash in what is to be their destiny.

THE RIGHTS OF PASSAGE

Inga, remains unconscious as she bounces roughly on the travois. It takes about six hours for the small raiding party to get to the Indian village since the warriors are extra careful about covering their tracks through the foothills.

As the raiding party enters the village they are greeted first by dogs and children, but the novelty of having a white woman captive immediately brings out all villagers. Even the sick and elderly are aided to the village center for a view of Lone Wolf's entrance.

Lone Wolf rides proud through his people brandishing Hartvig's rifle and wearing his gun belt, accepting graciously the yells of praise for his accomplishment. But he knows where he is going with his prize as he heads directly toward Spotted Deer's teepee.

Spotted Deer, an Elder Society woman in her fifties, is standing outside watching Lone Wolf as he approaches.

"Here! Take care of white woman. She pregnant. Do what you want, but save the baby. He may be good Sioux warrior," says Lone Wolf as he motions to one of the braves to leave the horse and travois by Spotted Deer's lodge.

Spotted Deer walks quickly to Inga and feels her stomach. She then turns to several other Indian women standing nearby. "Help get white woman in lodge. Hurry! Be gentle!"

The women move Inga inside the lodge. Lay her on three buffalo robes and begin to wash and clean her. Another of the elder women begins to make herbal medicine tea from roots, which they later force down Inga's throat. After several hours of intense care the women sit around Inga in a semi-circle and begin to chant. This ritual goes on all night and continues throughout the next day.

It is two days later that Lone Wolf appears again at the lodge of Spotted Deer. His attitude is arrogant and aloof, but also one of curiosity. "How white woman?" he asks demandingly.

"Still in long sleep, but well. We feed her small portions of medicine and food," informs Spotted Deer.

"Good! How long she carry baby?"

"Maybe three months. Maybe four months," guesses Spotted Deer.

"You take care of baby. Watch her during time of sun and moon."

Spotted Deer nods her head affirmatively, but talks defiantly to Lone Wolf. "Yes, but you stay away! You bad omen! I tell you how baby and her be. But you stay away! Spotted Deer is adamant about this as Lone Wolf just looks at her with disgust, turns, and walks away.

The Indian women take turns caring for Inga. Every hour they wash her face and body with cool water, give her a massage, and a medicinal drink. Before and after each group of women come to take care of Inga, they sit in a semi-circle, burn sage for purification, and chant to Wankan Tonkan (Great Spirit).

It is early morning in August, 1864, as the sun begins to slowly appear over the small butte on the east side of the encampment. The slight breeze periodically drifts though the teepee of Spotted Deer as she and two other women sit diligently massaging Inga's legs and arms. Their conversation is in low tones as they discuss the situation. "White woman been here fifty-two suns now," says Spotted Deer. "She have long sleep."

"Yes," says Sun Flower, "but how can she have baby when she sleep?"

"She have time yet to wake," cites Spotted Deer. "She healthy. No broken bones, breathes good, no fever, baby heart good. She wake up soon."

Sun Flower starts to voice her concern, then hesitates. She looks at Spotted Deer, then at Inga. "Maybe we give her hot smoke to nose?"

Spotted Deer looks at Inga, hesitates, then turns to Sun Flower. "Yes, maybe that help. You prepare tonight?"

"It take time, but I have ready by time sun come up," says Sun Flower.

"Good, I prepare lodge," concludes Spotted Deer. "We begin as sun come over hill."

Lone Wolf, heeding the words of Spotted Deer remains away from the lodge during the days the women tend to Inga. However, his curiosity is intense. Each day that he rides to and from the village he deviates his path near enough to Spotted Deer's lodge to take a look. Not having a son of his own, he envisions Inga having a baby boy that he can raise and train to be a warrior. He fantasizes about how he will teach his "son" how to hunt and trap, and later teach him the skill of bow hunting and horseback riding; skills he will need to be a good warrior. He has, in his mind, a vested interest in the white woman he has captured. She is now technically his property, and so will be the baby.

As Spotted Deer prepares the lodge for the medicine ceremony, Sun Flower selects the ingredients for her hot smoke, a combination of herbs, spices, sage, sweet grass, and peyote. This mixture is normally used when warriors would fall unconscious from wounds sustained in battle. But Sun Flower thinks that this medicine might work on Inga's long sleep and is cautiously mixing what she perceives will be the right combination to use on a pregnant woman. She also realizes that too much might put both the white woman and baby into a state of shock. Consequently, she is aware of her responsibility.

It is just before sunrise that Spotted Deer, Sun Flower, and three other Sioux women of Elder status enter the lodge to take their turn to care for Inga. They know that giving her this medicine is a risk. Both the white woman and baby could die if the procedure is not done correctly.

Spotted Deer props Inga's head and holds her mouth open as one of the Elder women pour small amounts of water down her throat. The other women assist as they set Inga in a more upright position and hold her firmly.

Sunflower approaches slowly, carrying a small bowl with the special mixture. Spotted Deer sits next to Inga with a twig, which she lights from the small fire burning in the center of the lodge.

"You ready?" asks Sun Flower, as she places the bowl across Inga's chest for Spotted Deer to light.

"Yes," affirms Spotted Deer.

Spotted Deer lights the mixture in the small bowl as Sun Flower lets the flames subside into a smoldering smoke. Spotted Deer then chants a few words and passes the smoke directly under Inga's nose. She does this several times but still there is no response from Inga.

"Wait," says Spotted Deer. "We give time to take effect."

Sun Flower waits several minutes and repeats the procedure. Suddenly, there is a uniform sound of awe from the observing women. Inga's right eyelid moves slightly.

"Again!" yells Spotted Deer.

Sun Flower then passes the smoke back and forth under Inga's nostrils three more times. Again, the sound of awe from the Elder women as both of Inga's eyes blink and her head turns slightly.

"It's working," says Spotted Deer calmly.

Sun Flower nods her head as she winks at the other women. "Give white woman smell one more time," Spotted Deer whispers to Sun Flower, who passes the smoking bowl under Inga's nose. This time Inga responds to the medicine mixture as her eyes slowly open and she begins to look at the women and surroundings of the inner lodge.

"Get her water!" exclaims Spotted Deer. "Woman will be well in two days! She will rest now. Medicine will make her sleep real sleep."

As Inga falls back into a restful sleep, the women smile at each other and begin a silent form of congratulations. It is not proper to show too much feelings, for hugging and joyous proclamation is strictly forbidden. But the women happily acknowledge to each other the fact that they have saved the white woman's life.

As predicted by Spotted Deer, Inga awoke from her sleep in two days. At first Inga is groggy, frightened, and confused as to where she is, and who the women are that are sitting next to her. But the kindness and constant washing of her forehead and arms by the Indian women assure her that they are not going to hurt her. Within the hour Inga again falls asleep for another fourteen hours. During this time the Elder women brush Inga's hair and dress her in one of their own soft doeskin dresses and a pair of moccasins.

The next time Inga awakes, eight Elder women are sitting around her, two of whom are gently braiding her long blond hair. The Elder women are fascinated with Inga's hair since none of them has ever seen blonde hair before.

"Hello," says Spotted Deer at first in Lakota, then in broken English.

Inga responds with a quiet, but very cautious hello, but then a hint of a smile embraces her lips. Inga suddenly and instinctively relaxes as she feels the soft buckskin dress. She knows that somehow these women have helped her through some tragedy, but as of yet doesn't know quite what it is.

During the ensuing days Inga slowly gains her strength back and starts to eat the dried buffalo jerky and broth the elders give her. Although there is no verbal communication, the women seem to understand one another and Inga, unsure of her situation, allows herself to partake in the comfort offered by the Elders.

Spotted Deer finally informs Lone Wolf that the white woman has gained consciousness and is doing well. Acting quite pleased at this, Lone Wolf demands that he visit Inga. This request Spotted Deer flatly refuses.

"You wait! Maybe ten suns, maybe more," orders Spotted Deer. "Elder women take care of white woman … so she not scared. You come in lodge, you scare her. We introduce her to Council … you see her when we say."

"How baby?" inquires Lone Wolf.

"Baby fine. Woman fine. Now you stay away!" Spotted Deer demands as she turns and walks back to the group of women in front of her lodge.

As the days pass, Inga becomes more and more comfortable with the village women, especially the Elders who have taken care of her. She is troubled, however, by the fact that she doesn't remember how she got to the village or even who she is. Her memory of Sweden, Hartvig, the wagon train, and why she is in this place, is completely gone.

During the next two and a half months the women of the Elder Society take protective care of Inga. They obtain this authority by a meeting with the Tribal Council and Tribal Chieftain, Two Crows. Lone Wolf accepts this decision, knowing that after Inga has the baby and remains in good health, he can then appeal to the Council to exercise his rights to Inga and in turn, the baby … if it is a boy.

It is mid-October, 1864, when the tribe begins to move its location to a chosen area one-hundred-fifty miles to the northwest. The grass, water, and wooded areas are plentiful in that valley, and the high hills will act as a windbreak from the cold northwest winds of winter.

It takes almost two weeks for the band of four-hundred-thirty-five Lakotas to move their horses and equipment this distance, but it is done efficiently and effectively. Another reason for moving is to avoid any winter engagements with the U.S. Army. But there is no real fear of the soldiers since they are very few and the nearest fort at this time is more than two-hundred miles away.

The only white men that are causing any problem at all are the few wagon trains passing through, some settlers in remote towns, and a few homesteaders. At this period of time, most of the Lakota's conflicts are with other Indian tribes, such as their long hated enemy, the Crow.

Once at their select site at the southwest foothills of the Supra Papa, or Black Hills, the tribe begins to establish their new camp. It takes less than one full day for the entire camp to be erected by the Sioux women in accordance with established procedure and custom. The location of lodges is determined by the rank or position within the tribe, the Tribal Chieftain, Council members, and the Shirt Wearers having select sites closest to the center of the whole encampment.

As a leading member of the Elder Women's Society, Spotted Deer has much say in the matter of the encampment. It is the women who run the village and the lodges. Whereas it is the man's job to hunt, take care of the horses, and make war.

Although Inga senses each day that there is something different in her heart from what she is learning while in captivity, she can't pin point it. Consequently, she assumes that she has been here all her life and has just lost her memory of the Sioux language and customs. She also knows she is pregnant, but no one talks about who is the father. For the most part Inga just does what she is told, doesn't ask any questions, and basically accepts her role as a member of the Lakota's.

One thing she does know for sure is that she is near the time to give birth. Spotted Deer and Sun Flower spend more and more time with her in these last two weeks, especially during the moving process. It is just a matter of days now and all the women are preparing for the birthing occasion. This will be a time for private ceremony and ritual.

Lone Wolf is also keeping track of Inga as best he can. In fact, as a leading warrior of the Warrior Society, he is becoming a little too interested in what the white woman is doing, at least according to his fellow warriors. His nickname becomes Lone Dove, and he is teased relentlessly. But Lone Wolf knows what he wants and that he was lucky the day he came across Hartvig's overturned wagon on the remote, open prairies.

It is the morning of October 28, 1864, when Inga goes into labor. Spotted Deer, Sun Flower, and six of the other Elder women are present. Inga feels as comfortable and secure as can be, for she has learned over the last several months that she can trust these Indian women. She also knows that they did their best to prepare her for this birthing and so far all seems to be going as normal as possible.

And it does. At 10:05 a.m. Inga gives birth to a healthy eight and a half pound boy. All the Elder women are smiling, talking fast to each other, and attending to Inga. Inga is overjoyed as she first views her new born son and looks into his bright blue eyes. This is also a moment for tribal celebration as Inga is now considered a member of the clan and officially given the rights of other women of the Lakota.

Lone Wolf also secretly celebrates. It is as his vision quest has reveled to him. It is just a matter of time and he will assert his rights according to Tribal laws and custom. He will train and educate his "son" in the ways of the Lakota warrior. His short-term destiny has been granted.

THE CLAMOR OF FEAR

The two hunter/trappers are cautious as they come over the hill. They know from experience that a small Sioux war party will hit and run in a surprise attack on the reverse slope. Although there has been no recent incident with any of the various bands within the Territory, caution is the primary concern on the prairie.

As they come to the crest of the hill the lead rider raises his hands as a signal to stop. "Looks like there may have been some trouble down there," says Jim Fraser, a tall, lean man in his forties. "Best we circle around on the ridge ... give us a better look."

"Yup," agrees Ol' George, a scraggly, tough looking mule skinner and trapper who is hitting on seventy-years-old. "Never know what be hiding on either side of these here hills."

The two carefully ride the high ground looking on both down slopes for any sign of Indians or other riders. "Let's cut down that gully 'n swing up on the backside of that wagon. Looks like there's been some kind of accident or somt'n," says Frazer, as he knees his horse in the girth.

"Ya, siree!" Ol' George agrees. "Some settler I betcha. Probably got lost, tipped his wagon on the hill and just left it thar. We'll see."

As the two riders approach the wagon their faces freeze with horror. They have seen many dead, rotting animals in their life and quite a few dead humans, but never a site quite like this.

Hartvig's body is decomposed almost to the bones. What the animals couldn't tear apart, the maggots and other bacteria did. The five arrows are still protruding from Hartvig's rib cage and back, his rotten clothes barely covering his bones.

"What the hell do you think happened here?" Frazer asks Ol' George.

"Damned if I know for sure, but reckon he found himself a Sioux war party. Them Sioux arrows. Wonder why they didn't pull them out of his body and keep 'em?"

"No matter," says Frazer. "This means is we got problems com'n with Injuns. Know that for sure." Frazer and Ol' George just sit on their horses momentarily and survey the situation.

"Do ya think he fought back, Jim?" Ol' George asks curiously.

"Don't know for sure," Frazer replies.

"How long you think he been dead?"

"Don't know that either. Maybe four months, maybe six."

"Ya think him by himself?" Ol' George asks curiously.

"Looks like it. He's the only dead body here. Looks like the poor fool musta went loco and just drove aimlessly until he tipped the wagon ... then the Sioux found him. Horses musta run away or died somewhere in the distance. Doesn't make any difference though, critters will have done the same thing to them as they did to this lost soul."

"Maybe," says Ol' George, "but this looks unusual. Wanna check that old trunk o'er there?"

"Naw, think we best leave all alone. Might be cholera or somt'n in that stuff. Let's just let everything be. No need to do not'n for him now. Sure doesn't need any buri'n," Frazer analyzes to Ol' George. "Suppose we should ride into North Platte and report this. Someone might know who this lost pilgrim is ... might even have family somewhere."

"Damn toot'n!" agrees Ol' George. "More important though, he was killed by hostile Injuns. Best alert the townspeople."

The two hunters leave the unsightly scene as they had found it and head directly to North Platte, Nebraska Territory. Ol' George and Jim Frazer, feeling it's their moral duty to report this incident to the proper authorities, end up in the mayor/sheriff's office of this bustling little town of four-hundred-twenty people.

"Chris' sake! You're telling me that there's a rotting body with arrows in it just forty miles north of here?" inquires the Mayor, Jim Ashley, a short, stocky, but scholarly looking man in his thirties.

"That's right. Don't know how he got there. Musta gone loco and got lost. Know one thing for sure. He's dead ... and killed by Injuns!" adds Ol' George with one eye closed.

The Mayor looks terrified. Just the thought of warring Indians thirty to forty miles away is of serious concern. "Didn't know there were Indians in this area," queries the Mayor.

"Didn't either. But they must be migrating this way from Minnesota and the Dakotas ... don't know for sure. Maybe they're just after buffalo," relates Fraser.

"Buffalo! Then why'd they kill that settler out there?" asks the Mayor.

"Don't now. Don't know what they're up to. Just know if they kill one white man, they won't hesitate to kill a lot more," says Frazer.

"You bet!" confirms Ol' George. "You best inform the Territory Gov'nor there, son."

"Ya damn right I will! I'll do that now," replies the Mayor with serious concern.

The rumors associated with the discovery of Hartvig's dead body and the evidence of an Indian attack escalate into outlandish proportion. Homesteaders, small ranchers, almost everyone sought refuge in numbers by moving to the nearest town or combining families of at least ten or more on one ranch. The memories of the Minnesota massacres of 1862, better known as the Great Sioux Uprising, are still fresh in the minds of all settlers on the western plains.

It is several days before the Mayor gets a response from the Territorial Governor:

> November, 1864
> Territory of Nebraska
> Office of the Governor
>
> Dear Mayor Ashley,

Understand your concern ... Am putting as much pressure on the army as I can ... They're seriously undermanned at both Fort Sheridan and Fort Hays and can't spare troops ... I, along with several other businessmen, have telegraphed the President of the United States ... We have also enlisted the assistance of the Territorial Governors of the Dakotas, Montana, and Wyoming, to request protection by the army ... At present, do the best you can and stay in large, well armed groups ... Good Luck!

James Baldwin
Territorial Governor

After receiving the telegram, Mayor Ashley calls a meeting of the City Council at the Mercantile store.

"What the hell kind of response is that?" says the local blacksmith to the Council of Concerned Citizens.

Several of the members shake their heads. "Down right stupidity. What the hell kind of a Governor we got?" declares Peter Wench, a small homesteader about five miles south of North Platte. "He should know we can't live like this. My wife and little girls are petrified that these Indians will steal them away one night!"

"I know what you're saying," says the Mayor.

"But if they can't send troops, what are we gonna do? Sit here and wait to be scalped! Best start tak'n some action now!" says Wench. "Maybe if we get the word out and everybody in the region gets scared enough of these savages, we might get some politician to respond."

"You mean spread more rumors than we already got?" says Sheriff Ricky with a smile.

"Damn toot'n!" exclaims the Mayor. "We'll get army protection out here one way or another. Even if they have to start building hundreds of forts."

"Well, sure a shoot'n, anything's worth a try!" agrees Wench. "We don't' want what happened to that man out on the prairie to happen to us or any members of our families. How we gonna get this started?"

"For one thing we're a Territory of the United States and we want statehood, right?" declares the Mayor. "All present shout in agreement."

"Then we'll keep the pressure on the Territory Governor. We'll send our own representatives to Washington directly," adds Mayor Ashley with a sense of confidence ...

"I agree," comments Wench. "We can't live in constant fear. We need protection now! However we get it!"

"Maybe the senator from the new state of Minnesota will help. They just received statehood in 1858. Surely he will understand the terror we live in out here. Specially after what the Sioux did there in '62," interjects the storekeeper.

"Got not'n to lose. He's probably our best bet to get troops out here," adds the blacksmith. "Okay, I'm all for it! Let's do it now, then."

All of the regional citizenry are seriously concerned and agree adamantly with the decision of the Council at North Platte. Within several days they have more than five-hundred letters and telegrams sent to Washington, and have enlisted the support of most regional politicians.

By late November of 1864, the Union Army is on the verge of victory in the Civil War, and by April of the following year the South will surrender. However, this is not the time to lobby Congress for an army in the west. Most available men are tired of fighting and by June of 1865, the army of the United States will be reduced to less than twenty-five thousand men.

The letters and cries for help from North Platte, Nebraska Territory, and other towns in the Dakota Territory, basically fall flat. The U.S. Government just doesn't have the manpower to provide protection to settlers this year. As a consequence, each Territory assembles a token army of volunteers under their Territory Constitution ... an Army Reserve of sorts, albeit, loosely structured and totally undisciplined. The essence of their organization is termed the vigilante army.

During the next two years Lone Wolf and other Sioux warriors manage to avoid any outright hostilities with the sparse white population. The death of Hartvig is all but forgotten and he is never identified. The clamor of 1864/65 sets the stage for United States Government action in 1868. More and more settlers are entering the Great Plains and the periodic conflicts with the Sioux are beginning to take a serious tone.

Again the citizenry begin screaming for Federal Government protection and the polarization between cultures starts again. With the intense intrusion of passing wagon trains, Indian raids increase. Their raids are not only on the trains, but extend into raids on small homesteads for horses and cattle. They produce casualties among the defenders and further cries for revenge from the citizenry.

On May 18, 1866, the first serious discussion about what is happening in the west begins in the U.S. Senate Chamber. This debate will set the stage of history in the west for the next twenty-five years.

It is the Senator from Minnesota, James Mitchell, who still carries the banner for the Plains Territories. He has assembled a vast amount of information on the Sioux Indians and their allies, the Cheyenne and Arapahoe. Many settlers in his state, especially near Blue Earth County, have personally experienced the atrocities of the raiding Sioux. Mayor Ashley, who has become deeply involved in Federal politics and had written the Minnesota senator weekly, is now a close friend of Senator Mitchell.

It is the morning of April 10, 1866, when Senator Mitchell begins his argument on the Senate floor. "There's a war developing on the central plains," he begins. "The combined forces of the Sioux and other bands of "hostiles" are harassing and stealing livestock from the settlers by the thousands. They're asking for help and we as members of Congress carry the responsibility to provide them some semblance of law and order out there."

As the Senator envisions what has happened in his own state, he becomes more emphatic. "The United States Government purchased that land from France with the intention of getting it settled. We have an obligation to those brave people!"

The Senator from New York stands to be recognized. "I address this comment to the Senator from Minnesota, Sir." He turns from the Speaker to the Minnesota Senator. "Most of our military manpower has been disbanded. We cannot call these men back to military service. We have barely enough of an army left to protect Washington, Senator. How do you suppose we can protect settlers in an area as vast as the Great Plains?"

"That's precisely the point, Senator," replies Mitchell. "We need an army out there. I propose that we consider increasing our military strength, especially the cavalry. Authorize the formation of new units and build some decent forts for supplies and protection. This is in our national interest and you know that!"

The Senator from Virginia stands and is recognized. "Where do you propose we get these men, Senator?"

"There are thousands of immigrants landing in this country daily. They seek jobs and adventure. They will fill part of the ranks. Also, remember that during the Civil War many blacks fought on the side of the North. According to my information, these ex-soldiers will also serve."

The Senator from Georgia stands and speaks with his slow drawl. "Pleased to address the Senator from Minnesota.

Now, Sir, we have some of our southern boys in the regular army and honorably serving out west. What makes you think they will serve with coloreds after what has happened over the last seven or eight years?"

"I don't believe we will have a problem there, Senator. The policy should remain as it did during the Civil War. Blacks served in all black regiments. They have proven themselves as excellent soldiers and their record overall is highly commendable. Furthermore, white or black, we are under an obligation to build America into a land for all people."

"I believe blacks take that same pride as a race and will fight for America," continues Senator Mitchell. "Many of these people need a job that offers them a career. I believe in this idea and God knows those people out there need help!"

It takes more than four months of debate and argument on what is needed in the western Territories, but the relentless pursuit on the issues by Senators from Minnesota, Illinois, Indiana, and Oregon, finally convince the United States Congress of the need to authorize an increase of military strength by a hundred-thousand men and ten new Cavalry Regiments. Two of these regiments will be black Cavalry.

President Johnson and War Secretary, Ulysses S. Grant confer for more than an hour on the legislation passed by Congress. Grant, having been a General in the Civil War, is well versed concerning the military. He supports any legislation that will re-establish the strength of the United States Army. It is President Johnson who is hesitant about anything dealing with the military, as his philosophy borders on pacifism.

"Sir," directs General Grant, "the west is growing faster than a young colt. It is clear that we need more soldiers out there ... many more soldiers, and we need them now. I recommend that you sign this bill. It is also healthy for the economy. A good political move, Mr. President."

"I've got to think of my political future, General. I don't want the general public to get the idea I'm a warmonger."

"I understand that, Sir," appeases Grant. "But this is a serious consideration in regard to the fact that you are the person in charge of fulfilling America's destiny."

Pleased by this comment, President Johnson seeks out further advice from General Grant on the problems in the west.

"The Territorial Governors are screaming for protection and statehood out there, Mr. President. This is a prime time political move on your part and it is for the good of the country."

"Mr. President," Grant continues, "Congress has approved this bill. It only requires your signature to become law. Think of the monumental benefits both to your administration and to the Unites States as these Territories join the Union statehood. Your political base will triple. I bet even your previous boss, Abraham Lincoln, will approve of that!"

"Well, General Grant, who should command this vast area?"

Grant thinks for a moment, then replies, "General Olson. He will be an excellent choice to command all of Indian Territory. Also, Sir, since we're on the subject, I would like to recommend Colonel Novak to command a Regiment of the newly formed Tenth U. S. Cavalry Regiment ... the proposed colored Regiment. He's experienced in black relations in the army having led a regimental unit in the Civil War. Those are my two best recommendations for success, Sir."

President Johnson stands, paces a few steps as he ponders the situation. After a few moments he turns to his War Secretary, General Grant. "Take care of it, General. This better work with these colored soldiers, or I may not have a political future!"

"Yes, Sir!" replies Grant. "I didn't let President Lincoln down, and I won't let you down." "Give me a pen, General. I'll sign the bill"

CHAPTER NINE
THE STRONG YOUNG MEN

During the next seven years the United States takes on a new consciousness: that of "rugged individualism." The Civil War has torn the country apart and creates a new era of "escapism." This movement has a logical place to migrate and that is west; to California, Oregon, or any place in between the Mississippi and the Pacific Ocean. The culture conflict that develops among the indigenous native Americans and the land rushers, becomes a battle for territory and rights.

The migration to the western territories, owned now by the United States Government, is unstoppable. All persons feel they have an inherent right to the vast land, and this idea sets many different codes of conduct. It just depends on who the teacher is. This is especially true in the developing youth of both Henry Washington and a young white Indian named White Hawk.

A CHILD'S EDUCATION

It is April of 1872, Bishop Jackson has just completed his annual budget request to the Episcopal Church Board of Directors in Atlanta, Georgia, which includes funds for college and work programs for the children in the orphanage. It is his sincere desire that all the orphanage children be given a good education and gainful employment. His personal opinion is that these children will then not only be an asset to their race, but to the state and nations as well.

A charismatic man, now age sixty, with graying hair, he never lets up on his pursuit that the children of the orphanage should strive for excellence, both in academics and lifetime goals. In fact, that is exactly what Andy Simon, the school Superintendent and he are discussing this morning.

It is school policy to concentrate on the upcoming senior class members and prepare a program of transition for each into their chosen endeavors during their final year.

As they sit in the Bishop's office reviewing senior student files, Andy Simon places a file in front of Bishop Jackson. "Bishop, this young man is truly remarkable. Especially considering his traumatic beginnings."

Bishop Jackson reaches for the file and instantly nods in agreement. "He certainly is that. I'd go even further in my assessment. He has been an outstanding student and such a pleasant young man to work with." Bishop Jackson ponders for a moment, then continues, "I remember the first day I laid eyes on him. Such a tragic event."

"Yes, I remember," comments Superintendent Simon. "His coping skills and his adjustment emotionally have certainly been amazing. He gets along well with both his fellow students and the staff. His grades are excellent and he has obvious leadership skills. He's been elected president of several school clubs and captain of the ball team."

"I agree," adds Bishop Jackson. "But what about his future? He will make an excellent physician, or college professor."

Andy Simon interrupts with a chuckle as Bishop Jackson looks over his bifocals curiously.

"Sorry for interrupting you, Bishop, but I don't think Henry has that kind of career in mind."

"Don't tell me," quips Bishop Jackson. "Is he still on that soldier idea?"

"You know he is, Bishop."

Bishop Jackson smiles and sits back in his chair.

Andy Simon leans forward to the Bishop's desk and continues. "In fact, he's expressed interest in enlisting in one of those black regiments the army has."

"Enlisting?" exclaims Bishop Jackson with disgust...

"Yes, remember, he's been wanting to be a soldier since the first day you found him and that desire has not subsided. He's even more determined than ever. I thought you knew that."

"Well, Andy," begins the Bishop, "I do. That's why I've been in constant correspondence with Senator McBain during the last two years."

"Senator McBain?" Andy Simon queries.

"Yes. Henry is intent on being a soldier and I know that. For him to enter the army as an enlisted man is understating his potential. There's no future for him in the ranks. He's officer material."

"I certainly agree with that, Bishop, but what are you getting at? What's Senator McBain got to do with this?"

"West Point, Andy! West Point Military Academy!" Bishop Jackson relates excitedly.

"You're serious, aren't you? How'd this come about?"

"I've been following Henry's development for how many years now, ten, eleven? He's a leader, a dedicated student and has the potential to be anything he wants. In this case, he wants to be a soldier and I believe he has the qualifications to be one. The first black officer in the United States Army."

"Well," says Andy Simon, somewhat surprised at he Bishop's statement, "this is a surprise. Does Henry know about this yet?"

"No," confesses Bishop Jackson. "But all the paperwork has been completed and the assignment to West Point confirms upon his graduation. It's just a matter of Henry signing the papers now. It's a conditional appointment. He must make the grade his first year. But I believe he will."

Andy gets up from his chair and walks back and forth in front of the Bishop's desk, thinking about what has just transpired. "I can't tell you how excited I am personally about this, Bishop Jackson. Henry will be a credit to our race, I'm sure of that!"

"Remember," interjects Bishop Jackson, "three other blacks previously, from states other than Georgia, have tried to graduate from West Point. They all failed for one reason or another. We must give Henry our maximum support in this ... if he accepts and I'm sure he will."

"Definitely! Definitely!" says Superintendent Simon with a big smile. "When are you going to tell him?"

"I'll talk with him tomorrow," states Bishop Jackson.

"I'd love to see his face when he hears this."

"You can, Andy. Just be in my office by ten o'clock tomorrow morning," adds the Bishop.

The conversation about Henry possibly going to West Point interrupts the senior student reviews for the day, but that is fine with Andy Simon. He is excited and highly elated as he thinks about one of his students going to the United States Military Academy.

Henry, now sixteen-years of age, has grown to six-feet tall and has developed a sinewy build through sports competition, especially running. On this particular morning, he sits on the bench in front of Bishop Jackson's office wondering why the Bishop has summoned him. He hasn't done anything wrong that he knows of in the last year. It has been over a year since he put a snake in one of the freshman's bunk beds and he has worked off his punishment for that. Henry chuckles to himself as he recalls the incident for he thinks to himself, it was kinda funny.

At ten o'clock sharp, Andy comes out of Bishop Jackson's office and invites Henry in. "Please come in, Henry."

Henry, dressed nicely in a shirt and dark pants, enters the Bishop's office, greets the Bishop, and takes the seat offered him in front of Bishop Jackson's desk.

"Good Morning, Henry," greets Bishop Jackson. "How's your day so far?"

"Going quite well, Sir," replies Henry.

"Well, son, there's a good reason I asked you to come here this morning. I have something important to talk with you about."

"What's that, Sir?" Henry asks curiously.

"Soon you'll graduate from this school, Henry. I know that over the past couple of years we've talked about what you might want to do when you graduate, and now I wish to inquire once again."

Henry thinks for a moment, does his usual chair shifting before speaking, then comments. "The army now has black regiments and I've been think'n about joining a Cavalry regiment and going out west. I think it will be exciting, Sir. I've always wanted to be a soldier."

"I'm aware of that, son. So is Mr. Simon here." The Bishop hesitates for a moment, then continues. "You mean to tell me that you intend to enlist?"

"Yes, Sir," replies Henry.

"So you're still very serious about this?"

"That I am, Sir. I've wanted to be a soldier ever since I can remember."

"I believe you, son. I think you will make a good soldier, in fact I think you will make a good officer!"

Henry is taken back by the word "officer." "Officer, Sir?"

"Yes, Henry, I said officer. Do you think you can apply yourself enough to be an officer?"

Henry is shocked at the mention of being an officer. "I never thought about being an officer. Well, once I did, but not very much. What are you saying, Sir? I don't quite understand."

"Well, Henry, I'm talking about West Point."

Henry is aghast as he shifts quickly in his chair. "West Point, Sir? Are you serious?"

"As serious as can be, Henry."

"Wow! West Point! I don't know, Sir, I don't think I can qualify to be an officer. I really don't ..."

Bishop Jackson interrupts Henry. "Are you interested Henry? Andy and I know you have the qualifications."

Henry hesitates for a brief moment. "Well ... well, yes, Sir! But I never expected to be ..."

"Henry, from this day on we will prepare you to enter West Point, agreed?"

Henry, at first is cautious, but relents. He just can't believe what he is hearing. He instantly realizes that this may be his golden moment.

"Yes! Yes, Sir! I'll try, Sir. I really will, Sir. I just can't believe it!"

"It's true, Henry," interjects the school Superintendent Andy Simon. "It's real."

Bishop Jackson then brings the meeting to a close. "Go now, Henry. We'll work the rest out with Senator McBain. I'll inform him of your intentions. You have a nice day."

"I will, Sir! Thank you. Thank you so much for this opportunity. I won't let you down, Sir. I just won't!" Henry exclaims excitedly before he turns, then runs out of the office all the way back to the dorm to tell his friend Leon.

Bishop Jackson looks to Andy Simon and smiles. "Looks like we've got work to do, Andy. Maybe make some history. Who knows?" Both men smile and congratulate each other on their choice.

Henry is yelling for Leon even before he gets to the dorm. "Leon! Leon! Where are you?" Henry runs into the building and down the hall to his room, screaming for his friend, excited to tell him the news.

Henry throws open the door, sees Leon taking a nap and jumps on top of him. Leon, abruptly awakened, is startled and upset. "What the heck is wrong with you, Henry? Get off me!"

"Leon! Leon! Guess what? Guess what!"

"Okay, Henry. I give up. What?" Leon scowls in an irritated tone of voice.

"I'm gonna be a soldier! I am! Really! I'm gonna be in the army!"

"You gotta be Josh'n! Are you going loco? Just let me go back to sleep," Leon says forcefully.

"No! I'm serious, Leon. Bishop Jackson just talked to me about going to West Point Military Academy. Honest! Mr. Simon, the school superintendent was there. He heard it!"

Leon is now half convinced that something along that line took place, but still has reservations about Henry being temporarily nuts. "When did all this take place?" Leon inquires.

"In the Bishop's office at ten o'clock this morning. I was shocked too. I couldn't believe my ears when he said West Point. I was just going to enlist after I graduated, but now … Wow! Can you believe it?"

Leon stares at Henry, but is starting to believe what Henry is telling him. "Darn, Henry! That's really something. Not many people get a chance like this. Holy cow! How'd the Bishop do it?"

"Don't know for sure, Leon. Just know he has talked to a Senator McBain and he helped."

Leon is now smiling. Even Henry can't help smiling as he looks at the plump cheeks on Leon rise to his eyes when his mouth curves up. "Henry, let's go to the ball field and tell the others! Hey! If I get work in Washington D.C. we won't be far from each other!" exclaims Leon with enthusiastic hope.

"That's right, Leon."

"A soldier, an officer soldier. Wow! Don't let us down now, Henry. You always said you wanted to be a soldier. Now's your chance!"

"I won't Leon! I only wish my Ma and Pa were alive so I could tell them."

"They'd be proud of you, Henry," Leon says seriously as both boys instantaneously rush out the door to the ball field.

WHITE HAWK'S GIFT

It has been seven years since Inga was first brought to the Lakota village. During this period of time she integrates completely into the tribal society. Her fluency in the language is now excellent and her seven-year old son has adapted well in his role with the other Indian children. He is accepted in all the games, and to the members of the Tribe and regional ally tribes, like the Cheyenne and Arapahoe, he is considered Indian.

Inga still carries the protection of the Tribal Council and the Elder Women's Society. She is not allowed to be involved with any of the warrior clan. This is considered necessary by unwritten traditions, for to violate this law will mean serious punishment. Too often conflicts arise involving jealousy on the part of men and even the women. The Council, in accordance with this wisdom, strictly enforces that policy.

For the most part, Inga seems content and happy. She has developed many friends among the village women and is diligent in her duties. Inga's memory of her past life has not returned. But she knows she is different because of the color of her skin and hair. This is also apparent in her son. His fair skin and blue eyes are markedly different from the other children. But all is fine otherwise. Her son plays and competes well in the games the children play, especially the youth game of brave and soldier. But there is a serious purpose in this game. It is the first part of training in a long series of training that it takes to become a true Warrior.

It makes little difference to Lone Wolf that he cannot see Inga. His interest is in the development of her boy. Since all children are, in essence, members of an extended family within the Tribe, Lone Wolf will have the opportunity to be the boy's teacher, and also, as the one who brought him into the village, the right to give him his name.

Lone Wolf is intense, as is his nature anyway, over the influx of the settlers or "white eyes" into the traditional hunting areas. As the settlers keep settling, the buffalo keep moving farther west. This means the village will keep moving with the herds' migration.

The periodic raids against the Crows and certain white homesteads are not done with the intention of creating a war with the soldiers. For the most part Lone Wolf and his followers originally did this to prove themselves as warriors to their own people. Raids against the Crows, for example, are mostly over territorial disputes and normally include from ten to twenty braves. The Sioux tactics are usually of the hit and run variety with a "coup" (touching a live enemy in battle) more important to their social status than an outright kill.

But during the years of 1864 to 1871, Inga's son is the focus of Lone Wolf's existence. If he can teach this boy the way of the Sioux warrior and the boy becomes successful, Lone Wolf will attain a coup of a different nature ... one just as honorable as any in battle. A son of this nature will bring him great honor among his people, and great honor is what Lone Wolf seeks in all of his endeavors.

It is the right of the teacher to give a child a name that he will keep forever. This ritual usually occurs between three and five years of age. In Lone Wolf's mind, he has seven years to pick out a name for Inga's son and when the time for presentation comes Lone Wolf will act the part of a proud teacher and father.

Under the guidance of the Tribal Council, a time is chosen for the small ceremony. It is of no particular importance to most of the Tribal members, but the blood relatives of Lone Wolf will be present.

It is on the morning of June 18, 1871, when Lone wolf brings gifts to the Tribal Chieftain, Two Crows, and also to Inga. The ceremony of initiation is simple with fifteen relatives (Those who have close association with Two Crows' family and thus, Inga), or extended family, who gather to sit in a symbolic circle of the earth.

Lone Wolf, in accordance to tradition, sits in the middle of the circle. He chants a few secret words before he rises up to present Two Crows with a gift of five horses and ten buffalo robes. Although it isn't required, he also presents Inga with a doeskin dress and two fine blankets.

After his presentations, Lone Wolf returns to the circle center, takes out a brown and white hawk feather from his parfleck, raises it to the sky, and begins to chant and dance. He turns first to the North and with both hands presents the feather skyward. This he does to each of the four directions of the earth.

When Lone Wolf is finished, he motions for the boy to be brought to the circle center. When the boy stands before him, Lone Wolf begins his final chant, stops, then sits down in front of the child.

"Here!" Lone Wolf says in a low, firm voice. "A feather of the Great White Hawk, whose sharp eyes and quick speed give him great honor as a hunter among the Flying People."

He presents the feather with both hands to the boy who reaches out to receive it. "You, my son, will become like the Great Hawk, a great hunter and warrior among the two-legged people. Your name shall be WHITE HAWK. Soon you begin to learn like a baby hawk learns to bring honor to the Flying People, you will learn to bring honor to the two-legged people of the Lakota Sioux and to me."

Lone Wolf then stands, towering above the boy, and points in the direction of Two Crows. White Hawk turns and runs excitedly to his mother.

Inga now has no choice in his son's lifestyle. This is under the direction of Lone Wolf as approved by the Council and the traditions of the Lakota's. Inga is later given the name White Deer, representative of her association with Spotted Deer and her white colored skin. Her life will carry the duties of the other Lakota Sioux women; to carry water, skin the animals, prepare pemmican, sew leather clothes, do beadwork, erect and tear down teepees, among other duties of the women.

White Deer is kept in hiding when members of unrelated tribes come to visit. It is the Tribal Councils' decision that to alert the outside world of a white woman in their midst will eventually invite trouble and possible deception, even among themselves, as any ransom that might be offered for her will be tempting.

White Hawk's education begins immediately. Lone Wolf will instruct him how to hide and creep silently in the children's games; games like stalking and shooting rabbits, shooting small arrows at a rock to see who can get the closest, and even at seven years of age, riding a horse in a game called "knock off." These activities are almost a daily occurrence and strongly encouraged. It is part of the education that will hone the skill of the future warrior.

Lone Wolf is not only obsessed by his own desire to become famous as a warrior, but wants it known that his teachings are the best ... this will be shown in the person of his son, White Hawk.

It is on the morning of October 29th, 1871, when Lone Wolf and twenty of his most trusted followers attempt their most daring raid. It is his way of celebrating White Hawk's birthday and he intends to bring his son a new horse, along with the many others he wants. In his mind it is not wrong to take from the white eyes. His past history of such activities, dating back to the Stevenson farm in Minnesota, are becoming legendary among both the settlers and the Lakotas. He is thought of as ruthless by both factions.

His objective is more than one-hundred-fifty miles from the Lakota encampment; a Morgan horse-breeding farm near Fort Hayes that was established for the sole purpose of upgrading the army remounts. Lone Wolf has seen these horses on several occasions and covets them more than any other horse he has ever seen. He has also heard that Generals in the Great White Father's War, or Civil War, ride these horses. In his mindset, if a general will ride one of these horses, so should he.

His raid, he thinks, is well planned. He and his followers will attack quickly in the early morning dusk. Kill the ten settlers with arrows identifying another tribe, take the twenty best horses, including a bay stallion, and travel the back trails home.

At two-thirty a.m. his followers stealthily walk into the ranch yard. Ironically enough no one is up and he has the element of surprise as his followers systematically burst into the bunk house and main home at the same time. The attack takes the rancher and cowboys with such surprise that not a shot is fired. The silence of the arrows and knives entering the bodies is almost anti-climatic as far as combat goes.

"Take all weapons, bullets, and one best horse each!" yells Lone Wolf. "Leave all rest! No scalps. We leave now!"

The braves strip the dead cowboys of their gear and weapons and quickly rush to the horses. Each picks out the Morgan they want, attach a rope to its neck and muzzle, and lead them away. The whole incident is over in a matter of twenty minutes.

"We head north, then back west on the rocky ground!" orders Lone Wolf. The other braves say nothing, just accept what Lone Wolf instructs. They choose to follow him as he is the organizer. The Council has also approved him to lead this raid. It takes six days of fast travel through the foothills and rock beds before the raiding party gets back to the village. They leave no tracks.

The reception at the village is enthusiastic, and Lone Wolf and his party ride in proud. This is even a better reception than when I bring white woman in, he thinks to himself as he rides gallantly to the village center to be addressed by Two Crows.

Two Crows acknowledges Lone Wolf's accomplishments as does young White Hawk, who stares with wonder and awe.

Lone Wolf jumps off his horse holding the lead rope to the beautiful, but gentle bay stallion. "Here, White Hawk! This horse for you. You ride him like the wind and be proud!"

White Deer just stands watching as her son accepts the horse. Her stomach seems to ache deep inside as she watches him. She knows that he is no longer her little boy, and that Lone Wolf controls his attention.

White Hawk is overjoyed and from this day on does all he can to please Lone Wolf. He listen intently to every word Lone Wolf says to him and does everything possible to emulate his warrior father. White Hawk's youthful values begin to focus around those of Lone Wolf's, and not on the overall values of the tribal elders.

By the time White Hawk is ten, he has learned to ride his horse with such skill that he can knock off all the children of the tribe. This feat allows him to be chosen to practice being a decoy for the Warrior Society's raids and ambushes. His ambition and determination to be a warrior like Lone Wolf is obsessive. White Deer witnesses this behavior in her son and is becoming distraught and bitter toward Lone Wolf. However, for her to show emotions is not tolerated by either the women or men in the tribe.

By the time White Hawk reaches thirteen years of age, he is adept at everything Lone Wolf and his uncles, or warrior society braves, have been teaching him. He can pull a sixty-pound bow and shoot six arrows with accuracy seventy-five yards within sixty seconds, kill a buffalo with one arrow at a full gallop on his horse, skillfully lead small raiding parties in ambushes, and skin a rabbit in less than sixty seconds. It won't be long, thinks Lone Wolf, and White Hawk will begin his final tests into manhood. Then he will be ready for the ritual of the sweat lodge and seek his vision quest. But White Hawk now wants more than that.

CHAPTER TEN
AN OFFICER AND A GENTLEMAN – A CODE OF CONDUCT
WHAT PRICE, MY SON, DO YOU PAY FOR GLORY?

It is early afternoon when Henry looks in the mail box reserved for senior students and becomes instantly excited.

"Gol' darn!" he exclaims loudly. "It's here!" He gazes intently at the envelope for several moments, his mind reeling with both joy and fear as Leon nonchalantly approaches at his side.

"What is it, Henry? Your letter from West Point?"

"Ya!" replies Henry seriously. "How'd you know?"

"Well," Leon replies sarcastically, "you've been waiting for it every day for a month now. So aren't you going to open it?"

"Ya, I am. But what if ... if they say no?"

"Don't be silly, Henry. How can they say no if you've been appointed by Congressman McBain?"

Henry, trying to be calm, is obviously nervous at the prospect of opening the letter. "I'll open it when I get ready, Leon. Don't rush me."

"If you're scared, let me open it for you. I'll read it to you."

Henry thinks for a moment, his hands shaking. He quickly hands the letter to Leon. "Okay, here! You open it, but don't read it to me if it's bad news."

Leon looks at Henry and smiles mischievously. "Com'on, Henry, don't worry so much. You're as nervous as a scared rabbit."

"Just open it and read the letter, Leon!" Henry blurts.

"Alright! Here goes," says Leon as he slowly opens the letter.

"Hurry up, Leon," Henry demands. "Don't take so long!"

Leon purposely pulls the letter out of the envelope very slowly, further irritating Henry. "Leon, get to it! Read what it says."

Leon opens the letter, scans it briefly, then looks to Henry for a moment with a somber look on his face.

"What's it say, Leon? What's it say?"

"Well," starts Leon, "it says ..."

Henry starts fidgeting and excitedly interrupts. "Says what?"

"Just let me finish, darn it!" Leon barks. "It says ...

> United States of America
> Department of War
> West Point Military Academy
> West Point, New York
> Sir;
> You are hereby informed that the President has ..."

Leon looks at Henry with a frown on his face.

"What, Leon? What? What?" screams Henry.

Leon puts the letter down at his side for a moment, then lifts his right hand to Henry's shoulder. "I'm sorry, Henry ... do you want me to continue?"

Henry's eyes look bewildered. He looks Leon in the eyes, then drops his head to the ground. "I didn't get it, did I?" Henry murmurs in a low voice.

"I'm sorry to be the one to tell you this, Henry/"

"It's alright, Leon ... darn it! Darn it!"

"But someone has to do it, right, Henry?" Leon says masterfully.

"Ya," mumbles Henry.

"Then let me finish. 'The President has conditionally selected you for appointment as a Cadet at the United States Military Academy …'"

Henry looks at Leon for a good five seconds, then breaks into relaxed excitement. "You Do-Do Leon! You dumb Do-Do! You had me thinking …"

Leon starts laughing loudly and interrupts Henry, "Couldn't help it! I just couldn't help it."

Henry, now more excited than ever, grabs Leon and gives him a strong bear hug, lifting Leon's one-hundred-fifty-plus pounds almost four inches off the ground. "I'll never forgive you for this, Leon. Never!"

"Yeah, ya' will," Leon chuckles as he hands Henry the letter.

"Com'on, Leon, let's go see the Bishop. Wait till I tell the Bishop what you just did!"

"You better finish reading the letter, Henry. Never know what else it might say."

As Henry finishes reading the letter, he turns to Leon. "Says here, that if I desire this appointment I must report in person to the Superintendent of the Academy between May 25th and 28th."

"That's not too far away," Leon comments as he slaps Henry on the back. "But you'll be there in time, Lieutenant!"

Henry looks at Leon with a smile as wide as if it were carved on a giant pumpkin.

It is less than ten minutes later when Henry and Leon knock on the Bishop's door. "Come in!" yells the voice in a moderate tone from behind the door.

As Henry and Leon enter the Bishop's office, they see several of the teachers and administrators seating in a semi-circle around the Bishop's desk. Somewhat surprised at the group's presence, Henry speaks abruptly. "Unh .. we're ... we're sorry, Sir. Didn't know you were in a meeting ..."

The Bishop stands up and interrupts Henry. "That's fine, Henry. We were rather expecting you."

Henry looks around, unsure of the situation. "Expecting us, Sir?" he questions.

"Well, not the two of you, but that's alright since you're such good friends. Would you both care to sit down for a moment?" Henry and Leon nod to each other slightly and move to the open chairs in front of the Bishop's desk.

"We were just talking about you, Henry. In fact if you hadn't shown up, we were prepared to summon you."

"You were?" Henry politely interjects.

"Yes. We have a letter from the Superintendent of West Point and we thought ..."

Henry interrupts Bishop Jackson as a smile comes to his face. He pulls his letter from his coat. "Like the one Leon read me, Sir?"

Bishop Jackson, unsure of what Leon read to Henry, doesn't quite get the jest of Henry's statement. "Well, I'm not sure. What did Leon read to you?"

"Oh, nothing, Sir. Just a little joke between him and me," Henry chuckles contentedly.

Bishop Jackson looks curiously to his staff, then back to Henry. "Anyway, Henry, since you already know of your appointment, be it a conditional one, we in this group have something of importance to discuss with you."

Henry looks puzzled, but agrees. "Sure. What might that be, Sir?"

"It's something called undue publicity, Henry. The fact is that the newspapers are going to have a heyday with this, especially in regard to the issues of you being an orphan and a person of color."

"What do mean, Sir?"

"Well, we think that it is in your best interest to be as low profile about this as possible. Not that you aren't capable of withstanding what some of the major papers in the nation might say, but just that you are going to take on a tremendous responsibility. Every concerned eye in America will be following your entrance and progression at West Point."

"I believe I understand that, Sir," replies Henry firmly.

"That may be true, Henry, but I just want you to know it will not be easy and that we in this group will do all we can to assist you through to graduation. God knows, son, you have the background and talent."

Bishop Jackson walks over to Henry, puts his hand on his shoulder, bends over, and looks into his eyes. "Go now, Henry, and prepare yourself as best you can according to the requirements instructed to you on the appointment letter. We have some preparations of our own to make concerning your registration. If anything out of the ordinary transpires concerning this issue, please let me know immediately."

"I will, Sir," Henry replies as he and Leon get up to leave.

After Henry and Leon leave, Bishop Jackson sits down at his desk, sighs, and addresses his staff. "This has been a long awaited moment for this young man, and this appointment will not only be a test of his character and determination, but a test of him as a representative of the Black race. There is no doubt in my mind that he will become as written about in the papers, good or bad, as the President of the United States."

Less than a week after Henry met with Bishop Jackson, several of the local southern newspapers picked up on Henry's appointment to West Point. For the most part all editorials and articles written speculate that he will never graduate. Their view is that it is a waste of a West Point Appointment to send a Black to the Military Academy.

Henry's first encounter about his appointment immediately follows the Atlanta Constitution's neutral newspaper editorial about a colored from Georgia receiving a Congressional Appointment.

Henry has just mailed his letter of intent to the Academy at the post office and is leaving when a well-dressed gentleman in his forties approaches him. "Good day, Mr. Washington," the man relates courteously.

Henry, responds in kind. "Good day to you, Sir."

"Mr. Washington, let me introduce myself. My name is James Baldwin. I'm a physician from Atlanta and happen to have read about your appointment to West Point ... a good article on you. Congratulations, son."

"Thank you, Sir," Henry replies politely.

"Mr. Washington, may I talk with you candidly for a moment on that issue?"

Henry, unsure, hesitantly agrees. "I suppose. What is it you want, Mr. Baldwin?"

"I'd like to discuss something that might interest you. Sort of a proposal."

Henry is suspicious of this strange man, but not wanting to offend him, agrees to listen. "What is it that you propose, Sir?"

"I have a son your age, Mr. Washington and he has always been interested in the military. He, like you, has just graduated from preparatory school. Of course, as we well know there are only so many appointments to the Academy. Isn't that right, Mr. Washington?"

"Yes, Sir," agrees Henry. "But what is your point, Mr. Baldwin?"

"I'll get to the point, Mr. Washington. I'm willing to offer you the sum of five-thousand-dollars in cash in trade for your appointment to West Point ... in order that my son may go. Does that at all interest you?"

Henry, stunned at the offer and the amount of money, hesitates only for a second. "Sir, I appreciate the offer, but I can't accept money for my appointment. Like your son, I've wanted to be an army officer all my life. That's just something that I could never do. Not for any price."

"Are you sure, Mr. Washington? You realize don't you, that no colored man has ever graduated from West Point and the likelihood of you becoming the first is highly remote."

Henry doesn't respond, just looks to the ground and fidgets a bit.

"Son, don't you think that this large amount of money will allow you to go to any other school of your choosing and let you pursue a career of your choice?"

"Sir, I'm sure it will, but you see, I've had this dream since I was four. I can't just give it up, not for any amount of money, Mr. Baldwin. I'm sorry."

"I see you have your mind made up then,"

"That's correct, Sir."

"Okay, but here's my address. You think about it for a while, you may change your mind ... in fact, I'll double the amount to ten thousand. Stop at my office or write me if you change your mind. My offer may be the best thing that will ever happen to you, Mr. Washington."

Henry glances at Dr. Baldwin's address.

"Think about it hard, Mr. Washington. Good day!"

Henry is perplexed at this chance meeting, especially the offer of such a large amount of money. Ten thousand dollars is more money than he has ever thought about having in a lifetime.

Leon is studying for his final history exam as Henry bursts through the dorm room door. "Leon! Leon!" Henry shouts. "Guess what!"

Leon is irritated at Henry's excited interruption, as they have occurred constantly over the years for the smallest reason. Leon turns to Henry and responds sarcastically, "Okay, I give up. What?"

"You won't believe it! You won't believe what just happened!" Henry is excited and talking rapidly, but is quickly interrupted by Leon.

"Slow down! What you talking about?"

"This man ... a doctor ... at the post office. Dr..." Henry fumbles for the paper note. "Ya, Doctor Baldwin. You just won't believe it!"

Henry sits down on his bunk bed, trying to contain himself.

"Believe what?" Leon demands.

"Ten thousand dollars. He offered me ten thousand dollars!"

"For what? I don't know what in tarnation you're trying to say, Henry. I can't understand you."

"The doctor! He offered me ten thousand dollars to buy my ..."

Leon stares at Henry as he interrupts. "Are you crazy? You're mind is gone. Who in the heck would offer you ten thousand dollars for anything?"

"He did, Leon. Honest! Here's his name and address."

"For what? What have you got that's worth ten thousand dollars?"

"West Point!" replies Henry. "He wants to buy my appointment to West Point ... for his son."

Leon looks at the piece of paper and then to Henry. "This is serious, Henry! No one comes up to someone and offers that kind of money for anything."

"Well, he did!" replies Henry instantly.

Leon thinks for a moment. "Maybe I believe you now. But what you gonna do about it?"

"Don't know what to do, Leon. Nothing I guess."

"Horse crap!" exclaims Leon. "You're gonna go talk to the Bishop 'bout this."

"No, I don't think this should be mentioned."

"Henry, this is illegal or something. Maybe you're being tested by the newspapers. You got your life at stake here and you best think about that. What are you do'n even talk'n to the man for?"

Henry doesn't say anything, just sits there with his hands on his knees looking down at the floor.

"Com'on, Henry. You remember what the Bishop said about anything out of the ordinary. You owe him that after all the years he has spent helping you."

"Yeah, I know, Leon." Henry states firmly. "But what will I say to him? I'm scared. I don't know if I can handle this ... the publicity and all. I don't know if I can even make it through West Point."

"You well better think you can after all your demands of everyone for the last twelve years. That includes me, putting up with your strange dreams and rude interruptions!" Leon looks to Henry in a very serious manner, then speaks in an authoritative tone of voice. "Com'on, Henry. We're gonna go see the Bishop. Now!"

Leon opens the door of the dorm room and stands there defiantly. "Com'on! Let's go!"

Leon has never seen Henry display such doubt and lack of confidence before. As his long time friend and roommate, he is proud of Henry's accomplishments at the school. He thinks he has some grasp of understanding about Henry's emotional makeup, but this situation is of serious concern. Leon knows this is a turning point in both of their lives.

As they walk across the orphanage grounds, Leon ponders in his own mind about West Point. What if the newspapers crucify Henry and he doesn't make it through his first year. That will be devastating. Then what? Leon senses Henry's fear and wonders himself if he will enter into such a complicated and demanding life; a lone Black at an all white military school. Especially with a lot of Southern boys there who still will not accept a black man on their social level. This situation requires some serious soul searching and Leon feels an obligation to his friend.

It is three o'clock in the afternoon when Bishop Jackson arrives back to his office. Henry and Leon are sitting quietly on the bench outside, both thinking their private thoughts.

"Looks like you two have something on your minds," queries Bishop Jackson as he stops to open his door. "Are you here to just sit outside my office or would you like to come in and discuss what's on your thinking?"

Bishop Jackson chuckles briefly but notices the serious looks on their faces. "Com'on in. We can talk inside."

Leon takes the initiative, gets up, taps Henry on the shoulder, and motions him in first.

"Have a seat," says the Bishop as he motions Henry and Leon to the two chairs at the front of his desk. "I'll be with you in a moment. Let me put these papers away and we can get down to whatever it is you're here to see me about."

Bishop Jackson realizes that Henry and Leon are not in his office for a casual chat. After filing his papers he walks to the door, puts his head outside, and informs his assistant that he is not to be disturbed.

"Now, what can I do for you, gentlemen?" the Bishop comments as he walks over to take a seat at his desk.

Neither Henry nor Leon volunteer a response. Bishop Jackson then leans back in his chair and looks at each of them for several seconds. "I presume you're not here to talk to me about the nice weather we're having ... so, what's on your minds?"

Leon hesitates, then looks to Henry. Henry is looking at the floor again. Leon gives him a gentle nudge.

"Uh, Sir, I think Henry has something to tell you. We've already discussed it and I think ..." Henry interrupts, "I'll tell the Bishop, Leon. Just be quiet and give me a chance." Henry looks to Bishop Jackson as he nervously rubs his hands. "Sir, I don't know how to tell you this ..." Henry breaks off into silence, and again looks down at the floor.

"Tell me what, Henry? queries Bishop Jackson.

"Well, Sir, remember in our last meeting you said if something out of the ordinary occurred that I should let you know?"

"Go ahead, Henry."

Henry looks to the Bishop. "Sir, you know I've always said I wanted to be a soldier." Henry hesitates and swallows. "But I don't know if I can be one. At least not a West Point Officer, Sir. I don't know if I can take the pressure."

Bishop Jackson sits up and leans forward on his desk. He anticipated some doubt in Henry's mind about his appointment, but feels this meeting is more serious than just questioning a new educational challenge and environment.

"Henry, I think I can understand some of your hesitations, that's not unusual. What is it that you and Leon discussed. I presume that's why you're here."

Henry looks to Leon, who gives him an affirmative nod, then back to Bishop Jackson.

"Uh, well, Sir, I heard all you said about me being strong and that the newspapers will jump on my appointment and stuff, but I didn't expect something that happened this morning at the post office." Henry hesitates as he clears his throat.

"What's that?" inquires the Bishop.

More composed now than he was a few hours earlier, Henry relates his encounter with the doctor from Atlanta. Bishop Jackson listens intently, but does not express any emotion. As Henry completes citing his experience, he looks to Bishop Jackson who says nothing, then to Leon.

The room is silent until Bishop Jackson finally stands up. "Are you telling me that you considered selling out your dream for money, Henry?"

Henry is embarrassed by the question and sheepishly responds. "No, Sir."

"Good," replies the Bishop. "You have more at stake here than all the money in Georgia. You have your character at stake. The very moral fiber that makes up your personality and reputation. In essence, your life and self-respect. Do you know what I'm talking about, Henry?"

Henry hesitates as he thinks about what Bishop Jackson is saying, then responds, "Yes, Sir. I believe I do. I remember my father talking about that."

"I'm glad you do, Henry, for it's a true test of a man in almost every way. There will be many temptations in life that will lead you away from your goals and beliefs: money and power are only two."

Henry listens intently, as does Leon. Bishop Jackson reaches in his desk drawer, pulls out a single page of paper, and lays it next to him.

"I'm glad that you're here too, Leon. There is nothing more interesting for me to see than two young men who have a common loyalty and bond. It seems to me that you two have been positive antagonists for each other." The Bishop then smiles.

Both Henry and Leon seem more relaxed as they look to each other with a slight smile.

"I have something else I would like to say to you both, especially to you, Henry. Each accomplishment you believe you have obtained in life may be offset by some kind of personal disappointment. They somehow have a way of balancing out. Even during severe times of stress and adversity, believe in yourself. Some divine guidance may be necessary, but ultimately it will be you who decides what is right for your life. Even adversity can be good, because that too, can build character."

Bishop Jackson looks to both young men with a serious, but pleasant look on his face. "Now, Henry, I know West Point is not going to be easy. In fact, it will be damn tough, especially for you. You are going to be taunted, yelled and sworn at, and possibly belittled in many ways. But your goal has been, as far back as I can remember, to be a soldier. So do you want to give that opportunity up? Do you feel that all your goals and ambitions should be cast away in your own doubt, without trying?"

The Bishop looks to Henry directly and hesitates, as if waiting for a response. Henry doesn't know if the Bishop is waiting for an answer or just letting him think about what he has said. Somewhat surprised by the question, the conversation stops. Henry then makes an awkward response. "No, Sir, I shouldn't."

"Okay, Henry, one last comment. I know part of your motivation and determination to be a soldier is derived from the death of your mother and father, isn't that true?"

Henry thinks briefly before responding. "Not really, Sir. I think I wanted to be a soldier before they were killed."

"Really? inquires the Bishop. "That's an interesting statement."

"Yes, Sir, I liked playing soldier as early as I can remember."

"That too is interesting, Henry. But now I have something for you. You're not going to West Point to play soldier. You are going there to become one. Do you think you can face up to that reality ... to that responsibility?"

Again Henry ponders briefly, then answers, "Yes, Sir! I can."

Bishop Jackson walks back behind his desk, sits down and picks up the paper on his desk. Glancing at the hand written page, he turns to the window. "It certainly is a nice day out there, isn't it?"

Both Henry and Leon look toward the window and nod affirmatively to the Bishop's strange question.

"Here, Henry, I want you to have this," continues the Bishop.

"What is it, Sir?" Henry inquires.

"It's a Code of a Gentleman. Written by someone, no one knows who, but I would like you to have it. Read it once in awhile and it may give you some idea of what a man's character can be." Bishop Jackson hands the paper to Henry.

"Henry, I want you to think about what has happened to you today and our conversation, even though I did most of the talking. If in the next few days, you have any questions or think this assignment to West Point is beyond your capabilities, then please let me know. You have less than a month before you must be at West Point. If you decide your goal is to be abandoned, I feel you have a moral obligation to inform me of such and at the earliest possible time. I will then write a letter to Congressman McBain explaining the situation. Do you have any questions?"

Henry, somewhat shocked at Bishop Jackson's firmness, looks to Leon and then to Bishop Jackson. "No, Sir. Thank you very much for your time, Sir. I'll read this paper."

"Then have a good day, both of you. It's a beautiful day for the two of you to contemplate your future."

Once outside Bishop Jackson's office, Leon immediately asks Henry to see the paper given to him by the Bishop. Henry, who has only just glanced at it, suggests that they go to a large tree in the center of the orphanage, sit down on the grass, and read it.

"Let me read aloud to you what it says," Henry comments to Leon. As they both get comfortable on the grass, Leon makes a comment on sitting down and getting up again, but Henry ignores it.

"Here it is, Leon. The Code of the Gentleman." Henry looks at the paper momentarily, then begins to read.

"A gentleman is …" Henry clears his throat, "… a man whose conduct proceeds from goodwill and an acute sense of propriety; a man who speaks with frankness, but always with sincerity; a man who thinks of the rights and feelings of others rather than just his own; a man who does not flatter wealth, cringe before power, or boast of his own possessions or achievements; a man who does not make the poor man conscious of his poverty, the obscure man his obscurity, not any man conscious of his inferiority or deformity; a man who appears well in any company; a man whose deed follows his word; a man with whom honor is sacred and virtue is safe."

Henry looks to Leon, then continues, "It says anonymous."

Both Henry and Leon sit silently contemplating what the Bishop has said and what the words on the paper mean. It is a matter of a minute or so before Leon turns to Henry. "You'll be a gentleman someday, Henry. An Officer and a Gentleman."

Henry turns to Leon and smiles slightly. "Thanks for being my friend, Leon. You're also a gentleman."

WEST POINT, NEW YORK
THE ARRIVAL

May 20, 1873, is an auspicious day. Henry shudders as he stands on the hill this sunny morning. It is his first look at the stone structures thereon, the pinnacle of military fame: West Point Military Academy.

Henry and Bishop Jackson have traveled all night, mostly to avoid newspaper reporters. The trip alone is harried and physically trying, but Henry is more exhausted from tension and anticipation.

"There it is, Henry. Your destiny stands before you," comments Bishop Jackson in a serious voice.

Henry stares at the site. "I don't know, Sir. My mind is so full of emotion and apprehension. What kind of treatment can I expect?"

"Well, I expect the Cadre will be firm, yet fair. The cadets, especially the upper classmen, will surely test your character."

"What do you mean, Sir?"

"From what I understand all first year cadets are called Plebes, or low life commoners, and subject to harassment."

Henry takes a deep sigh. "Bishop Jackson, I just want you to know that I'll do the best I can."

"I know that, Henry. That's why you're standing here. Maintain your dignity and stay focused. You'll do fine."

Henry looks to the Bishop with a somber face, then let's a hint of a smile cross his lips as he looks again at the awesome site of West Point.

"Are you ready, Sir? The carriage is waiting."

"Am I ready?" inquires Bishop Jackson. "My question is, are you ready, Henry?"

Henry takes a deep breath, then turns to the Bishop, "Yes, Sir. I am."

It's ten o'clock in the morning as the carriage pulls onto the Academy grounds. Henry watches the other cadets walking to and fro on the immaculate campus. The driver, following the Bishop's instructions, stops in front of the Adjutant's office. Henry gazes at the impressive surroundings for a moment before he dismounts from the carriage. As he walks to the back of the buggy to get his two bags, he feels sweat beads tingle over his whole body.

"Have you got your certificate of appointment?" inquires Bishop Jackson.

"Yes, Sir. Here in my bag, Sir. I feel kind of warm."

Bishop Jackson puts his hand on Henry's shoulder as he has done so many times in the last ten years. "This is it, Henry. Be strong and maintain self-discipline. May I remind you, that you, more than anyone I know, must demonstrate to the world around us your uprightness and intelligence. It cannot be otherwise. Through that you will ultimately gain respect and self confidence."

Henry puts his head down, then slowly raises it, tears in his eyes. "I'll miss you, Sir." He gives the Bishop a firm hug.

"I have one last thing to give you, Henry."

"What's that, Sir?"

Bishop Jackson hands Henry a small black bag. "It's the red Bible your mother and father had. I meant to give it to you upon graduation from preparatory school but then I thought this timing might be more appropriate."

Tears run down Henry's cheeks as he puts his hand out to accept it. "I don't know what to say, Sir."

"Don't say anything, son. Just do your duty. This is your opportunity. I must go now, but please write as often as you can. You have a lot of support back home."

"I will. For sure, I will."

"Good luck, Henry ... and goodbye for now. You'll be in our hearts and minds."

"Goodbye, Sir," replies Henry with a sad look. Henry watches as the carriage pulls out of sight, then picks up his two bags and begins the lonely walk into the Adjutant's office about one hundred feet to the front.

Several senior cadets are mingling around the building entrance. They have noticed Henry talking by the carriage and are waiting for him to pass by. One of the cadets named O'Hara, pokes his comrade. "Hey! Look what we've got here. A nigger! He musta taken a wrong turn somewhere," yells O'Hara in a loud voice.

"Yeah!" relates another cadet. "Hey, boy! What the hell do you think you're do'n here, anyway?"

Henry keeps on walking toward the entrance door and says nothing. He tries to ignore the jeers. It is as he expected, and he feels mentally prepared to accept the verbal abuse and racial slurs.

"You don't think you're gonna make it here, do ya', nigger? If ya do, ya got another thing com'n," taunts O'Hara as he turns to the other cadets. "Where do these bastards come from?"

The other cadets laugh as one responds sarcastically. "Africa! Didn't ya know? The dark continent."

Henry continues on through the entrance door and walks to the receiving station. A smartly dressed Sergeant seated behind the desk looks up at Henry with a surprised look on his face. "Well, what do you want?" the Sergeant growls.

"My name is Henry Washington. I have my certificate of appointment in my bag, Sir."

The Sergeant looks at Henry sternly. "You don't address a Sergeant with Sir, Mr. Washington. That's the first thing you best learn. Here you address the staff officers with Sir. Remember that!"

"Yes, Sir ... I mean yes, Sergeant."

"Let's see your certificate, Mr. Washington."

Henry fumbles nervously through his pack for his certificate. "Here it is, Sergeant."

The Sergeant takes the paper, reviews it carefully, then points to the registrar. "Sign here, Cadet Washington."

Henry bends over, signs his name, then stands up at a relaxed form of attention.

"Grab your bags and report to your barracks. You're in room one-twenty-two, down the hall, to the right. A senior cadet there will direct you. You will refer to yourself as Cadet Henry Washington from now on. You will also address all senior cadets as Sir. Do you understand?"

"Yes! Sergeant! Thank you, Sergeant."

The Sergeant looks at Henry, shakes his head and mumbles, "You're welcome."

While inside, none of the cadets mention a word as Henry walks down the hallway. However, their icy stares are more than obvious. Henry can feel the tension as he turns the hallway corner. There he notices the sign: DORM ASSIGNMENTS. REPORT HERE.

A senior cadet is sitting lazily behind a Spartan looking desk with his feet propped on it. Henry approaches, surprising him. "Cadet Henry Washington, Sir. Reporting for room assignment, Sir."

The senior cadet looks at Henry, then jumps to his feet, walks over to Henry and yells. "At attention, Plebe! How dare you come into the presence of a senior cadet officer in a careless and unmilitary manner!"

Henry is stunned. He isn't aware of any personal misconduct, but he Senior Cadet continues on. "Heels together and on the white line! Little fingers on the seams of your pants! Button your coat! Draw in your chin! Throw out your chest! Cast your eyes twenty paces to the front! Stand steady, Plebe! You've evidently mistaken your profession, Plebe! In any other service, or at time of war, you would have been shot to death ... without trial, Plebe, for such conduct."

Henry is flabbergasted. Trying to follow all the instructions both irritate and confuse him, but he knows this is part of the test.

The senior cadet barks additional orders. "Pick up your bags, Plebe! Get to your room! You don't deserve to be in the presence of a senior cadet. Now, Plebe! You report for orientation drill tomorrow at zero-five-hundred hours! Now march!"

Henry picks up his bags as fast and military-like as he knows how, searching for inner strength to overcome the frustration and animosity he feels for the senior cadet. A Plebe, he thinks to himself as he opens the door to his room.

The room doesn't look that unusual. It reminds him of his room at the orphanage school; two twin-type beds, two studying desks, two lamps, two chairs, two closets, two foot lockers, and a window. It is military décor at it's finest, but the setting brings back memories of Leon. I wonder how he's doing, Henry thinks to himself as he unpacks.

After organizing his room according to the instructions on his locker, Henry tries to make his bed in accordance with military standards. Best stay in here for the night, he thinks. No sense in going out to get harassed.

Henry has just begun to get the hang of making a bed military style when his new roommate enters the room. Before Henry can say a word, Fred Williams, a tall, white cadet from New York addresses him.

"Hey, boy! When you get done making that bed you can start on mine. I'm going back outside to say goodbye to my girlfriend and family. I should be back in an hour or so. Oh! Hang my clothes up too."

Henry, puzzled by these words, turns around and looks as Williams puts his suitcases on the floor and rushes back out the door. Henry shrugs his shoulders and chuckles. Strange people around here, he thinks to himself.

It is three o'clock in the afternoon when Fred Williams returns. Henry is reading the instructions for orientation drill. Fred stands silently with his hands on his hips looking at his unmade bed and unpacked clothes. Furious, he turns to Henry. "What the hell! How come my bed isn't made and my clothes unpacked?"

Henry remains silent and tries to concentrate on reading his military manual.

At Henry's non-response, Fred Williams becomes more irritated. "Who the hell do you think you are, boy? I'm talking to you!"

Henry refuses to answer under the circumstances, unsure of what kind of situation might develop in this unpredictable atmosphere. Besides, now Henry is getting annoyed.

Obviously angry and upset that his demands are not being met, Cadet Williams turns and storms out of the room, slamming the door hard.

Henry, trying to maintain his dignity, remains on his bunk and tries to relax. It is hard, however, as his thoughts waver between his home in Georgia and the anticipation of a serious struggle here. I must follow this through, he thinks to himself in the lonely solitude of the room, even if it means my life.

As Adjutant, Major Dibbs is an impressive looking officer. He has a three inch scar on his left cheek from combat, which just seems to add to the demur of his well built six-foot frame. A Civil War veteran, he looks like a soldier. Although not West Point educated, he has worked his way up through the ranks to become an officer. This experience earned him a well deserved reputation of being both fair and tough, but also one of following Academy rules to the detail.

Major Dibbs just poured himself a cup of coffee and is about to sit down when the door to his office flies open. Startled at the unexpected entrance, he reacts by standing up instantly and spilling on his uniform.

"What the hell! How come I've got a nigger for a roommate!" yells Cadet Fred Williams.

"Stand at attention, Cadet!" Major Dibbs yells in a loud, intense voice.

"You will at all times address me as Major Dibbs, Cadet! And if you ever have the opportunity to come in here again, you knock first. If I want to talk to you I will say enter, you then walk in, stand at attention, salute, and state your name with cadet in front of it!"

Major Dibbs walks toward Cadet Williams. "Do you understand me, Cadet?"

Apprehensive at his improper conduct, Cadet Williams relents. "Ah, yes, Sir, Major Dibbs!"

"Now you turn around, walk out of here in a military fashion, shut the door, and come back here tomorrow at 0800 hours, and with a more respectful attitude! Is that understood, Cadet?"

"Yes, Sir! It is, Major Dibbs, Sir!"

Cadet Williams turns and is immediately ordered to halt by Major Dibbs. "And you salute army officers, Cadet!"

Fred Williams immediately attempts a salute, but is shaking out of control.

"You're dismissed, Cadet!"

Williams walks out of the room as fast as he can. Once outside the door he takes three deep breaths. "Damn!" he mumbles under his breath. "Now what?"

Not wanting to walk where one of the senior cadets might chastise him, Williams decides to return directly to his room. As he enters his room, Henry is lying on his bed reading the red Bible the Bishop has given him.

Agitated by Henry's presence, Williams quietly unpacks his travel bag. As he opens his closet door he notices the strict regulations in which his garments are to be hung and displayed. Neither he nor Henry speak a word to each other the rest of the night.

Reveille sounds at 0500 hours sharp followed by a loud yell, "Cadets, turn out promptly! Now?"

Both Henry and Fred dress as fast as they can in their civilian clothes and rush out to the parade ground per the instructions of the senior cadets.

"Form a line Plebes! In order of your dorm assignments!" comes the command from the senior cadet drill officer.

All one-hundred-thirty freshman cadets line up, then divide into sections. "You will be assigned to companies as the orientation week continues," yells the drill officer. "However, today you will be told what is expected of you, issued uniforms, and given a schedule of classes and drills. You are to memorize these by tomorrow."

All the cadets stand in a rough semblance of a formation as the individual cadet company commanders order the platoon leaders to distribute information.

Henry stands directly behind Fred Williams as the squad leader approaches Fred in the front formation. Williams is tired from his lack of sleep and his irritation of having a Black roommate, and it shows.

"Atten-hut!" shouts the cadet platoon leader as he approaches Fred.

Startled by the order, Fred stiffens up quickly.

"Wake up, Mister! This is no trifling matter, understand?"

"Yes, Sir!" replies Fred.

"Don't talk to me in ranks, Cadet! You have until this time tomorrow morning to give me a one page report on why you don't address a Senior Cadet officer in ranks, Mister! Do you understand?"

Not knowing whether to acknowledge his understanding of the order or not, Fred nods his head up and down.

"You do not nod your head in ranks, Cadet! I want another report on that! Do you understand, Cadet?" The platoon leader looks into Fred's eyes directly and is nose to nose, as he yells the question, "Do you understand, Cadet?"

Fred does not move, nod, or say anything.

"Do you understand, Cadet?" the platoon leader yells again. Fred holds his stationary position quiet and firm. "Good, Cadet! I want those reports tomorrow!"

As the platoon leader continues his individual harassment of the front line, Henry can't help but notice how the platoon leader is picking on each and every man. So this is what I have to look forward to ... but I can't flinch, not without dishonor, he thinks.

"Cadets, after breakfast, withdraw to your quarters for your first inspection at 0800 hours," comes the order from the senior drill officer.

"Damn! I can't make that!" Fred thinks to himself. "I've got to meet with Major Dibbs. That's more important."

At 0800 hours, Fred knocks on Major Dibbs' door. "Enter!" sounds the firm voice.

Fred enters, still dressed in civilian clothes, walks up to the Major's desk, comes to a stiff attention, and awkwardly salutes. "Cadet Fred Williams reporting, Major Dibbs, Sir!"

The Major does not look up immediately as he shuffles through some papers. After more than five minutes of standing at attention, Fred decides to relax.

"I said stand at attention, Cadet!" Fred jumps back into a rigid stance. Major Dibbs puts his papers aside and gives Fred a hard, stern look. 'Okay, Cadet Williams, what's your problem?"

Fred, still standing at attention, speaks in a nervous tone. "Sir, I have a nigger for a roommate and I want ..."

Major Dibbs interrupts immediately. "You want! You want! Let me tell you something, Cadet. What you want and what the army wants may be two different things!"

Major Dibbs gets up from his chair, walks around his desk, and positions himself one foot to the right front of Cadet Williams. "If you want to be an army officer, you'll earn that title. That means you'll do what we tell you to do here. Maintain the grade and in four years you may graduate to that title. It's not what you want, Cadet! It's what we want!"

Major Dibbs walks around to the back side of Fred, observing his stance, then returns to a position by his desk. "And, Cadet Williams, if you have a roommate problem, you take that up with your roommate. If you have a pissing problem, you take that up with the Medical Officer. If you have a discipline problem, we'll take that up with the Administration Board." Major Dibbs hesitates for a moment and relaxes his facial expression. "It's my opinion the army doesn't need a cadet that has all kinds of problems. Do you understand, Cadet?"

"Yes, Sir. But what will the other cadets think? I don't want to be known as a nigger lover."

"Cadet Williams, you best start paying attention! Now get your ass over to room inspection or you needn't think about West Point at all. I see no need to visit with you again. You're dismissed!"

Major Dibbs walks around his desk to sit down. Fred is still standing at attention. "You're dismissed, Cadet! Now salute and march out of here."

Almost in tears, Fred gives a quick salute, turns around, and quickly marches out of the office. Disgusted and resentful, Fred stops outside Major Dibbs' office, trying to regain his composure. "Damn it!" he says in a low voice, "What the hell am I doing here?"

Suddenly he realizes that he has missed the first morning room inspection. Feeling exasperated and worried, Fred rushes across the parade grounds to his dormitory. Several of the upper-class cadets yell obscenities to him but he ignores their indignities.

Henry is remaking his bed as Fred rushes into the room.

"Damn it!" exclaims Fred as he sees all his belongings lying on the floor along with his bedding and mattresses. He glances over to Henry who looks at him and says nothing. "Who the hell did this?" blares Fred.

"The Cadre," comments Henry in a quiet voice. "We didn't pass inspection."

"Horse shit! They did this because you're my roommate!" infers Fred. "Damn it! I can't live like this!"

Henry stands upright and turns to Fred. "That's not the reason and you know it," says Henry in a firm voice.

Fred does not respond as he starts to sort through his belongings. He has just started making his bed as the order to report is called.

"All Cadets! Report to the Quartermaster Building to be issued uniforms!"

Again frustrated, Fred throws his mattress back on the floor and walks abruptly out of the room. Henry, feeling flustered, follows.

There are four lines of cadets in the receiving line, and Fred moves to the end of the third line once he sees Henry eight individuals behind him in line four.

Henry feels anxious as he patiently waits his turn to select his gear. It is obvious that many of the cadets are staring at him or at least glancing in his direction when he isn't looking. The mumbled conversations, although not clear to Henry, are obviously about his presence.

It seems what Bishop Jackson has said is right. The upperclassmen are intent upon harassment and that is expected. But what is also concerning Henry is that his own classmates are afraid to associate with him. There is prejudice of caste, as well as race, Henry thinks to himself.

As Senior Cadet James O'Hara enters the building, one of the other cadet officer's yells, "Atten-hut!"

O'Hara has a mean look about him. At five-foot-six inches tall, he is stocky and has a ruddy complexion, topped with bright red hair. As all the cadets remain at attention, Senior

Cadet James O'Hara steps on a chair and addresses the first year class members.

"My name is Senior Cadet James O'Hara. I am the Cadet Commanding Officer here, and all you Plebes will address me as such! In fact, whenever you see me or any other senior cadet officer, you will stop, salute, and stand at attention until we pass ... or until we tell you to carry on."

O'Hara looks at the group for a moment then continues, "Is that clear?"

The freshman cadets reply in unison, "Yes! Sir!"

"Let's try that again, Plebes. I can't hear you!"

Again, only louder, the cadets yell, "Yes! Sir!"

"That's better," O'Hara informs the group as he looks around. O'Hara notices Henry in line, jumps off his chair, and walks over to him. "I see we have a brunette in our midst." O'Hara looks around to the other cadets for approval. He then questions Henry directly. "What's your name, Plebe?"

Henry stands at attention and looks straight forward, remembering his encounter with the senior cadet the night before. "Washington, Sir! Cadet Henry Washington, Senior Cadet O'Hara."

O'Hara moves directly in front of Henry, looking him straight in the eyes. "Tell me, Plebe, how does a brunette get into West Point?"

Feeling challenged by O'Hara's questioning, Henry tries to maintain his composure. "An appointment, Sir."

"And who in their right mind appoints you to this white man's school, Plebe?" O'Hara snarls.

"The honorable Senator from my state, Sir!"

O'Hara looks stern, then continues his drill, "And what state is that? A state of insanity?" O'Hara chuckles to himself as he again looks to the other cadets. Henry does not reply. "Answer me, Plebe!"

"No, Sir, Senior Cadet O'Hara. The state of Georgia, Sir."

"A bad decision it seems to me, Cadet. I trust you realize that there are no brunette officers in the United States Army. And personally, I don't think there ever will be. It takes courage and determination to give orders, Cadet. I don't think you have that!"

O'Hara, steps back, turns to the other senior cadet officers, then looks to the freshman group. "Carry on, Plebes, and we'll see how long you can carry this brunette with you."

Henry is indifferent to the glares he receives from the other cadets. And although he is tempted to respond to Senior Cadet O'Hara's demeaning comments, he wisely brushes them off. I must remain disciplined and retain my self-esteem, he thinks to himself.

While Henry and Fred Williams are in the Quartermaster Building, three other senior cadets have gained access to their room. One of the upper classmen carries a bucket as the other two pull the blankets back from each of the beds. "Hurry up. We can't stay in here too long," quips the taller of three men. "Hell, if we get caught in here the cadre will have our heads."

"Bring the tar and feathers over here," commands the other cadet. "These chicken feathers should make for a comfortable sleep, don't ya think?" The three laugh as they remake Henry and Fred's bunks. "Let's get out'a here before anyone sees us. I'd like to see their faces after they crawl into these beds."

Fred and Henry return to their rooms at different times, but both are consumed with the tasks of getting their uniforms properly appointed with brass, and shoes shined for the next day's drill and inspection. Neither one talks to the other as they both maintain their own sense of space.

The evening meal call was uneventful compared to the afternoon quartermaster call, but the tension Henry feels seems ominous. From now on, all first year cadets are to line up outside the dormitory and march to all meals. This is the time in which the yells and catcalls by upper classmen are the most insulting and continuous for all the new cadets.

Mine is just going to be more interesting, but I can take it, Henry rationalizes to himself as he marches to dinner.

That evening is busy. Both Henry and Fred are preoccupied with preparation for the next day's full schedule; drill inspection in uniform, then lineup and march to breakfast, then room inspection, after which they are to get their class curriculum.

The sound of Taps indicates all lamps are to be put out and all cadets to be in bed. Henry and Fred rush to put their belongings in order before getting into bed. Both turn their kerosene lights out at the same moment and crawl into their bunks. Then a yell. "What the Hell! screams Fred.

At the same moment Henry lets out a yell. "Damn! What is this stuff?"

In the darkness of their room, both scramble to get a light on. As the light brightens they see each other, white feathers clinging to each of them.

"Shit! Just because I got a damn nigger for a roommate!" replies Fred, as he tries to pull the feathers from his body. "Damn you, nigger! Why'd you have to come here in the first place?"

Henry, trying to get the feathers off his own body, responds. "To be an Officer and a Gentleman."

Fred, still preoccupied with the tar and feathers on himself, asks in a delayed response, "What the hell did you say?"

"I said we're here to become Officers and Gentlemen."

"Ya, damn it! With chicken feathers."

Henry smiles for a moment. Looking at Fred with feathers all over his body is quite humorous.

"What the hell are you laughing at?" screams Fred as he experiences the feeling of embarrassment and vulnerability.

Henry reaches into his drawer and pulls out a large bottle of liniment. "Here, try some of this." Having no other recourse, Fred reluctantly accepts the bottle. "That stuff will remove the tar," comments Henry in a calm voice.

At 0500 hours both Henry and Fred appear at drill inspection. The three cadets who tarred and feathered their beds the night before, look on in amazement. "How the hell did they get clean so quick?"

"Damned if I know," replies the other cadet. "Let's wait until they're dismissed from drill."

Once drill is dismissed the three cadets approach Henry and Fred. As military protocol requires, Henry and Fred stop at attention and salute.

"Hey, did you salt and pepper twins sleep well last night? Ya know there's nothing better than feathers to make a bed more comfortable," shouts the taller senior cadet. The others laugh at the comment. He then continues, "Say, if you two need anything, count on us. There's nothing we enjoy more than making new cadets feel comfortable."

At this moment the bugle sounds the Assembly Call. All freshman cadets rush into formation. Henry and Fred take a quick glance at each other. Fred just shakes his head in disgust. "I want to talk to you after class orientation," Fred declares.

It is ten o'clock when Fred walks out of orientation. He knows Henry is still getting his class registration completed so he positions himself outside the doorway. *I've got to get this nigger off by back*, he thinks to himself as he reviews his new class schedule.

"Damn, look at this schedule of classes," he mutters under his breath. "Algebra, geometry, French, tactics of infantry/artillery, small arms, social behavior ... they gotta be nuts."

Senior Cadet O'Hara and five other senior cadets, including Senior Cadet Jerry Jensen, Assistant Cadet Commander, approach Cadet Williams. Startled, Fred drops his books and assumes a position of attention.

"Forgot to salute, didn't you, Plebe?" informs Senior Cadet O'Hara.

"Ah ... sorry, Sir," replies Fred, feeling nervous.

"Say, Plebe, where's that brunette roommate of yours?"

Fred, being resentful that Henry is his roommate, is even more upset by the fact that the senior cadets are referring to Henry as his roommate. In a fit of stubbornness, Fred decides to say nothing.

Senior Cadet O'Hara moves up to Fred nose to nose. "What's the matter, Plebe? Has your nigger roommate got your tongue?"

Fred stands rigid, but silent.

"I think we got a nigger lover here," adds Senior Cadet Jerry Jensen. "Don't you gentlemen agree?"

All the other senior cadets mummer their insults as one of them notices Henry walking out of the class orientation building. "Hey, O'Hara, look what's com'n."

O'Hara turns to see Henry walking out of the building in their direction. He turns back to Fred. "Here comes your lover now, Plebe. You better call him and ..."

Fred's right fist hits O'Hara on the jaw before he can finish his sentence. The other cadets react immediately by attacking Fred, knocking him to the ground and kicking him.

Henry notices the scuffle, then sees that it's Fred on the ground out-numbered. He immediately drops his books and runs into the fight, knocking Senior Cadet Jensen to the ground with a hard left hook. O'Hara, who originally wanted revenge on Fred Williams, now wants his chance at Henry. It doesn't quite come.

Just as Henry and Senior Cadet O'Hara are about to square off a loud whistle blows, indicating the Cadre are coming. All cadets immediately discontinue their engagement as Major Dibbs comes running up. "Freeze at attention!" he screams.

All the cadets involved in the fracas stand firm and silent. Both O'Hara and Williams are bleeding from the nose and all seven cadets have either torn or dirtied their uniforms. The Major is blatantly angry. The veins in his neck are about ready to pop.

"What the hell do you bastards think this is? I'll tell you something and you all better listen close! If any of you even breath wrong, your ass is gone. Now what happened here?"

None of the cadets move, nor do any say a word. All stand at attention, silent. Major Dibbs has been in this situation with cadets many times before. It isn't unusual to him that they remain silent. That is their unwritten code, but he still doesn't approve of it. "Okay, if you want to play games, I have one for you. It's called West Point Discipline. And I'd like to teach you the rules."

Major Dibbs walks slowly up to each of the cadets and glares into their eyes. "The first rule is that each of you are hereby restricted to your rooms until I say otherwise. The other rules of this game will follow, one by one."

Major Dibbs then walks over to Senior Cadet O'Hara. "How many times have you been disciplined now, O'Hara?"

O'Hara remains silent.

"You had your final warning several weeks ago, didn't you?"

"Yes, Sir!" replies O'Hara loud and clear.

"As a consequence of this action, O'Hara, I have a special game for you. It's called meet the dismissal board. We'll see how that plays out." Major Dibbs looks to the other cadets and speaks in a firm, rational voice. "And if any of you other cadets display this type of behavior again you will suffer serious consequences. Am I understood?"

All the cadets yell in unison, "Yes! Sir!"

"Good. Now get your little asses to your rooms and remain there until further notice. Move!"

Back in their room, Fred is wiping the blood off his mouth and uniform when Henry breaks the silence. "Never thought you'd have a black man for a roommate, did you Williams?"

Fred, surprised at Henry's comment, responds in a somewhat reverent manner. "Hell, it's not your fault, Washington. It's just the times." Fred finishes cleaning himself and looks toward Henry, "Thanks."

Surprised at hearing this word, Henry inquires, "For what?"

"For helping me in that fight. I never expected a colored man would help out a white man."

Henry smiles slightly then looks toward Fred. "Well, it's like you said, Williams. It's just the times."

For the next several weeks both Henry and Fred, like most of the cadets, settle into the routine and lifestyle at the academy. The harassment of the upper classmen is forever present and it is even more prevalent for Henry as all the major newspapers are periodically attempting to get interviews or just running their own editorial viewpoints. Some of the Eastern papers outwardly support Henry, but most will suggest that his graduation will be socially and academically impossible.

During the next year Henry maintains his focus and optimistic outlook. It seems to him that each day is somewhat better than the previous one. However, the feeling of ostracism is continually present. In fact, it is so strong that any white cadet who dares to socially fraternize with him will be ostracized by the other cadets.

The first year Henry has no social friends, male or female. He and Fred become "tolerable" of each other, but their friendship grows very, very slowly.

Henry grows to appreciate the rigorous discipline of the Academy and spends most of his time studying. He is more determined than ever to keep his mind set on becoming an officer. I won't flinch from this, without dishonor, he tells himself each day, as he reads some of the newspaper's accounts of his activities.

"It's strange, all the things I've done, that I haven't done," he comments aloud to himself after reading the editorials. This becomes a weekly ritual with Henry, first to read the editorials, then read about the Indian Wars out west. He especially tries to follow the exploits of the all Black Tenth U.S. Cavalry Regiment under Colonel Novak. "That's where I want to be assigned when I graduate," he fantasizes aloud. Being alone much of the time Henry learns that it is good to talk to himself, especially, he thinks, if he is to go to the Great Plains.

I know now that I will make it, he writes in his Christmas letter to Bishop Jackson, and say "Hello" to Leon. I miss you all.

CHAPTER ELEVEN
"SHORTY" – A YOUNG RECRUIT

Emanuel Thomas, an energetic fourteen-year-old at five-foot-one-inch tall, is packing his small bag when his mother enters the bedroom. She is both surprised and shocked at what she sees. "Emanuel, where you think you be go'n?"

Emanuel turns around and smiles a sheepish grin. "I be signin' up fo' de' army ... Cavalry. I wont to be a soljur! Deys hirin' colored folks."

His mother stands there in amazement, her hands on her hips as Emanuel looks at her with pride. "Boy, you be 'bout knee high to a grasshopper. Ain't no army gonna hire no little colored boy. You stop dis foolishness ... we got chickens to tend to!"

Emanuel keeps the smile on his face as he continues to pack his bag. "I can make it, Ma. Ain't no job 'roun here fo' no black boy, and de army pays thirteen dollars a month."

"Where you learn that?"

"I heard it down 't the store. A man read it to me. It on a big piece 'a paper."

His mother takes a deep sigh, then sits down on the bed in front of him. Looking him straight in the eyes she puts her hand gently on his shoulder.

Emanuel looks to her with a serious expression. "You's gonna be proud of me, Ma."

Tears come to his mother's eyes as she speaks softly. "I'se already proud of you."

Emanuel hesitates for a moment then moves close to her and gives her a firm hug. Grabbing his bag in one hand and his mother's hand in the other he gently pulls her up. "Stop yo' cryin', Ma. You gonna have a boy in de army. De' Cavalry!"

Jefferson City is bustling with activity on this nice June day of 1872. Men, women, and children are walking or driving their wagons up and down the dirt street of this small Missouri town. A large banner hangs over the main street with army recruitment posters everywhere.

UNITED STATES ARMY RECRUITMENT HEADQUARTERS
TENTH CAVALRY REGIMENT–COLORED MEN ONLY
APPLY AT LIVERY STABLE.

Outside the livery stable are hand painted signs directing all applicants to a temporary office, once used as a large fouling stall, inside the barn. Black men by the hundreds are lined up outside or milling around talking. Some are dressed in nice clothes, others in torn shirts and pants. A few have no shoes. Every age group is well represented from eighteen to thirty-five. This is an opportunity for many to escape a life of drudgery and earn a minimum of thirteen dollars a month, plus, in the eyes of some, find adventure.

Colonel Novak, Commander of the Tenth Cavalry, is a fatherly looking type, even dressed in his uniform. At five-foot-eleven-inches tall, gray hair, and somewhat rotund, he doesn't look the experienced combat soldier that he is. Having commanded a Black regiment in the Civil War, he is very familiar with the mind set and steadfastness of colored troops. Now in his early forties, but still carrying a professional soldier image, it is appropriate that the men in his regiment refer to him affectionately as "The Old Man."

The men stand at the interview table, one by one, as Sergeant Ruben Waller takes down their names and ages. Having served with Colonel Novak since the Civil War days, he has attained the rank of Master Sergeant, one of the highest ranks afforded a Black soldier. He is also very proud, not only of his rank, but to serve in the Tenth Cavalry and with Colonel

Novak. He knows what kind of men will best serve in the regiment, but as usual, Colonel Novak will always make his comment, "Remember, Sergeant, we want only the most fit fo these men."

Sergeant Waller looks away from the man he is interviewing for a moment, and reaffirms the Colonel. "Yes, Suh! I be pick'n only de best, Suh!"

Colonel Novak smiles slightly, then walks to the small window to look outside. "There's still a lot of men out there, Sergeant. How many have we accepted so far?"

"Fifty-three, Suh."

"Is that all? We need at least one-hundred-fifty, and that's just a start."

"We'll pick 'em, Suh! You know dat."

As Sergeant Waller continues to interview men, Colonel Novak's curiosity perks as he sees a very short, young looking, colored boy standing in line with the other taller recruits. Hmm, he thinks to himself. That's interesting. Wonder what he's doing out there? After a moments chuckle, Colonel Novak walks to his desk and puts on his hat. "Sergeant Waller, continue the interviews. I'm going to take a short walk."

Sergeant Waller looks to the Colonel, puzzled. "Yes, Suh. I be do'n' that."

Colonel Novak eases himself through the line of men and walks outside the old stable. Squinting briefly at the bright sun, he casually walks over to the recruit he has observed through the window.

Emanuel is dressed in loose tan clothes and has his chicken feed'n straw hat on. He is inwardly excited as he watches the regular cavalry soldiers ride their mounts in the distance. It has taken him almost two weeks to walk to the recruiting station. During that time all he thought about was riding one of those cavalry horses. It never did occur to him that there are regulations to meet when joining the army, especially that of being a minimum height of five-foot-two-inches. But he knows the army accepts sixteen-year-olds.

"What's your name, son?" asks Colonel Novak as he approached Emanuel, unnoticed.

Emanuel, caught completely off guard, is startled out of his wits as he looks up at Colonel Novak. Quickly sticking his chest out and throwing his right hand up in an awkward salute, he replies in a very nervous voice, "Emanuel, Suh! Emanuel Thomas, Suh!" Still trying to get his two feet locked together and stand a little taller, Emanuel comes to an awkward form of attention. Colonel Novak has to turn his head slightly to the rear to hide his smile. Quickly, however, Colonel Novak resumes his military presence and salutes back to Emanuel. "How old are you, son?" he asks Emanuel in a serious, yet soft, military voice.

"I be sixteen, Suh ... really am, Suh!" Emanuel continues to hold his salute.

Enthralled with the situation at hand, Colonel Novak continues to question, "Are you intending to enlist today, son?"

"Yes, Suh!"

"Hmm. Why do you want to be a soldier, Thomas?"

Emanuel stands straight, his eyes beam as he responds with enthusiasm, still saluting. "Adventure, Suh! To ride in de cavalry 'n be a good soljur, Suh!"

Colonel Novak is noticeably taking an interest in the young man as he ponders for a moment. "Ah, yes. I'm sure you will be, Thomas. I'm sure you will be." The Colonel looks around to all the other troops who are watching him as he talks to Emanuel. "You can drop your salute now, Thomas."

Emanuel immediately drops his arm in a civilian military fashion. After all, he has been practicing his salute for over two weeks because he knows he needs that in the army.

"Can you ride a horse, Thomas?

"Well ... I rode a mule. I rode her three times, Suh!" replies Emanuel.

"How tall are you, Thomas? You know the army has a minimum requirement of five-foot-two-inches, don't you?"

Emanuel squirms a bit as he rolls his eyes at the sky. "I be five-foot-two 'n a half inches, Suh!"

"Are you sure?"

"Yes, Suh! My Ma tol' me."

Colonel Novak knows that he is drawing a lot of attention talking to Emanuel and decides he best curtail the conversation. "Okay, Thomas. Your interview will be coming up soon." Colonel Novak turns to walk away when Emanuel begins his salute again. After walking more than forty paces, Colonel Novak stops, then turns around. He looks at Emanuel for a moment, then yells, "You can drop your salute now, Thomas."

As the Colonel walks away Emanuel drops his salute, stands erect, and smiles at all the other recruits near him.

"Hey there, shorty, what did the Colonel want?" yells a tall black man up the line.

Emanuel is too engrossed in his own world to answer. *I met the Colonel*, he thinks to himself with satisfaction and a smile.

Upon re-entering the makeshift recruitment office, Colonel Novak throws his hat on his desk and walks back to the window. Somehow Emanuel Thomas has affected his emotion. As he looks out at the small boy standing among the older men, he shakes his head, then turns to Sergeant Waller. "Sergeant Waller, come here for a moment. There's something I want you to see."

Sergeant Waller tells the recruit he is interviewing to hold his position, gets up, and walks to the window. "Yes, Suh?"

"Sergeant, see that little recruit out there?"

Sergeant Waller moves closer to the window and looks at all the men lined up outside. 'De little colored boy, Suh?"

"That's the one, Sergeant."

"Yes, Suh. I see him."

"Says he's five-foot-two and a half inches tall, and can ride a mule."

Sergeant Waller shakes his head. "Suh, cain't even be five-foot. He be too little fo de cavalry, Suh."

"Says him name is Emanuel. I think he'll make a good soldier someday. You take good care of him!"

"If you say so, Suh." Sergeant Waller knows what the Colonel means, as he walks back to his interview station shaking his head. "What's this man's army com'n to?" he mumbles to himself.

As the line slowly moves on, Emanuel fantasizes about riding the fastest horse the cavalry has. His daydreams are abruptly interrupted when the Black man next to him gives Emanuel a quick poke. "Get your little black ass up there, shorty!"

Shocked and nervous, Emanuel walks up to Sergeant Waller. "Emanuel, reporting for duty, Sir."

Sergeant Waller doesn't know whether to smile or look stern. "What's your full name?"

"Emanuel Horatio Thomas."

"How tall are you, Thomas?"

Emanuel looks around, then responds confidently. "Five foot … two 'n a half."

"Com'on o'er here, Thomas. We need a measurement." Sergeant Waller stands Emanuel against the wall where there is a height chart. Emanuel, now very nervous, puts his chest out and stands tall.

"Heels down, Thomas!"

Sergeant Waller takes one look at the measurement, then backs away. "Just stand there for a minute, Thomas. I'll be right back." Emanuel's hopes of making five-foot-two are fading.

Sergeant Waller picks up a short board from one of the stalls and puts it next to Emanuel. "Here, Thomas. Stand on this." Emanuel hesitates, then steps on the board.

"Yup!" exclaims Sergeant Waller, "You be five-foot-two and a half, on de mark!"

Emanuel takes a deep breath, closes his eyes, then releases it quickly.

Sergeant Waller has Emanuel sign his enlistment papers and instructs him to go to the Quartermaster tent. "Sign here soldier, then go pick up your gear. They'll tell you what tent you'll be assigned to down there. You'll be leaving for Fort Concho in a couple of days."

Excited and smiling from ear to ear, Emanuel signs his mark and begins running out the door to the Quartermaster tent.

"Hey, Private Thomas! You forgot yor requisition papers!" yells Sergeant Waller.

Embarrassed, Emanuel runs back to Sergeant Waller's desk, grabs his papers, salutes, and runs back out the door.

It is a hot, sultry morning at Fort Concho. General Olson, Commander of Troops west of the Mississippi, and Colonel Novak watch as Sergeant Waller has the new enlisted men practicing training maneuvers on horseback for the first time. "How are these colored recruits doing, Colonel?"

"They're learning, Sir."

The drill isn't going very well as Sergeant Waller yells out his commands. "Keep that formation tight, you numbskulls!

Formation at a trot! screams Waller, as he shakes his head in disgust. "Thomas! Damn, you! Move up 'n down with the horse's hindquarters."

Emanuel just can't seem to get the posting position right at the trot. His bouncing motion is causing him to loose control of the horse, as his hat falls on the ground, then just as fast, Emanuel is on the ground.

"Looks like that short recruit out there has his problems," quips General Olson. "Never seen a cavalryman use two stirrups to mount before."

"He's a good recruit, Sir. These men are doing as well as can be expected." Colonel Novak then quickly changes the subject. "What we need, Sir, is better equipment and more sound horses. We also need repeating rifles, Sir."

Colonel Novak points to the horses in the training field before he continues. "How does the government expect us to do our job without being killed ... for lack of proper equipment?"

General Olson listens intently as he watches the men train. "General, these men are determined to be good soldiers," continues Colonel Novak. "This Texas sun alone has tested their grit. We need the proper ..."

"Grit, shit!" broke in General Olson. "If I owned Texas and Hell, I'd rent out Texas and live in Hell!" General Olson laughs at his statement then turns back to Colonel Novak. "I'll make sure you have proper supplies and decent horses, Colonel. In fact, I'll have some well bred Morgan stallions sent out here from the government-breeding farm in Vermont. You can upgrade your grade mare stock. Might even find your officers some good Morgan geldings."

"Thank you, Sir! That will add to the Esprit de Corps."

"When will you be able to take command at Fort Wallace, Colonel?" asks General Olson.

"I'm guessing about forty days, Sir. They're progressing that fast."

"Great! Oh, Colonel, better teach that short recruit out there how to ride a horse!"

Colonel Novak smiles as General Olson slaps him on the back. "There's something about that lad, General. Can't quite figure out what it is, but there's something."

It is thirty-eight days later when Colonel Novak leads four Companies, totaling two-hundred-thirty-two Tenth Cavalry troopers, down the trail to Fort Wallace, Nebraska. The soldiers look sharp and clean as they trot in column formation to the fort gate, the Tenth Cavalry flag flying at the forefront.

As flag bearer, Private Thomas rides directly behind Colonel Novak and Sergeant Waller.

It is an honor to be chosen to carry the flag, and Emanuel rides proud past the fort soldiers and civilians who have assembled to watch the all black regiment arrive.

Many of the two-hundred-plus spectators have never seen a Black soldier before and most just stand quiet, watching the new soldiers ride in.

"Column, Halt!" commands Colonel Novak as he turns to Sergeant Waller. "Take charge, Sergeant! Make sure the horses are stalled and fed, and the men quartered."

Sergeant Waller salutes. "Yes, Suh, Colonel!"

Colonel Novak then rides over to the Fort Headquarters building where five officers stand to attention. "Welcome to Fort Hays, Sir," says Major Baker.

"Thank you, Major," acknowledges Colonel Novak as he dismounts and hands his horse reins to a young Lieutenant. "Nice country 'round here. But we can talk about that later. Let's all go inside, get acquainted and comfortable. We have a lot of business to conduct."

CHAPTER TWELVE
MUD ON FACE

There are more than three-hundred lodges surrounding the village teepee of Two Crows. The normal daily activities are taking place. Women are skinning and tanning deer and buffalo hides as young children run naked, playing. Most of the Indian men are separated into smaller groups outside talking about their exploits, checking their weapons, or playing with their younger children. Most of the older children are playing "knock them off" with their horses. The exterior setting looks serene and peaceful as most of the horses graze lazily on the grass at the edge of the campsite.

As leader of the Cut-Head band of Sioux, Two Crows' lodge is always erected in the center of the village upon each relocation. Not only is this strategically convenient, but also a symbol of his power and leadership. As an Elder, and respected Chieftain, Two Crows likes to display his symbol of two large crows painted on each side of the entrance to his teepee. As usual, he also displays his lance of thirty-two eagle feathers just outside the lodge entrance to the right. This is his mark of distinction, displaying all the honors and coups he has accumulated in his years of battle against other tribes and the soldiers.

As the other members of the Tribe continue their daily activities, Two Crows, Grey Bull, an ancient medicine man, and other members of the Tribal Council are engaged in a serious confrontation with the behavior of Lone Wolf. As is social tradition in their culture, each male member of the tribe has the inherent right to independently pursue his own desires. Usually, without interference from others.

However, Lone Wolf's violent and murderous raiding activities are causing concern even among his own people. With the arrival of more soldiers in the territory, the Elders are contemplating the merits of a peace treaty with the White Father. The general course of conversation is not whether the male warriors want to fight or not, but that they should consider the hardship on the women and children. Although the idea of a treaty is not at all popular, the raging rampages of Lone Wolf if putting all the people of the band in danger of an attack by the U.S. Army, especially the newly arrived Tenth Cavalry.

"Who are these strange soldiers that have mud on face?" demands Lone Wolf.

"That not mud on face," replies Two Crows.

"Then what kind of war paint?" asks Lone Wolf.

Two Crows sits quietly as he looks to the other members of the Council sitting around the small fire. He turns to Lone Wolf. "The new soldiers dark white men."

Having never seen a Black man before, Lone Wolf displays a slight grin, but is intent and concerned. "Where do they come from?"

Two Crows waves his right hand slowly. "From across the great waters."

Lone Wolf's interest is insatiable. "How do you know this?"

"Because I have heard."

Lone Wolf's frustration is showing. But this trait is well known by the members of the Council. It is this exact behavior that the Council is concerned about, but they do respect Lone Wolf's fighting abilities. "I must see these strange warriors!" Lone Wolf says as he stands.

"Be patient, Lone Wolf. There are many. In days to come you will learn much about them," informs Grey Bull. "If you are to lead our warriors in battle, you must use good judgment ... be cautious and cunning, like the fox ... and do not reveal village location."

Grey Bull remains silent as he looks to Lone Wolf, then to the Council members. He then voices further concern. "Every step we take on Mother Earth is sacred, each step like a prayer. The power you seek only planted as a seed if the soul is pure and good. It can only grow in man's heart if he walks in holy manner. The Great Spirit will aid all who seek him with pure heart."

Lone Wolf looks confused. He isn't sure if this statement is directed at him or as a general prayer. That means nothing, Lone Wolf thinks to himself. I just want to see these soldiers. The other members of the Council grunt in approval of Grey Bull's advice and wisdom.

Although fiercely independent, Lone Wolf realizes that without the approval of the Tribal Council his chances of leading the main war party in any battle will be slim. Only a few braves will take a chance on defying the wisdom of the Elders. His mind then begins to think in terms of a raiding attack on an army patrol.

Two Crows looks at Lone Wolf. His eyes are clear and piercing as they gaze out from behind the deep wrinkles of his weather beaten skin. "Three days ride. Tomorrow you come with me Lone Wolf. I will show you."

Lone Wolf, appearing satisfied, nods in approval, showing unusual respect for the Elders on the Council.

"Remember what I say," comments Grey Bull as Lone Wolf prepares to leave.

The rough terrain conceals the four horses as Two Crows, Lone Wolf, and two of his followers crawl stealthily to the top of the hill. It is a good vantage point in which Fort Wallace is clearly visible from the distance. The crisp morning air provides a haze free view of the fort.

The morning reveille can be faintly heard in the distance as the soldiers prepare for their daily activities.

Company D, Tenth Cavalry is just beginning their morning patrol to check on the railroad crew that is laying tracks in their eastern district. As is common on these patrols, the men wear what is most comfortable, rather than the formal military uniforms of eastern forts. Some soldiers wear their military caps but many opt to tie them to their belts. The wool shirts are too hot and are also optional attire on patrol. It is a colorful patrol; blue pants with a yellow strip, and red or yellow undershirts, with yellow suspenders.

Lone Wolf's eyes are fixed on the soldiers as they leave the Fort. "Give me long glass," says Lone Wolf.

Two Crows hands him a telescope that was taken from a settler's wagon several months ago. Lone Wolf studies the Black soldiers for several minutes. "Strange soldiers," he comments in a low voice. "Like hair on buffalo's head."

Lone Wolf slinks back down behind the rocks and turns to Two Crows. "Buffalo soldiers! But are they strong like the buffalo?"

Two Crows remains quiet as he studies Lone Wolf's reaction.

Excited and deep in thought, Lone Wolf responds to his own question. "We shall see. I will test them."

As the scouting party begins their return to the village more than seventy miles to the northwest, Lone Wolf's mind fills with ideas. He is a man of action and what he wants, he wants now. During the overnight ride he contemplates constantly the different means of attack he can use on the soldiers. A Buffalo Soldier's scalp will bring honor to my lodge, he thinks to himself.

As the men camp the first night, Lone Wolf talks incessantly to his two followers while Two Crows sleeps. "We will use three decoys. They will lead the soldiers into our ambush."

Whatever Lone Wolf says, his two followers nod in agreement rather than take a chance on fueling his violent temper. But then most warriors in the band want to improve their social status by making coups, and Lone Wolf is proven as a brave warrior and leader.

As the scouting party enters the village the next morning, Two Crows departs in silence and rides to his lodge. Lone Wolf instructs his two followers to bring all warriors who wish to plan a raid on the soldiers to meet at his lodge. He is intense with anticipation on leading this attack and he decides it is time for his son, White Hawk, to be initiated in the way of the warrior.

White Deer is carrying fox skins to Grey Bull's lodge as Lone Wolf rides up at a full gallop, pulling his horse to a sliding stop. "Where White Hawk?" he yells as he flings himself off his horse in front of White Deer, momentarily stopping her.

Defiant and filled with anger for Lone Wolf's abusive nature, White Deer turns to walk away when Lone Wolf grabs her arm. "Tell me, woman. Where White Hawk? His time come!"

White Deer looks at Lone Wolf with defiant eyes. "You dominate him! You should know where he is!"

"Why you avoid me, woman?" Lone Wolf shouts as he tightens his grip on White Deer's arm and gives her a violent jerk close to him. "It good thing that you have protection of Grey Bull and Council!"

White Deer quickly turns her head close to Lone Wolf's, then spits in his face. CRACK! Lone Wolf's right hand instantly hits White Deer's jaw, knocking her to the ground. In a split second flashback she visualizes the times that Lone Wolf has tried to rape her and beat her. Her reaction to being knocked down is instant aggression as she reaches for her skinning knife.

"I kill you! I kill you!" she screams as she raises to her feet and lunges toward Lone Wolf slashing him across the side of his face. As Lone Wolf backs away from her, other members of the tribe come running over to the scene. "I kill you someday! I kill you!" White Deer screams with passion and conviction as she backs away toward Grey Bull's teepee.

Embarrassed by being cut by a woman and having witnesses to the event, Lone Wolf quietly mounts his horse and rides quickly to his own lodge. He knows that someday he will have to account for his actions; either to Grey Bull or maybe even White Deer herself. For the moment, however, his pride is injured and he knows that being cut in this manner is a bad omen. The raid on the soldiers at Fort Wallace will have to wait. Now will be the time to prepare White Hawk to be a "Water Bearer."

Lone Wolf has sat alone in his lodge for more than a week without venturing out. The deep four-inch cut to his right cheek has quit bleeding and is beginning to heal. He is ready to see White Hawk and sends word that he wants to see him.

A Water Bearer is an honor for a young Sioux boy, and the first step in becoming a member of the Warrior Society. It is this important role that will insure a war party has sufficient water prior to, and after battle. It is a first test.

It is early morning when White Hawk arrives at the entrance of Lone Wolf's lodge. "What you want, Father?" White Hawk asks in a loud voice from outside the teepee.

Lone Wolf has been waiting for this moment and quickly walks outside. Standing erect and proud, he looks at the son to whom he has shown the arts of manhood as is required for membership in his Society of the Pipe Carriers. He walks to White Hawk and firmly puts his hand on his right shoulder.

"You have been training well, I know," begins Lone Wolf. "The two-legged and four-legged animals fall before your arrows. You ride your horse fast like the wind. The Great Spirit has given you many gifts. Now, after all these moons, time for you to use them. To test yourself as a new warrior against the soldier who is your enemy."

White Hawk knows exactly what his father is talking about. It is his time to prove to all the other males of his age and the Elders, that he is the best of the young warriors, like his father Lone Wolf. He has been preparing for this day since he left his mother ten years earlier. He has been well instructed in the skills of tribal religion, ethics, hunting and tracking, raiding and warfare. He is honed into the environment. White Hawk is also ambitions. He knows that to achieve success and status in his society he must know well the skills of the Fasting Place, The Raid or Warrior Society, and become a member of the Council.

Now at age sixteen he is more than ready to enter the world of true manhood and gain his first coup and eagle feather ... a symbol that will show all that he is a warrior. His first of five steps is to be that of a Water Bearer or a Scout, whichever he is chosen for first.

"I am ready, Father. What you want me to do?"

Lone Wolf senses his son's aggression and eagerness to do whatever he is ordered. Suddenly, Lone Wolf feels a sadness in his heart he has never felt before. He, for he first time, feels the loss of that which is loved. He, like White Deer did years before, has lost the control he has over his son. White Hawk has passed through all the rights of passage; from child, through mother, through father, to self-attainment. A slight shudder runs down Lone Wolf's spine.

"Take your strong horse, water, and food," commands Lone Wolf. "Learn the honor of being Water Bearer and Scout. Go scout soldiers at fort. Observe everything like you do the animals, the rivers, the rocks, and the trees. Do not let soldiers see you. Do not fight. You will be tested."

White Hawk's eyes are bright with excitement. His heart and pulse begin pounding with the anticipation of proving to the tribe and himself that he is the best of warriors, and will be a leader like his father, Lone Wolf. What White Hawk doesn't know, are the secrets of his father's past.

CHAPTER THIRTEEN
THE DREAM CONTINUES

It is a perfect day. Just a slight breeze interrupts the warm, cloudless Sunday afternoon. The spring flowers and green grass add to the picture perfect setting among the immaculate stone structured buildings as Henry Washington steps out of his dormitory hall.

Looking trim and military sharp, Henry runs toward Bishop Jackson and Leon. Henry has longed for the moment he will wear the military dress uniform of an Army officer. Now he has it on and Bishop Jackson and Leon are there to see him wearing it.

Visiting Henry, along with Leon and Bishop Jackson, is Jeff Hill, a white journalist from the Atlanta Constitution, the largest newspaper in the South. Henry learned long ago to avoid newspaper reporters, but Jeff Hill is one of several individuals who has consistently given him support and encouragement during his four years at West Point.

As Henry approaches the small group, they give him a joyous welcome. Leon is the first to shake Henry's hand and give him the ol' bear hug. "Congratulations, ol' friend! I knew you could make your dream come true."

"Thanks, Leon. It means a lot to me that you and Bishop Jackson are here," replies Henry as he turns to shake the Bishop's hand, then gives him a firm hug. "So glad you could come, Sir," says Henry emotionally, as this is the first time he has seen either the Bishop or Leon in four years.

"Glad to be here, Henry. You make us all down right proud. You're the spitt'n image of an army officer. My how you've matured."

"Thank you, Bishop Jackson. It's been a real challenge, to say the least." Henry then glances over to Jeff Hill. "Mr. Hill, I didn't mean to ignore you."

"That's okay, Henry. I'd also like to congratulate you. An accomplishment in our time."

Again Henry takes a moment to think and reflect. "I guess during my first year I felt fear. I was really afraid. Not so much of the Cadre, they were fair and professional. It was more the other cadets ... my apprehension was such that I expected to be insulted or struck at almost any time."

"Were you ever struck?" asks Hill.

Henry quickly remembers the incident with his first year roommate, Fred Williams, and the fight with Senior Cadets O'Hara and Jensen. "Well, almost, but only once. I look back on that incident with a lot of chuckles today."

"What are you referring to, Henry?" asks Hill again.

"My first two weeks were definitely the worst."

Henry relates the fight incident and his initial experiences with Fred and himself.

"So how are you and Fred getting along today, as opposed to your first meeting?" inquires Jeff.

"Well, I'd say we're getting along pretty good. I've been asked to be the best man at his wedding this coming weekend."

Hill's eyebrows raise as the expression on Jeff's face is one of surprise. "Yes, I'd certainly have to agree, Henry."

Jeff then takes a minute to look over his notes. "Are there any specific instances that you recall, or that stand out in your mind, that indicate racism?"

Henry looks to Jeff Hill with a serious expression. "Yes, in my opinion there is, but the prejudice didn't stop my cadet peers from becoming gentlemen. I'll tell you why I think that. Some, like my roommate Fred, come from wealthy families and are motivated into West Point by family tradition. Others come from rural areas and are rough and uncouth, with only a rudimentary social education. Some just lack backbone ... but after four years of education and strict military discipline, attitudes did change."

"Yes, go on, Henry. I'm listening."

"Let me give you an example of what I'm trying to say, Mr. Hill. I was called nigger by one cadet in my class well into my second year. Then, during a routine horse drill down a steep slope, my horse started to fall. This cadet was next to me and grabbed me off my horse. Had he not done that, I would have surely been injured in the fall or possibly killed. Why he did that I'll probably never know, but he hasn't called me nigger since."

Henry contemplates as he shifts his seating position. "Overall, there was ostracism and prejudice, especially the first year. However, it seemed to diminish as the years went on and as I got to know more of the men. Possibly I just became an accepted fixture." Henry laughs.

"You do have a sense of humor, Henry."

"Yes, Sir, a lot better one now than I had four years ago."

"This is a serious question," begins Hill. "The nation is looking at you now. You carry an unusual responsibility. Do you feel you have equal rights?"

Henry ponders the question. He knows that he is taking a risk answering it, but decides to make the commitment. "Mr. Hill, equal rights will come for me in due time. I personally don't want equal rights now, but identical rights. I want to be a soldier. This is my life. I believe there must be a mutual dependence on races, not an independence, don't you think?"

Jeff Hill isn't ready for this answer and avoids it by asking Henry about politics. "Do you ever plan to get into politics?

If you can be the first black graduate out of West Point, why not the first black Senator from Georgia?"

Henry responds quickly to the question. "Like I said, Mr. Hill, I want to be a soldier in this life and be a good one. Nothing else."

"Do you have your assignment yet?"

Henry smiles. "Yes. I got what I requested."

"And what is that, Henry?"

"The Tenth U.S. Cavalry Regiment, Fort Wallace."

Knowing little about the army, Jeff is unimpressed with Henry's assignment, and knowing they are pushed for time, looks at his pocket watch. He notices it is close to ceremony time. "Almost time, Henry, but a couple last questions, then we best go. First one; what is your major?"

"Bachelor of Science in Engineering, with Spanish as my minor," replies Henry.

"Did you date while in school here?"

"No."

"On a very personal level ... what's your favorite kind of food?"

Henry laughs. "Anything that's not hot or spicy. I can't take hot peppers or anything like that. It's a good thing the army doesn't station me in Mexico."

"Well, thank you, Henry. You certainly are a rising star ... no pun intended." Both men laugh casually as they get up and walk toward the parade grounds.

As they arrive at the reviewing stand Henry waves to Bishop Jackson and Leon, who are seated in the audience. Henry takes his seat with the other cadets as the graduation ceremony begins. The Commandant of the Academy gives his so-called rousing speech, quite similar to those he has given in past years. The only difference is that no one knows this. These are new cadets to graduate, and new parents and friends in the audience.

What is unique in this graduation ceremony is that Henry is to get his Commission as a Second Lieutenant in the U.S. Army. The first Black person in the history of the United States to do so.

As Henry walks up to the podium to receive his degree and commission, all the other graduating cadets stand up and applaud. It is at this moment that it dawns on Henry that all signs of ostracism are gone and that these new officers have accepted him as a fellow officer, even the boys from the South. Henry has a good feeling in his heart as he walks off stage.

Immediately after the ceremony, Bishop Jackson, Leon, and Jeff Hill move through the crowd to find Henry. Excited as Henry is, he maintains his composure and new military presence. He is being completely surrounded by all the other graduates who are congratulating him.

Bishop Jackson has tears in his eyes as he turns to Leon and Jeff. "That scene touches my heart. Never in all my years would I have thought I would be witness to something like this."

"It certainly is a great occasion," comments Jeff Hill.

"Crip's! It's more than a great occasion, Jeff," interjects Leon. "It's a monumental occasion!"

As Henry exits from the crowd of other cadets, Fred Williams runs up to him. "Sorry I didn't get to talk to you before the ceremony, Henry. Lynda and my family got here late and I had to get them settled. Congratulations there, ol' roomy!"

"Never thought this day would ever come," relates Henry jovially.

"Me either, Henry. Had my doubts for at least three years."

"Fred, come over and meet the persons most responsible for me standing here today, will you?"

"Sure thing, Henry. Where are they?"

Henry points in the direction of where Bishop Jackson, Leon, and Jeff are standing, as he and Fred begin to walk, carrying on light conversation.

"Say, Fred, you got your assignment yet?" Henry inquires in a serious tone.

"Yeah, just came in three days ago. Originally thought about joining up with the Seventh Cavalry, Custer's old Regiment, but I wanted to serve under Colonel Novak, Tenth Cavalry. He's supposed to be a great Commander. How 'bout you?"

Henry smiles. "That's where I'm assigned!"

"Damn! We're in the same unit. Maybe we'll even be at the same fort ... Fort Wallace, I think. When you leaving?"

"Right after your wedding. I'll be taking the train. I've got two weeks leave but I'm anxious to see what it's like out there."

Henry directs Fred through the crowd of well wishers over to Leon, Jeff, and Bishop Jackson. "Bishop Jackson, Leon, Jeff, I'd like to have you meet my first and second year roommate, Fred Williams."

Bishop Jackson extends his hand. "Good to meet you, Lieutenant Williams."

"And you, Sir!"

Leon, immediately extends his hand. "And I'm Leon. Once a roommate of this character myself. Congratulations, Lieutenant."

"Thank you, Leon. Henry's quite a guy, huh?"

"Well, I don't know about that," puffs Leon as he lightly pokes Henry in the shoulder.

"And Fred, this is Jeff Hill. The reporter I told you about over the years."

"Good to meet you, Mr. Hill. Henry's told me a lot of good things about you."

"Thank you, Lieutenant. You've been a rather interesting part of Henry's life, as I understand it."

"You might say that, Mr. Hill. He's become my best friend."

The atmosphere is almost electric with happiness and enthusiasm. Even the normally very serious Jeff is relaxed and smiling. After the four have conversed for some time, Fred bids his farewell. "Henry, I know you want to visit with your friends. They've traveled such a long distance. I'll see you at the wedding this weekend. Don't forget to be there Saturday afternoon for the bachelor's party we have planned."

"I'll be there, Fred. Wouldn't miss it for anything!" Fred shakes hands goodbye with Bishop Jackson, Leon, and Jeff.

"Seems like a nice fellow, Henry," comments Leon.

"He is, Leon. But you should have witnessed our first week together." Henry then winks at Leon as he puts his arm around his shoulder.

"Wild, huh?" questions Leon.

"To say the least, Leon. To say the least."

Bishop Jackson is silent. He is enjoying the excitement he feels watching the camaraderie of Henry, Leon, and Lieutenant Williams. But at the same time he experiences a contented sense of peace and enjoyment. After all, dreams can come true, he thinks to himself.

Henry, Bishop Jackson, and Leon converse the rest of the afternoon as they tour the Academy, then have dinner together that night. The next morning they say their goodbyes at the train station.

Bishop Jackson shakes Henry's hand firmly. "Keep us informed as to your progress, Henry. And be careful! I hear the Indians out there are a formidable foe. Good luck to you, Henry."

Henry turns to Leon and gives him their traditional bear hug. "I'll write you, Leon. And you write me. Let me know how you like teaching at the school. The orphanage is lucky to have you."

"I will, Henry." Leon says with an emotional voice. "It is great seeing you again. I'll miss you."

"Same here, Leon."

"Best of luck to you in your new career, ol' friend," conveys Leon one last time with tears in his eyes.

Bishop Jackson and Leon board the train as an emotional departure takes place. Henry watches as the train pulls out o the station, then waves a final goodbye. Well, he thinks to himself, now what? Time to go back and pack, I guess.

CHAPTER FOURTEEN
HEAD'N WEST

The rhythmic sound of the train going down the track is putting Henry to sleep. Periodically, he glances out the Pullman car window at the countryside, but he is thinking of Fred and Lynda. A beautiful wedding, he thinks. I'm glad they're both coming out to Fort Wallace. At least I'll be serving with another officer I know and trust.

Lynda and Fred's wedding was beautiful indeed. Fred wore his army Dress Blues. Lynda was absolutely stunning in her long, white lace bridal gown. At twenty-one, Lynda is five-foot-three, slim and pretty. Her long brown hair pinned up in a bun and her large brown eyes are stand-out-ish in the white dress. Fred is spit and shine in his uniform. The two of them looked the part of a prince and princess.

Henry smiles as he thinks back on the weekend. Being a best man was enjoyable. All the people were courteous and happy. And what a nice home. No wonder Fred was such a spoiled ass when he first came to West Point.

Henry chuckles as he reminisces about the events of the last four years. But just as quickly his thoughts switch to what it will be like on the western frontier. The stories he has heard of drudgery, hardship, and loneliness don't seem to matter. He has chosen his career and he is proud of it. Now what is important is being a good soldier.

Many people stare, but no one talks to Henry on the train ride to Chicago. Just one old man that sat next to him for a couple of hours, and a curious Black conductor, who has been periodically looking at Henry.

"Never seen a black army officer before," says the Conductor. "You sure you'se not a fak'n?"

Henry, amused at the reactions he is getting, is used to this kind of comment. "No, I'm not faking," he replies to the conductor.

"Well, I'll be damned! Where you be headed? Out to Indian territory?"

"Fort Wallace," replies Henry.

"If'n that be way out west at one of them remote forts, I feel sorry for you. Them is desolate! I know. I hear from soldiers rid'n back east. No, sirree! That no place to be," concludes the conductor as he stares at Henry in amazement and shakes his head back and forth slowly.

"Thank you for that information, Mr.... What did you say your name is?" inquires Henry.

"Didn't. But just call me John. I been travel'n this here route now go'in on ten years. But them army soldiers tell me 'bout out west. Bad food, hot'n the summer, cold'n the winter, bugs, snakes, then the Indians. If'n you get wounded, got no doctor. Don't know why you want to soldier, 'specially out there!"

Henry smiles. "That's what we're trained for, John. Oh! Please tell me, how much longer until we arrive in Chicago?"

"Bout one hour, I think," guesses John. He then looks at his pocket watch. "Yup. Should be close to one hour. You be chang'n trains there, right?"

"I guess. My orders take me to Omaha Divisional Headquarters, then west to North Platte. I'll be met there by someone from the Regiment."

"Well, Sir, don't know where that is, but I sure be wish'n ya luck. If'n ya make it, sure hope to see you pass this way again. Alive, that is." The conductor gives Henry a quick wink. "Best get back to work, now. You take care, Lieutenant!"

"Thanks, John. Pleasant talking with you."

After two days of breathing black smoke from the engine, Henry is relieved to hear the words, "End of the line! No more tracks west!" He brushes the soot off his uniform as the train pulls into a small depot at Wallace City, Nebraska.

Henry picks up his satchel and walks slowly out of the car. A lot of open space out here, Henry thinks to himself as he is the only passenger to step from the train onto the wooden platform.

Henry is amazed as he surveys his surroundings. "Awful small town and a lot of open spaces," he mumbles under his breath as he walks to the baggage area and looks around. "Wonder where my transportation is?"

Private Emanuel Thomas has been waiting for nearly an hour. His back is beginning to ache as he sits on the buckboard seat. His orders specifically stated that he is to meet an officer and to take him to Fort Wallace, thirty miles to the northwest.

Emanuel didn't notice Henry disembark from the train, so he just continues to wait. Maybe he missed the train, or maybe he's talk'n to someone while they change engines, Emanuel concludes as he starts to doze.

About ten minutes later Emanuel feels a tap on his leg. Opening his eyes, he reacts both in surprise and puzzlement when he sees the gold bar insignia of a Lieutenant. Instantly, Emanuel stands up in the wagon, holding the reins in his left hand, and saluting with his right.

"Oh! Mornin', Suh! You be the Lieutenant? Tenth Cavalry?" Emanuel's eyes focus straight forward as he stands at rigid attention holding his salute.

"That's right, Private!" responds Henry as he returns the salute. "What's your name, Private?"

"Ah, ... Private Thomas, Suh!" Emanuel's nerves are causing him to shake. How could he be caught dozing by an officer, a Black officer at that?

"Drop the salute, Private Thomas, and tell me what's going on."

Emanuel turns and looks at Henry. Shocked at seeing a black officer, his look turns into a stare.

"What are you staring at, Private?" questions Henry in a firm, military tone of voice.

"Well, Suh. It's ... it's ..."

"It's what?" interrupts Henry.

"Well, Suh, it's ... I never 'spected ta see no colored officer ..."

"Get used to it, Private! Now drop the salute and help me get my bags!"

Emanuel instantly ties the reins and jumps off the wagon, following Henry into the train depot. "How long's the ride to Wallace?" inquires Henry.

"'Bout two hours, Suh!" Emanuel responds nervously.

"Well, let's get these bags on that buckboard and be on our way."

"Yes, Suh! We be do'n that right now, Suh!"

Emanuel rushes off the platform with Henry's bags and puts them in the back of the buckboard. Henry, at first somewhat irritated, watches Emanuel hustle, then shakes his head and grins. "Damn, a five-foot Private," Henry thinks to himself. How'd he get in the army?

Henry follows Emanuel to the buckboard and climbs up onto the passenger seat. Emanuel just sits there holding the reins, looking straight forward, his hands shaking slightly. After a short time of sitting, Henry turns to Emanuel, "Are we waiting for something, Private Thomas?"

"Oh! No, Suh! Just wait'n for your orders, Suh!"

Henry is becoming more amused by the minute with the short Private. "Well, then, move out!"

"Yes, Suh!" responds Emanuel as he snaps the reins on the horses back.

Henry is quiet as they travel on the dirt trail. He is amazed at the lack of trees and endless rolling hills in the distance.

Sure is different from back East, he thinks to himself as he suddenly feels a conflicting sense of fear and joy. It is obvious to everyone he knows that he is looking forward to his first assignment, but deep down in his heart he is already beginning to miss his friends.

Henry and Private Thomas travel a good three miles before Henry utters a word. "Sure is hot out here. Got any water on this rig?"

"Yes, Suh! Right under your seat, Suh. To the left."

Henry takes a couple of good swallows, then puts the cap back on the canteen. "What's happening out here, Private?"

Emanuel, still nervous about seeing a Black officer, having been caught dozing, and fighting a backache, attempts to maintain a military posture. His hands hold the reins directly in front of his knees. He stares straight forward as he replies. "Lot's be happ'nin, Suh. Dem Injuns got one chief warrior called Lone Wolf. Seem lak dey in control, scarin' hell out'a dem settlers and survey'n parties everyday."

Henry seems unconcerned as he looks at the countryside. "Seen any Indians around this territory?"

"Some skirmishes, Suh, last summer, and one winter patrol."

"Winter patrol?" questions Henry. "Isn't that a bit cold?"

"Yes, Suh! It be cold alright. Below zero. Both men and horses freeze. Some men lost fingers. Some lose toes. It make no differ', patrol'n is rough, 'specially if'n ya don't have de right equipment, Suh."

"And at the Post. How are the living conditions?"

"Dey be bad, Suh. Dat's why I likes patrol duty. Don't have ta sleep in dem damp barracks with mice an' bugs. But you be okay, Suh. You's got officers' quarters."

"How about the food?" continues Henry.

"Big'st complaint, Suh. Word go'in 'round that cooks kill more men than the Injuns." Emanuel lets a slight smile come to his face. "Just'a josh'n, Suh! But food be bad. The hardtack, it be lak a firebrick. Maybe dat's why the army exams the teeth careful. Should issue steel teeth, Suh ... 'n a file ta sharp'n 'em."

Henry laughs. "You have quite an imagination, Private Thomas."

"No, Suh! No 'magnation. It be true."

"How long you been with the Tenth, Thomas?"

"I join up when I be fourteen. Colonel Novak let me, but I think he be thinking I sixteen. Been wid da Tenth, Comp'ny C, nigh on to five years. I be nineteen now, Suh,"

"Colonel Novak, huh? What's he like?"

"I laks him a lot, Suh! Laks serving wid 'im. Think'n you might too, Suh."

Henry has read about Colonel Novak in the newspapers and is anxious to meet him. "Ya, I just might," replies Henry.

"What've I got for a horse, Private?"

"We rides mostly Bays, Suh. I pick'd out a gelding fo' de Lieutenant. Name's Chance. A Morgan horse, Suh."

"A Morgan, huh?"

"You be lakking him, Suh. He be a good'un."

As Fort Wallace comes into view, Henry comments to Emanuel. "So that's it?"

"Yes, Suh! Not too big n' not too small."

Fort Wallace covers more than twenty acres on its interior, with several hundred acres for pasture, gardening, and recreation on its exterior. The essential buildings, although made of logs chucked with mud, sand, and lime, are present; administration buildings, mess hall, a small hospital, store, recreation/dance hall, living quarters for officers and their wives, and barracks for enlisted men. The maintenance and laundry facilities are located to the rear across from the horse barns. The exterior portion includes a baseball diamond, horseracing track, and horseshoe pits on one side, with Crow and Mandan Indian scouts and their families living in teepees to the northern perimeter. It is, for the most part, a self-sufficient post. Incidentals of a personal nature are available at Wallace City, several miles to the south.

"No perimeter walls, I see," comments Henry.

"No, Suh. The Colonel think it be bad for troop morale. Says it be better to d'pend on breech loaders 'n 'lertness than 'hind walls."

"Well, I'm glad we're here. I need to shower."

Emanuel looks briefly in Henry's direction. "Ain't no showers, Suh. Need water for drink'n an de horses."

"You mean no one takes a shower here?" inquires Henry.

"Officer's sometimes, Suh. But not 'ofen."

"I'll be darned!" says Henry as he shakes his head.

As Henry and Emanuel approach the west gate entrance the two sentries salute. "Good afternoon, Sir," reports the guards. Henry returns a casual salute as he instructs Private Thomas to stop in front of the Headquarters building. All personnel, white, black, and Indians on post stop momentarily to watch as Henry rides in.

Henry doesn't see Lieutenant Jim Jensen standing by the blacksmith shop talking to Sharp Grover, an army scout of questionable character. Grover, a lean, lanky man does his best to fraternize with the officer corps. He is always easily recognizable in his fringe buckskin shirt and pants, but his most salient feature is the ugly, long scar on his face. Extending from his right ear to his left chin. Word has it that he received the scar in a fight with a Sioux Indian.

Lieutenant Jensen knows he remembers Henry from someplace: West Point, but has to take a studious second look to be sure. Somewhat shocked at seeing Henry, he interrupts his conversation with Sharp Grover. "Sheeeit, Grover! Do you see what's pull'n in?"

Grover turns to see Lieutenant Washington get out of the buckboard in front of the Headquarters building, "Damn!" Grover responds. "I didn't know they allowed Negroes to be army officers!"

"I knew him as a first year cadet at West Point. Didn't know he made it through. Son of a bitch! I can't believe it! I just can't reckon with a nigger being an officer."

"Ya, know what they be say'n, Lieutenant. A boost for the colored enlisted men, huh?"

"Don't know, don't care. Just don't need him in this unit ... or the army, for that matter!"

Private Thomas pulls the buckboard to a stop near the Administration Headquarters. "Colonel's headquarters is on de right, Lieutenant. He be expect'n you, and I be tak'n' de bags to yo' quarters right over der, Suh."

Henry nods approval as Private Thomas salutes. "Thanks, Private Thomas. Enjoyed the ride." Henry brushes off the fine dust and adjusts his uniform. He briefly looks around as he steps onto the wooden boardwalk in front of Colonel Novak's office, then knocks on the door.

"Come in!" responds the Colonel.

Henry walks in, comes to attention, and salutes as Colonel Novak stands up from behind his desk.

"Lieutenant Washington reporting for duty, Sir!"

"Good afternoon, Lieutenant," replies Colonel Novak as he walks around his desk to shake Henry's hand. "Welcome to Fort Wallace."

'Thank you, Sir."

"I trust you had a pleasant trip?"

"Long and uneventful, Sir."

"You're probably tired after the journey, so let's get you briefed and then settled into your quarters. We can get down to business later. Have a seat, Lieutenant."

Henry seats himself in front of the desk as Colonel Novak walks back to his chair. "Lieutenant Washington, I understand that you're the first of your race to graduate from West Point. Congratulations! That's quite an accomplishment."

"Thank you, Sir," replies Henry formally.

"Your records indicate that you did quite well at West Point. I'm glad you chose the Tenth. I think you'll like it here, Lieutenant. We've got a good bunch of officers and the enlisted men in this Regiment are as good as any in the west. We still have some problems with social mores here, but nothing like back east. The settlers and railroad personnel are just happy we're here, no matter what color the skin."

"I think I understand, Sir."

"We can talk more tomorrow. Right now get yourself acclimated. Later, I'll have Lieutenant Sandy show you around, then we can get you scheduled for your first patrol. So, get situated and rest up a bit. Oh, is there anything you need at the moment?"

"No, Sir. I just want to say I'm happy to be here and proud to serve under your command. Thank you, Sir."

"Glad to have you in this Regiment, Lieutenant. I'm sure you'll be quite an asset. You know where your quarters are?"

"Yes, Sir. Private Thomas pointed them out." Henry smiles slightly, then adds, "He's quite a Private."

Colonel Novak smiles and comments, "Yes, I know. He's a good soldier. I trust him. That's why I sent him to the depot to get you. You'll like him, Lieutenant." Colonel Novak then walks over to shake Henry's hand. "Get some rest, Lieutenant. I'll be seeing you tomorrow."

"Yes, Sir!" says Henry as he salutes, takes an about face, and walks out the door.

Henry ponders as he walks to his quarters and looks around at the activities on the Post. I've got a good feeling about that Colonel, Henry thinks as he walks slowly towards Officer's Row. This place is exciting. I'll check my quarters, and then I've got to see this Morgan horse. Wonder why they named him Chance?

Henry checks out his quarters and is amused. "Not too bad. Two rooms. At least I have some privacy," he quips out loud.

His thoughts then turn again to Chance. I've got to take a look at this Bay. Henry throws his bags on his bed and turns to walk out the door. His pulse quickens as he approaches the barn. He is aware that he is getting glances from most of the men around the fort. But that's common for any new officer, he rationalizes to himself.

Once at the livery stables, Henry sees a black Buck Sergeant. "Excuse me, Sergeant. My name is Lieutenant Washington, I've just arrived on post but I understand I've been assigned a horse here. A Bay. Name's Chance."

"Yes, Sir," replies the Livery Sergeant. "Right o'er here. He's quite the animal."

Henry breathes deep as he first sees Chance. What a horse, is his first thought. I can understand why they have horse thieves.

Chance is chewing hay, but his ears perk up as Henry calls him. "How ya do'n, boy?" Henry leans on the stall boards and admires Chance as the horse walks slowly towards him. What a beautiful animal; long black mane and tail, good hindquarters, short back, straight legs, good withers, and nice eyes. I'll have to thank Private Thomas for this one, thinks Henry as he walks in the stall to pet Chance.

CHAPTER FIFTEEN
PATROL DETAIL

It's 0500 hours the next morning when Henry arises. He is looking forward to talking with Lieutenant Sandy during their tour of the post and surrounding area, especially about life at Fort Wallace. All he knows of Lieutenant Sandy is that he is married, and that he and his wife reside in the married Officer's Quarters on the northwest corner of the post, one-hundred feet across from the Bachelors Quarters.

This is also his first opportunity to ride Chance and he is anxiously looking forward to this. But first he has to attend the morning briefing by Colonel Novak.

"Good morning, men," greets Colonel Novak as Major Baker, two Captains, and eight Lieutenants, including Lieutenant Jensen, settle into their seats. "I trust you have met Lieutenant Washington. If not, please introduce yourselves after this briefing." Lieutenant Jensen immediately looks at Henry with contempt.

Colonel Novak walks over to a map of the territory hanging on his office wall. "I've just got word from Divisional Headquarters that we have two new missions starting immediately. The first is to escort a telegraph repair party, and the second is to locate a small wagon train that should have passed this way two days ago."

He uses a three-foot pointer and begins circling areas on the map as he talks. "Lieutenant Sandy, I want you to take H Company out and search this area to the east. According to the latest communication this wagon train should be following the flat ground between the Sand Hills and the Republican River. Take Lieutenant Washington with you. This will be his first patrol and it'll be a good experience for him to go with an officer that knows the territory. You know the procedure, Lieutenant Sandy. Just locate the wagon train and bring them in. Any questions?"

"No, Sir," replies Lieutenant Sandy.

"Okay. Ready your Company and leave within the hour."

Lieutenants Sandy and Washington salute, and leave the room as Colonel Novak continues briefing the other officers.

"Well, Lieutenant Washington, this is one way to tour the area," jokes Lieutenant Sandy. "I'll have Private Thomas ready your horse and equipment. You best change into something more comfortable. It gets hot and dusty out there. I'll meet you at the stable."

"This should be interesting," replies Henry with enthusiasm as he leaves for his quarters.

"Yeah, it can be," quips Lieutenant Sandy.

Henry feels a rush of excitement as he anticipates his first patrol duty and on his new horse. After picking up his gear he walks directly to the stable. Henry notices Private Thomas standing near the corral gate holding two horses, fully saddled and equipped.

Private Thomas comes to attention and salutes as Henry walks up. "Yor horse be ready, Suh. Lieutenant Sandy ask'd me to make sure the tack be fitted properly."

Henry returns a brief salute. "Thank you, Private. Now can you tell me something about him?"

"He be rid'n good, Suh. You see, he's a Morgan."

Henry's eyes beam as he leads the horse a few paces and mounts. Chance stands quietly, ears alert.

"He be an easy mount. Do ya think, Suh?" questions Emanuel.

"That he is!" Henry smiles as he rides Chance to the front of the formation. Lieutenant Sandy looks back for a final check of readiness. "Okay, move out!" he orders as he throws his right arm forward and legs his horse.

Henry feels an immediate affection for Chance as the Company walks out of the post in file formation, then moves into a posting trot. Henry reflects back to West Point and the difficult time he had learning to post correctly with the up and down movement of the horse's hindquarters. He knows, however, that this is the best gait to cover a lot of ground without tiring the horses too quickly. Especially on a day like today; hot and no breeze.

The column is thirty-five miles out, near a deep ravine as Lieutenant Sandy, followed by Henry and Private Thomas, raises his hand to halt. Private Thomas is carrying the Tenth Cavalry, Company H flag, a small swallow-tailed Gideon. As flag bearer, it is his duty to stay close to Lieutenant Sandy at the front of the column. Besides, he knows the territory. "What ya think, Private Thomas?" questions Lieutenant Sandy as he halts the column.

Private Thomas looks around. "Look at all dem trees an' bushes. Does you hear what I hear?"

Henry looks around curiously as Lieutenant Sandy studies the terrain. "I don't hear anything, or see anything," concludes Lieutenant Sandy.

"Jus what I means, Suh. No sound of birds or nothin'. Too quiet fo' me. Not even a Meadowlark. Somethin's wrong!"

Lieutenant Sandy gives the signal for readiness as the patrol slowly moves forward. Suddenly the sound of shots comes from the ravine one-hundred-yards to the left of the patrol. Not knowing for sure from where the shots are being fired, Lieutenant Sandy orders his men at a full gallop to the top of the hill just above the ravine. In the process three Indian sentries, accidentally flushed from the thick brush, head out immediately in front of the patrol.

"There they are!" yells Lieutenant Sandy. "After them men!"

"Are you sure they aren't decoys?" yells Henry to Lieutenant Sandy, recalling the use of decoys as a common ploy used by a small force to lead overly aggressive or naïve soldiers into ambush by a larger Indian force.

"Maybe!" responds Lieutenant Sandy.

As the Indians scatter over the hill, Lieutenant Sandy splits his column into two, twenty-man patrols and orders Henry to take one patrol and come up on the flank of the hill. Lieutenant Sandy then proceeds around the opposite side.

As they both reach the ridge of the oblong sand covered hill, the two units re-converge. Instantly they witness the three Indian riders reining in at the edge of an encircled wagon train less than a mile down the hill.

"Shit!" yells Lieutenant Sandy. "They're sentries for the war party hitting those wagons below." Lieutenant Sandy waves his arm, the bugle blows, and the patrol gallops in full charge toward the wagons.

It is a matter of seconds before the Indians scramble to mount their horses, reacting to their sentries alert and the bugle sound. Lieutenant Sandy commands as he rides at full gallop, indicating to Henry to take his part of the column and pursue the Indians that are riding away.

Henry's adrenalin is pumping as he anticipates his first real combat experience and attempts to overtake the Indians in the far distance. Private Thomas splits into Henry's group after giving the Gideon to another soldier. Lieutenant Sandy rushes directly towards the wagons.

The Indians that Henry is pursuing split again, and he reacts immediately by ordering Private Thomas and ten men to pursue the five Indians heading into the riverbed. The six Indians that Henry pursued have too much of a head start and Henry knows that the horses can not maintain a full gallop for more than several miles, if that. Henry halts his group and turns to see Private Thomas and the men with him shooting their rifles with accuracy at a full gallop, killing three of the Indian raiders.

Henry is amazed at the ability of Thomas. "Damn!", he thinks to himself. I never thought anyone could ride and shoot like that! This image cements itself in Henry's mind as he rides up next to Lieutenant Sandy and the wagon master.

The wagon master, who is shot in the leg, is swearing at Lieutenant Sandy as Henry rides up. He sees settlers; men, women, and children, wounded and dead. Some of the horses are dead in their hitches and others lay dying. Henry is appalled at the site as he rides up next to Lieutenant Sandy and the wagon master.

"Where the hell you been, Lieutenant?" screams the wagon master at Lieutenant Sandy. "I damn near had ta shoot myself before the Indians scalped me!"

"Looking for you people!" replies Lieutenant Sandy.

"Well, ya' couldn't have been look'n too damn hard. We been fight'n those bastards for mor 'n half a day."

"Com'on, Sir, let's get that leg bandaged, and get you folks back to the fort."

Henry's mind is reeling with the events which have just taken place. He watches as the soldiers place the dead on one wagon and wounded on another. Wagons which can no longer be used are burned. Henry's heart beats fast as he watches the wounded horses being shot and dragged to the fire.

The Company First Sergeant rides up to Lieutenant Sandy, "Ten wounded, six people killed, and twelve unscathed. All civilians. One scalped, Sir."

Henry thinks about Chance for a moment. "You did alright, boy," whispers Henry quietly as he pets Chance on the side of the neck with his eyes fixed on the burning horses.

"Those Indians were too far ahead for us to catch them," comments Henry to his horse. Chance performed well but has not yet met his true test as a cavalry horse. This will come later.

It is early evening as Lieutenant Sandy organizes his men for the thirty-five mile ride back to Fort Wallace. Dark clouds have moved in from the west and the wind is beginning to gust. "Damn it!" mutters Lieutenant Sandy as he turns to Henry. "Isn't this the life?"

Henry doesn't respond. His facial expression is blank as he thinks to himself, "This isn't at all what I expected. I feel so helpless." Henry thinks back to the first dead man he ever saw, the man he saw hung on the Hooten Plantation, then thinks about his parents. "Wonder what my fate will be?" he thinks briefly before he hears Lieutenant Sandy call.

"Henry, com'on over here!"

Henry rides up along side Lieutenant Sandy, who is frustrated and uneasy. "What you need, Lieutenant?"

"Want you to ride back to Fort Wallace. Report this to the Colonel. Tell him we're com'n in with wagons of dead and wounded." Lieutenant Sandy spins his horse around and looks at the wagons, then continues, "Don't know if they'll all make it. Ask the Colonel to get the hospital detail together, and get the Contract Surgeon from Wallace City. We should be about three to four hours behind you."

"Sure will," replies Henry.

"Henry, take Private Thomas with you … just in case. There's gonna be a bitch of a storm. Private Thomas knows the way, Lieutenant! Get him and get going! We'll be along pronto."

The wind picks up with strong gusts as the rain starts pelting down in sheets. It's getting dark and the fierce storm is disrupting final preparations as the ground begins turning to mush.

Henry and Private Thomas make it back to Fort Wallace in what seems like a record run. It's closer to one o'clock in the morning as they gallop into the Fort, both horses white with sweat. "Take care of my horse, Thomas!" orders Henry as they stop in front of Colonel Novak's quarters.

Henry pounds on the Colonel's door until he opens it. Colonel Novak is surprised to see Henry, drenched with rain, and reporting at this hour of the morning. "My God! What is it, Lieutenant!"

"Sir! The wagon train was ambushed. We found them, but six are dead and some wounded. Lieutenant Sandy is still out there. He's bringing them in." Henry stops talking for a few seconds to regain his breath. "He says to ask you to get the hospital detail ready ... and a doctor from Wallace City ... don't know how many will make it, Sir! They're pretty beat up!"

Colonel Novak quickly gives orders to Henry. "Tell the Lieutenant on duty over in administration I'll be right there. Stable your horse and get over there right away."

"Private Thomas is doing that, Sir. I'll meet you there."

"Okay, Lieutenant," replies the Colonel as he rushes to dress.

Henry runs in the sloppy, soft ground to the Administration Building and alerts the Duty Officer. "I'll get the messenger to get the doctor in Wallace City, Lieutenant. Just you relax a bit."

Lieutenant Sandy is struggling to keep the wagons moving. The horses are slipping in the mud as the wagons burrow deep in the soft soil and water. Ropes are tied to the wagon as the men pull and push to get them up the long grade of the hillside. The soldiers push on through the night, using their own rain slicks to cover the wounded civilians. Between the darkness, mud, and the sweeping rain, both men and horses desperately move on, almost blindly.

Colonel Novak talks to Major Baker about cleaning out the hospital and making preparations for receiving the wounded as Henry abruptly interrupts. "Let me ride out and help them, Sir," requests Henry.

"No! You stay here, get some rest. There's nothing you can do," orders Colonel Novak. "Lieutenant Sandy knows what he's doing. And I've got three Mandan scouts heading out to meet them."

Henry remains in the Administration Office rather than going back to his quarters. Periodically he dozes off, but he feels a responsibility to be present when the patrol comes in.

Although the storm is freakish and severe, it blows over by five o'clock that morning. The air smells fresh as the sun starts to come up slowly over the eastern hills. The ground is still thick with a soupy mixture of soil and water as Henry walks over to the small building the troops referred to as sawbones hotel. The interior is more like a vacant room with several benches and long tables along the twenty-by-twenty foot walls.

Henry sits down and thinks back to the days when he was a child and he and his friends would play the game, "the Blue and the Gray." The innocence of childhood, he thinks reflectively.

It is 0800 hours before one of the regular scouts reports that the wagons and Lieutenant Sandy are in sight. While the wagons pull into the hospital area of the Fort, Henry runs up to Lieutenant Sandy. "Good to see you, Lieutenant. Was getting worried!"

"Damn rough go'in, but I think they all survived. See you got the hospital detail ready ... for whatever good they'll do. Can't do much for them arrow wounds."

Lieutenant Sandy orders his men to the stables as he hands his horse to the First Sergeant. "Where's the Colonel."

"Back in his office," replies Henry. "Com'on, let's put in our report to the Colonel. Can't do much here."

Soldiers detailed to take care of the survivors rush to unload the wagons. Post personnel watch the soldiers assist the wounded and unload the bodies. Henry and Lieutenant Sandy walk quietly to Colonel Novak's office as a two seated buggy carrying the doctor from Wallace City rolls in next to them.

"Too bad you had to arrive at such a terrible time," comments Lieutenant Sandy.

Henry turns and for a moment gazes silently at the crying women and children that were on the wagon train.

Lieutenant Sandy and Henry are conversing about what it's like to be wounded on the frontier as they wait for Colonel Novak to finish his meeting with Major Baker.

"You'll probably be taking over Company H now, Henry," informs Lieutenant Sandy. "I'm moving back to C Company and going to start training on some new artillery pieces. I plan on tak'n my First Sergeant with me, so you'll need a new Sergeant. You got one in mind?"

"Well, I've only been here a few days, although it seems like a year, and the only one I really know is Private Thomas."

"Well, Lieutenant, that's exactly who I was thinking about. He's qualified. I've known him for about a year and a half. He knows the territory, has survived several serious engagements with the Sioux and Cheyenne, is dedicated, and plans to make the army his career. He's loyal, and he appears to think well of you."

"I'll need the Colonel's approval," replies Henry.

"Yes, there's a story behind that also. Sergeant Waller can tell you that one someday. That's why I know the Colonel will approve it."

"Well, Thomas seems fine with me. I'd like you to back me up on this request."

"I'll do that. In fact we can make the request right after our debriefing," confirms Lieutenant Sandy.

"Thanks," replies Henry as Colonel Novak walks in. Henry and Lieutenant Sandy come to attention.

"Okay, gentlemen, let me have your reports. I need to know what tribe you encountered out there."

Lieutenant Sandy briefs the Colonel as Henry listens. After they talk for awhile, Colonel Novak summarizes, "They must be part of Lone Wolf's band. The arrows have the same markings as the arrows in other raids he's instigated. Is there anything else ... something unique that you can remember?"

Henry interrupts, "Yes, there might be. I didn't mention this before, but I'd like to know about the light skinned decoy they used."

"I don't know what you mean, Lieutenant Washington," quizzes Colonel Novak.

"The Indian I was chasing. He's different. His skin is more the color of a white man than that of an Indian. It's just an observation, Sir."

"Do you know anything about this, Lieutenant Sandy?"

"No, Sir. I wasn't that close or didn't pay attention to him. I was concerned about getting to the wagons."

"I'm not aware of any white captives in this district, but it may be something for you to keep in mind, Lieutenant Washington. A lot of strange things happen out here," reflects Colonel Novak as he continues. "Is there anything else, Gentlemen? If not, Major Baker and I have some serious business to discuss concerning this incident."

Henry and Lieutenant Sandy look to each other. "Well, yes, Sir, there is. Lieutenant Washington and I have been talking.

He needs a Sergeant for his troop, and well, we have someone we would like to recommend, with your approval, of course."

"And who might that be, Lieutenant?"

"We're thinking about Private Thomas, Sir. He'll make a good Buck Sergeant. You know him, Sir."

Henry intervenes. "Yes, Sir. I saw him riding after the Indians that attacked the wagons yesterday. He and the others stuck to their horses like flies and shot accurately at a full gallop. Never seen anything like it, Colonel. He's also brave and follows orders."

Colonel Novak thinks for a moment. "Hmm, so you mean, Lieutenant, that I can report to Washington that we have fast riding, sharp shooting coloreds in this unit?"

"Well, that's not exactly what I was trying to ..."

"I know what you're getting at, Gentlemen," interrupts Colonel Novak. "I've always had a fondness for Private Thomas. I think he deserves to become a Sergeant. I'm glad that you have recommended him and I certainly will approve of his promotion."

Colonel Novak walks to his desk, pulls out a pen and paper, and signs his name to the orders. "You can tell Private Thomas the news personally, Lieutenant Washington. It will be good coming from you as his new Company Commander. Here's the order promoting him. We can give him his stripes this afternoon. We'll make it a formal ceremony here in the office. How about 1400 hours?"

Henry is elated as Lieutenant Sandy slaps him on the back. "Now that didn't take long, did it, Lieutenant? You've got yourself a new Sergeant."

"When can I tell him, Sir?" questions Henry.

"Do it immediately." Colonel Novak then hesitates. "No, on second thought, why don't the two of you bring him in here at that time and we can surprise him."

"Good idea, Sir," concurs Lieutenant Sandy. "We'll notify him that he has to attend a briefing with us."

"Well, do you two Lieutenants need anything else?"

"No, Sir!" replies both Henry and Lieutenant Sandy in unison. Both men salute and walk outside.

"Let's grab some chow," says Sandy. "I'll tell you a bit about this place before we look for Private Thomas."

It is a hot, muggy afternoon as Henry and Lieutenant Sandy approach Private Thomas, who is cleaning stalls in the stable. "Hey, Private Thomas!" yells Lieutenant Sandy as he winks at Henry. "Get yourself cleaned up a bit. We gotta go to the Colonel's office for a briefing."

Surprised that he is to be included in a meeting with the two officers, Emanuel's eyes grow large. "Me, Suh. What's the Colonel want'n me fo'?"

"Don't know, Private Thomas. He just ordered it. Com'on now, hurry up. Can't keep the Colonel waiting."

"Okay, Suh. If'n you say so."

Emanuel quickly washes his hands and wipes his face with a barn rag. "Let me staight'n out my uniform, Suh. Then I be ready."

Emanuel's mind is whirling with ideas as to why he would be called before Colonel Novak. Army protocol knows that officers don't talk directly to lower ranking enlisted men, except through the Sergeant. The more Emanuel thinks the more nervous he becomes. "Wonder what I did wrong?" he ponders. "Maybe I bein' discharged."

As the three men walk into the Colonel's office, Major Baker is sitting next to the Colonel's desk.

"Detail reporting as ordered, Sir!" booms Lieutenant Sandy in an exaggerated command voice.

"Stand at attention, men," responds the Colonel. "I see you brought Private Thomas with you."

"Yes, Sir!" responds Lieutenant Sandy.

"Good," affirms Colonel Novak as he seats himself at his desk, then continues, "Private Thomas, Major Baker and I have just been talking about you."

Emanuel becomes nervous as the Colonel continues, "Private Thomas, I remember the first day you joined the army. It's been over four years now, hasn't it?"

Emanuel stutters a response. "Ye, yes, Suh!"

"And when you joined, didn't you tell me you were sixteen?"

Emanuel's hands are shaking as he now figures what the Colonel is about to say. The Colonel knows that I not be old enough. Maybe they be kick'n me out of de army, right now, he thinks fearfully. "Well, yes, Suh!"

"And you've performed those years without any infraction, or disciplinary action, is that correct?"

Emanuel just knows the Colonel is going to give him a discharge for lying about his age. "That be right, Suh, but I can 'xplain 'bout'n my age, Suh!"

Colonel Novak hesitates. "What about your age, Private Thomas?"

"Well, Suh, you see, Suh, when I join'd up, I wasn't ..."

Colonel Novak interrupts. "Private Thomas, you don't have to explain anything. We brought you here because we feel you've excelled as a soldier." Colonel Novak gets up from behind his desk, the three stripes in his hand. Emanuel is so nervous that he keeps his eyes fixed on the crack between the wall and the ceiling.

"Private Thomas, you were brought here today because of your exceptional record and performance of duty."

Emanuel isn't hearing what the Colonel is saying, as he is absolutely frightened that he's going to be discharged from the service because he lied about his age.

"Private Thomas, are you okay?" inquires the Colonel as he witnesses Emanuel's strange nervousness and the hundreds of tiny sweat beads on his forehead.

"Oh, oh, yes, Suh! I, I ... be fine. Just fine, Suh!"

"Okay, Sergeant Thomas, relax."

Emanuel still didn't hear the word "Sergeant", but remains at rigid attention, his mind reeling with fear of being discharged.

Colonel Novak motioned to Lieutenant Washington to step forward, then handed him the stripes of a Sergeant.

"You do the honors, Lieutenant." Still, Emanuel Thomas has not digested the fact he is being promoted.

Lieutenant Washington steps to the front of Emanuel in a precise military manner. "Private Thomas, let me formally inform you that you have been promoted to the rank of Sergeant, E-5 in the United States Army."

Thomas is shocked. His eyes gaze steadfast at Lieutenant Washington, his body begins to quiver. For a moment Emanuel says nothing. Then, as if he suddenly came out of a trance, he realizes what has happened. Lieutenant Washington gracefully hands the stripes to Emanuel, who now re-enforces his military bearing with a snap salute.

"Thank you, Suh!"

After the brief ceremony, Sergeant Thomas nervously approaches Lieutenant Washington. "Suh, if I may Suh, cain I talks with you?"

"Certainly, Sergeant. What's on your mind?"

Well, Suh, I cain't read 'n 'rite," Emanuel hesitates, feeling awkward. "Suh, this be a great honor. If'n you would Suh, would'n you help me write a letter to my ma? She ain't heard from me since I's join de army 'n I want'n to tell her about it.

Lieutenant Washington smiles, "Certainly, Sergeant Thomas. Let's just do that now while we have the chance."

It is about a month later that Mrs. Thomas receives a letter. She is ecstatic as she runs to Mrs. Yoney's cabin where she stops in the outside porch area to sit down.

"From Emanuel! Oh my God! I hope he be alright. I ain't heard from him since he join'd de army." Her hands shake as she tries to open the letter and can't. She hands it to Mrs. Yoney. "You know I cain't read anyway. Here, you open it 'n read it to me!"

Mrs. Yoney takes the letter and opens it gracefully, then addresses Mrs. Thomas. "Settle down, girl! Lordy, sho' I'll read it fo' yo. Quiet down fo' yo' body gives out!"

Mrs. Thomas anxiously listens as the letter is read to her.

"Dear Ma, This letter is from your son, Emanuel. I hope you are well. Life out here is tough, but I'm fine. The army has been good for me. I be proud to serve with the Tenth Cavalry, a horse regiment. It is an all colored unit, except for the white officers and one colored officer, who is my company commander. His name is Lieutenant Washington, a West Point officer. He recommended me for Sergeant and the Colonel approved it. I'm a Sergeant in the army now, Ma. I miss you and love you, and will write again sometime. Emanuel. P.S. Ma, the Indians call us coloreds Buffalo Soldiers cause we are tough and good fighters like the buffalo."

Emanuel's mother has tears running down her cheeks as the letter is read. When Mrs. Yoney finishes reading, Emanuel's mother wipes the tears from her eyes and sobs as she speaks. "He allus wont to be a soldier, but he be so little. I miss 'em so much. Wish his Pa wuz 'live to hear dis letter."

Mrs. Yoney gives her a handkerchief and puts her hand on Mrs. Thomas' forearm. "He growed up to a man and showed he can be a soldier. You has a right to be proud of him, girl. We can write him when you be ready."

CHAPTER SIXTEEN
THE DEATH DANCE

"Hey-A-A-hey! Hey-A-A-Hey. Hey-A-A-Hey," chants the Medicine Man as he sits in the darkness of the small sweat lodge looking at the glowing red stones, sweat oozing out of every pore in his body. "Grandfather! Great Spirit! Behold the granite rock created by Father Sky, energized by fire, which comes from trees and they in turn give of themselves who come from the sun. We pray to you Father Sky, for Mother Earth, all part of the Great Oneness." He then becomes silent.

It is Lakota Sioux tradition to retrieve their dead and wounded whenever possible, for spiritual reasons. The raid on the wagon train resulted in three dead warriors and two others wounded. But the warriors killed and wounded a good number more of the train people. The exact number isn't important, for the warriors have many coup. It is also a victory for they were able to get away with several good horses, twelve repeating rifles, and a substantial amount of ammunition. What is important now, is that the dead warriors must be honored. This is required for a peaceful travel to the Spirit World.

This is also White Hawk's chance to participate in his first Death Dance. He has done what is expected of him on his first raid and performed according to the Warrior Society's standards of bravery. Even Lone Wolf is pleased with his son's accomplishments and his heart is proud.

The usual daily activities of tending horses, cleaning skins, cleaning or repairing weapons is taking place in the camp by most of the men, women, and children of the tribal. The exceptions to the daily regimen are the relatives of the dead warriors and the Chosen Ones, who are preparing for the spiritual ceremony. The Chosen Ones are the elite of the warrior society and selected by their members on special ceremonial occasions, usually three men who performed the most daring deeds and earned coup during the battle in which their brothers have died.

While the ceremonial preparations are being made, Two Crows, Grey Bull, Spotted Wolf, and Lone Wolf conduct a War Council meeting in Two Crows' teepee.

It is quiet as they all sit down on the buffalo robes that encircle the fire pit at the center of the lodge. Two Crows, as Chief and leading Elder, has the honor to talk first. He sits silently and contemplates for more than ten minutes. His silence is for a reason. He firmly believes that when two-legged animals (human beings) meet in council, there should be protocol or a formal way to do so. To him, being hasty is inconsiderate, or being too bossy and dominating the conversation, are obstacles in his mind to entering the Spirit World. Two Crows' mind finally becomes focused. He is ready to speak.

"Black Soldier Chief and his warriors have good medicine. No fear, shoot straight ... three dead!"

Although Lone Wolf didn't participate in this particular raid he is immediately defensive and becomes arrogant at Two Crows' comment. He did plan the raid, but decided against going. He instead had a private council concerning White Deer with the tribal Medicine Man. A very superstitious man, he perceives it a bad omen to enter battle after an argument with a woman. But still, Two Crows' statement bruises his sensitivity and pride. He can't help but rebuke that. "They not have good medicine like Lone Wolf! Many times white man's bullet fly by me. None can kill me!"

Two Crows is use to Lone Wolf's ego boosting. But it is true, Lone Wolf has been in many battles and never been hit, not even a superficial wound. Two Crows, his face stone-like, is clearly irritated as he immediately responds.

"We not talk about you! We talk about battle at long wagons." Two Crows ignores Lone Wolf momentarily as he turns to the Elder chiefs. "We plan big attack with our friends the Cheyenne. There will be many warriors and much planning. It will be a great day!" Two Crows then turns back to Lone Wolf.

"You, Lone Wolf, will lead this battle. It will be your true test as a Warrior Leader. It will come soon. You will prepare yourself. We talk no more about this now. Now we go to honor our dead warriors. It is time to go to sweat lodge. Purify our spirits and pray for good medicine. Later, we dance to honor the spirit of our dead ... that they may be released in peace to the Great Spirit. That they may have a happy journey to visit the ancient ones. It will be a long night."

The Elders all nod to one another and rise to leave. Lone Wolf's mind is not concerned with the ceremony. He reflects back on his thoughts of the first time he saw the Buffalo Soldiers. I will kill many, he thinks to himself as the other Elders leave. I will prove my invincibility ... that I am the greatest warrior of all warriors. I will sit where Two Crows sits.

The four walk slowly and silently to the Sweat Lodge, a small round hut twelve feet in diameter, made of willow frame, bent in the shape of an igloo, and covered with buffalo robes. The entrance always faces east for spiritual reasons, to honor the morning sun. It is only two feet wide and three feet tall, with a heavy cloth drape covering it.

The preparations for the sweat is made by the three Chosen Ones from the Warrior Society. Their role is to build the fire of wood and place large rocks on it until they are red hot. This task takes several hours and was prepared earlier during the War Council meeting.

It is late afternoon as Two Crows, Grey Bull, Spotted Wolf, and Lone Wolf approach the Sweat Lodge. The Chosen

Ones have waited to prepare the purification smoke. As is required before entering, each must purify himself with the smoke of burning sage. After this is done they enter the lodge in order of importance; Two Crows, then Grey Bull, Spotted Wolf, and Lone Wolf. Two Crows sits next to the entrance on the inside and receives a deer antler with a hot rock on it. The rocks are continually handed to him one at a time. This procedure is repeated until Two Crows determines that there are enough rocks for the sweat. After the red, hot rocks are placed on the dirt pit in the center, a Chosen One hands Two Crows a bowl of water made of bone, and then closes the entrance cover.

It is totally dark inside, but before the flap is closed, each has positioned himself on the bare ground, ten to twelve inches apart around the hot rocks. All remain quiet as Two Crows begins to chant and pour several small streams of water onto the glowing rocks. The steam immediately fills the small lodge. After several minutes the lodge is intensely hot. The ceremony then begins in earnest according to tribal tradition.

Two Crows begins to pray to the Great Spirit. He prays to the four cardinal directions; north, south, east, and west. Then, after a brief interlude, to the four seasons of life; spring, summer, fall, and winter (birth, adolescence, adulthood, and old age/death). He stops for a moment, then prays for the dead warriors. He recalls their past and great deeds they made while living in oneness with Mother Earth.

"We pray for our ancestors who died in battle. We pray to you Wankan Tonkan for guidance. We pray to you Wankan Tonkan for victory over our enemies. We pray for all good people, both four-legged and two-legged. We pray to you Wankan Tonkan for the survival of our people. We pray you take our warriors on a peaceful journey."

Two Crows and the others begin to chant, interrupted only by the periodic pouring of water over the hot rocks. The temperature becomes so hot that Lone Wolf puts his nose to the ground to breathe minute amounts of fresh air that is filtered up through the ground.

The preparations for the burial are taking place per custom as the four leaders purify themselves spiritually and physically in the sweat lodge. The burial scaffolds are erected nine-hundred-feet away from the camp perimeter by the dead warrior's relatives. This is done as a protective procedure, mostly to prevent the bodies from being abused by wild animals. For, as they believe, if any part of the body is disturbed or mutilated, the warriors will have difficulty in their journey. Three death logs are placed on the ground at the center of each scaffold. The death logs are then purified with the smoke of sweet grass and sage.

At sundown the bodies, wrapped tightly in animal skins, are brought from the lodges of their relatives, then wrapped tightly in deerskins, and placed on the logs.

Two Crows, along with the others, emerges from the sweat lodge and walks to his teepee. There, he dresses meticulously. All the tribal members silently await his appearance. After more than half an hour, Two Crows, dressed in full headdress counting forty-five eagle feathers and finely beaded tan buckskins, walks out of the lodge and heads directly for the three dead warriors. All men, women, and children watch in silent respect.

Grey Bull then appears, also in full dress of the Tribal Medicine Man. His buffalo head headdress and eagle feather bustles, reveal his authority and position. He gives a foreboding appearance. It is his responsibility to start the death dance. He signals the drums to begin and they start to beat in rhythmic high and low tones. Boomboomboom, Boomboomboom, Boomboomboom, Boomboomboom. The evening is calm except for the drums that echo a dirge into the distant hills.

Grey Bull begins praying to the Great Spirit after which he starts his slow, rhythmic steps of the Death Dance. After fifteen minutes of dancing and chanting he is finished. He signals the drums to stop. He calls to all living things and all things that have once lived, that they will protect the warriors on their journey. He signals the drums to begin again and leaves for his lodge.

The whole tribe then begins to dance to the beat of the drums. First the men, then the women and children. Most dance throughout the night, each to the step of their own choosing. Ultimately, after hours of dancing, the drumbeats intensify. Some warriors seem to dance themselves into a hypnotic frenzy. It is first dawn before the drums cease and the dancing ends.

It is now time for just the immediate female relatives to be left alone to lament. The cries are loud. Some of the wives, daughters, sisters, and mothers of the dead warriors begin to mutilate themselves. Some cutting off fingers, others cutting and slashing their faces with knives.

White Hawk, still awake and sitting quietly at a distance, watches with little emotion. His thoughts concentrate on his future and that some day the tribe will honor him for battle and his first coup. I am not afraid of death, he pledges to himself.

CHAPTER SEVENTEEN
A NEW PATROL CONCEPT

Henry and Fred are excited to see each other again. It is a joyous occasion, however, brief. They don't have much time to renew acquaintances as each is immediately ordered on assignment; Henry, on a twenty-one-day wagon escort, and Fred on a four-day telegraph escort detail. They are, however, able to have dinner together at the married officer's quarters, plus one night at a band concert put on by a group of Black soldiers. They share their feelings confidently as they recall the past and anticipate the future. Henry, Fred, and Lynda discuss joys of traveling the west and make plans to take two weeks leave in the fall and visit the booming town of Denver. For Lynda, the social life is quite limited at Fort Wallace. Protocol dictates that all officers' wives not associate with other women at the fort, especially enlisted men's wives or Indian women who are considered "friendlies" of the army.

Gossip and worry at the Ladies Club is a daily activity with the officers' wives, especially if their men are on patrol duty, for they never know for sure if they will return. The main topic of social conversation is the increasing boldness of the attacks that the Sioux and certain factions of the Cheyenne Tribes are creating in the territory. The fact that a wagon train was ambushed only twelve miles away creates a certain element of their daily fear. Talk about a direct attack on the fort is a common topic, but in reality, unlikely even with the constant shortness of personnel. Unknown to these women is that attacking forts is not a method of Sioux combat. Even when on patrol, the soldiers themselves have little or no chance of finding an Indian encampment. It is virtually impossible for the soldiers to track, much less find the Indians, due to their constant movement. Indian main camps are usually hundreds of miles away from army fort activities.

Plus, the main camps move often, mainly to follow the buffalo.

General Olson is constantly being informed of impending atrocities by various factions of the civilian population, either through the Territorial Governors, Congress, or the War Department. In his mind, something has to be done. He feels he is forced therefore, by his superiors, to make a personal visit to Fort Wallace. Colonel Novak receives the telegram only one day prior to General Olson's arrival.

General Olson, a hardened Civil War veteran, determined to rid the west of the Indian Problem, is dead serious when he arrives at Fort Wallace. Colonel Novak, Major Baker, and two lead scouts, Jack Stillwell and Sharp Grover, are waiting in front of the Administration Office when he arrives.

Major Baker can't help but chuckle to himself as General Olson gets off his horse. He recalls how President Lincoln once described him as "a brown skinned, chunky little chap, with a long body, short legs, not enough neck to hang him, and with such long arms that if his ankles itched he could scratch them without reaching."

"Good Morning, Sir," greets Colonel Novak as General Olson dismounts.

"What's so damn good about it, Colonel? This is a damn, son-of-a-bitch'n trip out here!"

Colonel Novak nods his head in agreement and smiles slightly. "Yes, it is, General."

General Olson hands off his horse to his aide, and instructs his contingency of sixty men to rest their horses and get something to eat and drink. He then abruptly turns to Colonel Baker, a snarl in his voice. "Well, Colonel, let's get inside, have some coffee, and talk turkey. I didn't come all the damn way to this forsaken place to pay a social call."

General Olson, accompanied inside by his two senior advisors, a Lieutenant Colonel and a Major, takes Colonel

Baker's chair. General Olson slaps his feet on the Colonel's desk and leans back, frowns, and talks sharply. "Brief me on what the hell is going on out here, Colonel! All I'm getting is static from the damn War Department. Sons-a-bitches!"

Colonel Baker acts irritated as he taps his fingers on an old table that he normally uses for map reading. "General, it's rather simple. We just don't have enough men. Your department has ordered us on all kinds of special details, plus trying to maintain this post. How in the hell do you expect us to spend full time chasing these hostiles, when we don't even have the manpower to work post maintenance? And hell, we probably couldn't locate any Indians if we used all the personnel here anyway. Most of the men have never seen an Indian, much less Indian tracks. You know they're inexperienced."

General Olson, trying to act knowledgeable about the West and the Indian problem, responds with assurance. "I understand your situation fully, Colonel. But that doesn't solve my problem. I'm here to get a personal assessment from you and talk face to face. Once and for all we must come up with a solution to rid this territory of these damn Indians. Shit, my reputation depends on it!"

"As I mentioned, General, the Indians know this country. We don't! It's endless. They can appear and disappear at will. We can give chase but that's useless. If you want to stop these hostiles, we must find their main camp. Then we can run 'em on a surprise attack."

General Olson thinks for a moment, stands, then comments with some annoyance. "That Indian bastard, ah, what's his name?"

"Lone Wolf!" interjects Scout Grover.

General Olson, irritated by the interruption of a half-breed scout, continues. "Ya ... Lone Wolf. Shit! He seems to be running wild around here. Kill'n and scalp'n. Hell, by the time his antics hit the newspapers in New York and

Washington D.C., the rumors have him controlling all the land west of the Mississippi. Hell, I can't have that kind of pressure on me. I just want you to get him, Colonel, and I don't care how. It'd be a feather in the cap for the army."

Colonel Baker, acting outwardly calm and professional, is burning internally at the lack of knowledge and support from his superiors, especially now at General Olson's ignorance. Trying to remain polite, he answers, "Aside from killing their source of food, the buffalo, which the Eastern civilians are doing anyway, I have a suggestion. That's why I have these two scouts here."

"What's that?" queries General Olson impatiently.

Colonel Baker presents a detailed plan, of which the major objective is to first locate the main camp through a special scouting unit, and then destroy it with a ready reserve unit of four-hundred or more properly equipped horsemen.

"Okay. Let me review what you've just said, Colonel. You want a medium size patrol out there of forty-five; half 'specially selected soldiers, the rest Indian half breed scouts. Is that right?"

"Yes, Sir. They can move swiftly, spread out as they go, and recognize tracks and signs our regular patrols can't."

General Olson cautiously returns to Baker's chair. Colonel Baker moves closer to General Olson in an attempt to firmly convince him of the necessity to change former tactics. "This type of reconnaissance patrol is large enough to defend itself briefly if attacked, then retreat. Yet it's small enough and experienced enough to avoid detection. Which is what we want. The idea is that they split up into five-man teams, once every day or two and reconnoiter at night. If the Indian camp is located, the Commander can send out experienced scouts. They know the territory and can get back here expediently. Re-enforcements will be immediately sent while the patrol maintains a distant surveillance."

General Olson stands up and looks curiously to each of his aides. "Well, I don't know, Colonel. It's different. I like the idea of killing all the buffalo better. In fact, I intend to pursue that idea later. If nothing else we'll starve the bastards."

Colonel Baker becomes more emphatic. "This plan is more like they operate, General. This isn't the type of warfare we experienced in the Civil War. This is more of a guerrilla, hit and run operation. There's no large battles. Hell, our artillery is useless. We can't pull cannons over this rough terrain and chase them at the same time."

General Olson takes a deep sigh, walks over to the map on the wall, and looks at it studiously. "You mean you have no idea where in tarnation they are?"

"No, Sir."

General Olson's impatience begins to show in the tone of his voice as he turns back to Colonel Baker. "I'm not suggesting you're not doing your job, Colonel. I know you and your abilities too well. But your plan is highly unorthodox. It's against the army training manual, you know."

"I know, General, but the training manual is out of date, obsolete. It doesn't work out here. Besides, General, you promised more men, horses, and equipment."

"What the hell are you talking about? I had forty Morgan horses sent out here, and two of them top breed stallions."

"The Morgans are fine, Sir. But they're the only horses we've got that can keep up with the Indian horses and we've only got the forty. We've bred all the grade mares, but as you know, until they foul, those horses are useless to us. Then it's almost three years until the fouls are even old enough to ride without injuring them. If you want to get Lone Wolf and his band, I need your help!"

"Don't worry, Colonel. I'll get you more horses. I also ordered you the new Spencer repeaters. They should be here within a day or two. Two-hundred of them, plus a thousand rounds of ammunition for each."

"That will help, Sir. Thank you. But the rest? More men, more horses?"

"That too will be on the way. I'm giving you all the support I can. I see how remote this damn place is."

Olson sits down and looks to the scouts. "What's your background there ... what's you name?"

"Stillwell, Sir. Jack Stillwell. Grew up with the Arikara, Northern Missouri River, Northern Dakota, Sir. Ma's Arikara. Pa's Canadian. The Sioux used to raid our villages back in the 1850's and 60's. No love for them, Sir. Been trapp'n and scout'n ten years now, since I was fourteen."

General Olson then turns to Sharp Grover. "And what's your credentials?"

"Crow and French background, Sir. My tribe been enemies of the Sioux since I can remember. I have a personal reason to scout for the army, Sir."

"What's that, Scout?"

"My younger brother and sister were killed by a Sioux raiding party. I got no liking for the dog eaters."

General Olson acts surprised at the credentials of Grover and Stillwell. "Sounds like you have a couple of vengeful scouts here, Colonel. Best keep these two under control. I don't want to hear about atrocities committed under army jurisdiction. That'd ruin both our careers, fast."

"I know these men, General. They're two of the best, and they understand the sensitivity of what you're talking about. That's why I chose them."

"Okay, Colonel. I'll approve your plan and give you all the support I can, beginning immediately. So, what about recruitment? Do these so-called scouts you want to pick have any problem soldiering with the coloreds?"

"Not that I've witnessed. They seem to have an understanding of the other's plight."

"Okay, you've got my approval. When and where's this recruitment going to take place?"

"Made plans for Hays City, Sir. Starting in three days. Was just waiting your approval."

"Well, get on with it. I'll divert fifty of those Spencer rifles to your station at Hays City. Plus, take all your best Morgan horses you have here, or that are not on assignment. I'll try to have fifty or so more out to you within the next three months."

General Olson stands, is about to leave when he stops. "Oh! What officers are you going to have in charge of this operation?"

"Major Baker, here, will be in charge, and Lieutenant Washington second under his command."

Major Baker interrupts. "Excuse me, Colonel, but Lieutenant Washington isn't due back for another six to eight days and …"

"That's right, Major. Who do you suggest?"

"How about that new Lieutenant you have on telegraph detail. He seems quite able and the men work well with him. He'll be back tonight sometime."

"You mean Lieutenant Williams?"

"Yes, Sir."

Colonel Novak thinks for a moment then looks to Jack Stillwell. "What do you think, Jack? How's he get along with the scouts here?"

"A good officer, Sir. He's about as respected by the scouts and coloreds as any."

"Fine with me, Major. Get your hand picked troops together, then supply and ammo up. I want your contingent in Hays City in three days. General Olson, have you anything to add?"

"No, not really. I just hope to hell your plan works, Colonel! I'm putting my ass on the line, ya' know."

Later that night Lieutenant Williams pulls in from patrol and reports in to headquarters. Lieutenant Sandy is on duty and tells Fred about his new orders. "Shit, Jim. What'ya mean I've got to leave in two days? I just got in. I want to spend some time with my wife. I haven't spent more than five days with her since I got here."

"Colonel's orders, Fred. Or more so, General Olson's orders. Best get as much time with your wife as possible. Don't know how long a man can be out there on an assignment like this."

"An assignment like what?" replies Fred.

"A special assignment. Don't know the particulars. All I know is that it's some kinda search for Lone Wolf."

"Damn it!" growls Fred as he hits his fist on the wall.

Lynda and Fred spend the next twenty-four hours together talking. She is obviously worried. "How long are you going to be out this time?" inquires Lynda.

"Not sure, hon. Was just told we're forming some special patrol to seek out Lone Wolf."

Lynda, obviously frustrated with the post lifestyle, turns to Fred with an air of defiance. "I don't mind telling you, Fred, I'm getting pretty tired of this life. You're never here and the other wives are getting to be a real bore."

"I know. But you have to avoid the gossip and concentrate on yourself. I'll be back soon and then you, Henry, and I can take that trip to Denver. They have some nice theaters there and we can take a trip into the Rockies."

Lynda becomes adamant. "I don't care about the Rockies, theaters, or any of that! I just want to spend time with you. No matter where it is. I didn't marry you to never see you."

"Lynda, you know it's my duty. You knew that when you married me. Things are just in an upheaval now because of Lone Wolf and his followers. All that will soon end, then I'll request a transfer back east. I promise you that."

Lynda's near tears as she gives Fred a hug and kiss. "I know this is your career, honey, but I'm so worried that something's going to happen to you."

Fred tries to reassure her with a hug as he looks her in the face. "Look, Lynda, I will make all this up to you. In the meantime, just keep socializing as best you can. Maybe some of the women who have been here longer than you can help you."

Lynda starts crying profusely. "That's part of it! There's nothing to do and they don't do anything themselves. Without you here it's so lonesome, so desolate. I just can't stand it!"

Fred realizes that he must leave shortly to refit the horses and get the men lined up for movement.

"Honey, when I get back everything will be different. Colonel Novak understands these things. We'll take that trip and I'll request a transfer after my tour is up."

Fred hugs Lynda close and tries to comfort her. "Please cheer up. It bothers me to see you like this. Just realize, I love you and am proud of you … proud to have you as my wife."

Lynda tries to dry her tears, then looks to Fred. "I love you too and I'll be waiting here for you. Please be careful."

Fred smiles at her as he hugs her. "Don't worry, I'll be just fine and be back here before you know it." Fred kisses her passionately, then bids his farewell, his eyes gazing, almost staring at her, with a look that only real love can convey.

"Gotta go now. The men are waiting. Just know I love you, darling."

Lynda says nothing, tears roll down her cheeks and her pulse is beating fast. She has a feeling about Fred leaving, but doesn't know how to express it. Even if she could, she knows he has to go. She follows Fred to the door holding his hand. Fred winks at her and smiles. Lynda's heart pounds as she watches him walk his horse to the assembly area.

SCOUTS WANTED

Lieutenant Williams feels confident as the detail rides into Hays City, Kansas. He thinks of Lynda momentarily with feelings of joy and pride. "What more can I ask for?" he thinks to himself. I've got a beautiful wife and beginning a career of adventure and purpose. A smile comes on his face as he anticipates his future.

Hays City is a bustling small town with dirt streets and hastily constructed wood-frame buildings. This day, however, the street is muddy and slushy as a quick, hard rain has taken place about one hour earlier. Men, women, and children all lift their pants or dresses as they skirt off the road to avoid the soldiers riding in on their horses.

It takes two days to get the recruitment banners up and advertisement posters printed. Lieutenant Williams has sent telegraphs to cities and towns within a four-hundred-mile radius to be placed in local newspapers.

Major Baker establishes his recruiting headquarters in a shed next to the railroad station. A handmade sign hangs outside the building: "ARMY SCOUTS WANTED IMMEDIATELY!! FIFTY DOLLARS A MONTH! MUST HAVE OWN HORSE."

Although Major Baker planned to spend two weeks in Hays City recruiting, the response for new scouts is immediate. By the third day there are a vast assortment of a hundred or more men milling around outside the recruitment headquarters. Lieutenant Williams is amazed at the sight as he gazes at the ragged looking bunch; Indian half-breeds, full breed Crow, Mandan, Idatsa, and Cree, trappers, mountain men, and drunken army scouts that have deserted other posts. Some are old, some young, others fat and some robust. Some are quietly sitting and talking, others drinking whiskey, while others are just loud and boisterous. But they all have one thing of interest in common ... fifty dollars a month and they hate the Sioux.

Pete "Frenchy" Trudeau stands out among all the men. He is six-foot-eight, an extra large man with long, black hair, and a thick, salt and pepper beard. He keeps his hair tied in a pony tail with a long, bright red cloth he has gotten from the Crees in Canada. An imposing figure, he sits quietly alone, watching the activities, and smoking his pipe made from buffalo bone.

Inside the recruitment shed, Major Baker and Lieutenant Williams sit side by side at an old wood table, interviewing Doctor Moors, who is dressed in an old, shabby, black suit, and sits precariously on the other side smelling of alcohol.

"You say your name is what?" repeats Major Baker.

"Doc! Doc Moooors. I mean Doctor Moors ... shur!"

Major Baker smiles slightly, then continues to question, "And tell me, Doctor Moors, why are you interested in joining this expedition?"

Doctor Moors hesitates for a moment as he attempts to focus on Major Baker. "Cause I's know how to fix up the wounded." Doctor Moors smiles a sheepish grin as he looks toward Lieutenant Williams. "Haven't had much luck wissh the dead, tho."

Major Baker looks at the Doctor in a serious manner. "Looks like you've been fix'n yourself up a bit too, Doc."

"Darn toot'n, Sir. Today's my day off."

"Day off from what, Doctor?"

"From ... pracshice, Sir. From medical pracshice."

Major Baker looks to Lieutenant Williams, winks, then turns back to the Doctor.

The Major continues in a calm voice. "Tell you what, Doctor. If you can prove to me you're a genuine medical doctor, I'll consider taking you along ... that's if you can sober up."

Doctor Moors starts fumbling around in his coat pocket and pulls out a crumpled piece of paper. His hand shakes as he hands it to Major Baker who reaches out to take the paper, unfolds it, and after a brief moment, turns to Lieutenant Williams. "Says he's a doctor alright. Degrees from the University of Pennsylvania."

Lieutenant Williams looks at the old diploma, then to Doctor Moors. "Looks real, Doctor. What brings you out this way?" questions Lieutenant Williams as he hands him his certificate.

Doctor Moors straightens up and tries to talk clearly and seriously. "A woman, Lieutenant. You know. Ish's a long story."

Lieutenant Williams nods as Major Baker interrupts. "Okay, Doctor. You get yourself sober, and I mean sober. Be here in two days, at seven o'clock in the morning, and bring your medical bag. You have a horse?"

"Shuuur do!" slurs Doctor Moors as he struggles to fold up his diploma.

"Seven o'clock, Doctor! Day after tomorrow. If you're not here to be trained and fitted we won't be taking you along."

Doctor Moors braces himself on the table as he stands and attempts a salute. He then smiles, stumbles a military about face, and straddles out the door.

The Major shakes his head and calls to Sergeant Waller. "Next man, Sergeant!"

Frenchy Trudeau, dressed in beaded buckskins, bends his head as he walks in the door and takes a relaxed stance in front of the table.

Major Baker momentarily looks up in awe at this large man before addressing him. "Name?"

Frenchy Trudeau replies with a firm, strong French accent. "Mr. Pete Trudeau, Major. Just call me Frenchy."

"So what brings you to this recruitment station, Mr. Trudeau?"

"'Ol' Pete here knows territory ... and Sioux can no kill me, cause I disappear."

Major Baker briefly turns to Lieutenant Williams, raises his eyebrows, then turns back to Pete Trudeau. "How's that, Mr. Trudeau?"

Pete Trudeau stands more erect, looks the Major in the eyes, and speaks with the utmost confidence. "I trapped many times ... Canada, Dakotas', even 'round here. Injuns no can see me. I 'scape 'em."

Major Baker chuckles to himself under his exterior stone face. He leans back in his chair, looks seriously at Pete Trudeau, then speaks in a jovial tone of voice. "Okay, Mr. Trudeau, so the Indians can't see you. Tell me why you want to scout for the army?"

Trudeau leans down, places both of his large hands on the table in front of Major Baker, and stares him in the face. "Ol' Pete is good Injun fighter, right?"

The Major nods as he quickly glances at Lieutenant Williams, who remains quiet. "Right! I guess so," responds Major Baker.

"Hey, Ol' Pete here no like Sioux. I like fifty dollars a month. It buy many things for squaw and papoose ... see?" He then looks at Lieutenant Williams. "I Ojibwa. Sioux no friend."

Pete Trudeau stands erect, displays a slight smile on his face, and adds a final statement in a firm, rough voice. "And I help you find Injuns!"

Major Baker looks down at his note pad, scribbles himself a memo and looks to Pete Trudeau. "Alright, Mr. Trudeau. As long as Indians can't see you, I'll hire you. I take it you have a horse?"

"I do. A good one!" replies Trudeau.

"Then pack your gear. The army will supply you with a Spencer rifle and ammunition. Be here with the rest at seven o'clock in the morning, ready for training and supply."

"I be here!" confirms Trudeau as he extends his huge hand to the Major.

As Pete Trudeau leaves, Lieutenant Williams turns to Major Baker shaking his head back and forth. "Wow! Where did he come from, Major?"

"Ya' know, Lieutenant, this should be quite an interesting trip."

Lieutenant Williams chuckles. "I agree, Major ... a drunk Doc and an invisible Indian Frenchman. What more do we need?"

Major Baker smiles, then calls to Sergeant Waller. "Next man, Sergeant!"

It is exactly two weeks later when the final scout is selected, supplied, and trained. The special patrol is finally organized and prepared to leave Hays City. Now is the time to begin the test of this new operation. It is six o'clock a.m. as Major Baker and Lieutenant Williams sit on their horses watching as Sergeant Waller assembles the soldiers and scouts in formation. Once this is done, Sergeant Waller rides up to Major Baker. "Men are ready, Suh! An interest'n bunch!"

"I know, Sergeant. And not a one has any army discipline."

Sergeant Waller winks, shakes his head in agreement, salutes, and returns to the head of the column.

Major Baker checks over the column, determines they are ready to move out, and turns to Lieutenant Williams. "Well, time to get this show on the road, Lieutenant. Sound the bugle."

Lieutenant Williams signals to Sergeant Waller to bring the men forward. The bugler sounds and the men all begin to ride forward.

"Column ho!" yells Lieutenant Williams as he and Major Baker take their place in the front of the column.

The patrol of twenty-six scouts, twenty black soldiers, and Doctor Moors, follow Major Baker, Lieutenant Williams, and Sergeant Waller as they make their parting parade through the city of Hays. Doctor Moors takes up the rear of the unit and waves continually to the crowd of people that line the street, watching.

It is late afternoon and the special patrol has traveled fifty-six miles west toward the Republican River when Major Baker orders a halt. "Lieutenant, we'll stop here for the night. Put out guard post sentries. One man every hundred yards."

"Yes, Sir! Do you want scouts out on patrol, Sir?"

"Yeah, might as well get 'em started. Let Stillwell, Grover, and that Frenchy scout start out. They can sleep wherever they can find cover tonight. That'll put them several miles in front. If there are Indians ahead of us they should find them."

"Yes, Sir," replies Lieutenant Williams as he turns to call the three scouts. "Stillwell, Grover, Trudeau! Com'on over here a moment. The Major wants some scout'n done."

As the three scouts approach Lieutenant Williams, Frenchy Trudeau bellows out a sarcastic remark in his French Canadian accent. "Hey, Lieutenant! How many scouts you need?"

"Major wants you three to scout on ahead for tomorrow. Sleep whenever, wherever you like."

Frenchy Trudeau, as one of the first scouts hired, had two weeks to get to know Jack Stillwell and Sharp Grover. "Ya' know, Lieutenant, I go, but I want you to know it be me and Stillwell that can track Injuns."

Lieutenant Williams, about to comment, is interrupted as Frenchy Trudeau winks to Jack Stillwell and continues, "Me and Stillwell can do Scout'n'. Grover, here, no can track a herd of a thousand buffalo. Maybe he lead us on wild buffalo chase, aye?" Trudeau laughs a loud, boisterous laugh, irritating Sharp Grover. "Speak for yourself you fat, French half-breed!"

Frenchy Trudeau steps forward toward Grover as Lieutenant Williams intervenes. "Com'on you two. We've got enough problems without you fighting."

"Horseshit, Lieutenant!" exclaims Grover. "Tell the Major I can scout this one alone, without either of these two spike whores."

"That's not what the Major ordered! You've been briefed on your responsibilities back at Hays City. Now is the time to earn your pay. You three get your equipment, saddle up, and do as you're ordered. And as one last piece of advice, you all just might need each other out there!"

Grover takes one last glaring look at Frenchy Trudeau before he walks back to his horse. Jack Stillwell and Frenchy Trudeau smile at one another, then turn to Lieutenant Williams. Jack Stillwell attempts to inform Lieutenant Williams of the situation. "Just testing him, Lieutenant. I've worked once before with Frenchy, here, know what he's like. Don't know Grover. Don't trust him."

"That's alright to a point, Stillwell. But we all have to work together. It could mean our lives."

"I understand, Lieutenant," confirms Stillwell.

"I follow orders too, Lieutenant!" adds Trudeau.

As the three scouts mount up, Lieutenant Williams turns to the other scouts. "You other men take rotation on sentry duty this evening. Sergeant Waller will call your names. Four, two-man watches every two hours. No talking. No fires. No smoking."

It is two o'clock in the morning when newly hired scouts Art Lombard and Bill McJohn start their shift. Both are in their early twenties, but have impressed Major Baker with their experience as wagon train sentries. This is their first expedition as army scouts, but both are like the rest, intrigued with the pay and the excitement of adventure.

Although the rocky hillside position of the camp site offers a good field of vision in the day, it becomes impossible to see more than several feet in the dark moonless night. The evening is still and quiet until about three o'clock in the morning. Suddenly there is the sound of a lone wolf howling in the near distance. Bill McJohn immediately whispers to Lombard. "Do ya think that's a wolf or an Injun out there?"

"A wolf," replies Lombard confidently. "Relax you dandy. There isn't an Indian within fifty miles of this place. What! You scared?"

"Hell to you, Art! I never been scared."

"Shit, Bill, you been scared since the day you were born. Relax. We'll be relieved at daylight."

It is five a.m. when camp breaks and the men begin saddling their horses. All the sentries, except McJohn and Lombard, have reported in by four-thirty a.m. as Sergeant Waller takes morning roll call. Concerned, but not immediately alarmed, Sergeant Waller calls to Lieutenant Williams. "Lieutenant! Have you seen scouts Lombard and McJohn?"

"No, they were on last sentry. Should be in by now. 'Spose they might be sleeping? Don't worry, Sergeant. I'll tend to it," replies Lieutenant Williams as he turns to ride over to Major Baker.

Major Baker responds nonchalantly. "That's the trouble with these damn civilians. No discipline. Just can't seem to follow orders. Go out and tell 'em to get their asses in here!"

Lieutenant Williams turns his mount and gallops slowly out to the sentry post. As he rides up to the two men he sees them sitting back to back with their heads down. "Hell! The assholes are still sleeping," he thinks to himself.

"Hey! You men! Get you fat asses up! We're ready to move out."

There is no response from either Lombard or McJohn. Lieutenant Williams walks his horse so close to McJohn that the hooves spray rocks on his hands. Still no movement. It isn't until now that Lieutenant Williams notices massive amounts of blood on the front and shoulder areas of their coats. Dismounting quickly, he shakes McJohn. This movement knocks the hat off McJohn's head, showing a raw, bloody, gruesome sight. Shocked, Lieutenant Williams turns his head away. His pulse is throbbing.

"Damn it! They've been scalped!" he mutters to himself in a low voice. Hesitating for a moment, he puts the hat back on

McJohn's head, quickly mounts his horse and gallops full speed back to Major Baker's position.

"Major! Major!" yells Lieutenant Williams as he rides in, "The scouts ... they've been scalped! I think they're dead, Sir!"

Major Baker knows what this means, but remains calm as he responds immediately by grabbing the reins of his horse. "Calm down, Lieutenant! Let's go see. Sergeant Waller, hold the patrol here till I get back."

Upon arriving at the sight, Major Baker dismounts and checks both men for any sight of life. "They're dead. Must've been a scouting party."

The Major takes a deep breath and lets it out slowly. "They know we're here, Lieutenant. The main force can't be more than one-hundred miles away and that's a guess."

Lieutenant Williams, still sitting on his horse, just stares at the two dead men. "Christ, Sir! Is this what they do? Are they that sly?"

"Sometimes, Lieutenant. Depends on how much time they have. It certainly appears they had the time here."

Major Baker quickly surveys the terrain. "Lieutenant, quit staring at the bodies. Let's go. When we get back, have Sergeant Waller assign you three men to bury the bodies. I'm going to start the patrol. You can catch up when you're done. They won't attack today."

Both officers gallop their horses back to the camp. Lieutenant Williams takes his three-man detail with shovels, back to where Lombard and McJohn lie. Major Baker, hoping to pick up an Indian trail, sends out his peripheral scouts, then orders his patrol forward, due west.

As the patrol moves out at a walk, the men are quiet and alert. They periodically talk in a low tone of voice. One of the new recruits riding next to Doctor Moors mumbles to himself, "I hope we find those bastards. I could use a scalp for my bunk."

Doctor Moors can't help but hear the comment of the young scout. "Don't let the Major hear that, son. You know he's against scalp'n."

The patrol continues on horseback at a steady, walking pace, and are unusually quiet. Major Baker had ordered that morning to wrap in leather anything that might rattle. Every man in the patrol knows now that events could be deadly serious and that the enemy can move with stealth.

CHAPTER EIGHTEEN
AMBUSH AT THE ARIKARA

As the army patrol starts out the day after the killing of McJohn and Lombard, the Sioux and the Cheyenne are already in Council. Chiefs Two Crows, Grey Bull, Spotted Wolf, and Lone Wolf meet with Dark Sun of the Cheyenne. The meeting is intense and ideas clash as all know of the coming army patrol.

Lone Wolf is loud and defiant as he speaks of killing the soldiers and scouts. His eyes are red like burning coals, and his voice carries a message of vengeance and hate. He is even violating the traditional Indian code of respect and honor towards his Elders as he talks incessantly with rage.

"We have many more braves than do white eyes. We kill all who come to our land! They have fifty men ... forty-eight after I take two scalps and Spencer rifles."

Lone Wolf raises a rifle in the air, and puts his right fist on his chest. "Look at me! No white man's bullet can touch me! Many white man's bullets come my way, but they not kill me! I have good medicine."

Grey Bull interrupts Lone Wolf with a firm, steady voice. "Yes, Lone Wolf. But these strange new soldiers are not the white soldiers of the past. They are Buffalo soldiers and half Indian scouts. They shoot straight! They have Spencer rifles! They have good medicine!"

Lone Wolf becomes more defiant and defensive as he immediately addresses Grey Bull. "You say, old Medicine Man, that Lone Wolf, great warrior leader of the Lakota Sioux and Cheyenne allies, is not good medicine against the blue coat ... soldier scouts?"

Lone Wolf glares at the Elder leaders as Grey Bull answers. "The army scouts of the old days are one thing, but today we have different kind of blue coat to fight. They think they fight for freedom like we do. They know not our way of life. They caught between the past and the future."

"What you say, Medicine Man?" inquires Lone Wolf, not quite comprehending what Grey Bull means.

Grey Bull leans forward in the direction of Lone Wolf and begins to speak calmly, and deliberately. "You, Lone Wolf, must go to sweat lodge alone. Pray to Wankan Tonkan (Great Spirit) for good of your people. Then you must go to the high hill, seek a vision. Carry the sacred peace pipe with you in your vision quest. Pray to all directions for victory. Pray for wisdom and patience in leadership."

Grey Bull passes the red stone peace pipe, with two attached eagle feathers, to Two Crows, who passes it to Lone Wolf. Grey Bull then raises his arms up towards the sky and holds them there as he speaks. "All powers of the world, the heavens and the star peoples, listen. All red and blue sacred days, all things that move in universe, in rivers, listen. All trees that stand, all grasses of our grandmothers, all sacred peoples of universe, listen." Grey Bull chants briefly, slowly rises to his feet still holding his hands toward the heavens.

"Hey-H-H-H-Hey! Hey-H-H-H-Hey! Hey-Hey-H-H-Hey! H-H-Hey Hey! ... Wankan Tonkan, a sacred relationship will be asked of you by Lone Wolf. That his generations will increase and live in a holy manner. That his warriors will be not afraid and be brave in battle. Let him have his vision." Grey Bull quietly sits down and resumes his silence.

Two Crows, as Elder Chief, then follows tradition by making the final speech to all present. "It is way it must be. Lone Wolf must seek his vision and find good medicine. He must be at peace with himself to fight in this battle. He must come to us when pure of heart."

Two Crows looks at each member of the Council in a slow deliberate manner. His eyes fixed directly and seriously on those who will make the decisions in this upcoming battle. He speaks with authority. "We prepare for battle. I lead our warriors until Lone Wolf has vision."

Lone Wolf is now confused. He has been denied his chance for glory ... momentarily.

The camp is filled with excitement as the warriors beat their drums and scream. The women are busy painting the horses with war paint, creating designs that not only represent past feats of the rider in battle, but designs that are intended to intimidate any foe. In many cases, the war paint on the horse is a direct copy of the war paint on the warrior's face.

The drums continue to pound loudly, creating a feeling of intense power and excitement among every brave.

DAY ONE

It's early afternoon as the army patrol rides at a silent walk along the Republican River. Sergeant Waller rides next to Major Baker and Lieutenant Williams. The sweat dripping from the men is equaled only to the wet necks and flanks of the horses. Sergeant Waller looks around nervously and whispers to Major Baker. "Suh, I has a bad feelin'. Feels lak' der may be a fight com'n' on."

Major Baker responds confidently, trying to calm the Sergeant. "Relax, Sergeant. We haven't seen but a few pony tracks in the last few days. Probably are from the Indians that killed the scouts. There's no indication of any major force in this area."

Sergeant Waller, still acting nervous, re-enforces his feelings. "Jes a feelin', Suh. Where you think be Stillwell and de others?"

"Don't know, Sergeant. They'll be along. If there's a problem they'll let us know."

The patrol continues on quietly, each man looking eagle eyed at each crevice and blade of grass as if through a microscope.

Unknown to the men in the patrol, more than six-hundred Indians under the leadership of Two Crows are moving southeast, following the Republican River and advancing toward them. The two forces are less than five miles apart, and probing Sioux scouts have brought word that the patrol is advancing northwest towards them.

Two Crows divides his force into three groups. One group to come up behind the patrol and attack on horseback. The second to hide in the ravine at the mouth of the Arikara River where it meets the Republican River, and the last to stay north of the patrol and attack head on. This tactic he hopes will force the soldiers to dismount and fight on foot. If this happens, reasons Two Crows, the fight will be quick and the soldiers killed without much of a fight.

Scouts Stillwell, Trudeau, and Grover have little luck in finding any substantial Indian tracks in the hilly, rocky terrain to the west and are returning to the main patrol. As they are coming down a high hill off to the northwest of the Republican River, Frenchy Trudeau yells to the others. "Hey, my friends, Ol' Pete sees dust out there ... beyond that ravine. The Major's com'n to meet us."

Trudeau laughs as he continues to talk. "We must tell the Major we scare Indians out of territory, ya?"

Scout Stillwell, who is looking toward his left to the river and the deep ravine, is suddenly shocked at what he sees. "Bull shit, Trudeau. Look at what's in that ravine!"

All three scouts look to the ravine and are stunned. "Halt your horses!" yells Stillwell.

"Shit!" screams Scout Grover.

All three momentarily just look at the sight of hundreds of Indians in the ravine between them and Major Baker's patrol.

"Holy, Jesus! Ambush!" yells Scout Stillwell. "There must be thousands of them! How the hell did we miss that?"

"Don't give a shit!" yells Scout Grover.

Scout Trudeau is yelling at the same time. "We warn Major now!"

All three spur their horses into a full speed gallop and head down the hillside straight towards Major Baker's location.

Two Crows notices the three scouts coming down off the hill. He realizes that he has lost the element of surprise in his ambush and yells to his warriors. "Attack now!"

Unmounted warriors scramble to their horses. More than fifty ride out to intercept the scouts. Two Crows waves the main force to immediately attack the patrol.

Lieutenant Williams is the first to notice the three scouts coming down off the hill, riding at a full gallop and waving their hats in the air. It is less than ten seconds when he sees the Indians, some coming out of the ravine in front of the patrol and others swinging out on the high ground, to intercept the scouts. He yells frantically to Major Baker. "Major! Major! Look what's coming at us!"

Major Baker is astonished and bewildered.

Lieutenant Williams looks to the rear. "Sir! Sir! Over there! They're coming up behind us on the back hill! Look! Look! Where the hell did they come from?"

Major Baker spins his horse around. The scouts are in near panic.

"Orders, Sir! What's your orders?" Lieutenant Williams is frantic as he turns to the Major.

"Sir, we're surrounded! There's hundreds of 'em!"

Major Baker is quickly trying to assess the situation. He realizes immediately that to dismount and fight in the light cover provided on the hill will be suicide.

"Sir! We've got to take a defensive position. Now! We can't out run them!"

Major Baker, although frustrated, holds on that order and thinks for a few more seconds before giving his orders. "Lieutenant! Order the men onto that river island below! Now!"

Surprised at the order, Lieutenant Williams hesitates. "Sir! The island, Sir?"

Major Baker displays his anger at the Lieutenant's question. "Immediately, Lieutenant! Damn it! It's our only chance! Do it!"

"Yes, Sir!" yells Lieutenant Williams as he gallops by the men giving the order to head for the Island on the river eight-hundred-yards away down the hillside.

The scouts charge for the Island, a sandy area in the river about one-hundred-yards long and fifty-yards wide. The only cover there being some prairie grass about three feet tall. But there is the water and the open area for defense that it provides.

Doctor Moors is the last of the forty-eight men scrambling down the hill at a full gallop.

Lieutenant Williams sees the doctor is having problems and halts his horse. He turns and screams at the doctor. "Doc, let's go! Hit the river!"

Doctor Moors finally gets his horse moving at a full gallop following the scouts, but doesn't have the staying power to ride the terrain like the scouts. Lieutenant Williams sees him fall off and tumble down the hill, his horse running after the pack.

"Damn it!" yells Lieutenant Williams as he turns his horse back up the hill to get the doctor. "Climb on, Doc! No time to waste!"

Doctor Moors exerts every ounce of energy he has to climb on the back of Lieutenant William's saddle. Lieutenant Williams struggles to pull him up. "Hang on, Doc! Hang on! We've got to make that island!"

Doctor Moors grabs the Lieutenant's waist tightly as they gallop and almost stumble down the hill to the water's edge.

The river, from three to four feet deep, turns into a splashing barrage of water from the horses. Some horses and riders stumble and fall, and are hit head on by the horses immediately behind them. The situation is total pandemonium as hundreds of arrows and bullets are flying at the fleeing patrol. Those that reach the island first are frantically trying to find something, anything that they can, to hide behind. Some of the horses fall wounded or dead and are used as temporary shields from the deadly barrage of oncoming arrows and bullets. Those who fall in the water scramble to the small island.

Stillwell, Trudeau, and Grover are the last to cross, right behind Lieutenant Williams and Doctor Moors.

Major Baker's horse takes two arrows. Barely making it to the island himself, he starts screaming orders. "Dig in! Use your hands, spoons, knives! Dig as deep as you can!"

Lieutenant Williams and Doctor Moors reach Major Baker's side and sprawl in the sand. As Lieutenant Williams positions himself to shoot, he yells to the Major. "Sir, they're dropping off on the north end! I can't see them because of the tall grass!"

The gun fire is intense and loud. Horses are falling fast from their wounds. The combined eerie, high pitched screams of the animals in pain creates a sound even more deafening than the gunfire. The men, covered with wet sand, hastily pull the dead horses into semi-circles. The screaming of the horses, and the yelling of the men desperately trying to regroup, cause total havoc for more than twenty minutes. The sound is almost unearthly. None of the men can hear Major Baker as he yells orders.

Scout Trudeau crawls more than thirty yards on his belly to Major Baker's position. "Major! We got seven horses alive. Rest are dead or wounded. On man's holding them but they'll be shot soon if we don't let them go!"

"Shoot them!"

"What, Major?"

"Shoot them! We need them as a shield! Do it! Now!" orders the Major as he tries to access what is happening.

"I follow orders, Major!"

Many of the scouts give up firing their rifles as they are jammed from the fine sand. The best they can do for the moment is hide near the dead horses and dig into the sand. They know their pistol fire is ineffective due to range.

Just as quickly as it started the attack stops. The air is quiet except for a few moans and screams of the last dying horses.

It is less than a half an hour from the initial run to the island to the last bullet being fired that Major Baker can yell any clearly heard orders.

Lieutenant Williams crawls closer to the Major. "Why'd they stop, Sir?"

Major Baker raises his head cautiously over his dead horse's stomach. "Don't know." He then yells to Scout Trudeau. "Trudeau! What the hell are they up to?"

Scout Trudeau holds up an arrow that he pulls out of his horse's neck. "They tease us, Major. They know we no place to go."

Major Baker doesn't react to Trudeau's statement but Lieutenant Williams, partially in shock, feels a shiver run down his spine. "How can this happen?" he thinks to himself.

"Lieutenant!" yells Major Baker. "Give me a report on dead and wounded!"

"Yes, Sir!" responds Lieutenant Williams as he regains his focus on the reality around him.

"Sergeant Waller!" continues the Major. "How much water we got?"

"Don't know for sure, Major. Maybe two days. Maybe three. Most lost com'n' cross the river."

Jack Stillwell moves closer to Major Baker. "Can't drink the river water, Sir. Too salty and too dirty."

The Major raises to his knees and tries to look above the grass. "Where's the Doc?"

"In dat group dead horses to yo'r right, Sir," replies Sergeant Waller. "He be alive."

Lieutenant Williams crawls back to the Major's position. 'Three dead, Sir! Eight wounded. Four seriously."

"Get all the horses bunched up in seven piles on all four sides, Lieutenant. Six men or whatever, to a pile. Get what ammo we have left and redistribute it. Make sure the men clean their rifles."

Still recovering from the shock of the surprise attack, Lieutenant Williams replies nervously, "Yes, Sir."

Major Baker watches briefly as the men follow out his orders and dig deep into the sand with their bare utensils.

He gazes to the hills and bluffs on both sides of the river. There for the first time he gets a first glance of his adversary. He pulls out his binoculars for a closer look. On the bluffs overlooking the river he sees a sight he never thought possible.

Two Crows, Dark Moon, and Grey Bull sit on their horses quietly looking down at the small, trapped patrol. Almost all the Indians that attacked the patrol are now lined up on the bluffs on both sides of the river. The men on the island just stare at them in the distance.

"Damn, Major! Never seen so many Injuns in my life!" yells Scout Stillwell.

Major Baker slowly moves his binoculars along the ridge lines.

"What you seeing, Major?" inquires Lieutenant Williams.

Major Baker puts down his binoculars. "I'm just guessing, but there must be three to four hundred on each side of us."

Lieutenant Williams takes a deep breath, holds it for a moment, then blows it out. But his heart continues to pound.

Two Crows signals to his lead warriors on both sides of the river. They acknowledge by raising their right arms that they are to contain the soldiers and scouts on the island through the night. Two Crows turns to Dark Moon and Grey Bull. "Soldiers have good rifles. Fire power great. We take them tomorrow! It be Lone Wolf's day. He finish vision quest tonight."

The three chiefs turn their horses away from the river and ride down to a temporary village set up by the women who have followed them.

FORT WALLACE

Lieutenant Washington, leading H Company, rides into Fort Wallace tired and exhausted. The soldiers and horses are all sweating, dust caked into dry mud on the sweat. Lieutenant Washington's patrol comes to a halt in front of the livery stable as Lieutenant Washington addresses Sergeant Thomas. "Take charge, Sergeant. I'll make my report to the Colonel."

"Yes, Suh!" replies Sergeant Thomas.

As he makes his way to the Administration Building, Lieutenant Washington reviews the frustrations and low morale evident on the escort detail: poor food, bad water, hot weather, and the constant flies, snakes, and dust.

Colonel Novak greets him with a smile. "How'd it go out there, Lieutenant?"

"All is quiet, Sir. No evidence of Indians. Just a bunch of scared settlers and railroad workers. I'll detail that to you in my written report later, Sir. Just want you to know we're all back in one piece."

"No hurry, Lieutenant. Go clean up and get some rest. You'll get new orders as I see them."

Lieutenant Washington turns to leave then stops. "Excuse me, Sir. Is Lieutenant Williams on post? I haven't had much time to talk to him since we've been out here and ..."

Colonel Novak interrupts gently. "I know, Lieutenant. He's a good friend of yours and I know you want to take leave together to Denver. He's already mentioned that." Colonel Novak leans back in his chair and momentarily recalls his best friend at West Point years before and the plans they had made before the Civil War started.

"He's out on patrol right now but I expect them back in a week or so. And don't worry about your leave requests. I'll grant them."

"Thank you, Sir!" replies Henry.

Colonel Novak gets up, walks over to Lieutenant Washington and pats him on the back as they both walk towards the door. "You're both excellent officers. I'm just glad to have you two in my command. Now relax and take it easy for a day or two."

Henry walks outside, takes a little jump off the wooden walkway and laughs. "Denver, here we come! I've got to tell Lynda."

As Lynda opens the door of her officer's quarters and sees Henry, she acts with surprise, then joy. "Henry!" she exclaims. "What a surprise! Where you been?"

"Just got back from escorting a telegraph crew. They're hanging wire east of here. How you and Fred been?"

"Alright, but I worry about him."

"He'll be okay, Lynda, especially when you give him the news."

"News about what, Henry?"

"Denver. The Colonel approved our leave for Denver. Two weeks. It's not just a dream anymore."

Lynda's eyes immediately light up as she dances with delight. "Are you sure?"

"Sure am! The Colonel just told me. So get your fancy clothes ready, 'cause when Fred gets back we're gonna have the time of our lives."

Lynda takes a deep breath and sighs. "This is such welcome news, Henry. I just can't wait."

"Well, keep up those spirits, Lynda. I gotta get back to the men now ... tell them they have a couple of days off. Surprise Fred as soon as he gets back."

"I will, Henry. You bet I will! Thank you."

DAY TWO

The fires on the hills have burned all night and the echo of the constant drumbeats allow the men on the island little peace. As daylight comes and the sun rises over the bluffs, the men on the tiny island scan the horizons. What they see is an imposing sight. Earlier that morning Two Crows' Warrior Leaders positioned all the warriors in line at the top of the bluffs and along the river's edge to the north and south, just out of rifle range. All of the warriors sit quietly, looking at the island. The men on the island stare, almost frozen, at the frightening sight.

Doctor Moors is the first to say anything. "God, Major! Look at that!"

Major Baker grabs his binoculars. He looks three-hundred-sixty-degrees around him. "There must be six-hundred or more out there," he comments in a low, emotionless voice to Doctor Moors.

"Lieutenant Williams, Sergeant Waller, Stillwell! Come over here!" All three men move to Major Baker's position.

"It looks like they're going to attack soon. Lieutenant, tell the men to shoot fast and make every shot count. If they don't we'll be overrun."

Major Baker takes another look and mumbles to himself. "It looks like we're gonna have one hell of a hot day."

"You talk'n weather, Suh?"

"Ya, that too, Sergeant ... Sergeant! Make sure all the dead horses and packed in tight. Cover them with as much sand as you can ... it'll reduce the fly problem and increase the cover."

"Be do'n that now, Suh!"

Major Baker wipes the lens of his binoculars, then scans the bluffs and river bed. Suddenly he sees Two Crows sitting on his horse, easily distinguishable with a long eagle feather war bonnet. He focuses in and watches as Two Crows begins to raise up a long feathered lance. Two Crows holds the lance above his head for a good two minutes.

"Get ready, men!" yells Major Baker as he closely watches every movement Two Crows makes. Suddenly he sees Two Crows throw the lance straight and hard into the ground. "They're com'n'!" screams the Major. "Fire at will! Shoot their horses if nothing else!"

Two waves of Indians gallop head on into the shallow water from each side of the river, dividing the firepower. The yelling and screaming of the warriors as they attack is almost drowned out by the rifle fire and the splashing of hundreds of horses in the water. Splashing water, combined with tumbling horses and warriors, stop the Indians' momentum. Volley after volley from the Spencer repeaters gives the army defenders the advantage as the attacking force becomes bottled up in the river. But the attack is relentless. Some of the attackers, whose horses have fallen into the river, scramble for the island, others are shot. As the intensity of the battle begins to hit its peak, the Indians again suddenly withdraw.

Major Baker, acting surprised, yells, "Cease fire!"

For a brief moment all is quiet. Not even the ripple of the river can be heard. Major Baker looks through his binoculars at the many dead and wounded horses that are left in the river. Most of the dead or wounded Indians have been pulled back to the bluffs, even in the heat of the battle.

Frenchy Trudeau hastily scrambles to the Major's side. "Major, Injuns on north end. Saw them when their horses fell."

"Okay, Trudeau. You go get them. Take five men. Keep low."

Trudeau points his fingers at five scouts, motions them over to his position, then whispers. "Be careful. They be two feet in front of you 'n you not see them. Maybe five Injuns, maybe six." The scouts fan out and slowly crawl into the sand and tall grass.

All the men are quiet as they cautiously tend to the wounded and their rifles. Suddenly the sound of rifle fire causes them to react for another attack. No Indians can be seen, either near the water or on the bluffs. Moments later Frenchy Trudeau and the five scouts come walking in upright in the tall grass.

"Hold fire! It be Frenchy!" yells Scout Stillwell.

Scout Trudeau heads the incoming scouts and is carrying several scalps in his right hand as he approaches Major Baker. "Others must got away. But no more Injuns on this island."

Major Baker eyes the scalps with disgust. "God! Did you have to do that, Trudeau?"

"Aye, Major! Ol' Pete here lucky he didn't lose his."

Sharp Grover looks at the scalps and recognizes one of the hair braids. "Hell, Major! I knew that Sioux. His name was Bad Heart."

Trudeau holds the scalp up, looks at it closely, then shakes his head back and forth. "It no matter. Bad Heart, good heart ... it no work now!" Trudeau laughs with a gruesome, guttural sound to his voice. He walks over to Major Baker with the scalps. "Here, Major. We win today, Major. We take more scalps tomorrow."

Upset at the scalping, Major Baker turns to Doctor Moors. "Tend to the men, Doc. We'll need all who can shoot."

DAY THREE

The night is quiet, except for the sounds of slapping gnats and flies, and the constant beat of loud drums just over the bluffs. The drum beat is a constant reminder that the enemy is just beyond sight. The sounds themselves are having an effective psychological effect on the soldiers and scouts.

The ninety-plus-degree heat during the past two days has created an overwhelming thirst in the men, and the water supply, although rationed, is now depleted. The situation is now so serious that they might die of thirst before being killed by the enemy. Lieutenant Williams brings this concern to the attention of Major Baker. "Sir! We're almost out of water. What we have left won't last through the afternoon. You know we can't drink river water ... it's too salty. And there's no hard tack."

Major Baker responds to the situation. "Cut the throats of those dead horses. Drain the blood into the canteens and water bags as best you can."

Lieutenant Williams is shocked and surprised. "You can't be serious, Sir! We'll die drinking that ..."

"I'm serious, Lieutenant! Get a detail and do it. Now!"

As Lieutenant Williams slowly begins to move out of the pit, Major Baker continues, "And have the men cut some flanks. We'll need food."

"Yes, Sir!" comes the reply with hesitance.

Lieutenant Williams walks by Sergeant Waller and tells him what they must do, then adds his personal comment. "I don't know, Serge ... think maybe the Major's go'in' crazy?"

With no imminent danger of being attacked a detail of six men cut the throats of the dead animals and carefully drain the blood into the canteens and burlap water bags. Blood gushes out of the arteries, half going into the canteens and half on the men's clothes or on the ground. After more than two hours of attempting this task, Lieutenant Williams reports back to Major Baker. "Canteens filled and bags filled, Sir. The flanks look kind of rancid, Sir."

"You don't have time to worry about that, Lieutenant."

This evening is the same as the other two. The men have a lot of time to think about things as gnats, flies, and drums work on their reflections.

DAY FOUR

Again the Indian warriors line up on the bluffs above the island. But on this particular morning, Major Baker notices a large number of Indians on foot at the tree line and rocky areas of the river's edge.

Without warning, volley after volley of arrows fly into the patrol's defensive position. Hundreds of arrows fall into the sand in and around the pits, some sticking into the bodies of the now rotting horses. At the same time the Indian horse warriors begin their attack in mass. The bullet and arrow barrage is so thick that the men have difficulty getting their heads above the sand and horse barriers to shoot back.

Suddenly Doctor Moors sees Major Baker fall. He yells to Lieutenant Williams above the sounds of gunfire. "Lieutenant! Lieutenant! The Major's hit!"

Doctor Moors scrambles to the Major's side, places the Major's head in his lap, and attempts to wrap the wound to the Major's back side.

Major Baker, temporarily stunned and in pain, looks at Doctor Moors. "I'm okay, Doc. We can pull the arrow later. Get me to the horse cover. Watch so you don't get hit!"

The patrol fires volley after volley at the oncoming attacks, sometimes coming from four different directions at once. Again the attackers are repelled and the Indian Warriors pull back.

"Think they're done for this round, Major. Got to get that arrow out of your side."

"I need to know how many casualties we took, Doc. Where's Lieutenant Williams?"

"He's coming now, Major."

Lieutenant Williams sits next to Major Baker. "Sir, you okay?"

"Just give the report, Lieutenant!"

"We took some casualties. One dead, six wounded. Musta been twenty-five or more Indians killed, maybe fifty wounded. Hard to tell, Sir."

Major Baker passes out in pain as Doc Moors attempts to cut the arrow out of his side. Scout Stillwell rushes over. "Here, let me pull off his boots, Doc. He never did like army boots. They hurt his feet and he always stated he didn't want to die with his boots on."

Once Doctor Moors finishes removing the arrow from Major Baker's side he attends the other wounded scouts and soldiers. Lieutenant Williams repairs the defenses as best he can. The emotions and fears of the soldiers and scouts is beginning to take its toll.

DAY FIVE

Exhaustion and fatigue are showing on the soldiers. Some are hard to wake even though it has been daylight for more than an hour. The nightly fights with the bugs are minor now, compared to the stench from the rotting bodies of horses and men. Even the dead soldiers have to be covered with sand to prevent the flies from congregating in overwhelming masses. Major Baker is still unconscious.

On this particular morning, the soldiers and scouts witness a somewhat different sight on the hills and bluffs. Although the drums continued to beat through the night and into the early morning, hundreds of Indian women have lined the ridges, separated only slightly from the warriors. Some carry papooses on their backs, others stand waving colored cloth and ribbons. It is quiet on both sides until the women begin to chant in unison.

"What the hell are they doing now?" asks Lieutenant Williams as he quickly turns to Jack Stillwell.

"It's a form of picnic, Lieutenant. The women have come because it's safe for them to do so ... and it gives them a rare opportunity to see their men win coup and honors in battle."

Lieutenant Williams lies back down in the sand for a moment as he thinks. He then props himself up and looks Stillwell in the eyes. "Are you afraid, Stillwell?"

"Damn right I am! Ever see what they do to a man after they kill 'em?"

Lieutenant Williams shudders for a second. "No. What do they do?"

"They mutilate the body so that the person will have to live that way in the spirit world. That's how they believe."

"Damn, Stillwell. Do you think we can get out of this alive?"

"Only if we can get word back to the fort. And that's the Major's decision. Whoever takes the risk of leaving this island with all those Injuns out there sure doesn't have good odds."

Stillwell notices that the chanting has stopped. "Well, Lieutenant. Looks like their gonna hit us again. You ready?"

"I don't know, Stillwell."

Again the tactics are the same. Indians on foot try to get close and pepper the patrol with arrows while the horse warriors ride on full frontal attacks shooting and yelling. The squaws start singing a high pitched trilling sound, "Yiyiyiyiyiyigiyiyiyiyiyiyiyiyi," that can be heard even above the sounds of gunfire and screams. The Indian attack is bold this time, as twelve reach the island itself and remain on their horses.

Quickly regrouping, the patrol switches firepower to its flank position as the Indians attack from the north end. Four reach the defensive position of the pits and jump off their horses to engage in hand to hand combat. One soldier takes a knife to the stomach as other soldiers fire into the Indian's back.

Doctor Moors, attempting to aid the soldier, takes a bullet in the side of the head and falls near Sergeant Waller, who just seconds before, shot the last Indian rider with his pistol.

"Lieutenant! Lieutenant! Stay down!" screams Sergeant Waller as he turns to see Lieutenant Williams staggering across the sand to Major Baker's pit.

Sergeant Waller checks the safety of his position and starts to move in the direction of the Lieutenant.

"I com'n, Lieutenant! Get down!"

It's then that Sergeant Waller sees the stunned and glazed-eyed look on Lieutenant Williams' face, blood running down the front of his uniform. He watches helplessly as Lieutenant Williams falls into Major Baker's defensive sand pit.

Sergeant Waller, putting his own life in jeopardy, crawls as fast as he can in the sand to the Lieutenant. He removes Major Baker's blanket and places it under Lieutenant Williams' head. "Be easy, Lieutenant. You make it. Just you hang on!"

Still semi-conscious, Lieutenant Williams opens his eyes and looks at Sergeant Waller for a moment. Being sure that he recognizes the Sergeant, he speaks in soft, low tones as he gasps for air. "I won't make it ... Sergeant. This is my death wound. Tell my wife ... I love her."

"You make it, Lieutenant! You make it. Hold on! Just rest." With both officers seriously wounded, Sergeant Waller takes command. The attack, although intense, is once again repelled, mainly due to the fierce fighting power of the Spencer rifles and the determined resistance to fight to the death on the part of the soldiers and scouts.

So far the attacks have been routine. One attack a day and in the early morning. The time between attacks gives both sides time to reassess what has taken place. For the soldiers and scouts it means continual re-fortification and rifle cleaning, and for the Indians, time to Council.

Sergeant Waller pulls Doctor Moors into the same pit as Major Baker and Lieutenant Williams. As acting commander of the soldiers and scouts, it becomes his job to make the decisions. He calls Trudeau, Stillwell, and Grover into the Major's pit.

"How the Major, Doc, and Lieutenant, Sergeant?" inquires Trudeau.

"Not good. Doc hit. Never been in command before. What you scouts think?"

"Well, let's hope the Major comes to soon. But either way, we'll never make it without someone getting off this island and git'n help," comments Stillwell.

Trudeau, sitting next to Lieutenant Williams, leans over to check on him. Suspecting something might be wrong, he puts his hand on Williams' chest. "Sergeant! I think Lieutenant dead."

Sergeant Waller becomes more frustrated. "He tell me last words. He say ... tell my wife I love her. Yo' all 'member dat!"

FORT WALLACE

It's later in the afternoon as Lieutenant Washington approaches Colonel Novak in front of the officer's day room. "Good afternoon, Colonel," greets Henry warmly.

"Good afternoon, Lieutenant."

"Sir. Have you any word on the patrol yet?"

"You mean Major Baker's?"

"Yes, Sir."

"Not yet, Lieutenant. But I'm still not real concerned. They were to go out for at least ten to twenty-one days. They left Hays City about ten days ago. The Major's got the best soldiers and scouts he can find. I'm sure they're okay."

Henry smiles slightly. "Thank you, Sir. If you hear anything will you let me know?"

"Sure will, Lieutenant."

DAY SIX

During the night, the soldiers and scouts, with the minimum of utensils, dig the pits as deep as they can without letting mud develop in the bottom. Shallow runways are also dug connecting most of the pits together for a quicker transfer of firepower without undue exposure to bullets and arrows.

The raw and rancid meat previously cut from the dead horses is now uneatable. The only form of nutrition sustenance left is the blood in the canteens. The sight of blood on the lips of the men is in itself gruesome.

Major Baker regains consciousness during the night and although in pain, is alert enough to resume his command. His pain is obvious, as he talks to Sergeant Waller and Scout Stillwell. "Never expected the Indians to be so well armed ... or so many."

Scout Stillwell, sweat dripping from his face from the humidity, responds quickly to the Major's statement. "Sir, they're the same tribe that trapped Captain Traman at Fort Kerny. They got all the army supplies and weapons."

Major Baker seems unconcerned about this. His mind is thinking in terms of getting help, realizing if he doesn't that they will all be slaughtered.

"Stillwell, we've got only one choice left. No matter what happens we can't last here much longer than two days. I need two volunteers to sneak off this island under cover of darkness. If I lose consciousness, you're in charge of the scouts, Sergeant Waller the soldiers."

Major Baker looks at the flies hanging around the bodies of Doctor Moors and Lieutenant Williams. "Sergeant Waller, put some more sand on those bodies. The smell is atrocious."

"Yes, Suh! Suh, 'fore I forget. Lieutenant Williams' last words is, "tell my wife I love her.""

"I'll remember that, Sergeant Waller."

Major Baker tries to shift positions to look at the bluffs and in doing so opens his wound.

Jack Stillwell, concerned for the Major's welfare, volunteers to help. "I'll get some cloth off a pair of pants, Major."

"What's the situation with the Indians, Stillwell?"

"They won't attack today, Sir. Seems they're having a serious powwow. Even the women are quiet. Must mean something."

"Now's the time, Stillwell. Sergeant Waller, call in all the scouts and men not on sentry. How many we got left?"

"Twelve dead, twenty-two wounded, Suh."

Stillwell gives a prearranged whistle signal and six soldiers and seven scouts crawl to the Major's pit.

Major Baker, weak and in pain, tells the men his assessment of the situation. "Men, we've only one chance left. To stay here without help means we all will either die of starvation or by an Indian weapon. I need to ask for two volunteers. Somehow we have to get word of our situation to Fort Wallace."

No one says a word for a moment as most of the men keep their heads in their hands, faces to the ground.

"I go!" booms Frenchy Trudeau. "If I get trouble I become invisible, ya?"

Jack Stillwell smiles, slaps Trudeau on the back. "I'll go with him," Stillwell adds. "We can do it, Major. We'll go tonight. Right, Frenchy?"

"Aye! We go tonight, Major."

Major Baker looks to both of them with a feeling of hope. "God speed both of you. And make sure you take your boots off ... they'll track you for sure."

"Know that, Major ... we leave tonight, Major."

At slightly past midnight, Scouts Trudeau and Stillwell slip quietly into the water on their bellies, weapons and ammunition wrapped tightly in leather and waterproof rain gear.

DAY SEVEN

Major Baker is weak from loss of blood, but his spirit picks up a bit with the absence of any Indians on the bluffs.

Sharp Grover and Sergeant Waller take turns on watch in the Major's pit. The night has been exceptionally quiet and a slight wind pushes aside much of the smell. Although there is no major force lining the bluffs, Indian warriors can be seen periodically riding on both sides of the river and crisscrossing sides further downstream.

Major Baker, although extremely exhausted, is alert as he questions Sharp Grover for information. "Grover, why do you think there's no preparation for an attack?"

"Don't know for sure, Major. But I have a suspicion they might be in serious council. We've held them off so far and they've taken some heavy casualties. My guess is there's some arguing going on."

"Why's that?"

"Well, Major, from my knowledge of these people they all have the right to do what they want. Not even a Chief can tell another warrior what to do, not even in battle. That's why they hit hard and if beaten back some just don't want to fight anymore that day. They're funny that way ... and very superstitious. They call is bad medicine."

Major Baker turns to Sergeant Waller. "How the wounded doing over there?"

"They hangin' on, Suh. Dey got some mor' fight in 'em."

Concerned, Major Baker turns back to Scout Grover. "Do you think Trudeau and Stillwell made it?"

"Hard to say, Sir. They may have. Know one thing for sure tho."

"What's that, Grover?"

"If they hadn't, the Sioux would be parad'n their scalps up and down those bluffs."

Later that day, five warriors ride at a fast gallop and rein their horses into a sliding stop in front of Two Crows' teepee, screaming. Two Crows, in council with Grey Bull, Spotted Tail, Dark Moon, and several of the Warrior Chiefs, halts his meeting for a moment, then steps outside.

The braves are excited and elated at their prize; a black, long haired scalp with a long red ribbon tied to it. "We have scalp of French Indian!" yells the brave who carries it. "Other white eye get away!"

The young brave tosses the scalp to Two Crows and the five ride away yelling and screaming.

Two Crows looks at it for a moment, but is more concerned about what the brave said about a white eye escaping. He returns into the lodge and sits down quietly. The other Elders look at him and the scalp in his hand, but ask nothing.

Two Crows remains quiet as he positions himself and looks at the scalp. He thinks for a moment, then speaks as he holds the scalp above his head with one hand. "This means that soldiers from fort will come. This man dead. Other escape."

Grey Bull then speaks. "This why we here? Warrior, Lone Wolf ... his heart not true! His medicine weak!"

Spotted Tail, who is usually quiet, is upset and speaks firmly. "Lone Wolf sit on hill many day now, like woman afraid! His vision no more. Take too long! Warriors now question leadership. All soldiers and scouts should be killed five suns ago!" He raises five fingers. "I say my words!"

Grey Bull speaks in a solemn, sincere voice. "You tell him this, Two Crows. His honor like sun setting ... about go dark."

Two Crows fully understands what the Elders are saying and the reason for their disappointment. "I go to him," confirms Two Crows. "I have bad feeling. He not take responsibility. My honor at stake."

Two Crows leaves the teepee with irritation and humiliation. As he rides his horse to the high hill he thinks of what he will say to Lone Wolf. Somehow he feels deceived by the words that come from Lone Wolf's mouth.

Lone Wolf sits on the hill overlooking a great distance and is chanting as Two Crows approaches. The sound of the horses hooves, although distinctly clear, does not move Lone Wolf.

Two Crows dismounts and leads his horse the final steps to Lone Wolf. Nothing is said. Finally Two Crows addresses him. "Braves who fight the white eyes wait for you. But here you sit. Why?"

Lone Wolf arches his back and sits up straight. His face is stone like, with no emotion. "My medicine good now. I have vision tonight. I lead all nations into battle. I kill all white eyes on island."

"I tell Council," concludes Two Crows as he wastes no time in remounting his horse. "Lone Wolf, look at me."

Lone Wolf turns slowly to the elder Chief. Two Crows throws Frenchy Trudeau's scalp onto his lap. "Here! Scalp good omen. You use!"

Lone Wolf looks at the scalp with disgust. Two Crows leans over his horse's neck slightly towards Lone Wolf. "You make peace with White Deer. She not your woman. She good woman."

Lone Wolf ignores the Elder Chief's comment and begins chanting. Two Crows, frustrated with Lone Wolf's indignation, spins his horse around and gallops toward the temporary encampment.

Lone Wolf, tired and becoming more exhausted, continues his vigil into the night. No moon appears, but the sky is clear with thousands of stars visible as Lone Wolf continues to seek his vision. He looks anxiously into the darkness calling on all his inner strength to find some truth in his purpose. Suddenly he sees a small flicker of light slowly coming toward him. His senses perk up as he focuses on the increasing size of a small ball of brightness approaching him from the distance. As the light draws continually closer and closer he sees the vague image of an Indian woman dressed in a white buckskin dress. Her long, black, braided hair is wrapped with colorful bands of beads. Her headband and wrist bracelets display precise decorations and symbols made of small beadwork. As she draws close to him he sees her dark brown eyes and perfect features. Her hands reach out to him as she begins to speak in a soft, musical voice.

"Lone Wolf! Behold me! Behold me! In sacred manner I come to you. I come to give your soul peace and understanding."

Lone Wolf stares at her intensely, as if in a trance. The woman continues to speak to him in a serene manner. "Lone Wolf, you remember me? I came to your people, the Ancient Ones, many, many moons ago. I gave your people the pipe of peace, that there be goodness and abundance among all."

Lone Wolf is attentive and eager to impress her as he sits straight and acts confident. He reaches out to touch her, but she slowly backs away.

The woman continues to speak to him in a tender way. "Lone Wolf! Lone Wolf, do you not recognize me? I am of your people. I am the Earth people. I am of the Sky people. Do you not recognize me?"

Lone Wolf tries to answer, but his voice is mute.

"I am White Buffalo Calf Woman. I come to you, Lone Wolf, that you may do good for your people. Do you not want to be a warrior of peace, Lone Wolf?"

Again Lone Wolf tries to answer, but he cannot. He can only listen as she continues to sway gently back and forth in front of him.

"Your destiny is before you, Lone Wolf. Listen to the teachings of your Elders, who are wise. Listen to the teachings of the Ancient Ones, who are universal. Listen to that part of your heart that is good. Listen to the voice of the Great Spirit that you may rid yourself of anger and hate."

Lone Wolf tries to reach his hand out to her again but his whole body is immobile.

"I leave you now, Lone Wolf. I leave you to your destiny. I leave you to your own heart."

Lone Wolf tries desperately to address her, but his voice and body cannot move. Only his eyes can see as he watches her slowly move away from him, then stop. His focus intensifies as he watches her slow transformation from the beautiful Indian Maiden into a white buffalo calf. The small white buffalo calf lingers for a moment, then slowly fades into the background of the stars and into the universe.

Lone Wolf, startled, quickly jumps to his feet, Frenchy Trudeau's scalp still in his right hand. He blinks his eyes, trying to focus into the darkness.

"Was she real?" he thinks to himself as he looks briefly at the scalp he is holding. Regaining his old composure, he tightens his grip on the scalp and begins to walk confidently back to the camp. Lone Wolf is unsure of what his mind has seen.

DAY EIGHT

The morning sun is already hot as the remaining soldiers and scouts prepare for attack. Many are wearing cloth wrappings around their noses stuffed with grass in an attempt to minimize the smell of rotting flesh. More sand is hand shoveled on top of the carcasses. It is ten o'clock in the morning and still there is no show of force by the attacking Indians, just several warriors who are seen riding the bluffs.

Major Baker lies exhausted, but conscious in his sand pit. Scout Grover sits next to him with his hands over his face talking to himself. The Major tries to pull himself upright, but falls back onto his side, wincing in pain. He addresses Scout Grover with some difficulty. "Grover, how many left?"

"Ten, Sir. Eighteen dead, twenty wounded, not including you. Seven seriously."

Major Baker's jaws tighten as he again tries to look over the top of his pit. "Damn this smell! Are all the dead covered?"

Scout Grover, his head resting in his hands, mumbles a dejected response. "Yes, Major, but who gives a damn?"

"Grover, if I pass out again, you know you're in charge."

Scout Grover mumbles a discouraging remark. "Ya, I know, Major."

"How long can we hold out?"

Scout Grover rubs his eyes and looks listlessly to the sky. "Don't know, Major. Maybe a day. We have little left to drink, nothing to eat, and maybe enough ammo left for one more attack."

Jack Stillwell's feet are raw and bloody as he limps toward Fort Wallace. His yells for help are heard by the sentries and relayed to the night Duty Officer who assembles a detail of men to assist Scout Stillwell into the post.

Colonel Novak is alerted that a scout from Major Baker's patrol is being brought in. Upon hearing this information Colonel Novak orders that Scout Stillwell be taken to the medical building and to inform the scout that he will be there as soon as he gets dressed.

Scout Stillwell, exhausted and excited, is soaking his feet in salt water as Colonel Novak walks in. Stillwell immediately begins to describe the emergency situation that exists only fifty-five miles to the west. "Ya gotta help them, Colonel! They can't last much longer, if'n they're not already dead!"

"I've got two companies preparing to ride now, but tell me what's happened."

Scout Stillwell, impatient and still in a semi-state of shock, relates his version of the attack and what has happened up to the time he left the island. "Frenchy and I got caught off guard by some Indian sentries, or whatever you call them, and he took a bullet in the leg! We knew the only chance for the men on the island was to get word back to you. It was getting dark and Frenchy stayed as a decoy while I snuck out through a small ravine filled with underbrush. I don't know if they got him or not. He's one mile straight east of the Arikara. You gotta get men out there, Colonel. Now! They been hold'n onto that island for eight days."

Colonel Novak turns to the night Duty Officer, Lieutenant Sandy, "Get Lieutenant Washington in here immediately!" He then turns back to Scout Stillwell. "Hate to ask you, Stillwell, but are you well enough to lead the troops back there?"

"Sure will, Colonel. Just get me a good horse!"

As Lieutenant Sandy pounds on Lieutenant Washington's door, Henry quickly responds. "Who is it?"

"Lieutenant Sandy! Got an emergency!"

As Henry opens the door, Lieutenant Sandy is frantic. "God, Henry! Major Baker's patrol was caught in an ambush. They're surrounded by hundreds of Sioux on some island on the branch of the Republican. Colonel wants to see you. Immediately!"

"How's Lieutenant Williams?"

"Don't know! Hurry up! Colonel's in the hospital building with Scout Stillwell."

"Be right there!" says Henry quickly as he turns to get his clothes and gear on.

"They'll tell you more when you get there!" yells Lieutenant Sandy as he rushes back to the hospital room.

"Lieutenant Washington's on his way, Colonel!" reports Lieutenant Sandy as he rushes into the hospital room.

Colonel Novak continues to question Scout Stillwell as he waits for Lieutenant Washington.

"How many Indians, Stillwell?"

"Don't know exactly, Colonel. Maybe five-hundred, maybe seven-hundred."

Henry rushes over to the hospital and comes through the door excited. "What's happened, Colonel?"

"Major Baker was ambushed on the Arikara. Take H and F Companies out there tonight. They've been alerted. Scout Stillwell will lead you. Prepare to leave immediately!"

Henry has a fearful look on his face. "Yes, Sir!" He looks to Scout Stillwell. "Stillwell, is Lieutenant Williams alright?"

Scout Stillwell is unsure how to answer this question as it might cause an emotional over-reaction on the part of Lieutenant Washington. "Don't know for sure, Sir. Just know he's been hit."

This statement raises Henry's cause for concern. "You ready to go, Stillwell?"

"Yes, Sir."

"Let's go!"

Henry doesn't wait for an answer from Scout Stillwell. "I'll be leaving immediately, Colonel."

It's still dark as the two companies of cavalry move out of Fort Wallace at a steady, fast trot. Lieutenant Washington knows that he has a long march ahead of him and to start out at a gallop will only tire the horses in the end. He knows it is a life and death situation, and it concerns him deeply that his best friend may be dead. He paces the men to the limit and luckily is guided by Scout Jack Stillwell.

DAY NINE

Major Baker is unconscious and Scout Grover and Sergeant Waller talk with little emotion.

"Sergeant, we have ten men left and don't know if Stillwell or Trudeau made it to Wallace." Scout Grover looks at the unsightly area and shakes his head. "This just may be our last fight, Sergeant. There still must be five to six hundred braves out there and they intend to hang our scalps from their lodges ... 'specially, they like Negro scalps."

Scout Grover laughs his nasal, snorkeling laugh. Sergeant Waller's reaction is mixed. He never seriously thought about being scalped before, but has heard of many atrocities done to captives by the Sioux prior to being outright killed.

"Hell, Grover," reacts Sergeant Waller, "yo' hair be so thin no one wont it for scalp." Sergeant Waller chuckles nervously at his own statement as his eyes pick up an Indian waving on the high bluff.

"Hey, Grover, look! Up dat bluff. Who dat be waving his rifle in de air?"

Grover spins around fast to look, then grabs the binoculars. 'Damn! Thought he was dead. Where the hell's he been?"

"What you talk'n 'bout?" questions Sergeant Waller.

"Lone Wolf! Shit! That's him! He's the main warrior!"

Suddenly hundreds of Indians line the bluffs, much like the first two days of the attack. Sergeant Waller looks to the eastern side of the river. "Grover! They's on dat side now!"

Grover yells to the men. "Get ready to fight to the death! They're gonna hit us hard!"

More than a half an hour goes by and the Indians just stand with mounts in their positions above the river. No one on either side makes a sound or moves from their position.

Sergeant Waller is openly becoming more nervous as the quietness continues. "What dey wait'n fo'?" His eyes open wide as he freezes still and stares. Without moving his head he taps Scout Grover on the shoulder and quietly whispers, his voice trembling. "Grover, look! Der's more of dem!"

The scouts lay in the small pits, first looking to the bluffs on the west, then to the ones on the east. Lone Wolf has brought all braves to the forefront with no reserves holding back.

Sergeant Waller grabs the binoculars to look at Lone Wolf. "Grover ... Grover! What Lone Wolf be wavin' on his rifle?"

Grover quickly takes the binoculars and focuses in on Lone Wolf. "Shit! Shit! Shit! He got Ol' Pete's scalp! That bastard. That sons-a-bitch! They scalped Trudeau!"

Scout Grover is frantic and enraged. Sergeant Waller then takes a look. "Dey got his scalp for sure! I see de red cloth he tied in his hair." Sergeant Waller puts the binoculars down slowly, afraid and shaken by the sight of Scout Trudeau's scalp. He turns to Scout Grover. "Grover, if dey overrun us, you kill me quick! Don't want me no Scalp'n'!"

The men wait and wait. The tension mounts with each minute as the Indian warriors continue to look down upon them.

Suddenly there is a loud single shot and all the soldiers and scouts cower down instinctively. Then all is again quiet.

At first the men wonder where the shot came from, but they quickly understand as they see Sergeant Waller lying dead, next to his pistol, a pool of blood forming near his head.

Just as abruptly their attention turns to the sound of an army bugle charge, the familiar sound of Boots and Saddles. The remaining nine men look toward the south end of the river and see the distant flicker of a swallow-tailed Cavalry flag.

Grover grabs the binoculars and looks. His eyes can't believe it as he sees the colors of Companies H and F and several hundred black soldiers charging down the riverbanks. He yells, "They're here! You men! Look! They're here! Look at all those beautiful white teeth shining in those black faces!" All nine men are standing and yelling, waving, and jumping up and down.

Lieutenant Washington and his two companies are at full gallop through Indian lines and only slow down as they turn into the river to approach the island.

The Indians on the bluffs don't move, but stare in awe at the sight of these freshly arrived, well armed troops. Two Crows, Grey Bull, and Dark Moon sit on the opposite side of the river where Lone Wolf watches, what is even to him, a spectacular sight. Two Crows' face is emotionless, but he is inwardly churning and upset as he turns to the two Elder Chiefs. "Buffalo Soldiers! Many rifles! Much firepower! Too good medicine! We not fight today."

Two Crows does not raise his standard high to indicate attack. He turns to Grey Bull and Dark Moon. "Lone Wolf not follow his vision. His good medicine no more. He not lead warriors on first day and he not lead warriors this day. Today time for last talk at council."

Two Crows spins his horse around and rides to the lead warrior under Lone Wolf who was to lead the braves on that side of the river. "No fight today. Tell Lone Wolf to be in Council when sun is high."

The warrior rides to the north to gain safe crossing as Two Crows looks across the river to the western bluffs. There he sees Lone Wolf galloping back and forth. Disgusted, he talks in a loud, firm voice and points across the river. "Look! Lone Wolf has no guidance from Wankan Tonkan. He act like child."

Two Crows instructs the other warriors that they should continue to watch the soldiers below, but not fight. He knows there will be one last chance for a battle, for his warriors are ready and still out number the soldiers almost ten to one.

The nine scouts and soldiers are cheering wildly as Lieutenant Washington and his men ride onto the island. Sharp Grover runs up to him excited, but Henry, in an emotional mood, is first more concerned about what he sees around him on the island, and secondly, what he can observe strategically on the bluffs. Henry orders Sergeant Thomas to set up temporary picket lines for the horses. He then addresses Scout Grover in a firm voice. "Where's Lieutenant Williams ... Major Baker?"

"The Major's in the pit over there, and the Lieutenant is buried next to it ... under the sand, Sir."

Henry rushes to Major Baker's pit, calling Company F's contract doctor as he goes. He kneels next to Major Baker and quickly tries to comfort him. "You'll be okay, Major. A doctor is coming now."

Major Baker, barely conscious, grabs Henry's hand firmly. Henry looks to the many mounds of sand covering the bodies of the dead.

"Grover! Which one's Lieutenant Williams?"

"Twenty yards to your right, Lieutenant."

Henry gently puts the Major's hand down and scrambles over the sand pit to a mound of sand covering Lieutenant Williams' body. He begins to dig frantically with his bare hands. As Lieutenant Williams' bloated face appears, Henry pulls back in horror. The ghastly sight of his friend is more than he can bear. Henry reels back onto his feet as he stares at his close friend.

Sergeant Thomas runs toward Henry from the side and sees the hurt and pain on his face. He looks at the Lieutenant's dead body, then turns to Lieutenant Washington. "Sorry, Suh. I'se knows he yar bestest friend."

Henry shows no emotion as tears start forming at the corners of his eyes. After several moments Henry takes a deep breath and tries to regain his composure. He slowly turns to Sergeant Thomas and looks at him helplessly.

Sergeant Thomas feels compassion as he begins to talk softly. "Try git yo' self t'gether, Lieutenant. Dey's nothin' to do fo' him now. Dey's still a buncha dem Injuns out on dem bluffs, and we has gotta deal with 'em."

Henry starts to cry. Sergeant Thomas immediately shakes him lightly. "Suh! We needs a fortify dis island! Dey'll be 'nother attack, so what be yo' orders?"

Henry takes another deep breath, shakes his head, and wipes his eyes. He turns to Sergeant Thomas. "You're right, Sergeant! Secure the area, make sure the horses are tied securely." Henry takes one last glance at his friend then covers Lieutenant Williams' face with sand.

"Who's been in command here?" yells Henry.

"I have," comes the voice of Scout Grover.

"Starting now, Scout, you take orders from me. Take care of those men that have survived this ordeal. Give them some blankets and food from the pack horses."

"Sergeant Thomas! When you're done with the horses have the men cut all this tall grass. It obstructs our view if they get on this island, and we need to burn those damn awful dead horses. And, Sergeant, make sure each man has one-hundred rounds of ammunition and a clean rifle!"

The Indian camp is quiet as most of the warriors are on or near the river bluffs. It is common knowledge that there will be one more massive and final attack, for not only are the braves themselves becoming discouraged, but there is the question among the warriors of Lone Wolf's true leadership ability.

This evening Two Crows, Grey Bull, Spotted Wolf, Dark Moon, Lone Wolf, and three of the Warrior Society sit in Council. Their mood is solemn and serious. Two Crows begins. "There many Buffalo Soldiers now. We fought the white eye scouts and soldiers for nine suns, no victory."

Two Crows looks to each member of the council, then turns to Lone Wolf. He speaks in a firm, soft tone. "Lone Wolf! You disappoint me. You act like scared old woman, then like foolish boy. You avoid responsibility ... leave fighting decision to the Elders."

He takes a small red colored rock from his personal leather pouch and holds it up for all to see. "The Great Spirit has given me many things in life to warm my heart, including this sacred rock, which holds the blood of many warriors." Two Crows hesitates, firmly fixing his eyes on it before he continues to speak. "This rock tell me many things. It hold both good and bad medicine for all Indian people. It ... Mother Earth ... sacred to me." Two Crows hesitates again, then begins a brief chant. "Hey-Hey-R-R-R-Hey-Hey, Hey-R-Hey-Hey-Hey-R, Heeeya."

When he is finished he places his other hand on the rock and slowly presents it in the four cardinal directions: north, south, east, and finally west. He puts the rock gently down on a piece of cloth in front of him. He turns toward Lone Wolf and speaks in his low, gentle, but firm tone of voice. "This your time, Lone Wolf. Your medicine bad. Warriors that follow you, let them. That their choice. I have spoken."

Two Crows looks to Grey Bull who speaks his turn. Grey Bull raises a three-foot wood stem and red stone peace pipe, decorated with fox fur, glass beads, leather, and fine braided horsehair wrappings. He looks to Lone Wolf and holds the pipe above his head as he begins to speak. "Wankan Tonkan, the pipe, the stem our backbone, the bowl our head, the stone our blood, red like our skin. The sacred pipe good medicine brought to us by Buffalo Calf Woman."

Grey Bull gently lays the pipe on a piece of soft, white buckskin. He chants briefly before addressing Lone Wolf. "Lone Wolf. See with the eyes of your heart, not with the eyes of your head. If you cannot lead the Sioux and Cheyenne warriors to victory against the Buffalo Soldiers, tell us now. Your truth before you."

Lone Wolf, feeling alienated, says nothing as he picks up his six-foot battle Standard of many feathers. He stands erect before the Council, looking each of them in the eyes. He turns and stoops as he walks out of the teepee. The Elder chiefs look at each other in silence.

"Let him go!" speaks Two Crows firmly.

As some of the younger, more hotheaded warriors see Lone Wolf, they yell his name. Most run to their horses which are painted for battle, mount, galloping around him and the camp? The excitement and yelling is contagious as more of the braves who are not manning the bluffs, join in. Lone Wolf walks among them proud and defiant.

Observing Lone Wolf's behavior and actions is White Deer. She still carries the hatred and animosity she feels for Lone Wolf in her heart. After years of abuse and despair at the hands of Lone Wolf she knows him well. She has waited for this moment for a long time.

This opportunity couldn't have been planned better if I'd done it myself, she thinks as she watches Lone Wolf display his egotistical mannerisms and vocal statements to the young warriors. She becomes even more resentful as she watches White Hawk scream and yell as he rides his black horse back and forth in front of his father.

During the years she has been in the village she has observed Lone Wolf's traits and behaviors. She is not only aware of his strong ego, but his serious belief in superstition. As far as the Warrior Society goes, she knows they believe that anything a woman touches which is considered personally sacred brings bad medicine to that warrior.

It is common knowledge that her argument with Lone Wolf earlier has affected his self-esteem, and she knows now that he is to lead the warriors in the next day's battle or lose face forever within the tribe.

As she gazes steadily at Lone Wolf among the braves, she concludes that touching his war lance will be an unforgivable act, possibly even her death. But her feeling of antagonism for him is so strong that even death will be a friend if she can destroy him. All she has to do is touch his lance in public view of others. With this thought in mind she walks to Two Crows' lodge to find out what time the warriors will leave for the morning attack.

DAY TEN

At sunrise the warriors begin to paint their faces and check their equipment. Most of the women are walking to the bluffs to watch with much anticipation the destruction of the army soldiers.

White Deer remains in the village with the mounted Indian braves as they ride around the village displaying their daring acts and waiting for Lone Wolf to appear from his lodge. White Deer knows, as Lone Wolf has always done, that he will place his lance in the ground as a rallying point for his followers. This will be her time.

As predicted, Lone Wolf walks out of his teepee dressed with the attire for battle; buckskin pants and moccasins, armbands, and a leather head band that secures four eagle feathers. His hair is tightly braided on both sides and an arrow quiver and bow are strapped on his back. In his left hand he carries a repeating rifle of six shots and in his right hand, the symbol of his past feats ... the six-foot lance with Frenchy Trudeau's scalp. He waves the lance at the several hundred warriors who greet him, and as tradition dictates, he jabs it into the ground.

White Deer has been waiting for him to do this, but normally he would guard it from anyone's touch, especially that of a woman. However, this day, in Lone Wolf's mind, is to be his greatest. He gets caught up in his ego and the yelling, screaming braves. As he briefly moves away from his lance to shake hands and talk with the surrounding warriors, White Deer makes her way quietly and swiftly toward the war lance.

Lone Wolf's instincts suddenly make him aware that he has moved too far away from his coveted battle standard, and he turns to walk back to retrieve it. His body freezes in horror as he sees White Deer standing less than ten feet from him, holding his prized lance. Lone Wolf, seized with anger, lunges at White Deer with his knife. White Deer backs away with the quickness of a fox and stands defensively with the sharp point of the war lance pointed at Lone Wolf.

All and every activity of the braves stops instantly. The complete village is quiet as the warriors watch with startled skepticism the white Indian woman holding the battle standard. No one moves for a good minute as brave looks at brave and then back to Lone Wolf and White Deer.

Lone Wolf is furious and screams at White Deer. "I kill you! I eat your heart as food!"

White Deer screams. "You bad medicine!"

She throws the lance on the ground and attempts to run toward Two Crows' lodge. Lone Wolf steadies his knife and throws it hard, sticking it deep into the back of White Deer. She falls to the ground as if she has been hit by a thunderbolt, dead.

Embarrassed and wanting instant revenge, Lone Wolf becomes confused. Should he lead his warriors to war or cut up a dead hostile woman? His choice is obvious, especially in view of so many of his men. "We ride to battle now!" he yells as he picks up his lance and leaps on his horse.

The enthusiasm of the braves is nowhere near what it had been minutes before. Some braves elect to remain in the village. The doubt, based on strong superstition of Lone Wolf's bad medicine, has now been established. White Deer's action has done what she has wanted it to do ... create doubt in the minds of the warriors as to Lone Wolf's ability, and more so, create doubt and superstitious fear in the mind of Lone Wolf himself.

Lone Wolf rides out to the bluffs at a full gallop followed by loyal braves.

The fresh troops on the island have beefed up all defensive positions and cleared all avenues of possible rifle fire from obstruction.

Sergeant Thomas has done an excellent job of placing the soldiers at all edges of the island. The only way that the attackers can gain a foothold will be to overrun one of the heavily fortified positions.

Henry is looking through his binoculars and surveying the Indian movements on the bluffs when he sees Lone Wolf ride to the front of the positioned warriors. It is obvious to Henry who Lone Wolf is just by his actions of galloping back and forth in front of the warriors.

"There he is! That's Lone Wolf himself up there!" yells Henry to Sergeant Thomas. "He's trying to get them fired up for battle!" Henry keeps following Lone Wolf back and forth until suddenly he sees something that interests him and quits following the Indian warrior leader.

"There he is again!" yells Henry loudly.

"Who? Lone Wolf?" responds Sergeant Thomas.

"No! That light skinned brave. He almost looks like he should be a white man."

"Let'n me look, Lieutenant."

Henry hands Sergeant Thomas the glasses and points at the spot on the bluff.

"Yup! He shur 'enouff do. He luk like a white man if'in' I 'er see one." Sergeant Thomas hands the glasses back to Henry, who takes a second look.

"He's positioned right behind Lone Wolf now. Looks like he's going to run right after him on the attack."

"They startin' ta move now, Lieutenant! Best git de men ready."

"Go ahead, Sergeant. I want to keep my eye on this Lone Wolf."

Sergeant Thomas gets up and quickly checks all positions and gives the men Lieutenant Washington's battle instructions, then returns to his pit next to Henry.

Word has spread quickly among the Indian warriors about what has happened back in camp. In fact, even before Lone Wolf gets to the bluffs, several of White Hawk's close friends have already ridden out to tell him the story.

White Hawk, although well trained and taught by Lone Wolf, still has affection for his mother. What Lone Wolf has done immediately confuses and enrages the young warrior. As White Hawk follows closely behind Lone Wolf his resentments begin to build. Not only has Lone Wolf violated the tribal tradition of letting a woman touch his lance, an indication of bad medicine, but he has killed his mother for the deed. White Hawk's irritation with Lone Wolf grows into hate and animosity as he watches Lone Wolf parade as if nothing has happened. White Hawk's emotional state is beginning to boil as he thinks of revenge against Lone Wolf. He does not deserve to live any longer. He does not deserve to lead this attack, are the thoughts turning over and over in White Hawk's mind. However, fear and consequences of his acts stop White Hawk from putting an arrow in Lone Wolf at this moment.

Henry is still observing from his position on the island when he sees Lone Wolf raise his lance. "Any moment now, men! Ready your carbines!" commands Henry.

Finally Lone Wolf raises his war lance high for all to see on both sides of the river and thrusts it forcefully to the ground. He screams and heads down the embankment at a full gallop, immediately followed by White Hawk and hundreds of other screaming and yelling warriors.

From both sides it is like a suicide race to see who can get to the water and onto the island first. The noise of pounding hooves sounds like thunder amid the dust and screams.

"Ready carbines! Wait for my command!" screams Henry, with a sense of confidence in himself and hate toward the warriors. As the Indians converge on the river they spread out and come in from all sides, firing as they hit the water at a gallop, creating thousands of large splashes. The water slows the horses, but they keep on surging forward.

Henry and all the men are split seconds away from firing as the Indian horses slow down in the water. Henry times his volley right on the second. "Fire at will!" he yells.

The sound of eighty-plus carbines blast like a large cannon on the first volley. Round after round hit the attacking force. Both Indians and soldiers are being hit by flying bullets from cross fires and stray shots. Horses are falling almost every minute, Indian horses in the river and army horses on the island stake line. Men and horses are screaming in pain and the rifle power is deafening.

Lone Wolf survives the barrage of bullets and is the first to reach the island. His horse stumbles slightly and regains its footing. Lone Wolf hangs on and adjusts his reins, pulling the horse in a hundred-eighty-degree spin. As he legs his horse into an immediate gallop, Lone Wolf collides with one of his own men. The island is now swarming with Indians, some already into hand-to-hand combat with the soldiers. The battle is becoming an onslaught on both sides, but the many dead or wounded horses in the river slow the attacking warriors from completely over-whelming the island.

Lone Wolf spins his horse around again as he recognizes the gold bars of Lieutenant Washington, the Army Soldier Chief. Lone Wolf jabs his heels sharply into his horse's sides and heads for Henry.

Sergeant Thomas, trying to reload his rifle, sees Lone Wolf charge. "Lieutenant! Behind yo'!"

Henry turns quickly as he sees Lone Wolf less than thirty feet away, charging toward him and firing off two rounds, both zinging by Henry's head. It is a matter of split seconds as Henry is about to fire when suddenly Lone Wolf slumps to his horse's neck. The movement of his horse carries him within feet of Henry and throws Lone Wolf into the sand just beyond Henry's pit.

Henry immediately lays prone and aims at Lone Wolf, but something stops Henry from pulling the trigger. Lone Wolf does not move. All the Indians that have observed the falling of Lone Wolf stop fighting and immediately retreat. Within five minutes all the firing stops and most of the Indians return to the shoreline out of fire or on the bluffs, looking at Lone Wolf lying in the sand, dead.

Henry is extra cautious as he orders his men to remain in their positions. After a few minutes he slowly gets to his feet and looks around. Henry's first intent is to make sure Lone Wolf is in fact dead, not just wounded or faking.

Sergeant Thomas, rifle still ready, yells out. "Take care, Lieutenant! May be a trick!" Sergeant Thomas slowly stands up to survey the situation. As he looks around, he lets out with an exhausted sigh. He calls to the squad leaders as he watches Henry moving toward the body of Lone Wolf.

"Git count of de dead 'n wounded!" Sergeant Thomas continues to look around. Then his eyes become fixed. Under the body of another Indian not far from Lieutenant Washington's pit is the body of the white warrior he had seen through the binoculars. Sergeant Thomas carefully walks around other dead warriors to get to this one. As he turns the body over, he sees it is just a young boy, maybe sixteen-years-old. What strikes Sergeant Thomas as unusual is the young warrior has deep blue eyes. Sergeant Thomas is standing approximately thirty feet from Henry when he yells, "Sir! Des here boy might be intrestin' to yo'!"

"Be there in a minute, Sergeant. Scout Grover! Get me the after battle report!"

Henry confirms that Lone Wolf is in fact dead. But what is strange, he thinks, is that Lone Wolf has a bullet hole in the upper middle of his back which almost blew his heart out of his chest. A straight on, dead center shot, Henry thinks to himself. Henry continues to re-think those few seconds when Lone Wolf had shot at him. I know I didn't pull the trigger on him. The bullet came straight from behind.

Henry, puzzled how a bullet could have entered Lone Wolf from his back, continues to analyze the strange event. There were no soldiers behind him. Only the river and other attacking warriors. Surely his own men wouldn't have accidentally shot him, he was too well identifiable. And most of his warriors were to his left and right flanks.

Henry calls Sergeant Thomas over and asks him his opinion. "Well, Suh, de is only dem two dead Injuns o'er der 'tween de riv'r an us'n. Dat white Injun and a regular Injun. Way I fig're, one 'o dem musta shot de Lone Wolf chief by accs'dent. Dat's only way cain be, Suh!"

Henry shakes his head in amazement as he thinks to himself. "Damn! How lucky can I be? Lone Wolf might have gotten one or two more shots at me if he hadn't been hit from behind, and by one of his own men."

Henry takes a deep breath and a hearty sigh of relief before he turns back to the matter at hand. "Sergeant Thomas, check and see if the Major is still unconscious and tell all the squad leaders to come to my pit."

As Sergeant Thomas and eight squad leaders assemble around Lieutenant Washington's sand pit, Henry begins to review the battle and give further orders.

Most of the Indian warriors have retreated back to the bluffs and remain at a distant vigilance.

Henry, in preparation for another possible attack, scans the bluffs with the binoculars. He recognizes Two Crows by his long war bonnet and war lance with a trail of eagle feathers. Henry knows that each eagle feather represents a brave deed and thus, the person he is looking at has to be the Elder Chief, Two Crows.

What an impressive looking man! It would be an honor just to sit down with him and talk, thinks Henry.

Henry watches the actions of Two Crows for a good five minutes. He sees Two Crows lift his war lance high in the air. Henry's reaction is instinctive as he yells, "They're preparing to attack!" Henry keeps his glasses focused on the Chief, waiting for him to throw the lance into the ground as the signal to assault the island. Henry keeps looking and waiting for the lance to drop, but Two Crows keeps holding it above his head, waving it slowly back and forth. "What's he doing?" Henry wonders silently.

Two Crows continues to wave his lance in a non-vertical manner.

Finally Henry calls out for Jack Stillwell. "Stillwell! What's he doing up there?"

Stillwell looks. "Let me have your glasses, Sir. I can't really tell what he's do'n'." Scout Stillwell looks briefly, then turns to Henry and smiles as he puts the glasses down.

Henry, being somewhat anxious, waits for Stillwell's answer. "Well, Stillwell? What's so humorous?"

"He's calling for a cease fire, Sir! He wants a temporary peace."

"How do you know that?"

"He's wavin' his lance horizontally to the ground. It's not vertical. He's indicating to us and his warriors he has no intention of throwing it down ... or to give the signal to attack, Sir!"

"Be careful, Lieutenant. May be trickin' you," interjects Sergeant Thomas.

As Henry is talking, a warrior rides off the bluff displaying a white flag at the tip of his rifle. Within a few minutes he pulls his horse to a stop at the river's edge.

Henry, concerned at what is taking place turns back to Scout Stillwell. "Is this what I think it is?"

"I believe so, Sir," replies Scout Stillwell. "Want me to ride out and talk to him? It looks like he has a message from Two Crows."

Henry, heeding Sergeant Thomas' advice, looks around the bluffs. He turns to Scout Stillwell and talks seriously. "Go ahead, Stillwell. We'll stay alert here and cover you, just in case. Hope this is what it appears to be."

"I think it is, Lieutenant," adds Stillwell as he gets up and limps to his horse. Scout Stillwell's feet obviously bother him as he struggles to mount. Henry watches him on the river's edge with a feeling of hope and anxious anticipation as he talks with the Indian warrior.

It isn't more than ten minutes when Scout Stillwell breaks from his meeting and walks his horse back through the river. Henry's emotions in anticipation of peace are vacillating between hope and despair.

Henry stands up and walks a few feet toward Scout Stillwell as he approaches. Henry's face is stone-like as he confronts the scout. "What'd he say, Stillwell?"

Scout Stillwell looks at Henry seriously. He shakes his head back and forth for what seems to Henry like too long a time.

"What the hell did he say, Stillwell?"

Scout Stillwell winks at Henry, then breaks into a big smile. "To stop the fight, Sir! They want to know if the Buffalo Soldiers will allow them to pick up their dead warriors. Two Crows wants no more fighting today. They simply want to bring their dead warriors back with them. They have to give them a ceremony so they can go to the Spirit world peacefully. Oh! And Two Crows wants your promise that today they may go in peace. That the Buffalo Soldier Chief, I think he's referring to you, Sir, will promise this."

Henry thinks only briefly before he concurs. "I can certainly agree to that, Stillwell. We've got the same problem here as they do. Ride back and tell the messenger to tell Two Crows he has my word."

"I'll do that, Sir! You bet I will! Oh! And, Sir, Two Crows also says he sends his respect to the soldiers and scouts who died on this island."

"I don't know how to respond to that, Stillwell. I suppose that statement is just part of his culture. Just insure him I don't want to fight anymore today either!"

"Yes, Sir!"

Stillwell rides back to the brave. They talk briefly, then the brave rides up the bluff to Two Crows' position. Henry watches closely through his binoculars.

Two Crows yells to his followers and raises his war lance horizontally. He holds this position as all the Indian warriors slowly turn their horses away from the river and disappear from sight. Once all the Indians have left the bluffs, Two Crows slowly and systematically lowers his lance. He then raises his right hand, holds it momentarily, as a symbol of a salute. This done, he grabs his reins, turns his horse, and slowly disappears from the bluff.

Henry lets out a sigh. "It's over!" he yells to his men. "Let's get ready to leave! Squad leaders! Front and center!"

Henry presents his instructions for carrying of the dead and wounded and the preparations for evacuation. Once this is done he walks over to the doctor attending Major Baker. "How's the Major, Doctor?"

"Conscious. He'll live."

"I'd like to talk with him for a bit."

"See no problem with that, Lieutenant. Just make it as brief as you can. He's had one hell of an ordeal."

Henry sits down next to Major Baker. "How you doing, Major?"

He responds in a weak voice, but is able to smile slightly. "Okay, Lieutenant. Thank God you got here. Sorry about Lieutenant Williams. He was a brave officer."

Henry's eyes water at the name of his friend. "I know, Sir."

"Lieutenant, before he died he conveyed to several of the men a message."

"What's that, Major?"

"His last words were that he loved his wife. I think it would be appropriate if you were the one to tell her."

Henry, tears in his eyes, thinks about this. "I'll do that, Sir." Henry takes a deep breath. "I sure will."

The troops on the island make their final preparations to make the trip back to Fort Wallace, as the Indian warriors are making preparations for returning their dead back to their village.

Suddenly there is the distant sound of hundreds of drums. All the soldiers stop their activity and look to the western bluffs. Every soldier on the island who is able, watches as they see not warriors line the bluffs, but hundreds of women who start to lament. Their grieving sounds fill the air and the drums beat louder and louder.

Sergeant Thomas, carrying a military map vaguely outlining the Republican River and the Arikara tributary, walks over to Henry. "Suh, what dey call dis island? Don' see it no place on dis map."

Henry, fighting his feelings of Fred's death, thinks for a moment and looks to the bluffs. He puts his hand on Sergeant Thomas' shoulder and answers in an emotional, soft tone of voice, "Call this island Williams' Island, Sergeant Thomas. This is ... Williams' Island!"

CHAPTER NINETEEN
A SAD GOODBYE

As do the Indians, Lieutenant Washington orders his men to cut long poles and make travois' to carry their dead and wounded back to Fort Wallace. It is an unusual sight to see; two warring factions periodically intermingling in a quasi-peace to carry their dead warriors across the river. The only sounds are the thud, thud, thud of distant drums and the eerie wailing of the lamenting women on the bluffs.

It is 7:30 p.m., the day after the soldiers have left Williams' Island, that the column approaches within seven miles of Fort Wallace. Lieutenant Washington, quiet and depressed, turns the patrol and travois of dead and wounded over to Sergeant Thomas. "Bring the men in Sergeant. We're only a few miles out now. I'm going to ride in ahead and brief the Colonel."

"Will do that, Suh! Be follow'n right behind, Suh."

Although these are Henry's intentions, his real motive is to somehow break the news to Lynda. He feels that it is his responsibility to do this, and aching with the pain he holds in his heart, he also feels the need to grieve.

Henry rides at a full gallop into the fort at 7:50 p.m., slide stopping his horse in front of Colonel Novak's headquarters. Everyone in view of his entrance stops to stare.

"What happened out there?" yells Lieutenant Sandy from across the parade grounds.

"Tell you later," responds Henry as he quickly ties his horse to the hitching post and rushes into Colonel Novak's office, surprising him.

"My gosh, Lieutenant! What's happened? Where's the rest of your patrol?"

Frustrated and tired, Henry tries to explain the incident as quickly as possible.

"Slow down, son! Take a deep breath and get yourself together," consoles Colonel Novak.

Henry, in a semi-state of shock, stutters as he tries to explain, but just can't make any kind of report that makes sense.

"Lieutenant!" retorts Colonel Novak. "Calm down! That's an order!"

Somehow this statement takes effect on Henry's emotions. "They're com'n' in now, Sir, maybe five miles out! Lot of dead and wounded! Lieutenant Williams was killed, so was the Doc! Major Baker's seriously wounded! It is ..."

"Lieutenant! Which direction? Where they coming from?"

"Northwest, Sir," replies Henry, as Colonel Novak puts his gear and hat on. Henry, still emotional, continues to talk. "They should be in here soon! We had to make travois, Sir ... to pull them on ... like Indians."

Colonel Novak, obviously upset, yells for his aide. "Orderly! Orderly! Sound a general call!"

"Okay, now, Lieutenant. Try to calm yourself. Help will be on its way."

Henry's thoughts turn to Lieutenant Williams; the sight of him lying in the sand, face bloated, and dead.

"Sir! Let me brief you later. I've got to tell Lynda before they bring them in. Please, Sir!"

Colonel Novak hesitates at this request. Not because he doesn't empathize with their friendship, but it visibly seems to him that Henry is too emotionally shocked to convey such a sad message. "I don't know, Lieutenant. You're not in very good condition, emotionally or physically."

"I have to do it, Sir! Fred's last words were to tell her that he loved her. I've got to be the one to tell her."

Colonel Novak, an empathetic man, thinks about Henry's emotional state and how this in itself will affect Lynda. This incident brings back memories of a time during the Civil War in which he was in the same situation. Finally he walks over to Henry, puts his hand on Henry's shoulder and looks into his eyes. "I think I know how you feel, son. Go ahead. I'll take care of the situation outside. Be gentle. She's not going to take this well."

"I will, Sir. And thank you."

Henry starts moving toward the door as the Colonel calls to him. "Take your time, son. You can report later."

Henry nods and immediately leaves for Lynda Williams' quarters. During the five-minute walk to the Officer's Quarters section of the post, Henry reflects quickly in his mind all the moments of his friendship with Fred. Suddenly he realizes that it's really real. He has to tell Lynda that Fred is dead.

"How am I going to tell her this?" he thinks as he knocks on her door.

"Who is it?" Lynda questions.

Henry responds in a choking, low voice. "Henry, Lynda."

"Oh! Henry! I'll be right there," responds Lynda in a jovial, lighthearted manner.

Henry stands outside shaking, waiting for Lynda to open the door.

"Just one moment," says Lynda again, just before she opens the door and sees Henry. Lynda is shocked at Henry's dirty, unkept appearance. "My gosh, Henry! What's happened to you? You look terrible! Come inside … is something wrong?"

Henry doesn't respond as he walks in the door, but his behavior sends a sudden shudder of fear through Lynda.

"God, no! You didn't come hear for that did you? Please, Henry! Tell me Fred is still alive!"

Henry shakes as he looks down, his hands clasp each other tightly as he slowly looks up to Lynda with tears in his eyes.

"No! No, Henry! It isn't true! Please tell me it isn't true!" cries Lynda as she shakes Henry's coat lapels.

Henry stands there, not knowing what to do or what to say.

"Oh, God, Henry! Why him? Why him? We had so many plans."

"I'm sorry, Lynda. I'm sorry I have to be the one to tell you." Henry begins to choke as he talks. "His ... his last words were ... to tell you, Lynda ... that he loved you."

Lynda is hysterical and out of control with grief. Her sobs are interrupting any words that she tries to say. Finally Henry puts his arms around her and speaks softly. "He was gone when I got there, Lynda."

Lynda stops sobbing momentarily. Wiping the tears from her eyes she looks to Henry. "Take me to the hospital quarters. That's where they'll take everyone isn't it, Henry? I want to see him."

Henry is shocked that Lynda would ask this realizing the condition of most of the bodies. "Lynda," he says sympathetically, "I don't think you want to go there."

"Why, Henry?" Lynda asks between sobs and sniffles. "Why?"

"It's just not the place to go, especially now."

"Then I'll go there myself."

Henry doesn't want to tell her the condition of Fred's body. It is still etched in his own mind how terrible he looked.

"Lynda, wait until tomorrow, please."

"I can't, Henry. I'm going now."

Henry tries to convince her it's not a good time, but Lynda rushes out the door and runs to the post hospital. Henry rushes after her to little avail.

Once there, she witnesses the soldiers unloading the dead and wounded. She stops for a moment to look. It is then that Colonel Novak approaches her from the side. "It's not a pretty sight, Lynda. Best you wait. It's not just Fred in there, but many other soldiers."

Henry walks up to join Lynda and Colonel Novak. "Please listen to the Colonel, Lynda. This is not the right time."

"I don't care! I'm going in!" Lynda, determined and forceful enters the crowded hospital room. There she sees more than sixty men lying wounded or dead, some on the floor, others on old wooden dining hall tables. Colonel Novak and Lieutenant Washington follow immediately behind her. Colonel Novak knows she is determined to see Fred's body and decides to let her do so. He calls for the officer in charge. "Lieutenant! Lieutenant Mercer!"

Lieutenant Mercer immediately comes to Colonel Novak's position. "Yes, Sir! How can I help you, Sir?"

"Lieutenant, this is Lieutenant Williams' wife."

"Yes, Sir! I know." Lieutenant Mercer turns to Lynda, "I'm sorry, Mrs. Williams."

Lynda doesn't acknowledge the condolences as she looks around for what might appear to be Fred's body.

"Lieutenant, take Mrs. Williams to her husband's body."

Lieutenant Mercer at first hesitates. "Ah, yes, Sir! If that's what you want, Sir!"

"That's what I want, Lieutenant."

Lieutenant Mercer gently addresses Lynda. "Mrs. Williams, Ma'am ... if you will come with me." Lieutenant Mercer and Lynda walk slowly around the tables of the dead soldiers until they get to the back corner of the room. "He's on that corner table, Mrs. Williams. His head is toward the wall."

Lynda says nothing as she slowly approaches the table, her eyes frozen on the gray army blanket. She stops just as her dress brushes the table's edge. Lynda stand motionless for a few minutes then she slowly reaches for the blanket. Her hand trembles as she steadily raises the blanket to view Fred's gray and bloated face. Almost with a sense of fear she gazes emotionless at what was once her handsome husband. Her hands tremble as she slowly and systematically puts the blanket back over his face. She turns and begins to walk out of the hospital, her eyes fixed straight ahead with a glassy stare.

As she passes by, Henry reaches out gently to touch her hand. "Lynda, is ..."

"Please don't, Henry. I'm going home now. I need to be alone for awhile. Please respect that."

Henry agrees in a very low voice. "I will, Lynda."

Both Colonel Novak and Henry watch silently as Lynda walks at half steps to her quarters. Once on the steps she stops for a few seconds to look at the sign on the door:

OFFICER'S QUARTERS
First Lieutenant and Mrs. Fred Williams

Lynda stays in her quarters behind closed doors and windows for two days, crying and mourning. It is nine o'clock in the morning of the third day when she finally steps out of her quarters dressed in a long dark dress. The day is sunny and warm with just a slight breeze coming out of the northwest. It has a gentle, cooling effect on her face as she heads toward Colonel Novak's office.

The soldiers of H Company are grooming their horses as Lynda walks by the stable. Sergeant Thomas is the first to see her. "A-tten-hut!" he yells to the other men as she passes by.

Abruptly, all the men come to attention. Sergeant Thomas salutes. No words are exchanged. Lynda stops briefly to look at them and shyly nods. Before she continues on, a slight smile comes to her face, for she knows the salute from these men is a sign of respect for her dead husband. She also knows it was these brave black soldiers who faced the same danger in an attempt to rescue him.

Colonel Novak immediately stands up as Lynda enters his office. "Lynda, how are you? I've been concerned about you, but didn't want to disturb you."

Lynda holds back her tears as she suddenly becomes emotional. "I'm doing fair, Colonel."

Her eyes are red and swollen from crying, but she has tried to make her appearance presentable. "Colonel Novak, I've come here to let you know that I want to go back to New York and take my husband's body with me ... to be buried next to his father and grandfather." Lynda takes a deep sigh, then shows apparent signs of weakness.

Colonel Novak rushes to her and helps her sit in a chair. "Would you like a glass of water, Lynda?"

"No, thank you, Colonel. Just give me a moment to catch my breath."

Colonel Novak walks back to his chair behind his desk and looks compassionately at her. "How can I help, Lynda?"

"Colonel, will you assist me in getting his body to the train station at Wallace City?"

"Of course, Lynda. That's the least I can do. In fact, I'll assign Lieutenant Washington to escort you there if you wish. He's been out on the one-day-patrols, but I can certainly detail him for this assignment. I know he would like that."

Lynda regaining some of her composure, acts pleased as she wipes the tears from her eyes. She looks to Colonel Novak with a sense of strength in her eyes. "Are you sure, Colonel? That would be so nice. They were such good friends."

"I know, Lynda. I think it only appropriate. In fact, I think that all the men of H Company would like to escort you. I think they would consider it an honor to do so."

Lynda's eyes light up and a surprised look comes to her face. "Colonel, really? There's so many of them!"

Colonel Novak smiles. "Yes, but I'll arrange for it immediately. Tell me, when do you plan on leaving?"

"I'd like to go Wednesday, day after tomorrow, if that's not too inconvenient. I believe that's the day the train leaves from Wallace City."

Lynda looks around the office, then walks to the window. "I love it here, Colonel, except with Fred gone and ..."

"You don't have to explain, Lynda. I understand," interrupts Colonel Novak gently. "I know this is a difficult time for you."

Lynda sighs as she takes a deep breath, thinking of her husband. "Fred was so proud to be in the army and especially to be with the Tenth Cavalry. I guess he wouldn't have wanted to die any other way. It's just that ... it all seems so ... brief."

"I'm sorry this happened, Lynda. Fred was an excellent officer. If it's any consolation to you, I'm recommending him for the Medal of Honor, posthumously."

Lynda, appreciative of Colonel Novak's compassion, walks over to him and gently squeezes his arm. "You're a very kind man, Colonel. I thank you for that and I know that Fred, too, is somehow saying thank you. The military was such an honorable tradition with his family."

Lynda looks Colonel Novak in the eyes, tears again forming in hers. She gives him a gentle kiss on the cheek, then squeezes his hand one last time. "I best go now, Colonel. Thank you for everything."

"I wish you well back east, Lynda. I'll have your escort ready at sunrise Wednesday morning."

As Lynda walks back to her quarters, she once again passes the men of H Company.

"A-tten-hut!" yells Sergeant Thomas.

Lynda gives them a slight nod of appreciation.

Early Wednesday morning, Lieutenant Washington, Sergeant Thomas, and the men of H Company are in full dress uniform. Four of the enlisted soldiers of the Tenth Cavalry are carrying Fred Williams' coffin to the buckboard.

"What time is it, Thomas?" asks Henry.

"Zero-seven-hundred-hours, Suh!"

"Are all the men ready?"

"Shur 'ar, Suh!"

"Good. I'll go let Lynda. Oh! Are her bags on the buckboard?"

"Yes, Suh. Already put 'em on."

"Okay, here, tie Chance to the buckboard. I'll drive."

"Yes, Suh. Ah, Suh! How's his wound?"

"He's a tough horse, Thomas. Takes more than an arrow to keep him off duty."
"Know what ya be say'n', Suh."

Lynda rides next to Henry on the long trail to the train station at Wallace City. It is an impressive column of troops, as each member of Company H, Tenth U.S. Cavalry, looks spit and shine. They ride proud and silent except for the sounds of sabers jingling and horses moving. Lynda and Henry periodically talk quietly to each other as each recalls their experiences with Fred.

As they arrive at the depot, Lieutenant Washington calls to Sergeant Thomas. "Sergeant Thomas. Hold this team while I help Lynda off, and get a detail of six men to carry the coffin to the platform. Also, form the company up in 'charge ready' formation, at attention."

Lynda and Henry walk to the station platform in silence. Once there they stop. Lynda turns and watches as the detail of Tenth Cavalry troops carry her husband's body to a flat wooden table by the train car.

Suddenly the men of Company H begin to sing an old ballad, "Soldiers of the Lord". They continue to sing as Lieutenant Fred Williams' body is loaded onto the train car and the door is closed.

Tears run down Lynda's cheeks, but she attempts to maintain her presence. After the coffin is loaded, one-hundred-twelve men rattle their sabers. This sound sends a shiver up Lynda's spine as she begins to shake, both in grief and a sense of pride.

After this brief, impromptu ceremony, the men come to attention and a lone trumpeter plays Taps. The emotion of Lynda's heart is too much for her, and with tears in her eyes, she turns to Henry. Her voice soft, emotional, and sincere, "I'm going to miss each and every one of you."

Henry, maintaining military bearing, responds sympathetically to Lynda. "I'll miss you, Lynda, as I'll miss Fred. He was my best friend and I doubt if I will ever find another person I will trust like I did your husband."

Lynda looks Henry steadfast in the eyes, trying to contain her grief. "You're a good man, Henry. Honest, courageous, and a true gentleman. I wish you a fine and proud military career. You do the army proud! Especially the Cavalry."

Suddenly the train whistle blows and steam gushes out the side of the engine. Lynda looks around, sighs, then speaks softly. "Such beautiful country. Look at those white, puffy clouds floating in that beautiful blue sky, Henry. It's such a nice day to travel."

She gives Henry a gentle kiss on the cheek and squeezes his forearm tightly with both her hands. "Goodbye, Henry. May God be close to you out here."

She gives Henry one last look with tears in her eyes, then boards the train. Henry watches solemnly as the train moves out. His mind reels with thoughts, as his heart flexes with emotion. He feels confusion as he thinks of all that has just happened.

As the train disappears from sight, he looks to the sky momentarily, avoiding the bright sun. "They're gone!" he thinks to himself over and over as he looks at the soft, puffy clouds.

After taking a deep breath, he looks at the ground, then walks up to Sergeant Thomas, tears in his eyes. "I'll ride Chance back, Sergeant Thomas. Have one of the men drive the buckboard. Put the men in column formation, horses at a walk going back to the Fort." Then Henry, in a moment of emotional compassion, turns back to Sergeant Thomas. "Oh, Sergeant Thomas."

"Yes, Suh?"

"I love this horse you picked out for me."

Sergeant Thomas smiles. "Thank ya, Suh! He be a goodin'."

CHAPTER TWENTY
WALLACE CITY SALOON

"Grover! You're a coward at the Island! I know that! And all the men know that!" yells Jack Stillwell, as he puts his feet up on the table next to the bar.

Sharp Grover continues to lean on the bar with his back to the tables, talking to Lieutenant Jensen. "Tell that bastard to shut up, will you, Sir?"

"Tell him yourself, Grover. I've got no authority over any half-breed scout. Besides, he hates the Sioux. I don't give a damn about either of your personal problems as long as you two can scout."

Grover takes a drink and turns back to Lieutenant Jensen. 'Except, Sir," he begins sarcastically, "that son-of-a-bitch brunette Lieutenant. He wrote me a bad report at the island."

"You serious, Grover?" chuckles Lieutenant Jensen.

"Ya, I am. Why?"

"Well, that's the problem we got in this unit. That nigger officer! It still makes me want to shit every time I see him ride out on that good looking Morgan horse he's got. No nigger should be rid'n' that Morgan, much less, a nigger army officer!"

"Hey, Grover!" yells Scout Stillwell again, "You damn good fer nothin' piece of buffalo shit, you're a coward!"

Scout Grover, getting more irritated with the harassment by Jack Stillwell, slams his beer down on the bar.

"Just forget the kid, Grover, he's drunk," counsels Lieutenant Jensen.

"Ya, Lieutenant! Like you forget that brunette Lieutenant!"

"I'll take care of him in due time. Right now just ignore the kid. Don't want to lose a good scout over drunk talk."

"He's been jaw'n me all night, Lieutenant. You tend to your black officer, I'll tend to this baby bitch scout."

Grover turns from the bar and gives a menacing smile at Jack Stillwell.

"That's right, Grover, keep smiling. Cowardliness is always smiling!" yells Stillwell, then laughs at this statement.

Scout Grover's anger is becoming more apparent. "Tell you what, Stillwell. Best keep your little mouth shut. Ain't gonna' put up with some little kid cryin' fer long."

"Ya, Grover, ya piece of horseshit. 'Bout time ya show responsibility. If'n it weren't fer ya, maybe Lieutenant Williams and the doc would still be livin' … Frenchy too!"

Grover becomes intensely defensive at this statement. All the other scouts, soldiers, and prostitutes in the bar heard Stillwell's statement and know it is a challenge. Everyone moves back, stopping their own conversations. It is quiet in the bar. Everyone is waiting to see what the two scouts might do.

Grover spits on the floor and turns back to the bar, but speaks firmly and loud. "Leave me alone, kid. I can kill your ass in a second!"

Stillwell, drink in hand, slowly gets up from his chair and ambles over to the bar about ten feet from Sharp Grover. He leans on the bar and looks straight forward at the back bar mirror. Suddenly Scout Stillwell lets out a loud coyote call. "Ha! Don't think so! I'm not afraid of you Grover. You're too old. Whisky got your brain and reflexes. You're just nothin' but a lyin' cheatin' coward, half-breed Crow."

The anger shows in Grover's face as his hand clinches his bottle so tight that his knuckles turn white. Grover starts to stand a little straighter, rather than lean on the bar.

"Ya know, Grover," continues Stillwell, "ya're 'spose to be head scout on that island. All ya did was get men killed ... didn't do ya're job on the west end. Admit it! Admit to all of us. Ya were just a scared son-of-a-bitch!"

Sharp Grover tries to contain his anger by looking straight forward, but he knows that unless Stillwell shuts his mouth, he'll have to kill him. "Look, kid, don't want to kill ya. Don't want to answer to the Colonel fer kill'n' such a dumb shit as you that cain't read or write."

Jack Stillwell never had any kind of formal education and has been teased about this all his life. Scout Grover's statement tears into his very soul of self consciousness. This fact, plus the death of his friend, Frenchy Trudeau at the island, adds fuel to his hatred toward Scout Grover.

Stillwell turns to look at Scout Grover, then side-steps along the bar slowly until he is five feet away from him. Scout Stillwell raises his glass high above his head as he turns to the others in the bar. "Ladies and gentlemen! I want to propose a toast. A toast to a coward scout bastard named Sharp Grover." Stillwell pours the whole drink down his throat and slams the glass on the bar. He looks at Sharp Grover with hostility, then purposely takes a side-step in the direction of Grover.

Grover reacts quickly by standing erect and facing Stillwell. Scout Grover, anticipating Stillwell to pull his pistol at any time, keeps his eyes on the movement of Stillwell's hand.

If he lowers his right hand, I know he's going for his gun, reasons Scout Grover. "Best you go back to your bunk, kid. I'm patient most of the time, but not to no smart mouth'n snot kid whose mother is a whore." Grover is ready at anytime to draw his pistol.

Stillwell, angered by Scout Grover's last comment, instantly pulls a knife that is hidden in his coat and slashes Grover's face with a backhand. As Grover falls against the bar, Stillwell draws his piston and shoots Grover in the stomach.

Grover falls to the floor, bleeding profusely. Stillwell bends down slowly, picks up Grover's weapon and sneers. "It's over, Grover! Take the pain! You'll be dead in a matter of days. There's no Doc Moors in hell for you!"

Stillwell backs up, leans on the bar, grabs his drink, and looks down at Scout Grover. "Ya're one big coward, Scout!" Stillwell turns to the crowd. "Hey! Ya all saw this bastard pull his gun on me, didn't ya? Didn't ya?"

CHAPTER TWENTY-ONE
THE BONDING

On August 17, forty-five days after the Battle of Williams' Island, Colonel Novak gets new orders from General Olson. As a result, he calls five of his officers in for a strategic conference at Post Headquarters.

"Men, General Olson wants to pursue his winter campaign against the Sioux. He wants to hit them when they are immobile. Incidentally, as a note of interest, the General confirms in his last telegraph that he is pleased that fifty men of the Tenth Cavalry could hold off a good part of the Sioux nation, and is especially happy to learn that Lone Wolf has been killed." Colonel Novak hesitates for a moment, clears his throat, then adds a side comment. "I'll reserve my personal feeling on General Olson's statements for another day."

He then resumes the briefing of his officers. "Consequently, General Olson wants continued patrols out, more of a reconnaissance type who can keep an eye on their movement."

Colonel Novak moves to the map on the wall and with his pointer encircles an area for each of his five patrols. "Gentlemen, the railroad is coming through here next year and I don't need to tell you they are a powerful force in the development of this country. As soldiers, we don't get involved in the politics, we just follow orders as they originate out of Washington and filter down here." Colonel Novak returns to his desk and sits down.

"Lieutenant Washington, your patrol will be the first to go. I want to take two platoons of H Company and patrol the area northwest of the Platte River. Much of it is uncharted territory and I need it surveyed as accurately as you can.

Remember, you're not to engage the Indians. Our mission is to follow their movement only to record it. Remember, these patrols are in preparation for General Olson's massive winter campaign."

Colonel Novak continues at length on his briefing and the plan of having different patrols on a rotation basis. After two hours of meeting, he concludes. "You men are dismissed. Oh, Lieutenant Washington, remain here for a moment. I have some matters I would like to discuss with you."

After the other officers leave, he addresses Lieutenant Washington. "Lieutenant, how long you been out here now, three months?"

"Three months, twelve days, Sir."

"Have you heard from Mrs. Williams?"

"No, Sir. Not a word. Also, I haven't heard from my friend Leon in three months either ... mail is slow out here, Sir."

"That's for sure. Anyway, you're the most experienced officer I've got as far as contact with the Sioux is concerned. I expect that you will be patrolling at least once a week for a minimum of three days at a time. But there's something else I want to talk to you about."

Colonel Novak leans forward on his desk and talks in a serious, yet cordial manner. "With additional officers also going out on patrol, I need a capable officer to oversee the Quartermaster functions. So, I'm assigning you that position. The Quartermaster Sergeant can handle routine activities while you're gone, but I need an officer in charge."

"I have no Quartermaster experience, Sir. I'll try to do the best I can. What I don't know, I'm sure I can learn."

"Good! Now back to your patrol duties. I have a schedule here and I want you to follow it. Remember, I need a good description of the countryside and a detailed map made. Bring a surveyor with you."

"Will do, Sir. Per your instructions we'll be leaving at dawn tomorrow. Is there anything else, Sir?"

"Not right now, Lieutenant. Oh, speaking earlier of letters. I received one from Major Baker. He sends his best personal regards to you. He's doing well. Recovered from his wounds and is assigned to Divisional Headquarters in St. Louis. Ironically enough, under General Olson's command. An asset possibly. He just may be able to help us get the equipment and supplies we need out here."

"Good to hear he's doing well, Sir. Please give him my regards, Sir."

"I'll do that, Lieutenant. And one last thing, Lieutenant ... as far as we know, Two Crows has moved north. I'd tell you to be careful out there, but you already know that."

Henry smiles, then salutes. "Yes, Sir."

H Company rides two columns abreast for more than twelve miles before coming upon a ten-man railroad surveying crew. The day is hot and the August sun beats down relentlessly on both the men and horses. "Column halt!" commands Henry.

After inquiring who is in charge, Henry rides to the crew chief and begins talking. "Are you Mr. Vinson?"

"That's me, Lieutenant. What can I do for you?"

The crew chief is a large, tough looking man with sweat beads all over his face. He wipes his face and talks amicably.

"Just wondering how you're doing. Any problems?"

"No problems so far, Lieutenant. Why? Expectin' somthin'?"

"No, just patrolling the district and saw your men doing some mapping down here. Just stopped in to see if you're okay."

"Thanks, Lieutenant. Appreciate that. Always good to know we got some protection out here. Never know what might pop up. Too bad we can't get us some protection from that blazin' sun."

"Know what you mean, Mr. Vinson." Henry looks around and takes a good view of the area. "Say, Mr. Vinson. Does your surveyor have this place mapped yet?"

"To a point, Lieutenant, but only about two miles beyond here so far. Why?"

"Just wondering. We're trying to get our own survey and I thought our surveyors could match their notes, so to speak."

"Sure. That might be of some help to both of us."

After meeting for several hours, the two parties bid farewell. Henry directs the patrol in a northwesterly direction to a point twenty miles beyond the mouth of the Platte River. Henry marvels at the tall buffalo grass as it laps at the legs of the horses, like waves on a large lake. The clear view and vastness of the plains allows for a relaxed ride. Henry, therefore, permits the men to carry on conversations in a low tone of voice. This, more as a morale booster than for any other reason. Even Henry is relaxed and confident as he casually talks with Sergeant Thomas. "Do you know where we are, Sergeant?"

"Don't know, Suh! Never been this far out before. We not be on dis map I got. Scout Stillwell ought ta be wid us. No real need fo' da Colonel to confine him. 'Specially when we can use 'em!"

"Know what you mean, Thomas. Wish he were here too. He's young and cocksure, but he caused his own confinement."

Sergeant Thomas thinks for a while, smiles, and with a sense of humor turns to Henry. "Suh! Maybe we be in Mexico!"

Henry turns to Sergeant Thomas with a grin on his face. "Mexico, Sergeant. Where'd you get that idea? I'd never want to be in Mexico. Too hot. Too many scorpions ... and the food, I hear it's hot. My stomach couldn't take it. What made you think of Mexico?"

"Just a josh'n', Suh! But speakin' of food ... most anythin' better'n this hardtack the army feed'n us."

Henry nods his head in agreement as they ride side by side. That afternoon the patrol advances deeper into Sioux territory. However, the temporary situation of perceived security allows Henry and Sergeant Thomas to talk in a more informal manner than is normally done between the ranks of officer and enlisted man. "Have you heard from your mother, Sergeant?"

"No, Suh. De mail is awful slow in de south."

"It's slow here too, Thomas."

"Suh! Mind if'n I ask you a question?"

"I guess not, Sergeant. Depends on what it is, if you want an answer."

"Well, Suh. What it be lak at West Point? Never had me no educatin'. I jus' be curious."

"Well, Sergeant Thomas, it's an interesting place. Very formal. Everything there is prim and proper. But they don't teach the military knowledge that is needed out here. In fact, Sergeant Thomas, you could go back there and teach those officers something about fighting Indians."

Sergeant Thomas is surprised at Henry's comment. He straightens up in his saddle and thinks about it. "Me, Suh? Ya be a josh'n."

"No, Sergeant, I'm not. The establishment back there is behind times as far as teaching officers what they need to know out here."

Sergeant Thomas thinks about Henry's statement for a good five minutes before he asks another question. "Suh! What broht ya' in de army?"

"A long story, Sergeant Thomas. Just always wanted to be a soldier. Ever since I can remember, since I was four I think. Destiny I guess."

"Do ya' lak it, Suh?"

"Well, yes, I do. Living conditions aren't the best, as you know, but I intend to make it my career. Can't picture myself being a civilian."

"Me too, Suh. De army be my life. 'Especially de Cavalry. Ya ever think 'bout gitt'n hitched, Suh?" Henry turns to Sergeant Thomas with a smile on his face, then chuckles. "Now what kind of a question is that, Sergeant? A little personal, don't you think?"

Sergeant Thomas looks serious. "Just askin', Suh."

"I'll put it this way, Sergeant. I've thought about it. Time just isn't right now."

"Ya' ain't toot'n' Dixie on dat, Suh."

It is getting late in the afternoon when Henry decides to let the men camp for the night. He reasons he will start the patrol before daylight the following day, with emphasis on mapping, then return to Fort Wallace. "Send the scouts out to look for a campsite for tonight, Sergeant. We'll be stopping in about an hour."

Two Crows is in his lodge talking with Grey Bull when Jumping Eagle rides in at a full gallop. He reins his horse to a stop in front of Two Crows' lodge and quickly jumps off. Exhausted and out of breath he yells for Two Crows. "Two Crows! Two Crows!"

Two Crows immediately steps outside.

"My Chief! Buffalo Soldiers come this way. One day ride from here! Jumping Eagle takes a couple of deep breaths, then continues to inform Two Crows. "Black Soldier Chief lead them. One has good medicine. One that killed Lone Wolf!"

Two Crows acts surprised. His face takes on a curious, yet serious look. "Soldier Chief on the Arikara?"

"Yes! He come. Maybe one day! Not many soldiers ..."

"Go, Jumping Eagle. Summon the Council to my teepee."

Within an hour the Council is meeting and all braves in the camp have learned that the soldiers are coming. The sudden, unexpected chance for battle excites the braves, especially the younger, untested ones.

In Council, Two Crows acts pleased and relaxed. "Buffalo Soldiers look for us. Not know we here. They wander in search of wind."

Two Crows, his right fist closed, thumb up, makes a quick movement across his throat, indicating the throats of all soldiers will be cut.

"Jumping Eagle, it is you who will lead warriors tomorrow. That honor yours. Little time to get ready."

Jumping Eagle is excited at his first chance to lead a raiding party against the soldiers. In his exuberance he declares his strategy. "We send out decoys. Six braves. Braves lead bluecoats into trap at treed ravine. We show all soldiers who ride in Lakota country they meet death! It time. The Great Spirit sends us our enemy."

The Council agrees that this may be another opportunity to display Sioux superiority at the perceived territorial invasion. None of the Council dissents to an attack. Jumping Eagle then tries to change his plans. "We attack their camp in dark!" says Jumping Eagle.

"No!" replies Two Crows emphatically. "If a warrior dies at night, his spirit get lost in darkness. You attack at sunrise. Before they break camp." Two Crows, being somewhat reserved, remembers only too well the standoff at the island.

"Jumping Eagle shoot soldier horses! Men on foot easy to kill." Jumping Eagle listens intently to his Elders. "I surprise them! Take many Spencer rifles."

Two Crows knows that this attack is only a minor raid and purposely allows Jumping Eagle his actions of enthusiasm. "Do what you will, Jumping Eagle. This your raid. Maybe you take coup. Maybe not. Go now! And learn what you will from the experience."

Henry's men are tired from the long, steady ride and camp for the night atop a hill with tree protection. The patrol stops at five o'clock in the evening; they eat, tend the horses, and go to bed at sunset. Henry follows the normal procedures of sentry and perimeter protection. He wants his men rested for the morning. His plans are to go another ten miles northwest, swing back to the south, and return to Fort Wallace. He also knows that there will be no attack. This knowledge he learned from Scout Stillwell. But he wants his men saddled and ready to ride before daylight.

Jumping Eagle and his warriors move into position during the night. His plan is to attack at first light but changes to the decoy ploy upon seeing the soldiers mounted and ready to ride.

As they are preparing to leave, the outrider sentry thinks he sees something moving on the distant hill. He immediately alerts Sergeant Thomas.

"Must be strays," thinks Thomas. "Best tell de' Lieutenant." Sergeant Thomas pulls his horse next to Henry as the patrol is about to move out. "Suh! Five Injuns on dat hill."

Henry pulls out his binoculars. "You're right, Sergeant. Looks like decoys to me. They want to run us into a trap."

"How ya' know dat, Lieutenant?"

"They wouldn't let us see them if they didn't want us to. And that's just one of their tactics. Looks like we might see some action today."

Henry follows the five riders on the ridge with his binoculars. "They want us to follow them alright."

"What be ya' orders, Suh?" questions Sergeant Thomas in anticipation of seeing some action.

"We'll follow them to a point, then back off. If they get us in their ambush we're all dead. Best we stay in the open."

Jumping Eagle, an inexperienced warrior, is unaware of Henry's insight and moves his warriors into the ravine. The daybreak attack is spoiled.

Henry and his men follow the five decoys to the top of a series of three hills, then halt the patrol just short of the ravine. "Let them go!" he yells.

Upon seeing the patrol stop, several of Jumping Eagle's more independent followers break from the ravine in an attempt to gain personal coup. Other's then follow.

"Here they come!" yells Henry. "Head for the tree line on the knoll!"

The patrol, rather than engage in the open, speeds toward the tree line. But of surprise to Henry, about twenty Indians come up on his back side and ride well ahead of the main war party. The Indian fire becomes intense. Henry redirects his men as he spins Chance around and points to the tree line one-hundred-yards up the knoll. The men gallop their horses, slapping them with the reins to gain an extra bit of speed.

Henry legs deep into Chance's sides as the last of his men pass him by. The Indian rifle fire is now intense. Henry, the last in the patrol, is at full gallop and fifty yards from the tree line when Chance drops. Henry tumbles off and rolls back onto his feet. He scrambles back to Chance, who lies motionless on the ground, and uses him for momentary cover.

"Cover the Lieutenant! Cover the Lieutenant!" yells Sergeant Thomas.

The exchange of gunfire becomes voluminous as the soldiers with their Spencer rifles begin return volleys. Volley after volley of rifle fire causes the Indian war party to retreat. Henry immediately yells to Sergeant Thomas in the woods, "Any casualties, Sergeant?"

"Two men hit! Not bad, Suh!"

"Take care of them, Sergeant! Remount the troop! We're headed home!"

Henry inspects Chance. Blood is oozing out of his neck above the right shoulder. Not knowing the severity of Chance's wound, Henry grabs the reins and attempts to pull Chance upright. Chance struggles to his feet, stands for a moment then falls down. Henry's emotions go from hope to despair as Chance lies on the ground looking up at him. A slight whinny from Chance seems to say, goodbye, Lieutenant.

Sergeant Thomas rides up at quick time. "Is bad, Suh?"

Henry looks down at Chance and bites his lip. "Yes, Sergeant. Are the men ready? I need to report this skirmish and location."

Sergeant Thomas waves the patrol over to Henry's location. Henry kneels by his horse, tears in his eyes. He looks into the deep blue eyes of Chance, his revolver in hand. Hesitantly, Henry puts the gun to Chance's head. "I'm sorry old friend," whispers Henry. Then "Bam!" The echo of that single shot rings loud in Henry's ears.

Chance lies quietly on the ground as all the men in the patrol watch in silence. Sergeant Thomas speaks calmly, knowing the love Henry has for his horse. "Men be ready as ordered, Suh."

"Get me another horse, Sergeant. Double up two of the men."

"Yes, Suh!"

Henry unsaddles Chance, folds the saddle blanket and gently places it under the horse's head. Henry looks up to Sergeant Thomas and speaks with emotion. "He was a good one, Sergeant."

Two days later the patrol arrives at Fort Wallace. "Take over, Sergeant. Get the wounded to the hospital. I'll make my report to the Colonel."

Henry salutes as he walks into Colonel Novak's office.

"Morning, Lieutenant! How'd it go out there?"

"Sir, Two Crows is camped somewhere straight north of the Big Fork, I think about twenty-five miles from here. We ran into a few of his young braves trying to prove themselves. Figure they didn't travel more than five miles out of his camp."

Henry walks to the map on the wall and points to a blank area. "It's not on the map, Sir. But according to our survey and rough draft map it should be up in this area. The surveyor will get that to you, Sir."

"How many braves?"

"About sixty attacked us. I imagine he has three or four hundred in camp."

"Good job, Lieutenant. I'll have Lieutenant Fletcher go out tomorrow using the information you just provided."

Colonel Novak notices that Henry isn't his usual self and is acting somewhat melancholy. "Lieutenant, is something wrong? You don't seem to be your normal self."

Henry looks solemnly at Colonel Novak. "Nothing really, Sir. Just a horse ... a horse named Chance."

Colonel Novak is unaware of the personal emotion Henry was feeling inside and speaks in a manner he thinks might cheer Henry up. "Oh, Lieutenant! There's an officers party and dance on Saturday night. It's an annual event and it would be good if you would attend."

"Thank you, Sir. I'll try and make it, Sir," answers Henry with a disinterested attitude.

"You'll enjoy it, Lieutenant!" concludes Colonel Novak as he walks with Henry to the door.

CHAPTER TWENTY-TWO
A NIGHT TO REMEMBER

It is a gala affair. A social like this one is but a once a year affair. Twenty of the twenty-six officers on post are in attendance, twelve with their wives. The atmosphere is formal, yet jovial as the officers and their wives talk and drink wine in the old recreational building. The wooden beams and floor give the old building a rustic effect, despite the hand made paper decorations, and red, white, and blue banners that seem to hang in every crevice. A Tenth Cavalry flag hangs from the ceiling next to the American flag. Even dignitaries, such as the Mayor and City Council members and their wives from Wallace City, come dressed in formal attire. This is the great social event that everyone looks forward to each year. At least the officer's wives club thinks so.

Colonel Patrone, Divisional Adjutant from St. Louis, and his daughter Missi, traveled the great distance for this party and in his entourage are several other officers and their wives. For such a remote region it is quite an event.

By eight o'clock everyone is milling around; the band is just beginning to set up. While they wait, everyone toasts each other in their small group and snack on the pheasant, grouse, venison, and other wild game which was shot earlier that day.

The officers look sharp in their dress blue uniforms and the women are stunning in their formal, long dresses.

Lieutenant Sandy, who has spent the last few months on post in Administration, brought his wife, Mary. She is the president of the women's club and had been a good friend to Lynda Williams. Lieutenant Sandy has become a good friend to Henry since their patrol duty together. Whenever he and Henry did get together they talked extensively over a game of chess.

As the band begins to play, Mary comments on how good it is to have a social for the morale of the officers.

"Mary, let's not talk about this now. I hear it from you every day at home."

"Well, I think it is good for us. It's one of the few exciting events on post and it gives us women a chance to dress up and look pretty ... or as pretty as we can." She giggles as she looks around. "Say, Honey, where's your friend Lieutenant Washington? I haven't seen him yet this evening."

"He's probably still in his quarters. He's been quite solemn lately, losing Chance, to say nothing about losing his friend Lieutenant Williams. I think I'll go get him. He needs to socialize a bit."

"Jim Sandy. Open up, Henry!"

Henry slowly gets out of bed and walks to the door. As he opens it Lieutenant Sandy greets him. "Henry! Get dressed old friend. There's the big social tonight. Mary and I would like your company, as will others, I'm sure."

Henry wipes his eyes. "Oh, ya. I forgot. I'm sorry, just had some other things on my mind and musta dozed off."

"Are you coming? It's a once a year event. Band, dancing, good food. Com'on, Henry, it'll be fun!"

"Alright. I suppose I should at least make a showing. Guess the Colonel expects it."

"He sure does, but that's beside the point. A lot of the other officers are there plus maybe fifty or so townspeople. Never know who you might meet."

"Give me a few minutes. I see it's dress blues, huh?"

"Yup. Gives us a chance to dress like we did back at West Point." Lieutenant Sandy chuckles.

About half an hour later Henry and Lieutenant Sandy enter the dance hall. The music is playing and more than one-hundred people are conversing and laughing.

"There's Mary over at the far table by the dance floor. Com'on, Henry. We'll sit there. Grab something to drink first. No service here tonight. We can eat later."

Colonel Patrone's daughter Missi and her friend Pat are bored as they walk around the food table. Missi, a shapely, blond, sixteen-year-old, has never been to a western frontier fort before. She brought her friend Pat along as company. Like Missi, Pat is young and attractive with brown eyes and brunette hair, but much more shy and introverted. Missi is outgoing and dominates her relationship with Pat.

Both girls are dressed attractively and are searching for something to occupy their time. "This is the most boring dance!" declares Missi. "I don't know why we're here. All these men are married."

"I know. There's certainly no boys here I'm interested in. If it weren't so dark out I'd rather be horseback riding."

"Me too!" agrees Missi. "I think I'll go in the powder room and fix my hair. Are you coming?"

On the way Missi and Pat pass by Henry and Lieutenant and Mrs. Sandy. Missi looks at Henry out of the corner of her eye, then rushes Pat into the powder room.

"What's wrong with you, Missi? You didn't have to pull me like that!"

"Pat! Did you see that lone, young colored officer sitting at that table? Betcha he's not married."

"Doesn't make any difference. He's at least twenty-four years old and 'sides, he's colored."

"I don't care! He's an officer! That means he's educated, right? And if he's single, nine chances out of ten he's got no girlfriend out here."

"You're just look'n' for trouble if you start eye'n him, Missi."

"I'm not eye'n him. I just want someone to dance with that's not married, and a man who is more mature. What's wrong with that?"

Pat shakes her head. "I'm not getting involved with you in this one, Missi. The last time was a total disaster."

"Com'on, Pat. You're my friend, now help me. Why don't you go introduce yourself to him, then you can introduce him to me, and I'll take it from there?"

"Missi, I don't want to."

"Okay then, Pat. I've got an idea. I'll bump you as you walk by the table and you accidentally, on purpose, drop your hanky. Maybe he'll pick it up and give it to you!"

"Darn you, Missi! Why do I always get caught up in your little games?"

"You'll do it then? Please!"

"Alright. But that's it. You have to do the rest if you want to meet him."

Missi starts to giggle as she anticipates her introduction to Henry. "You're such a good friend, Pat. I'll pay you back somehow. I promise I will!"

As the girls leave the ladies powder room, they execute their plan accordingly. Missi bumps Pat and Pat drops her handkerchief near Henry's chair as they pass by. Neither Henry nor Lieutenant Sandy and his wife notice.

"Now what, Missi? They didn't even notice!"

"Well, walk over and pick it up. Then introduce yourself."

"Darn you, Missi!"

Pat walks over to where Henry is sitting and coyly excuses herself. "Excuse me, I dropped my handkerchief as I was leaving the ladies room."

Henry and Lieutenant Sandy don't respond. Only Mrs. Sandy makes any comment. "That's okay, my dear," then returns to the personal table conversation.

Pat walks back to Missi shaking her head. "It didn't work!"

"Well, we'll just have to try something else, Pat!"

Missi is to the point of pouting when she sees the officer's wife with whom she is staying walk in. "Stay here, Pat. I'm going to ask who that colored officer is." Missi walks over to Major Shaw's wife and starts to converse with her. After fifteen minutes she scurries back to where Pat is standing.

"His name is Henry Washington. He's a Lieutenant with H Company of the Tenth Regiment. He's a West Point graduate and he's never been married. He's also a hero, I guess. He saved some men on some island out in Indian country."

"That's impressive," comments Pat nonchalantly. "So, how you going to meet him?"

"I don't know yet. But I'll figure out something."

"Why don't you just use the direct approach, Missi? Go over and introduce yourself to him," states Pat in an irritated tone of voice.

Missi thinks to herself as she turns around, hands clasped in front of her with a daydream smile on her face. "Okay, Pat. Let's go!"

Pat is stunned and surprised. "What do you mean, let's go? You're just gonna have to do this yourself, Missi."

"Please, Pat. I'd do the same for you. Pleeease. Pretty please!"

Again Pat shakes her head, then agrees. Both girls walk slowly over to where Henry and his friends are sitting.

"Ah, excuse me. Is your name Lieutenant Washington?"

Henry turns to the two girls. He is taken by surprise, as are the others at the table. They instantly stop their conversation.

Missi, ignorant of social protocol, continues her forced, self introduction. "My name is Missi Patrone. I'm new here and I've heard a lot about you. So, I thought you wouldn't mind if I introduced myself to you. This is my friend, Pat."

Henry smiles, then stands up. "Good evening, ladies. Pleased to meet you."

Missi's teenage behavior shows as both Pat and she act coy and giddish. "I hear you're a great soldier. That you lead army patrols into Indian country."

Henry smiles as he momentarily turns back to Lieutenant and Mrs. Sandy with raised eyebrows. Unsure how to answer Missi's question, Henry replies modestly, "Well, yes. I've been out on patrol a few times ..."

"Do you like fighting Indians, Lieutenant?" Missi interrupts. "I hear it's exciting!"

Henry clears his throat and again looks towards his friends at the table. "Well, yes and no, Ma'am."

Missi is almost to the point of blushing she is so excited. Pat notices she is being a bit overbearing and pokes Missi gently in the back. Missi ignores Pat's signal and pursues the conversation. Acting very girlish, she holds her hands in front of her and sways back and forth to the soft music in the background. She then talks in a sweet, seductive voice. "Do you dance, Lieutenant?"

Henry is slightly embarrassed as he turns back to his friends at the table. Lieutenant Sandy leans back in his chair, smiles, and winks at Henry. "Of course he does, Missi!"

volunteers Lieutenant Sandy. "He's a great dancer. Aren't you, Henry?"

Mrs. Sandy adds her opinion. "Henry, as an officer and a gentleman, you're not going to turn down the request of a pretty young lady are you?"

Taking the suggestion lightly, Henry looks at Missi. "Of course not, Missi. Do you like to waltz?"

Missi is ecstatic as she responds. "Yes, Lieutenant, I do. That's my favorite dance!"

"Well, young lady, do you have a favorite song? Maybe the band will play it for you," suggests Henry politely.

"I do like the Old Timer's Waltz ... and Askam Farewell." Missi immediately turns to Pat. "Pat would you please ask the band to play those two songs?"

Pat eyes Missi with a condescending look. "Yes, Missi. I'll go ask them. Just you relax!"

Henry formally introduces Missi to his friends. Mrs. Sandy asks Missi a few questions as the band begins to play her requested songs, but Missi breaks off the conversation quickly as she grabs Henry's hand and leads him onto the dance floor.

Lieutenant Jensen's animosity grows moment by moment as he watches from behind the bar. Seeing Henry dance with Missi strikes a deep, sharp cord with the southern raised officer. He turns to Lieutenant Haun in frustrated anger. "Haun, look at that son-of-a-bitch'n nigger dance'n with that white girl! What the hell! Doesn't she have any morals?"

"Seems to me they dance well together, Jensen," comments Lieutenant Haun.

"Not if I have anything to say about it. That bastard Lieutenant Washington has got to go ..."

"You've got nothing to say about it!" injects Lieutenant Haun with authority as he grabs Lieutenant Jensen's arm firmly and holds on to it, restricting him from going to the dance floor. "Listen to me, Jensen! He's earned his right to be here. He's a good officer and the Colonel likes him. Let it be!"

Lieutenant Haun squeezes tighter on Lieutenant Jensen's arm, pulls him close, and talks directly into his ear. "Look! He's lonely enough out here. Let him have some enjoyment. Just leave him alone!"

Lieutenant Jensen looks at Lieutenant Haun's firm grip on his arm, then pulls it off. "Go to hell, Haun! Washington will see his enjoyment alright and he'll see it soon. You just wait!" Lieutenant Jensen, angry and upset, glares at Henry before he walks directly outside.

Henry and Missi dance their two dances, then walk toward the table. Before they get off the dance floor, Missi pulls on Henry's arm and speaks softly. "You're an awfully good dancer, Lieutenant. Would you like to dance another song?"

"I think that's enough for now, Missi. I best get back to my friends."

Missi acts upset and immediately starts thinking about how she can get to know Henry better, so she begins a new approach. "Lieutenant, you must know this territory really well?"

"I know it a little, yes. Why?"

"It's such beautiful country and I haven't seen hardly any of it. My father says I can't go riding unless someone responsible takes me out. Will you take me sightseeing tomorrow?" Missi looks directly in the eyes with a pleading look as she sways back and forth, slowly twisting and acting coy.

"I don't know, Missi. I'd have to think about that."

"Well, how about if I get my father's permission and he says that you can be that responsible officer?"

Henry chuckles and smiles as he begins to wonder what he has gotten himself into.

"Please, Lieutenant! Surely you wouldn't let me go back to St. Louis without seeing a small part of this territory, would you?"

Henry hesitates and looks around. He looks over to Lieutenant Sandy who simply gives him a thumbs up. "Missi, give me some time to think about it. I have some other things that I have to do tomorrow and …"

"Lieutenant, you go sit at your table and I'll be right back!"

Missi shuffles off the dance floor as Henry sits back down at the table, curiously watching to see where she is going.

"I think you have an admirer, Henry," laughs Lieutenant Sandy.

Henry shakes his head. "Ya, she's a spitfire all right. Very insistent! I don't know, but she acts like she's a Colonel's daughter."

Lieutenant Sandy and his wife laugh as they nod their heads in approval of Henry's comment.

As Henry turns back toward Missi he sees her talking with Colonel Novak. "Holy cow!" quips Henry as he taps Lieutenant Sandy on the shoulder. "Look who she's talking to."

"Got yourself a live one, Henry!" laughs Lieutenant Sandy.

After a few minutes, Missi comes trotting back to the table and asks to talk to Henry in private. "Lieutenant Washington, your Colonel, Colonel Novak, says he sees nothing wrong with you escorting me for a two hour ride tomorrow."

Henry doesn't know how to react. "Missi, I wish you wouldn't have …"

Missi boldly interrupts. "Puff, Lieutenant Washington. Don't be coy with me. I'll be ready at sunrise. If you'll be so kind as to have the horses ready. I'll be in my quarters at Major Shaw's place."

Missi smiles and does a brief, formal curtsy. "I'm going to get some sleep now, Lieutenant Washington. But I want to thank you for the dance. I'll see you in the morning. Goodnight, Lieutenant."

"Goodnight, Missi," says Henry in a quiet, surprised tone of voice.

Missi runs over to Pat, and the two immediately leave the dance hall as Henry walks back to his table.

"What was that all about, Henry?"

Henry, somewhat taken back by the incident, looks to Lieutenant Sandy and his wife. "Looks like I get to give a tour to a teenager tomorrow."

"I think she has a crush on you, Henry," laughs Mrs. Sandy. "Remember now, she's a Colonel's daughter. Best you watch your p's and q's."

Early the next morning Henry walks to the stable to get two horses for the tour. It is a beautiful day with a clear blue sky and little wind. Henry leads the two horses over to Major Shaw's quarters, ties them to the hitching rail, and knocks on the door. Missi answers immediately and acts overjoyed.

"Good morning, Missi. It's a beautiful day. Are you ready for your tour?"

"Sure am, Lieutenant Washington! I thought about it all night."

Henry and Missi mount up and walk their horses through the post to the exterior perimeter. Sergeant Thomas and another Black trooper stand in the background, watching. Sergeant Thomas shakes his head as he turns to the other soldier. "Man, da Lieutenant won't never live dis down, no matter how in'ocent it be. Sometimes I wonder where his head be!"

Many of the other soldiers of Company H stare at the two as they ride out toward the hills. "Yup, Sergeant. I know what you be say'n. Tak'n' dat white girl for a ride can cause him some serious trouble 'round here."

Lieutenant Jensen and Lieutenant Haun stand by the post hospital supervising construction repairs as they watch Henry and Missi ride to the top of the hill. Lieutenant Jensen looks at Lieutenant Haun, sneers and speaks in a vindictive, hostile tone. "I'll fix that cocky SOB. Just you see, Haun! I won't rest till I do."

CHAPTER TWENTY-THREE
AMERICAN JUSTICE

The massive winter campaign against the Sioux Indians is disastrous. Two Crows has moved more than three-hundred miles from Fort Wallace and the first attempt by the Cavalry at locating him results in dead horses and freezing soldiers, some who must have their limbs cut off.

It is March 1, 1878. Post maintenance has taken priority, and the summer campaign is yet to be organized. For all the men at Fort Wallace it has been a dismal winter and the closed environment did more than cause simple cases of cabin fever.

In Henry's case, most of the officers have come to like and trust him. However, there is still a small faction of southern officers that can not accept a Black man into their ranks. Although the Tenth United States Cavalry Regiment is an all black enlisted unit, it is still led by white officers ... with the exception of Henry Washington.

Henry reports in at the Duty Officer's station after coming in from patrol. Lieutenant Sandy quickly walks up to him. "Henry, the Colonel wants to see you. It's urgent."

"Something wrong?" inquires Henry.

"Don't know. Just know that he wants to see you as soon as you report in."

Henry shrugs his shoulders slightly as he pours himself a cup of coffee. "I'll fill out this report and then go over there. Maybe he's got some good news from back east."

Henry enters Colonel Novak's office and salutes. "Lieutenant Washington reporting, Sir. I understand you want to see me."

Colonel Novak sits at his desk without returning his usual pleasant greeting to Henry. "Sit down, Lieutenant. I need to talk with you. It appears we have a serious problem on our hands."

Henry, aware of Colonel Novak's tone of voice becomes concerned. "A problem, Sir?"

"Personally, I know you're a good officer and I trust you implacably, but it has been brought to my attention that there is a serious shortage of money in the Quartermaster funds."

Henry is surprised and shocked at what he has just heard. "A money shortage, Sir?"

"Yes, General Olson has just brought to my attention that more than a thousand dollars is missing."

Henry immediately becomes anxious, then upset. "That can't be, Sir! I've checked those books daily since you assigned me the position of Quartermaster Officer, Sir!"

"I believe you, Lieutenant. Unfortunately it doesn't matter what I believe. What matters is the money was missing when the Divisional Headquarters accountant audited the fund."

Henry is upset and confused. "Sir, I don't see how that could happen unless someone else had access to the funds while I was on patrol!"

"I'm sorry, Lieutenant. I believe you, but at this level it is out of my hands. I'll help you in anyway I can, but I can't stop the charges that are being brought against you." Colonel Novak takes a deep breath. "Formal court martial proceedings are scheduled in two weeks."

"I don't believe this, Colonel! You know I would never do something like this!"

"Lieutenant Washington, I'm in your corner and will investigate this myself. But for now I must inform you that you are currently relieved of duty."

"Colonel Novak, Sir. I didn't steal any money. According to my last calculations all items and monies were accounted for."

"I can't change what Divisional Headquarters is doing. I'm sorry. For now, you are restricted to the post, pending the trial. The General's Adjutant wanted to come out here and arrest you. I told him that wasn't necessary ... that I would take personal responsibility for you."

Henry doesn't say anything, but his mind is raging with anger. "How could this happen?" he keeps saying over and over in his mind.

"Lieutenant Washington, we'll talk tomorrow. Now you must go to your quarters. I'm going to do some investigation on this matter myself."

Henry is enraged, but doesn't dare act in an unmilitary manner. "Yes, Sir!"

The feelings of anger and disbelief fill Henry's mind. "I've given my life to being a good soldier! It's my life! How could something like this happen? I can't believe this!" he thinks to himself as he paces around his quarters, trying to analyze the situation.

As night falls, Henry can not sleep. His feelings of frustration and despair continue to mount. "This is my career! My life! It's all at stake," he thinks as he lights a small lantern on his table. Finally tears come to his eyes and his feelings of loneliness and fear are combined. Henry momentarily starts to hyperventilate. He takes five or six deep breaths and focuses all his mental strength on regaining his composure. He walks over to the top dresser drawer and pulls out the red Bible Bishop Jackson gave him almost six years earlier.

Henry sits at the table and begins reading verse after verse, and as he does he remembers many of the values that he learned in the orphanage, especially the paper that Bishop Jackson had given him on the True Gentleman.

The next morning Henry wakes up lying on his bed fully dressed with the red Bible on his chest. Somehow he feels stronger, even though he has had only three hours of sleep.

For the next two weeks Henry stays in his quarters reading the Bible, writing letters, and reviewing accounting documents from the Quartermaster records. On occasion he takes a walk around the post grounds, but the feelings of embarrassment and distrust make him keep mainly to himself within the privacy of his quarters. He talks at length with his friend Lieutenant Sandy about the situation and this is of some support. But much of the time he thinks of Fred and Lynda and how different life has become since Fred's death and Lynda's leaving.

It is the morning of April 15th. Henry is in full military dress as he is escorted to the Administration Hall which has been prepared for the trial. As he enters the court room, General Olson, two full Colonels, and a Major are seated behind a large oblong wooden desk. Henry notices the large United States flag draped on the wall behind them, flanked by the flag of the Tenth Cavalry, plus other things, such as a table full of military documents.

The atmosphere is highly formal in the sparsely furnished room. There are two Lieutenants who sit at two separate tables and four guards are posted around the room. Henry is told by General Olson to take a seat next to the Lieutenant on his left. Henry first, according to proper military protocol, walks in front of General Olson, salutes, then takes his seat.

It is a strange feeling since Henry doesn't know anyone in the courtroom, not even the other Lieutenant he is sitting next to. Suddenly the sound of a gavel hitting the table brings total silence. Henry and the two other Lieutenants stand at attention. General Olson looks at Henry with piercing eyes and speaks in a serious tone of voice.

"This Court is convened under the United States Military Code of Justice. The charges have been formally initiated by the United States Army, as Plaintiff, versus Lieutenant Henry Washington, as Defendant. Lieutenant Henry Washington, do you understand the charges against you?"

Henry standing to attention, replies in a firm voice. "No, Sir! I do not understand these charges at all, Sir!"

General Olson picks up a file from the table and pulls out a document. He begins to read in a formal, military manner. "Lieutenant Washington, I will cite to you the charges that have been brought against you: One, you are accused of falsifying records; two, you are accused of embezzlement in the amount of one-thousand-two-hundred-ninety-four-dollars; three, you are accused of deception; four, you are accused of conduct unbecoming to an officer. All charges are filed under the Uniform Code of the Military Justice, under which law you shall be tried."

General Olson stares at Henry, then continues in a firm, authoritative voice. "How do you plead, Lieutenant Washington?"

Henry swallows hard, then replies in a strong voice. "I plead not guilty to all charges, Sir!"

General Olson sits back in his chair while Henry remains at attention. "You may sit down now, Lieutenant Washington." General Olson looks to the officers next to him. "Are we ready to proceed?"

All three nod in agreement.

"Prosecutor, proceed with the Government's case."

The Lieutenant acting as prosecutor, rises slowly from his chair. He picks up a file of papers and carefully shifts through them. As he chooses several documents, he moves to the table where the General Officers sit. Waving the papers for all to see, he starts his argument.

"Sir, the United States Government has convincing evidence in these documents that Lieutenant Henry Washington intentionally and deceitfully diverted, or more appropriately stated, embezzled one-thousand-two-hundred-ninety-four-dollars from the Quartermaster fund of the Tenth United States Cavalry, stationed at Fort Wallace."

The prosecutor returns to his table, opens several more documents, holds them up for all to see, then walks back to the front of General Olson. "Look at these documents, Sir!" clamors the prosecutor as he hands the papers to General Olson for inspection.

"Lieutenant Washington's signature is on each page. These records are not accurate when you make comparisons with the originals. Sir, based on these documents alone, his crime is blatantly clear, Sir. The documents speak for themselves. It's quite obvious, Sir. I have no other evidence to present, Sir. The government will rest its case."

General Olson looks at the documents studiously, then gives them to the other officers on his judicial panel.

"Prosecutor, I accept these records as evidence."

General Olson turns to Henry and his Counsel. "Will the Counsel for the Defense please make its case."

The Defense Counsel, also a Lieutenant, is initially awkward and timid as he fumbles through his papers in a state of panic.

General Olson becomes impatient and speaks harshly. "Will the Defense make its statement!"

The young Lieutenant reacts nervously and replies quickly, "Yes, Sir! One moment, please, Sir. I have the records you want here someplace, Sir."

Henry, sits quietly, trying to put into perspective exactly what is taking place. "This trial seems so haphazard and rushed," he thinks to himself. "I don't even know this Defense Counsel."

"I have the information, General!" The Defense Counsel walks up to the table of officers and begins his initial opening statements. "Sir, I'm not an attorney, but having been appointed Defense Counsel, I'll follow the Uniform Code of Military Justice in my rebuttal."

The Defense Counsel presents documents on Henry's military career to date. "Look at Lieutenant Washington's record. He is dedicated. He cares for his men. He has an excellent military record. He has served with distinction in all facets of military duty. There is nothing in his background that will even suggest that he is capable of considering embezzlement. He is a career orientated soldier and obviously an asset to the Army Officer Corps."

The Defense Counsel then opens the large book of the Army's Uniform Code of Military Justice. "There is nothing in this book that meets the elements of the crimes of which Lieutenant Washington has been charged!"

The Defense Counsel lays the book on the table before General Olson and the other officers, open to the page to which he is referring. "Furthermore, Sir, if Lieutenant Washington did what he is accused of, wouldn't his lifestyle have changed somewhat?"

The Defense Counsel looks General Olson and the other Judicial Officers in the eyes. "Surely, he would have purchased some new clothes or a personal item of some kind that his current salary would not allow. But that is not the case! He has not been found in possession of any stolen goods or monies, much less any newly purchased possessions!" The Defense Counsel walks back to Henry. "General Olson, it is obvious there is some kind of a mistake on these charges. Possibly there has been a set-up by jealous, prejudiced officers and/or civilians who had access to the Quartermaster books and facility when Lieutenant Washington was on patrol or off duty."

The Defense Counsel continues to speak with more confidence as he continues to present document after document of records which accurately account for all material and monies connected with the Quartermaster section.

"General Olson, Sir. This court has to conclude on the evidence before us. The evidence presented by the United States Government is shabby and inconclusive. It is not even close to the records you have before you. It appears, Sir, that other persons or just one other person, had access to these funds."

The Defense Counsel continues with another approach to the same argument. "Sir, none of these charges can be proven beyond a reasonable doubt. Not even close! Look at this, Sir." The Defense Counsel points to a specific section of the UCMJ and brings it close for all the officers to read. "The Uniform Code of Military Justice requires SPECIFIC PROOF OF INTENT to commit a crime of embezzlement. You cannot convict this honorable officer on speculation and obviously trumped up charges!"

The Defense Counsel lays the book down in front of General Olson and steps back several paces. Again, with a sincere gaze, he looks into the eyes of each of the General Officers. He then offers his most convincing argument.

"Sir! This is a court of justice and honor. And according to the rules of evidence in the Uniform Code, it is impossible to find Lieutenant Washington guilty on any charge. I believe as you make your final review you will see that these charges stem from the malicious intent of another party or parties, possibly just because he is colored. Place yourselves in a position like Lieutenant Washington's before you consider your findings on this case. I thank you for your attention. The Defense will rest."

As the Defense Counsel sits down next to Henry, General Olson makes a brief statement. "Thank you, Defense

Counsel. I'll confer with the members of the Judicial Panel. I don't see any need to go with further argument in this case. We will be back in a short time."

As the Judicial Panel leaves, the Defense Counselor turns to Henry. "Lieutenant Washington, it's impossible for them to find you guilty of embezzlement or any of the other charges. It's so obvious that someone else manipulated these records."

Henry has been nervous and tense throughout the whole three hour proceeding. The last comment by the Defense Counsel gives him a reprieve. He feels better at the moment and confident that he will be vindicated. All Henry thinks about is getting back to duty and continuing on with his career as a Cavalry officer.

Exactly twenty-two minutes later the Judicial Panel re-enters the room. Henry, along with the Government Prosecutor and the Defense Counsel, rise to attention. Henry feels a shiver run up his spine as General Olson asks him to approach the panel.

Henry rises slowly and deliberately. The palms of his hands are moist and the brow of his face is covered with tiny, minute sweat beads.

"Lieutenant Washington! Will you step forward with your Counsel? We have made our decision."

General Olson then reads the decision as it has been formally recorded in the judicial chambers. "Lieutenant Henry Washington! After reviewing all accounting records with your signature on them and other documents provided by your Counsel, we find the following: Charge one, Falsifying Records, not guilty! Charge two, Embezzlement, not guilty! Charge three, Deception, not guilty! Charge four, Conduct unbecoming of an officer, guilty!"

Henry's knees go weak as he starts to collapse, but is held up by the Defense Counselor. He can't believe what he has just heard and his heart starts to beat rapidly. A cold sweat forms over his whole body and he feels dizzy as General Olson continues to address him.

"Please stand at attention, Lieutenant Washington. I have more to say. It is the decision of this Court not to discipline you with a term at Leavenworth Penitentiary, or to fine you, or to consider that you make any form of restitution. However, this Court finds you totally lacking in judgment and responsibility." General Olson looks briefly to the other officers on the panel then speaks in a firm, strictly formal tone of voice. "Therefore, it is this Judicial Court's decision that you be Dishonorably Discharged from the United States Army and no longer be considered a soldier of the United States of America or retain any privileges thereof!"

Henry is shaken as General Olson speaks. His mind and emotions are charged with confusion and frozen on the words "Guilty" and "Dishonorable Discharge".

"Your discharge papers will be prepared for you within one week. You will remain in your quarters, under guard, until such time of discharge. This Court is dismissed!"

Henry is devastated and shakes uncontrollably. He is silent as tears roll down his cheeks and the emotions scramble in his heart and mind. Then reality seems to grab hold of him as he breaks down and cries.

A crowd of onlookers have formed in front of the Administration Building and suddenly a newspaper correspondent yells, "It's a guilty verdict!"

The reaction of the crowd is mixed as Henry walks outside, escorted by four military guards. The catcalls and accusations are minimal, but each derogatory word digs into Henry's soul like a piece of hot steel.

As Henry is escorted to his quarters, reporters follow, yelling questions and taking photos. Henry remains silent and maintains his dignity as best he can under the pressure and emotional strain.

The men from H Company watch from their barracks area in silent respect. Most of the men are in some form of shock as each and every one of them knows in their hearts that their Company Commander is innocent.

Lieutenant Jensen is the only individual in the crowd of more than one-hundred that has an expression of contentment on his face. He first glares, then forms an exaggerated fake smile on his face as Henry is escorted past him.

"Got what you deserve, you son-of-a-bitch!" yells Lieutenant Jensen. He gives Henry an obscene gesture before he turns and walks toward the blacksmith shop.

The telegraph office in Wallace City is packed with reporters who scramble to get their news account out to their respective newspapers. The telegraph keys click in rapid succession as the information on Henry Washington's Court-Martial spreads across the United States.

The headlines in the *St. Louis Dispatch*, *Washington Post*, *New York Times*, and other newspapers are essentially the same with slight variance.

- ♦ First Negro Officer to Graduate From West Point receives Court-Martial!
- ♦ Lieutenant Henry Washington Receives Dishonorable Discharge!
- ♦ America's Only Colored Army Officer Accused of Embezzlement!

The sensationalism created by the reporters and newspaper editors creates a false image and an inaccurate report of what actually transpired at the court-martial, but the effect is the same. Henry Washington has been a victim of the times and politics, and the fact that he is given a Dishonorable Discharge is not reversible.

Henry knows he has not committed any crime, much less committed any offense as far as conduct is concerned. It is hard for him to comprehend how a court of military justice can justify their decision or warrant the destruction of his career by an obviously planned scheme.

Henry walks into his quarters as the guards remain outside. He feels devastated by what has just taken place and is trying to comprehend how, after all the dedication he has committed to becoming an officer, something like this could take place. Henry has tried to maintain some semblance of honor as he walked from the court room, but at this moment he doesn't know where to turn or what to do. He shakes and trembles as he pulls his red Bible from the table and puts it close to his chest. He begins praying aloud, asking God for guidance, but the words barely stutter out of his mouth.

Twenty minutes after the guards have brought Henry to his quarters, Colonel Novak knocks on his door.

"Who is it?" asks Henry in a low, sad, monotone voice.

"Colonel Novak, Lieutenant!"

Henry thinks, "How ironic! He's still calling me Lieutenant."

"Com'on in, Sir."

Colonel Novak enters and Henry comments immediately in a sad, yet bitter voice, "I no longer carry that title, Sir."

"Henry, I can't tell you what an abomination of justice was just carried out. I'm doing everything I can to get the court to reconsider. But in the meantime, I want to talk with you in private."

Henry's emotions of despair, anger, and hopelessness become apparent. "What's to talk about, Sir? I'm ruined! I don't have a prayer of making a life in the United States ... not with all the newspaper coverage nationwide ... and being a man of color. It's hell! Everything I've ever strived for is gone!" Henry looks away with disgust, his hands folded and his head bent toward the floor.

"Let me say something to you, Lieutenant! You're the best officer I've ever served with! And that includes my Civil War duty. A better day will come for you! A man like you can never give up hope!"

Colonel Novak pulls up a chair and sits next to Henry. "I don't believe for a minute you are guilty. To be discharged for a false charge of misconduct is criminal on the part of the judiciary. What's happened here is the same thing that transpired in the south after the Civil War, prejudice and politics."

Henry looks to Colonel Novak with aura of helplessness and sadness in his eyes. A look that Colonel Novak has never seen before, not even on the face of dying soldiers in the Civil War. "Tell me about it, Sir. But what the hell can a black man with a Dishonorable Discharge from the army do in America?"

Colonel Novak ponders seriously as he looks directly into Henry's famished eyes. "You speak Spanish! You're a civil engineer by education! You're a cordial man and you're well disciplined. Let me introduce you to a man that is much like you and very successful."

Henry stares at the ceiling and takes a deep breath as Colonel Novak continues. "His name is Thompson. His company works with land reform and mining on the Texas-Mexican border. He's a good businessman and quite honorable. He cares about the people he works with. I know he can use a man like you."

Henry acts disinterested and remains quiet.

"He lives in Nuevo Laredo, Mexico. I can telegraph him. Consider it, Lieutenant! It just may be a whole new life for you. Maybe this is what your destiny is really about."

Henry reacts defensively. "Hell, Colonel! I don't know if I can come out of this!"

"I'll contact him anyway. It's a good option. Think about it. Maybe God has a new responsibility for you now."

Henry's mind is not concentrating on what Colonel Novak is talking about. His mind reels with emotions, ranging from despair to rage.

"Lieutenant Washington! I have the utmost respect for you, remember that. I'll do whatever I can to vindicate you, but in the meantime I want you to consider seeing Mr. Thompson. It just may be that you can do more for yourself and society working in his company than you ever can being caught up in this forsaken place and the sick politics of the army."

Henry has tears in his eyes as Colonel Novak stands up. "I've got to go now, Lieutenant. Think about what I've just said."

Henry regains his composure slightly and realizes that Colonel Novak means well and is sincere in what he has been talking about. Henry stands up and looks Colonel Novak in the eyes. "Thank you for stopping by, Colonel. It means a lot to me. It's just that right now I want to be alone. I'll think about what you've said."

"Good, Lieutenant! It may be a whole new future and career for you."

"Oh, Sir. Will you please say goodbye to Sergeant Thomas for me? He's an excellent Sergeant, Sir. I hope you will treat him well."

"Lieutenant Washington, I've known him longer than I have you, and I think of him as I think of you. He's about the best enlisted man in the whole United States Cavalry. I'll do the best I can to help him in his army career, and I will surely give him your regards."

That night Henry reads his red Bible and ponders the circumstances that brought him to this time in his life. "Maybe I do have a destiny beyond the Army," he thinks.

The next morning Colonel Novak hears a knock on his office door. "Come in."

Henry, dressed in civilian clothes, walks to the front of Colonel Novak's desk, stands at attention and salutes. "Sir, I've been thinking ... maybe I do have a life beyond the Army."

"I think you do Lieutenant. How about Mexico?"

"I've thought seriously about that, Sir ... I'm ready to go there."

"Good, I'll wire Jim Thompson today that you're coming ... he's already expecting you. I've already secured your documentation. Are you packed?"

"Yes, Sir!"

"Well, how about if I have Sergeant Thomas give you a ride to the station. Be ready at 0500 hours."

Henry acts somewhat relieved at this decision. "Thank you, Sir. I'll be ready."

One the way back to his quarters each enlisted man he encounters stops, stands at attention and salutes, "Good morning, Sir!"

At 0500 hours the next morning, Henry opens his quarters' door to see Sergeant Thomas waiting with the buckboard, hitched to two of the post's most beautiful Bay Morgans.

Sergeant Thomas comes to attention and salutes. "Good Morning, Sir!"

"I see we're ready to go, Sergeant."

"Yes, Sir!"

As they begin to leave Sergeant Thomas drives the horses past Colonel Novak's Headquarters building. There stands

Colonel Novak and his officer staff. As Henry passes, all the officers salute. Then comes a loud yell, "Regiment, Ten Hut!"

Gathered at the post interior entrance are the men of the Tenth Cavalry Regiment. Small tears form at the corners of Henry's eyes as he takes his last look of the men he served with. The emotions within him are overwhelming.

Henry stands upright in the buckboard as he passes by and gives his old regiment one last farewell.

The trip to Wallace City is much like the one when Henry first came to the area. He was quiet for most of the ride.

"You like it here, don't you, Sergeant?"

"Yes, Sir, it be my home now Sir. Don't know what'n else I do. The Army be my life, Sir."

"Know what you mean, Sergeant," replies Henry as he takes his last look at the rolling hills. Nothing more was said until they came in view of Wallace City.

"There she be, Sir! Train's a chugg'n. We'se be ther' right on time, Sir."

Sergeant Thomas pulled the buckboard up to the station platform, and then jumped off to tie the horses.

"I be gitt'n de bags, Sir."

Henry walks to the station office for his ticket. In the background the conductor yells, "You're the only passenger outa here! You about ready to go?"

Henry walks to the passenger car where Sergeant Thomas waits with his baggage. "You be hav'n a good trip, Sir."

Henry, being somewhat emotional about the situation thanked Sergeant Thomas and shook his hand goodbye. "You're a damn good soldier Sergeant. It's men like you that are the backbone of the Army. I wish you well ... and who knows, maybe we'll see each other again someday."

As Henry boards the train, Sergeant Thomas gives his last salute.

"Oh! Take good care of those Morgans, Sergeant!"

"I be a do'n that, Sir!"

CHAPTER TWENTY-FOUR
MEXICO – A NEW LIFE

Henry takes his seat as the conductor approaches. "Your ticket, Sir!"

Henry is startled. His mind had been on vague thoughts of his future. "Yes, I have it here someplace." Henry searches his coat pockets as the conductor looks at him in a curious manner.

"I seem to recognize you from someplace," comments the conductor as he punches Henry's ticket. "Just can't place it. Maybe it was a picture ... a wanted poster maybe?" queries the conductor. "Ah! No matter. I'll think of it later."

As the train continues down the track the sound of the rhythmic click/clack, click/clack induces Henry to fall asleep. The past several weeks have been a severe emotional drain on him, and in a small sense, Henry welcomes the quietness and privacy on the train.

It takes five days of changing trains to make connections into Nuevo Laredo, on the United States and Mexican border. Henry is sweating slightly and changes clothes just before the train stops. "Damn! It's hot down here!" Henry comments to himself as he carries his bags to the train platform. As he looks around he sees the Mexican border Customs Information and Identification Office. "Thank God Colonel Novak got me proper identification and papers before I left," he mumbles.

Henry stands on the platform for a few minutes observing the festivities and people around him in ethnic dress. The sounds of music from different guitars comes from several directions and the people are talking loud and fast.

Once at the Customs gate the guard speaks firmly and directly to Henry. "Your identification, Sir! And your purpose in Mexico?"

Henry responds in Spanish as he presents his credentials. "Business. I'm here to visit the Mexican/American Institute on Land Reform."

The Customs Guard looks at Henry, then laughs. "Land reform? The Mexican Government knows nothing of land reform, Señor. Possibly you should be a revolutionary. They talk of land reform."

The Customs guard stamps Henry's passport, then looks serious. "Be careful, Señor. It's obvious you're new to this country. I'll give you some good advice." The guard leans close to Henry as he speaks, "Be careful who you trust here, Señor. You can get yourself killed!" The guard backs away and smiles. "Land reform?" voices the guard as he shakes his head and chuckles. "Good luck, Señor!"

For the most part, Henry ignores the guard's comments as he walks to the street looking for a black carriage that is to pick him up. As he waits, he watches the people go about their business in what appears to him, a relaxed, jovial manner. Standing there also brings back memories, such as his conversation with Sergeant Thomas. He smiles slightly as he particularly recalls the time Sergeant Thomas joked about being off the map and in Mexico. Henry turns as he hears someone call his name.

"Señor! Señor, Washington?"

There is his driver in a new Phaeton carriage and a beautiful black horse.

A nice carriage, Henry thinks as he picks up his bags.

"Hello, Señor Washington. My name is Pedro Gonzales. Mr. Thompson sent me to give you a ride to his office."

"Good to meet you, Pedro. This looks like an interesting place."

"It can be, Señor!" replies Pedro in a serious voice. "Mr. Thompson would like to meet you, so I take you to his place of business, yes?"

"That's fine, Pedro. I'll just look around as we go."

Henry is sweating in the ninety-seven-degree heat. He takes his suit jacket off, leans back in the seat, and marvels at the uniqueness of the people and the town's adobe style architecture. It's going to take some doing to adjust to this, he thinks as he continues to look at his new surroundings.

After a twenty minute ride, Pedro stops the horse in front of a neatly manicured lawn with hundreds of flowers neatly placed on the landscape. At the end of the one-hundred-foot walkway is a light tan stucco building with a large courtyard. Printed on the side of the structure is a company logo: MEXICANA/AMERICANA INSTITUTE-LAND REFORM

Henry gets out of the buggy and looks around the area as Pedro speaks. "Leave your bags in the buggy, Señor. We will take them to your hacienda later. You may walk inside. The secretary will help you."

Henry isn't used to the pleasantries he has received thus far and is still hesitant about being in Mexico. It will be years later when he will realize the significance of his decision to come to Laredo. Henry stops after his first four steps inside. The interior décor stuns him with its natural, simplistic beauty.

As he gazes at the fine interior stonework and neatly sculptured walls, a pretty Mexican woman in her early twenties, approaches him. Henry is surprised by her kind attitude, yet very business like demur. "Good afternoon, Señor. My name is Juanita. May I help you?"

Henry can't help but notice how pretty she is with her deep brown eyes and long, black hair tied in a braid, both distinctly enhanced by her cream colored dress. "Ah, yes. My name is Henry Washington."

"Your purpose of business, Señor?"

"I'm here to see Mr. Thompson. I just arrived from the United States. I believe he is expecting me."

"Oh! Señor Washington! Just one moment please. I'll let Señor Thompson know you're here."

Juanita walks into an adjacent room while Henry returns to his visual inspection of the room. He scans all the paintings on the wall and is about to walk over to one labeled "THE ALAMO," when Juanita walks back into the room.

"He'll see you in a few minutes, Lieutenant Washington," Juanita catches herself quickly. "I mean, Mr. Washington. I'm sorry."

Henry smiles as Juanita acts embarrassed. "That's okay, Ma'am," states Henry candidly.

At that moment the office door opens and John Thompson, a handsome, tall man of Mexican/American decent appears. At thirty-four-years of age, his rugged features belie his pleasant personality. Henry immediately notices the gentle look in his eyes.

"Henry Washington! Let me shake your hand. I'm so glad you're here. I've been expecting you."

John Thompson shakes Henry's hand firmly and talks in a pleasing, confident manner. "Colonel Novak told me so many good things about you. He and I grew up together in east Texas, but I hadn't heard from him in several years until he contacted me about you."

Henry acts shy and conservative, but feels relaxed by the cordial mannerisms of Mr. Thompson.

"In his letter he stated that you're an outstanding individual and an exceptional soldier. Please, come into my office. We can talk more there."

As they walk into John Thompson's office Henry becomes more enthralled as he looks around. The walls are covered with volumes of books. The room is furnished in a unique Spanish flavor with two soft leather chairs, a colorful stone laid floor, a glass chandelier, and behind a large desk are several original paintings, signed by John Thompson. It is the most professional appearing office Henry has ever seen, one of an obviously astute man.

John Thompson walks behind his large, hand carved desk which is piled with paper work and motions for Henry to be seated. Henry sits down slowly into a leather chair in front of the desk and feels the soft leather with his hands.

"I understand your major at West Point was engineering, with a Spanish minor, Henry ..." John Thompson interrupts his own conversation for a moment to light his cigar, then continues. "... the kind of background this institution needs in an individual."

Henry continues to admire several of John Thompson's original paintings as he quickly responds. "Yes, Sir. That's correct. You're quite an artist, Mr. Thompson."

"Please call me John, Henry. Painting is a hobby of mine. I'll give you a couple of paintings of your choice for your office, but for now, I must briefly orientate you to our public mission. Also, we'll be working relatively close together on certain projects, so we may as well dispense with formalities."

John Thompson takes a couple more puffs off his cigar as Henry acts slightly ill at ease in his new surroundings. "Henry, are you aware we're about to have a major revolution in this country ... not today, or tomorrow, but possibly within a few years?"

Henry looks at Mr. Thompson with interest. "A revolution? What kind of revolution?"

"Ultimately, an out and out war ... for the land, or as some like to call it ... independence. No matter how you look at it, it will be the peons against the patrons. I'm sure it will affect our intended purpose somewhat, but that's the nature of this country."

Thompson gets up from his chair and walks to the window. "I see the carriage is still waiting. Tell you what, why don't you get yourself situated. We can discuss business and politics later. As a military trained man, I'm sure you will be interested in what's developing here." John Thompson walks to his desk and lays his cigar in an ashtray.

"I've arranged to have you stay in a small house down the road. I think you'll like it. I'll have Juanita take you there. Get yourself settled and rested. Tomorrow we can talk business and then have dinner in the evening."

Mr. Thompson walks with Henry to the reception area and calls to Juanita. He shakes Henry's hand firmly. "Good afternoon, Henry. I'll see you tomorrow. I've got to get back to work, but Juanita will answer any questions you may have. She knows our business well."

Henry politely says goodbye to John, and as he turns to Juanita, she formally addresses him in an apologetic manner. "Mr. Washington. I didn't mean anything by calling you Lieutenant. It just slipped out. Mr. Thompson mentioned several times that a Lieutenant from the United States Army was coming here, so I ..."

Henry smiles as he interrupts. "That's okay, Juanita. I rather miss that title."

Juanita smiles back as she gives Henry his keys. "These are the keys to your casa. I'll show you where it is." Henry and Juanita walk outside and have walked part way to the carriage when Henry stops. Henry gazes at all the sites around him, then turns to Juanita and talks in a soft, deliberate voice, as if he has felt some kind of relief. "This place is not what I expected. It's really beautiful here."

Juanita smiles and agrees. "Yes, it is, Mr. Washington. But someday maybe you will tell me what it is like where you come from."

Henry smiles as they step into the carriage.

For the next year Henry perfects his written and oral skills in the Spanish language, and studies land and property law as it applies to Mexico. He and John Thompson develop a close business and personal relationship as both are intensely interested in the social and economic development of the region, and also have a common love for horses.

It is the first time in Henry's life that he feels some individual freedom of expression and has earned enough money to purchase his own horse and carriage, along with other items of personal need.

Although Henry's relationship with Juanita is clearly of a business nature, they work well together and become close personal friends. Periodically, Henry's thoughts revert back to the days when he was with the Tenth Cavalry. However, as time goes on, he becomes more interested in his duties with the Mexican/American Land Reform Institute and unknowingly, becomes more and more deeply involved in the politics and conflicts of the Mexican people.

Henry's home is small and simply decorated, but it affords him the privacy he has learned to love and appreciate. His office, done in a Spanish décor, is small and Spartan-like but has a good selection of history and economic books, as well as three cavalry paintings given to him by John Thompson. On the wall, behind his desk, Henry has framed and encased his brass insignias of the Tenth United States Cavalry, this being the only outward display of his military service.

It is a cool April evening as Henry and Juanita are about to conclude five months of work on researching original land titles recorded in the Province of Chihuahua. More than twenty books and legal documents have been piled on one of three desks as the two labor through the pages of others. Both are tired, as they have been working since early that morning in preparation for a business trip to Saitillo, Mexico.

Juanita closes her book, yawns, and sits back in her chair. She looks at Henry for a moment, then speaks in a soft, quiet manner. "Henry, let's call it a day. I'm tired and hungry."

Henry looks up from the book he is studying and blinks his eyes several times for a short distance focus at Juanita. "Yes, I agree. I think we're about as prepared as we can be for the trip to Saitillo tomorrow, don't you?"

Juanita yawns again as she stretches her arms. "I think so."

Henry closes his book, rolls his shirt sleeves down, and stands up. "I've got the files ready. I need to get some sleep. We can review everything on the train. Hopefully this should be a very productive trip."

"I think so, too. Oh, Henry, would you like to get something to eat?"

Henry looks at his pocket watch. "Seven o'clock. Sure. I've got an hour or so before I want to get some sleep. Do you know nice, quiet place?"

"I know a place just down the street. It's quiet and the food is good."

"I'm starting to like enchiladas, Juanita. Do they have good enchiladas?"

"Muy Bueno, Henry! They're the best in all of Mexico."

Henry and Juanita talk amicably about their business as they walk for ten minutes, then enter a small business district. "There it is, Henry, that little restaurant on the corner."

"I don't see any restaurant."

"That's just it, Henry. Not many people know it's there. Just the local people go there. I first went there when I was a young girl."

As they walk up to the building, Henry looks for a sign of some kind, but the only indication that anyone can even enter the small building is a sign by the door, "Restaurante. Entra!"

The interior is dimly lit by lanterns on the walls and candles on each table. An older lady, dressed in a beautifully embroidered white dress, approaches as they walk to a small reception area in the interior court yard. "May I help you?" she inquires politely.

Juanita leans forward and whispers in her ear. The lady nods a yes as both women giggle. "Come with me, Señor."

Henry follows Juanita and the lady into a small private room with a table set for two.

"Is this like the quiet place you had in mind, Henry?" asks Juanita.

Henry looks at the setting as the lady lights the candles. Soft music from a guitarist plays in the background. "Well ... yes. It's a little more than I expected."

TRAIN TO SAITILLO, MEXICO

The next morning, Juanita is waiting at the train station as Henry arrives.

"Good morning, Juanita! Did you get a good night's rest?"

Juanita smiles and acts confident, "Sí, I did, Henry, and I'm especially looking forward to this trip. I hope after all this work we can get the information we need."

"Me too," replies Henry as he changes the subject. "I want to thank you for introducing me to your friends last night ... and the food! It was great!"

"I thought you might like the place. Oh! Oh! The train's getting ready to leave! Best we get on board before we're left here," comments Juanita with a smile.

Juanita and Henry sit with business papers on their laps and original land titles on the adjacent seats as they ride the train to Saitillo. Henry becomes frustrated as he shakes his head while studying a legal document. "I just don't understand this ... this legal description and title holder ... this doesn't sound right."

"I know what you're thinking," comments Juanita. "Each time we have a new government in this country, the titles change names, almost overnight."

Henry holds up a file document entitled LEGAL DESCRIPTION. Frustrated, he waves it at Juanita. "We've been working on these legal descriptions and titles now for more than a year, and honestly, I don't know who owns any of this land!"

"It's confusing, I know," confesses Juanita. "The government talks about the peons owning it. The revolutionaries talk about the peons owning it." Juanita sighs, then continues with an emotional statement of conviction. "But in reality, the ownership lies with whoever has the most guns and power. In this country, the poor get poorer and the rich get richer. But the rich get the land ... El Presidente Camillo and his henchmen. That's reality!"

Henry looks closely at the document in his hands. "I thought we were here to change that!"

"We are, Henry, but it's more involved than you yet know!"

"Then what do you know about this man named don Abraham?"

Juanita rolls her eyes expressively. "don Abraham! Huh! I know some. He's a wealthy Hacendado, or land owner. During the Yaqui War he sided with El Presidente. When the Yaqui's were defeated their land was divided up among the friends of the El Presidente. Those Indians that were not killed became virtual slaves. don Abraham is one of those people. He has no honor. He is a bastard!"

Henry hands Juanita the document. She looks at it briefly, then shakes her head. "Henry, this is not unusual. A peon has no rights. don Abraham is instrumental in that. He is …"

Henry interrupts as he reaches in his sashay and pulls out several more documents. "But look! These documents give don Abraham's address as 127 Rue St. Jacques, Paris, France."

"That's probably correct, Henry. Many Hacendados live in another country, even America. They have overseers who manage the property or ranches and carry out the Hacendados' orders and they work the peons to death. It's been going on for so long now. The government allows this to happen."

Juanita sighs, then takes another breath. Her frustration and anger begin to show on her face and in her voice. "Men like don Abraham will sell their souls to the devil! They don't care about Mexico or the people … just themselves. They're very greedy men!"

Henry is anxious as he becomes more curious about the political dealings and apparent covert theft of land and resources. "The revolution that John talks about … what will happen to a man like don Abraham?"

Juanita leans forward, looks at Henry seriously, and speaks candidly and firmly. "He will please who he must, like a chameleon, he will change his colors. If the government remains strong, he will support that. If the revolution becomes strong, he will support the revolutionaries. Either way, his goal is to gain more land and power."

Juanita leans back in her seat as she throws her hands up in disgust. "Whatever direction the wind goes, so goes don Abraham. He is a man without a spine, a man without integrity, a man without a soul."

Suddenly there is a knock on the compartment door followed by the conductor's voice. "Saitillo! Five minutes!"

Henry and Juanita step from the train, then walk to a large adobe building that is used as a court house. Juanita walks to the reception desk and talks to the receptionist. "Excuse me, Señora, we're looking for some information on land tracts, mostly legal descriptions and land titles."

Although curious about why they are in Saitillo looking at legal descriptions, the woman politely directs Juanita to a room off to the left. "All legal descriptions on land should be in that room, if there are any," comments the woman with an air of sarcasm.

The room is full of old, legal property books and title documents, most loosely bound. "Looks like the place, Henry. There's a table and two chairs. Let's get to work."

Both Henry and Juanita systematically and studiously forage through volume after volume. After more than five hours Juanita lets out a short scream. "This is it! I think I've found it, Henry!"

Henry quickly gets up and leans on the table next to Juanita. "Damn! An American company ... out of New York!" exclaims Henry.

"That's right, Henry! American Industrial Mining. It shows here that they own thousands of acres in the state of Coahuila and Chihuahua. And guess whose name is on each piece of land and listed as title holder?"

"Don't tell me ... don Abraham Castillo!"

Juanita looks at Henry and smiles. "Right! And don't tell me there isn't an American interest in what happens in Mexico. This is just the tip of the iceberg, Henry. We've got something here! This information in itself, can cause a revolution if it were publicly known."

"No wonder these people are poor and scared! With the amount of money involved here, anyone who gets in the way will be killed!"

"Let's write all this information down, Henry. We can still catch the evening train back to Nuevo Laredo. John Thompson and the other members of the coalition will be interested in this!"

Henry and Juanita sit across from each other in a contented silence as they listen to the click/clack of the train roll over the tracks. Juanita's eyes are fixed out the window at the countryside, she is pleased at what they have discovered. However, she can't help but notice the poverty of the small towns as the train slowly passes through. Juanita looks at Henry as he appears deep in thought. "What are you thinking, Henry?"

"Oh, I don't know. A lot of things I guess. I keep remembering how a Sergeant once told me, in a joking manner, about Mexico. I was just wondering how he is doing."

Juanita sits upright. "You miss the army don't you?"

Henry thinks seriously about this question for a good minute. "Yes, I guess I do. But I've put much of that behind me. I think now that I may be destined for a different life than what I thought."

"Well, Henry, don't put those military experiences and knowledge too far in your past. There's going to be a revolution here someday. Like John says, it may be a few years away, but it will come. These documents certainly give reason for it."

Henry looks at Juanita with a gentle gaze. He has admired her from the day he met her. In his mind she is a woman of grace and compassion, filled with honesty, goodwill, and guts. "You're a revolutionary, Juanita."

Juanita looks surprised as Henry says this. "Me? No, I'm just a simple woman who seeks justice in my country. There are many ways to fight for justice."

"Yes, that's true. But what I like about you is your willingness to fight for what you believe in, or rather do not believe in."

Henry leans forward and puts his hand on Juanita's knee. "We've been working together for more than a year now and I have come to trust you, possibly with my life. I remember a piece of paper that a Bishop once gave me long ago called the Code of a True Gentleman. It says a lot about a man's code of conduct. It is a code impossible to live up to for most, including me ... but when I think of it, I think of you as a woman who can live up to a code like that. Let me call it your code. The code of the true gentlewoman."

"What does it say, Henry?"

"Well, let me cite it to you, interchanging the word man with woman." Henry then cites Juanita the Code of the "True Gentlewoman" as he remembers it.

Juanita listens intently and when Henry finishes she sits silent for a moment. "That's beautiful, Henry! You have memorized it!"

"That I did, the day after the Bishop gave it to me. I've carried that doctrine or set of principals in my mind almost every day since."

"Henry, I think you're a gentlemen in those ways and more. You have deep compassion for others and are so understanding. And you too, stand up for what is right and just. Maybe that's why we get along so well."

Juanita remains silent for a moment then adds, "Henry, be proud of yourself. You have good traits that other's seek. There is a reason you have come to Mexico."

Henry remains quiet, seriously thinking about the current situation as he listens to Juanita.

Finally Juanita slowly leans forward, puts her hands on Henry's and looks into his eyes. "Henry, are you okay?"

"Juanita, I must tell you something. I trust you with my soul. There is only one other person I learned to trust before. His name was Fred Williams ... a Lieutenant in my Regiment. But what I have to say goes beyond that."

Juanita's interest and compassion for Henry multiply as he talks. She listens to every word he says, then Henry abruptly stops talking.

"What is it, Henry? Feel free to confide in me," states Juanita.

"I don't want to confide in you, Juanita. I guess I ... I guess ..."

Juanita is anxious and interrupts. "You guess what, Henry?"

Henry swallows hard at what he wants to say. "I guess I want to tell you ... I love you."

Juanita reacts with a smile and a strong squeeze of Henry's hands. "I'm glad you said that, Henry. Because I feel the same about you. I think I fell in love with you and your fine qualities the day I met you in the reception room of Mr. Thompson's office."

Henry's whole body relaxes on these words from Juanita. His fear of possible rejection by her is gone as Juanita continues to talk. "Henry, you represent all the good qualities I would ever want in a man and more."

Henry becomes excited and lets his emotions flow. "Juanita, will you consider marrying me?"

Juanita smiles, then chuckles as her heart seems to flutter. "Henry, I'll do more than consider it. I'll commit myself and do it." Juanita squeezes Henry's hands again, then jumps to the seat next to Henry and kisses him. "Yes! Yes! Yes! I'll marry you, Henry!" exclaims Juanita excitedly.

"Wait 'til John hears about this!" laughs an excited Henry Washington.

John Thompson is pleased and happy for them. Four months later he sponsors their simple wedding in a small chapel next to a river at the edge of the Pasque Mountain Range. Juanita looks elegant in her long white dress. Her deep brown eyes and dark hair simply enhance her beauty. Henry also looks distinguished and happy. He still has that military bearing, even while dressed in a gray civilian suit.

The ceremony is short, with only a handful of personal friends invited. But the depth and commitment of love between Henry and Juanita is impossible to put into words or to express in any verbal form. This undying love and trust in one another will solidify their passion for justice and goodness in the violent years to come.

John Thompson sums it up at the end of the reception. "You two are truly meant for each other, probably more than you presently know, for I believe your union will have an impact in this country beyond description."

For the next several years Juanita and Henry work diligently on a comprehensive program for land reform in Northern Mexico, a program that brings additional financial and political support from the United States Christian based "Help the Little Children."

The Mexicana/Americana Land Reform Institute subsequently increases their political base and influence, not only with the people, but with a new wave of honest businessmen and politicians. Even the Catholic church in Mexico endorses the Institute's neutral position of new and equitable laws under a new Constitution. However, the deepening splinter between the Mexican government and the embittered peons of the region is creating a political abyss, and the Mexicana/Americana Land Reform Institute is about to be caught in the middle.

CHAPTER TWENTY-FIVE
CAUGHT IN A REVOLUTION

The involvement of Mexicana/Americana Reform Institute in the political and economic affairs of Northern Mexico deepens daily. Juanita, a descendant of a Yaqui Indian, has solidified her fight to return original ownership of the land to her people and creates a system of schooling for the Indian children. Her dedication results in Henry's loyal support, but he too becomes entangled in the deepening quagmire of political affairs in Mexico.

Between the years of 1900 and 1908, Mexico becomes a breeding ground of dissent on internal political and economic issues, resulting in massive social upheaval. On one side is the consolidation liberal faction of the revolutionary front, later led mainly by Poncho Diaz in the northern provinces. On the other is the conservative Cientifico backed government of President Camillo. The Cientifico's, or scientific orientated elitists of economic development, have exploited the Yaqui Indians and other rural Mexicans of their land and resources, then subject them to peonage. The Cientifico's philosophy is simple. If the people resist, they will be liquidated. They especially target the Yaqui Indians and others who originally held vast tracts of land and mineral resources. This policy, led by a handful of so-called "educated men" from the richest of Mexican families and totally influential in the Hernandez dictatorship, is clear; either accept the position of the government's political and economical abuse or be crushed. No opposition is to be tolerated.

The relentless task of keeping the Mexicana/Americana Reform Institute on a neutral political basis is getting more and more difficult. Henry and John Thompson work tirelessly to continue the development of the Institute's policy for National Reform. This includes a proposed National Convention on Constitutional law to be held in late October.

Incidental to the dangerous activity of representing a new National Coalition of Legitimate Interests, Henry and Juanita find themselves involved in an unexpected event. Juanita surprises Henry, early in March of 1898, when she informs him that she is pregnant. Henry, now in his forties, is shocked at the news, but the feelings of joy and the anticipation of being a father creates a new spirit in him. From this day on Henry's attitude changes even more than it did with his marriage to Juanita. His very soul seems to energize him as he continues to develop his goals and his life.

"Juanita, you have given me everything a man can wish for. You're a wonderful wife, and now you give me a child. What more can I ever ask for?"

Juanita looks at Henry, her eyes bright with happiness and joy. "It is you, Henry, that has given my life meaning. You are strong and brave, yet tender and compassionate. It means so much to me that you are this way, for it is your moral strength and depth of character that the people of Mexico have come to love you. It will be that way with your daughter also."

"Henry's facial features take on a strange appearance. "My daughter? How do you know the baby is a girl?"

"I know, Henry. I just know."

Henry smiles, walks to Juanita, and holds her close.

"A girl or a boy. Either one is fine by me. It just makes me want to cry, I feel so happy."

Juanita gazes into Henry's eyes with the same look of love and affection she had the day they were married.

"I'm happy too. Do you have a name in mind if it's a girl?"

Henry thinks for a moment, then replies confidently. "Yes! How about Carmen?"

"And if it's a boy?" asks Juanita gently.

"Well, I haven't thought about that."

Juanita smiles and squeezes Henry's hand, which has become one of her continual ways of touching and showing love. "Now more than ever we have a reason to work for truth and justice in our country, Henry ... for the sake of our child as well as countless others."

Carmen is born in December of 1898. To Henry's delight he is the proud father of a beautiful and healthy eight-pound baby girl with coal black hair and dark brown eyes. He displays his joy openly to all his associates and friends. Henry spends many of his spare hours playing with Carmen and throughout her formative years he guides her diligently. Even John Thompson, who Juanita and Henry named as Godfather, has to caution Henry on being an over protective father. But it is evident to all who know Henry, that he is a proud father, and a loyal and faithful husband.

As Carmen grows older it is obvious she has much of the physical and mental stamina of her father. But his years of involvement and commitment in politics and social change demand more of his time. Juanita then, lessens her involvement in the affairs of the Institution to care for Carmen.

Every Sunday is Henry's and Carmen's time together. As time progresses and Carmen grows older she becomes more devoted to her father. He is her hero and she is proud of him as her father, as Henry is proud to have Juanita and Carmen as his wife and daughter.

It is a Sunday afternoon in South Laredo when there is a knock at the home of Juanita and Henry. Henry is talking with Carmen, who is now fourteen, as Juanita rushes in. "Henry, word has come from a Yaqui messenger that Poncho Diaz is meeting with don Abraham in Chihuahua Province!"

Henry reacts quickly as he turns to Juanita. "That means the factions are splitting! More splinter groups. Damn!"

"There's more, Henry. Diaz thinks you're against him now."

"I've never met the man," replies Henry as he tries to calm Juanita's anxiety.

"With him it doesn't make any difference. You know his history don't you?"

"Just from what he's done in the last eight years, why?"

"He's for himself!" states Juanita. "I've known of him since I was a little girl. He's been a fugitive from the Federales since he was sixteen. He shot a rancher who he claimed had abused his sister. Diaz has been hiding out in the mountains since that time."

"I didn't know that," replies Henry with an air of surprise.

"It's true. His popularity with the peons was originally because he's anti-government ... against Hernandez. Not because he represents the peon's overall legal or land interests or well-being. He steals from them as easily as he steals from Presidente Hernandez. He fights the Federales for personal vengeance, not the good of Mexico. And now it appears you threaten him by being vocal in a legitimate reform movement."

"I'll talk to John Thompson about him tomorrow. There's nothing I can do today," states Henry casually.

Carmen interrupts her parents' conversation. "Papa, you must be careful of a man like him! My friends say that he is no longer to be trusted ... that he has raped Mexico of her soul."

"Carmen, I think you know your father better than that. I have survived more in life than the personal vendetta of someone like Poncho Diaz."

"Just the same, Papa, I worry about you."

Juanita gives Henry a serious look, then moves close to hug him. "It's true, Henry!" adds Juanita. "He is not a man to be reckoned with. It is his ignorance and stupidity that makes him dangerous."

Henry, in order to please Carmen and Juanita, pledges additional caution on his business trips.

"For the love of you both, I'll take your wishes to heart. I promise from here on out not to publish or publicly announce my travel plans. Only those persons with whom we are negotiating will know of my whereabouts."

Poncho Diaz is a stocky man at five-foot-nine-inches tall, who wears a heavy moustache and consistently dresses in vasquelare attire. His face is shadowed under the sun by his large sombrero and his spurs jingle as he walks to the window. He stands silent as he looks out at the mountains.

Don Abraham is sixty-three-years old now, and has gained much weight, almost to the point of being obese. However, his neatly combed gray hair and well dressed appearance gives him a somewhat distinguished look. He impatiently watches Poncho Diaz at the window as he rapidly puffs on his cigar. "I ask you, Captain ... Captain! What are your plans? You told me ..."

Poncho Diaz interrupts harshly as he turns to don Abraham and glares at him with silent intimidation. "Why you call me Captain? I am a bandit, Señor. Some say a murderer ... other things."

Diaz walks back to the window and stares out in silence for a moment before he continues his reasoning for his behavior. "You know, Señor! I have lived in these mountains for twenty years. Even the fierce Rurales, or the Mexican Rangers couldn't hunt me down! Yet, I am still a free man!"

Don Abraham quickly interjects his thoughts. "Señor Diaz, I know your history. The Federales still have a price on your head, but you are still the man to lead the oppressed people of Mexico against this regime."

Poncho Diaz's justification of himself continues. "President Hernandez, the Federales, the Rurales, all are corrupt. More than me!"

Diaz turns to don Abraham as he sits on the sill of the window. With a quizzical, but hostile voice, Poncho Diaz confronts him. "So, what do you want with a bandit? I support the peons, but I live my own code."

"We want you to organize the peons to fight! President Hernandez must be killed. It is the only way he will give up the comforts of his office. You must defeat the Federales! Free Mexico! Change ..."

Diaz interrupts don Abraham and shows the distrust and contempt he holds for all wealthy landowners. "You're asking me to overthrow this government for a corrupt bastard like you? You're more crooked than El Presidente! You don't care about the peons. Just the money and land ... power, maybe."

"No, Señor Diaz! I work to free our people. We need the land reform."

Poncho Diaz thinks hard. He bites his cheek as he walks back and forth by the window, thinking about this rare opportunity. "Okay! I know you lie, but you get me money to buy rifles, horses, and artillery. I will create havoc for El Presidente and destroy everyone connected with the government ... maybe you too!"

Diaz laughs, then walks up to don Abraham. "Maybe I become a Robin Hood, hey? Or El Presidente of all of Mexico. Even your boss! Who knows?"

For the next three years Poncho Diaz assembles thousands of men under his command with the promise that they will regain their land, and that their children will be schooled.

The distinction of the various factions is now more evident than before: the Catholic Church, the large landowners, the foreign capitalists, the federal government, and the peons. Unfortunately the peons have been lied to by all factions, and the splitting of forces within the revolutionary ranks creates further distrust of all leaders. Most however, still believe in the words of Poncho Diaz.

The last bastion of real honesty and truth, as felt by some of the peons and province businessmen of integrity, is the Mexicana/Americana Land Reform Institute. However, the Institute does not support armed insurrection, only diplomatic suggestions and solutions. This makes no difference to Poncho Diaz as he has determined in his own mind that the Mexicana/Americana Land Reform Institute is a spy group for the United States Government. Consequently, Diaz orders the assassination of Henry Washington and John Thompson.

The revolution spreads rapidly with the main forces in the South led by José, and with Poncho Diaz in the North. As these combined forces finally defeat President Hernandez and his forces, Juan Camillo comes into power. More counter revolutionary forces form and as the Hernandez government begins to immediately collapse, the Revolutionaries themselves begin an internecine struggle for power.

Poncho Diaz is still the most popular leader in the North. However, his raids are loosely organized and tend to be more of a rape and pillage victory than reformation. The months and months of attacking forces wane hard on the people.

The yearly theft and destruction of the villages is best described by Juan Ortiz, who from the age of twelve into manhood was a Diaz freedom fighter. "Poncho Diaz and his men, I was twelve when I first saw them, were a wild looking bunch of men. No discipline, half clothed on half starving horses. Obsolete weapons, ammunition belts across their shoulders, pistols in their belts, in their hands, shooting."

Ortiz hesitates for a moment, his eyes sad and bloodshot from crying. "In the beginning they rode in as heroes, freedom fighters. Pretty girls met them with kisses and flowers. The people rejoiced naively ... for it represented a false victory of the people. We didn't know."

Ortiz moves his head slowly from left to right several times, then stops as he covers his face with his hands. "They took everything from the towns, including the young women. In the end they were worse than the soldiers. I will remember this always! Always!"

It is a quiet afternoon in Diaz's hacienda, a rather plush hideout in the mountains, which is furnished from the looting and raiding of villages in the region, and on several occasions, raids on the United States border towns.

The only sound in the hacienda patio garden is the soft breeze blowing through the trees and a single Morning Dove cooing. Suddenly the sound of bristling spurs and boots tromping on a stone walkway and argumentative voices interrupts the peaceful setting.

"What the hell are you doing?" asks don Abraham as he takes a seat at a round wooden table in the court yard. "Are you out for your own personal gain or are you going to fight the Federales?"

Don Abraham is adamant in his statements. "You steal from the people, take their women. Some think you are worse than the Cientificos!"

Diaz occupies himself with a glass of tequila as he looks in the trees for the dove. He is disinterested in what don Abraham is saying, but turns to respond. "I have never been a soldier or never trained as one, Señor. Nor am I a politician. I am what you and the others have made me!"

Diaz walks slowly toward don Abraham, the steady clang, clang of his spurs breaking the otherwise moments of silence between the two. Diaz stops in front of don Abraham and looks down at him. "Señor Abraham, I've been chased by more uniforms than there are town whores in Mexico. For me, it is easier to know an enemy than a friend, my friend!"

Don Abraham remains silent as Diaz walks to a low hanging tree laden with flowers and gently picks one. He smells of the fragrance, smiles, and turns back to don Abraham. "Señor Abraham, I don't know if this revolution is good or bad, but it makes me money. It gives me women ... and it gives me power! I do as I want! Viva revolution! Death to the Federales! Viva Poncho Diaz!" Diaz laughs in a crude, loud, and boisterous manner.

Don Abraham becomes frustrated as he feels emotions half way between fear and anger. "Señor Diaz, you made a promise! You promised to destroy the Camillo Government, not the villages and the very people who joined your army! I can't even get peons to work under threats of death."

Diaz's voice becomes rough and guttural as he talks back in a firm, direct manner. "Don Abraham, you know I am not an educated man. I just know how to fight."

He takes a chair at the opposite side of the table and continues to talk as he stares don Abraham in the eyes. "That is my life. You pay me to fight! I give you much money ... you take the land. But I know that you are also a greedy, dishonorable man!"

Diaz sits back in his chair, relaxed, a broad smile forms under his large mustache. "I will run the revolution as I see fit, Señor Abraham. Now I pay myself to fight! You will listen to me or I take back what I give you and your friends, sí?"

Poncho Diaz slowly takes a cigar out of his vest and lights it as don Abraham sits quietly, powerless now, over the man he has created. His internal anger swells at each word Poncho Diaz speaks. "Señor Abraham, but there is a way you can help me."

Disgruntled, but surprised at the turn in the conversation and Diaz's request, don Abraham replies with anxious animosity. "What's your request?"

Diaz puffs several times on his cigar, then smiles. "There is one man I want. A man whom I want to see dead more than any other and you can help me."

"And who is that?"

"The Negro American spy! The one who reports my raids into the United States for supplies and weapons. The bastard of a whore who directs policy for that land reform institute in Nuevo Laredo ..."

"What's his name?"

"Señor Henry Washington. He travels, now mostly in secret, to the cities in the northern provinces. He tries to establish legal aid for the people. He is against me and the revolution. He causes me much pain."

Don Abraham quickly seizes upon this new opportunity. "So you want me to find out his travel schedule?" Don Abraham thinks for a minute as he scrambles for a political trade-out. "I can do that, but you must do me a favor in return, Señor Diaz."

"And that is what?" responds Diaz immediately.

"Five-thousand-acres outside the village of Leon. I'll get Señor Washington's travel plans for the next two months through a friend who has contact with the Institute. You raid the village and secure the land for me."

Diaz smiles as he thinks of the deal. "That will be no problem, Señor Abraham. I can take land at the snap of my fingers, but this Señor Washington is evasive."

"It's a deal then, Señor Diaz?"

Poncho Diaz laughs a hearty laugh, smiles, and walks over to don Abraham. "It is a deal, my friend! And I believe you are my friend, right?"

Don Abraham nods and smiles as he tries to quote Poncho Diaz. "It is better to be friends and make deals than to be enemies and make none. Isn't that what you once said, Señor Diaz?"

Both men shake hands as don Abraham prepares to leave. "I'll have the travel schedule of this Señor Washington to you within the next two weeks."

It is three months later when Henry, Juanita, and Carmen are enjoying their train trip to Monterey. Carmen is her vivacious self as she jokes with Henry about a young boy she has met just hours before at the train station. Her long dark hair, large brown eyes, and slim build are only an outward indication of her true beauty. Henry and Juanita have instilled an educational and moral format in Carmen that evolved into her loving and caring personality.

This particular day is a happy one for all, as Carmen has never been to Monterey and is looking forward to visiting the Huasteca waterfall and going to the Federale building with her father for his meeting with the representatives from the state of Chihuahua.

Henry is dressed professionally for the occasion in a business suit. His slightly graying hair gives him a distinguished appearance. And Juanita is especially gorgeous in a bright yellow skirt that accents her light brown colored skin and dark hair. Their conversation is lively and happy, mainly due to Carmen's outgoing personality and constant questioning of her father.

Juanita brought along a small basket of apples and juice she squeezed from oranges, which Henry is sipping on between his comments and opinions to Carmen. "I hope this meeting goes well this afternoon. I have more than fifty-five-hundred signatures calling for a Constitutional Law meeting of the adjoining states and don Ortega promised …"

Carmen interrupts Henry with a big kiss and hug. "Daddy, when we get to Monterey, where are we going to stay?"

Henry is just about to answer his daughter's question when Juanita excitedly interrupts. "Henry! Those men out there! What are they doing?"

Henry quickly shifts to the window and looks, instantly recognizing the developing situation.

"Revolutionaries! Get down!" screams Henry as he quickly tries to figure out an avenue of escape.

"Wham! Blam! Blam!" comes a series of explosions from preset artillery on the nearby hill. Machine gunfire rips through the upper half of the passenger car as another explosion hits the train engine, overturning it. Hundreds of men come running down the hill dressed in white clothes, some on horseback, and others on foot. As they run, their yells and screams intermingle with the constant gunfire.

Other passengers on the train are screaming in panic. Chaos becomes instantaneous. Henry is frantic as he tries to get Carmen out the passenger door. As he looks outside, several bullets hit just above his head. Both sides of the halted and damaged train are now covered by revolutionary forces.

Henry yells at Juanita and Carmen frantically. "Stay down! Crawl to the compartment! Hurry!"

Outside, the revolutionary forces have killed all of the Federal soldiers who were guarding the train, and are systematically robbing, then shooting the civilians. It is only minutes before the train is completely overrun, and Henry scrambles to get Carmen and Juanita hidden.

Revolutionaries swarm over each car, indiscriminately killing the people as they find them, yelling and laughing at their slaughter.

Henry pulls a gun from his business bag, and with concern for his wife and daughter, posts himself in front of the compartment door. "Stay in there and stay low!" he yells.

Suddenly bullets rip through the car as ten revolutionaries enter through the front and rear entrances. Henry shoots the first three men who enter, but is shot three times in the back and arm from behind as revolutionaries come in from the other direction. He immediately drops to the floor.

It is a matter of minutes before the Revolutionaries find Carmen and Juanita and drag them outside as they scream and struggle in vain. Carmen yells for her father. "Daddy! Daddy!" she screams, crying. "Please, help us!"

Henry lies motionless on the floor of the passenger car.

"You bastards!" screams Juanita as she kicks and continues to struggle.

Carmen begins crying uncontrollably as one of Diaz's officers walks up to her. "Hey! You woman! Shut up! My name is Fierro. You remember that!"

Fierro has his men hold Juanita down as he rapes her, then he turns his attention to Carmen. After raping both Juanita and Carmen he stands up and laughs. "Such fine women to die! Too bad!"

Fierro takes his knife and quickly cuts Carmen's and Juanita's throats. "I hated to do that," boasts Fierro to his men, "but my boss, Poncho Diaz, he would never forgive me if I had not!" He laughs.

Fierro orders his men to strip all the bodies of their personal effects. "Take the gold from the Federale car! Then let's go!"

Fierro yells several times as he mounts his horse and watches. Carmen and Juanita lie motionless, their blood pooled around them on the gravel at the base of the railroad track just outside the passenger car.

It is early morning of the following day when Federale troops arrive at the scene.

"Check for any survivors!" yells the Captain.

All the soldiers systematically check the bodies, then pull them one by one in a single row onto the rock bed at the side of the tracks. Juanita and Carmen are laid next to each other at the far end.

Suddenly one of the soldiers yells out of a window of one of the train cars. "One in here, alive! He's badly wounded, sir!"

The Captain rushes into the passenger car to find that Henry, although seriously wounded and unconscious, is still breathing. "Get this one to the hospital in Monterey! Immediately!" yells the Captain.

STATE OF REVENGE

Luckily for Henry, the Federale Captain had some experience in medical maintenance of combat wounds in the field. The twenty-five-mile trip to the hospital in Monterey in a supply wagon is a long, rough ride. Henry has lost a substantial amount of blood, but the timely use of tourniquets and medical supplies carried in the field by the soldiers is lifesaving for him.

Henry is still unconscious as he is rushed into the emergency room. Two doctors and three nurses use the best surgical methods they know of to remove the two small caliber bullets lodged in Henry's upper and lower back. The bullet that hit his left arm shattered his elbow. After more than three hours on the operating table the doctors claim their operation a success, at least in saving Henry's life.

"He'll probably remain unconscious for a few days. But I believe he will live," says Doctor Valdez to the nurses. "His vitals have stabilized. Keep him on the tranquilizer and make sure he has liquids every hour."

"How about his arm, Doctor?" inquires the nurse.

"Not much we can do for that. It's shattered beyond our ability to repair it. It will have to heal on its own as best it can. Just keep it strapped tightly to his side. Does he have any next of kin?"

"I don't know, Doctor. According to the soldier's report there was a woman and a young girl, apparently his wife and daughter, both had been killed and were lying outside the train car."

"His identification papers give his name as Henry Washington and list him as a representative of the Mexicana/Americana Institute in Nuevo Laredo," relates the nurse.

Doctor Valdez thinks for a moment, then instructs the nurse to contact the Institute. "I know the director of that Institute, John Thompson. Get a telegraph to him immediately and let him know Mr. Washington is here and in stable, but critical condition."

"I'll do that now, Doctor!" replies the nurse with a sense of urgency.

Fierro and his small revolutionary army have just returned to their camp, hidden high in the Pasquelo mountains, when one of Poncho Diaz's messengers arrives. "Señor Fierro! Poncho Diaz orders you to his hacienda, pronto."

"I'll be there when I get there! Tell him that! And tell him that his enemy, Señor Washington and his women are dead! Tell him all on the train were killed!"

"What about the money? The gold that the train was carrying?" inquires the messenger.

"Tell him I will bring it to him first thing in the morning."

The carrier rides the five miles deep into the mountains and immediately reports to Poncho Diaz who is grooming his favorite dog on the hacienda patio.

"Señor Diaz! Señor Fierro reports that Mr. Washington is dead, as are his wife and daughter, and all the train passengers. He has the gold and will bring it tomorrow."

Diaz waves the carrier away, sits down in his patio garden and lights a cigar. A smile comes over his face as he thinks of his adversary dead. Too bad his wife and daughter were killed, but that's the way it is, Diaz thinks to himself as a feeling of satisfaction replaces the hostility he has held toward Henry.

It is three days after Henry entered the hospital when John Thompson arrives in Monterey. Henry is still in a state of semi-consciousness, but is slowly improving according to Doctor Valdez, as he and John Thompson talk.

"Señor Thompson, I'm glad you're here. Señor Washington was badly wounded but I think he will live."

"Doctor, do you think he's aware of what happened to his wife and daughter?" inquires John Thompson with concern.

"I don't know. He's been unconscious. My guess is that he doesn't. He's been through severe trauma, physically, so far. I can only guess how he'll react emotionally once he learns of their fate."

"When do you think he'll regain consciousness?"

"Señor Thompson, your guess is as good as mine on that one. Maybe a few days, maybe a week. We want him resting. He took some serious wounds. He's lucky they were small caliber bullets."

"There's a reason I ask. Who's going to tell him about his wife and daughter?"

Doctor Valdez looks at John Thompson for a moment, then responds in a low, serious voice. "Señor Thompson, I had hoped it would be you. The realization of his personal injury, plus learning of the loss of his family, will be traumatizing."

Doctor Valdez hesitates, looks at John Thompson with sincere compassion, then addresses him seriously. "You're his friend and he's going to need you. It's hard to say how he'll react upon learning of their deaths. There's no easy way in a situation like this."

John Thompson stares at the doctor with refrain. He knows Henry well enough to know the rage that will come once Henry learns of his wife's and daughter's deaths. The doctor is right. There is no easy way to tell him, thinks John Thompson.

John paces the hallways of the hospital for hours. Thoughts of Henry, Juanita, and Carmen occupy his mind constantly. He reflects on the first day he met Henry, on Juanita and Henry's wedding, and then the birth of Carmen.

"Such a beautiful family to end up like this!" thinks John Thompson over and over.

Doctor Valdez gives John a room next to Henry's. Between the nurses and John, Henry is under constant surveillance.

Henry has been in the hospital six days before he regains consciousness. At first Henry is confused as to where he is, as if he is just waking up from a bad dream. But as his awareness increases he focuses on his wounds. It suddenly becomes apparent he is in a hospital. His initial reaction is one of panic and shock. Henry immediately begins yelling and screaming for his wife and daughter as he struggles to get up.

"Juanita! Carmen! Juanita, where are you?"

The nurses run into the room and try to first calm Henry, then restrain him. "Doctor! Doctor! We need help!" yell the two nurses.

Two nurses arrive immediately and strap Henry to the bed. John Thompson and Doctor Valdez arrive at the same time. The Doctor orders the nurses to give Henry a shot of morphine. The drug takes effect quickly and Henry soon relaxes and seems to rest calmly.

"We're going to have to keep him restrained for a while. I can't let him tear those wounds open," comments Doctor Valdez to John Thompson. "In fact, the way he's acting, it just may be best to tell him about his family while he's semi-conscious with the drugs and strapped down. It'll give him time to think about his loss without injuring himself or others. And, Señor Thompson ... it will give you time to talk to him one-on-one about his recovery ... physically and mentally."

The next day, as John Thompson sits next to the bed, Henry begins to regain a semi-conscious state. He calls for Carmen and Juanita several times before John puts his hand on Henry's and begins talking to him in a low voice. "How are you, Henry? It's me, John. Can you hear me?"

Henry turns his head toward John and responds in a weak voice. "John, where's Carmen and Juanita?"

"We can talk about that later, Henry. First you must get well, get stronger."

Henry makes a brief struggle to sit up and realizes he is restrained. "What's this? Why am I tied down?"

"You were reacting violently, Henry. The Doctor had to do it to keep you from tearing your wounds open."

After struggling against the straps several more times, Henry lies his head back on the pillow and looks at the ceiling for a moment, seemingly relaxed. "I can only remember the revolutionaries coming into the car ..." Henry then instantly recalls Carmen and Juanita hiding in the compartment. "What happened to them? Where are they, John? Tell me!" Henry again struggles violently against the straps to the point of exhaustion as he yells for Carmen and Juanita.

The nurses respond quickly per Doctor Valdez's orders, and give Henry another shot of morphine to calm him.

"I'm afraid you're going to have to leave him for now, Señor Thompson. He needs to rest!"

John Thompson slowly leaves the room, pondering how he is going to tell Henry, if Henry doesn't already assume that his wife and daughter have been murdered by Poncho Diaz's "butcher," Fierro. He just knows Henry won't take this information well. Instantly a thought occurs to him. "If I can get Colonel Novak involved, he might be able to make a difference in Henry's reaction."

John Thompson immediately leaves the hospital and telegraphs the situation to Colonel Novak, who has been appointed as Undersecretary in the United States Department of Interior, Washington D.C..

As John waits for a response to his telegram, he continues to sit with Henry daily. It has been more than two weeks since Henry has sustained his wounds, which are healing fast under bed restrictions. Still, Doctor Valdez wants Henry semi-conscious for just one more week. John knows he soon has to reveal to Henry what happened at the train attack. He makes the decision to tell Henry four days prior to the doctors decision to take Henry off the morphine. That day arrives quickly.

"Henry, you're healing well. You should be able to leave the hospital in another week or so," whispers John into Henry's ear.

Henry awakes into a lazy consciousness. "John, where's Carmen and Juanita?"

"We must talk about that, Henry."

"Are they okay? I can't remember what happened to them."

John hesitates as he wonders how he should continue. There's no easy way to tell him this, he thinks. He then talks gently to Henry. "Henry, I don't know how to tell you this, but I must."

"Tell me what, John?" responds Henry in a half conscious voice.

Again John Thompson hesitates, then clears his throat. "Juanita and Carmen are not with us any longer, Henry."

Henry doesn't respond for a moment, then as if everything clearly registers within his mind he responds with hostility and anger. His voice becomes forcibly stronger and he struggles violently against the straps. "What do you mean they're not with us? What the hell are you saying?"

John has to force his words out as tears come to his eyes. "Henry, Juanita and Carmen were killed during the attack on the train. I'm sorry, Henry."

Henry becomes frantic. His anger and sorrow combine as he screams to be released and struggles violently against the straps. "I'll kill those bastards! I'll kill those murdering bastards!" Suddenly his resistance wanes and he begins to cry profusely as he has used up all his physical and emotional strength in one burst of hatred. Again the nurses give him another shot of morphine to calm him and he falls into a state of unconsciousness.

John Thompson requests to see the doctor, who later comes into the room. "I don't know what to do now, Doctor. He's now aware of the loss of his wife and daughter, but I'm afraid he may withdraw into a state of shock, or deep depression, or even do something drastic," relates John in a voice that shows fear and worry.

"You stated earlier that you had written to his Army Commander back in the United States. Have you heard from him?"

"No. Not yet."

"Well, your answer may be in Henry's response to that telegram. He just may gain some strength and hope from that. I've witnessed soldiers responding to a renewed call to duty in battle after serious personal losses. Possibly this Colonel can instill some of that military discipline and moral support in Henry's case."

"I'm afraid to think what will happen if this doesn't work," adds John Thompson in a sympathetic tone. Doctor Valdez shakes his head.

John continues to visit Henry every day, and sits by his bed silently as Henry will not talk. Every attempt to get Henry to respond to a comment or a question is the same. Henry remains silent and disinterested, even after the discontinued use of morphine. It appears that Henry has withdrawn into the deepest and most remote part of his subconscious mind.

Except for his left arm, Henry's wounds have healed well and the doctor indicates to John Thompson that Henry will be eligible for discharge in one week.

It has been two weeks since John Thompson has sent the telegraph to Colonel Novak and he is beginning to get concerned. John had planned to go down to the Telegraph office that afternoon, when a message comes from a nurse that he has a message from the United States. John instantly rushes down to the telegraph office. It is there ... Colonel Novak's telegram.

"John Thompson ...

Response to tragedy ... tell Henry not to forget ... his friends in the Tenth Cavalry ... Sergeant Thomas sends sympathy ... as do I ... and others ... remind him adversity has ... brought him character before ... we have faith in him ... to carry on ... for himself and his wife and daughter ... his courage has never failed him ... when he is ready ... I invite him to Washington ... men of the Tenth are proud ... of him and his accomplishments in social justice ... His bravery is unparalleled ... Sincerely ... Colonel Ben Novak."

John Thompson's face lights up with a smile as he reads the telegram. "Henry will know his unit still thinks well of him. God, I hope this will reach his desire to live."

That evening John enters Henry's room and takes his usual seat next to the bed. Henry, still strapped, lies silently, looking at the ceiling.

"How're you doing tonight, Henry?"

Henry doesn't respond.

John takes out the telegram he received from Colonel Novak. "Henry, I'd like to read you something from a friend of yours back in Washington, D.C."

Henry remains motionless as John Thompson clears his throat. "It's from Colonel Novak," adds John calmly.

Henry's head turns slightly toward John.

"I'll read what he says." John reads the telegram slowly and clearly. Each word seems to draw Henry's attention as John reads on. When he finishes reading, John sits quietly hoping for a positive response. Henry stares at the ceiling and doesn't say anything. After an hour of silence, John says goodnight to Henry. "I'll see you tomorrow, Henry," then leaves the room.

The next morning John enters Henry's room and stops. He is stunned and amazed as he witnesses Henry calmly talking to the nurse. John quickly backs out of the room without Henry seeing him. "What's happened?" John asks himself as he waits for the nurse to leave the room.

As the nurse leaves, John stops her in the hallway. "Is he okay? I thought I heard him talking to you."

"You did!" replies the nurse. "He just started talking like a normal person when I went in to change his bed pan this morning. He seems fine."

"You mean he isn't ranting and raving ... going to kill somebody or anything like that?"

"No!" replies the nurse again. "He just asked me how his wounds were healing and I told him fine."

John smiles. "Can I go in there now?"

"Sure. Just don't upset him."

John walks in as Henry turns his head. "Good morning, Henry."

Henry gives a slight smile and answers in a monotone voice, "Morning, John."

"How you feeling, Henry? You're looking stronger every day."

"Ya, the nurse just told me I might be leaving in a few days." Both men are quiet for a moment before Henry speaks. "Excuse my behavior, John. It's just that it's taken me some time to accept what has happened ... you know, about Carmen and Juanita."

"I fully understand, Henry."

"I guess I'll be able to continue on for them. At first I just thought of giving up. I felt hopeless and desperate, maybe even self-centered at my own sadness. I had a lot to think about lying here, especially after you read that telegram from Colonel Novak. Did he really write that?"

John Thompson feels relieved to hear Henry talking rationally. "He sure did, Henry. I sent him a telegram a couple of weeks ago and this was his response. Your friends in the Tenth Cavalry apparently miss you."

Henry smiles slightly, then responds, "I miss them too. I know it's going to take me some time to get over this loss, but if I can summon the courage I will carry on as long as I can for ... Juanita and Carmen. At the Judgment Day I want them to be proud of me."

"They will be, Henry. We have a lot of work that Juanita started that still needs direction."

Henry then looks serious as he puts his hand out to John Thompson. "Tell me, John. Who took care of the burial and where are they?"

"I did, Henry. I had their bodies brought back to Nuevo Laredo. They're buried at the Catholic cemetery about a mile from your house."

Henry squeezes John's hand, much as Juanita used to do to him. "Thank you, John. Maybe you'll take me there when I get out of here."

"First thing, Henry."

Colonel Novak's letter did have an impact on Henry's attitude and recovery, but a more compelling desire sustained his quick recovery, a desire for retribution. Henry thinks about this as John Thompson and he travel on the train back to Nuevo Laredo and then to the cemetery where Carmen and Juanita are buried.

As Henry walks to the grave sites his resentments and feelings of revulsion surface. He looks at the inscriptions on the gravestones as his soul grieves his loss.

JUANITA WASHINGTON

1875-1915

CARMEN WASHINGTON

1898-1915

REST-GOD WILL GIVE YOU ULTIMATE PEACE

Henry kneels by the graves and is quiet for a moment. He talks softly and quietly, as if he were carrying on a conversation with Carmen and Juanita. Tears form in the corners of his eyes as his voice starts to choke. "I pledge to you, my darlings, on my life, I will avenge your deaths."

CHAPTER TWENTY-SIX
EL PRESIDENTE'S COMMITMENT

Through Foreign and American financial sponsorship of the Mexicana/Americana Institute, Henry is able to continue his work. He also carries enough influence through that institution to gain a private hearing on the deaths of Juanita and Carmen with, then President of Mexico, General Victoriano Camillo.

Henry's influence through all the years he has been in Mexico has remained solid. He has a well-deserved reputation as a fair and honest man, and this image contributes to his ability to meet with and have the Ambassador to the United States, Mr. James Lind, present during the meeting.

President Camillo sits at the head of the table with two of his Justice Ministers present, as Henry and Ambassador Lind enter the Presidential office.

"Gentlemen, it is good to see you. Mr. Lind, will you please introduce your associate," invites President Camillo.

Mr. Lind introduces Henry and mentions some political pleasantries.

"How is it that I might help you, gentlemen?"

Henry speaks first. "Mr. President, as an American who took up residency in Mexico more than twenty years ago, I have some grave concerns about law and order in this country. I also recently suffered a serious personal loss; namely the murder of my wife and daughter at the hands of Diaz's revolutionaries."

President Camillo listens intently as Henry continues to address him. "As you may know, Poncho Diaz's soldiers first raped my wife and daughter, then brutally killed them. I want to know personally, from you, what you intend to do about this."

President Camillo acknowledges his concern. "Yes, Mr. Washington. I'm aware of your personal loss and I am truly sorry. We are doing everything possible to bring this bandit to justice. He is very elusive but we are concentrating our efforts solely on his capture. We want this man also. Please be patient."

Henry becomes irritated by the apparent intention of President Camillo to pacify him. "Patient! I've been patient! It's been more than a year now and I've seen no effort on the government's part to arrest this man. I know where he lives, certainly you do also ... or, if not, you should."

President Camillo, embarrassed by Henry's statement, has an immediate sense of irritation and animosity, even though, what Henry has said is in fact the truth. "Mr. Washington! Did you come all this way to insult me and my government? If so, I can see this is a waste of my important time. I have told you what we intend to do and ..."

Henry stands up. Disgusted and angry, he interrupts and speaks passionately, and from President Camillo's point of view, undiplomatically. "This government! This Revolution! Both sides ... represent little more than a bunch of greedy, murderous, self-centered bastards! I've spent a good part of my life in Mexico working for truth and justice and have yet to meet a government official or a revolutionary leader who is trustworthy!"

Henry's emotional state is quickly getting out of control as the Ambassador tries to calm him. Henry has said what he wants to say, with the exception of one last statement. "Mr. President! Since you can't take Diaz out of commission, I will! I mean that! I pledge that on the graves of my wife and daughter!"

President Camillo doesn't respond to Henry's outburst, but motions to his two ministers to follow him out of the room. Ambassador Lind moves to appease the Mexican President as Henry turns to him. "And you stay out of this, Mr. Lind, you phony ass!"

Two days later Henry is back in his office at the Mexicana/Americana Institute. John Thompson walks in and sits down in a chair at the front of Henry's desk. John says nothing, just stares at Henry silently, which ultimately irritates Henry.

"What the hell are you staring at me for, John?"

"Well, it appears you certainly made an embarrassment of yourself in front of the President of Mexico, and in turn, the Institute."

Henry defends his position adamantly. "You know, John, if it weren't for the seriousness of these atrocities, and I'm not just talking about Carmen and Juanita, I'm talking about the people of Mexico, this government ... this whole mess would be a damn joke!"

"Henry, calm down! Technically, I agree, but I also have word that the Camillo government will not last long. There is nothing the Federales or President Camillo could have done on your behalf. Just now, as we speak, Diaz has taken Chihuahua City with his rag-tag division of the North. It's just a matter of months before those two have control of all of Mexico. There's nothing you can do!"

"Well, John. How about the United States? What's President Wilson's position? What about U.S. intervention? General Funstun has seven-thousand United States troops outside Vera Cruz ..."

John Thompson speaks in a serious tone as he tries to relate to Henry the seriousness of the situation and that Mexicana/Americana Institute itself is targeted for elimination by

Diaz's forces. "I doubt intervention, Henry. President Wilson is only trying to protect what American interests there are in Mexico. He doesn't want a war!"

John gets up and leans over Henry's desk. "I don't think the Revolutionaries want a war with the United States either."

Henry, aggravated at the current political situation and the helplessness he feels, talks with a feeling of revulsion. "What about that bastard, Diaz? Who's going to bring him to justice?"

John Thompson stands up, walks back to his chair and sits down. "Probably no one."

"No one!" screams Henry.

"Let me say something, Henry, without you interrupting. First, the statement you made at the meeting with President Camillo has surely gotten back to Poncho Diaz. Probably sent to him by the Justice Ministers themselves."

"And number two?" interjects Henry.

"Number two is Americans are not popular here right now, especially with the Revolutionary leadership. So, if the Revolutionaries win, which they will, who knows what will happen to all American businesses and American citizens? For that matter, you and me!"

Henry remains quiet as he listens to, and thinks about the words John is saying.

"No American or American business is safe in Mexico, Henry. Poncho Diaz set you up for a kill once and, if he knows you are alive, which I'm sure he does by now, he'll come after you again. And he'll do it with aggravated personal vengeance, especially after you vowed to bring him to justice, which I believe you meant death by your own hands. Do you understand what I'm trying to say to you?"

Henry stands up as he grabs his still injured left arm and paces a few steps back and forth, angry at the whole

Mexican political situation. "Yes, it's true, that is my intention, John. If no one else can do it, I will. I made a pledge on the graves of my wife and daughter. I intend to keep it or die trying."

"I understand your desire for justice, Henry. If anyone deserves justice in this life it is certainly you."

John looks at Henry studiously for a minute as both men remain silent. Finally John continues, "What President Camillo told you is true."

Henry looks at John with a feeling of helplessness.

"You are but one man, Henry. The Federales, the Rurales, the Cientificos, and many others have tried to capture or kill Poncho Diaz. None have succeeded. Do you get the meaning? Do you realize Diaz's power?"

Henry walks back to his desk and sits down slowly and quietly.

"What are you thinking, Henry?"

"Nothing, John. Just thinking."

"You know we are moving this company out of Mexico to Venezuela, for obvious reasons ... don't you?"

Henry nods his head, but is immersed in his own thoughts.

"Forget about vengeance, Henry. You've done well with your career and implemented many ideas and programs that can be used in Venezuela and, maybe again, later be used in Mexico. Don't go out and do something stupid, like get yourself killed!"

Henry remains silent, to the point of irritating John.

"Damn it, Henry! Get Diaz out of your head! You must go on with your life ... for the sake of Carmen and Juanita ... and others. They would expect that of you. I don't like what I see you becoming."

Henry leans forward on his desk, his face stern as he looks John Thompson in the eyes; his voice takes on an emphatic tone as he blurts out the name, "Jesus Salas Barraza!"

Surprised, John looks at Henry quizzically. "Who? Jesus Barraza. Who's that?"

"Jesus Salas Barraza. You know, John, the state legislator from Durango. I must meet with him! Soon! At least before we leave for Venezuela."

"Are you talking about the Counter-Revolutionary? The one that's had a personal feud with Diaz over the years?"

"That's right John, that's to whom I'm referring."

"Damn, Henry. You're something else. I think you better take a good look at what you're getting yourself into!"

"I am, John. I certainly am!"

After three months of intensive preparation, the Mexicana/Americana Institute is packed and ready to move via ship to Venezuela. All business records, contracts, land and legal descriptions, including original titles, are smuggled out of Mexico before a raid by any factions of the Revolutionary forces can get to them.

Most of the Institute's personnel have decided to follow the movement of the organization to Venezuela and are at the Shipping Port in Tampico, Mexico the evening of departure.

The ship is scheduled for departure that evening at six o'clock and by five o'clock all are on board with the exception of Henry. He is still on the dock talking with Jesus Barraza, a distinguished looking and well respected businessman/politician from Durango. Henry is seated alone with Jesus Barraza in the back seat of his black Cadillac as they talk privately under the watchful eyes of Barraza's bodyguards.

Finally John Thompson yells from the deck of the ship to Henry. "Henry! Finish your conversation. It's about time to leave!"

Henry momentarily turns away from Jesus Barraza and yells back to John Thompson. "Just hang on! I'll be there in a moment!" Henry turns back to Barraza and speaks firmly, with conviction. "It's settled then! You can handle all the details?"

Jesus Barraza places his hands on Henry's shoulders and looks at him seriously. "I will do that, Señor Washington! It will be a glorious day. Not only for you and me, but for all of Mexico!"

"You will telegraph me in Caracas?" asks Henry in a serious voice.

"That I will, Señor! You can be assured!"

Henry and Jesus Barraza get out of the car, give each other a firm hug of commitment, and smile at one another. "Goodbye, Señor Barraza," says Henry graciously. "I'll wait for word from you."

"Goodbye, Señor Washington. Have a pleasant and safe trip. You have nothing more to worry about."

Henry walks up the gang plank confidently, a smile on his face as he yells to John Thompson, "Let's go to Venezuela, John!"

CHAPTER TWENTY-SEVEN
MORTAL CONSCIOUSNESS

Henry watches from aboard ship as Jesus Barraza drives away. His emotions are mixed as he wrestles with his moral convictions and questions his decision to make a pact with the Representative from Durango. On one hand Henry has pledged to Carmen and Juanita revenge for their brutal deaths, but on the other hand, he remembers what Bishop Jackson once told him; "vengeance lay only in the hands of God." But at this point Henry has no choice in the matter. It is out of his control now and, in a sense he rationalizes, that destiny will take its course.

For the next two years Henry and John Thompson work diligently on changing the Institute's mission for adaptation in Venezuela and establish the local groundwork for public education and land reform. Both Henry and John talk frequently about the day they will return to Mexico, but they also realize that unless the protagonists of the Mexican Revolution are killed or put in jail, their return to Mexico is unlikely.

Jesus Barraza is ruthless in his pursuit of Poncho Diaz. His Counter Revolutionary force is well trained and hand selected. Many individual people and foreign corporations have a vested interest in Barraza's success as he is able to solicit several million dollars in contributions. His success in restructuring a legitimate state government in his own province is mainly based on his reputation as an honest and sincere advocate of Constitutional Reform, much which was the groundwork of Juanita and Henry.

Barraza and his supporters plan their movements against Poncho Diaz's forces well. They monitor his every movement and calculate a precise timetable on Diaz's travels. After more than a year of secret meetings with former Diaz soldiers, who themselves are discouraged by Diaz's disorganized and self-centered leadership, these disgruntled men gladly contribute information on Diaz's daily activities.

Poncho Diaz has survived many attempts on his life through the years and knows well the need for loyal bodyguards and changing of his daily routines. However, one routine that he rarely changes is his one hour Sunday morning trip into the village of Sansio, Mexico. It is here that he has established a school for the children and has paid all the local citizenry annual payments. This token act of good will was designed to buy village loyalty and thus, surround himself with what he thinks will be a secure enclave of local populace support.

It is a beautiful Sunday morning. A slight breeze from the northwest carries a fresh aroma of flowers down from the mountains as Diaz travels down the dirt road to his town.

Four bodyguards squint their eyes against the bright sun as they ride on the running boards of the new Dodge car, two on each side of the car. The trail of dust can be seen from miles away as the car makes its way down the winding foothills on the dirt road entering Sansio, Mexico.

There was a time when every villager would run to the roadside to wave at Poncho Diaz, but on this day only a few line the road and they all stand silent.

Inside the car are two more bodyguards well armed with automatic weapons and straps of ammunition over their shoulders. The driver turns to Poncho Diaz on the passenger side and comments, "Mr. General! Did you ever think you would be traveling at forty-five-miles-an-hour?"

Diaz gives a grunt as his eyes are focused on the road and town ahead.

"In a machine? We make history, right, General?" continues the driver, but getting no response.

It is ten-thirty a.m. as the new Dodge car enters the city of Sansio. None of the peons have ever seen anything like this new, fancy, driving machine, which Diaz obtained only five days prior from the United States. As is his normal procedure, Diaz instructs the driver to continue at a fast, steady pace of thirty-miles-per-hour, a cautionary measure in case of unsuspected trouble.

Diaz begins his usual waving at the sparse crowd, but realizes something is wrong when not one of the people cheer. As the vehicle slows to turn a sharp ninety-degree-angle on the street next to a closed Cantina, Diaz looks around, suspicious at what he sees. Immediately he comments in a loud voice, "It's too quiet! There are no people cheering me!"

Diaz barely utters these words when the crack of rifle fire breaks the surrounding silence. Blam! Blam! Blam! A barrage of gunfire comes from the Cantina and three adobe buildings across the street. Bullets come ripping into the car from a three-way crossfire and into the exposed bodyguards on the running boards. As the bodyguards fall to the street the driver is hit in the head, causing the car to ram into a wooden water trough, then into an adobe building.

Diaz attempts to duck down and return the gunfire, but bullets penetrate the car doors and catch him in the chest, neck, and arm. The barrage continues for another minute, this time hitting Poncho Diaz in the side of the head below the ear and again in the chest. As suddenly as it started, all is quiet. Not even the sound of a bird can be heard as the passenger door of the Dodge slowly opens. Again, there is silence until a low, guttural moan comes from the vehicle.

Two men dressed in white pajama type clothing walk slowly to the car, red bandanas covering their faces, and guns pointed at the ready. As one assassin checks out the bodies of the guards strung out on the street, another cautiously approaches the Dodge. A loud moan comes from the passenger side of the car as the assassin approaches. Blam! Blam! Two more shots ring out in the quiet solitude of the street.

There are a few more moments of silence as the peons start to peek out from behind hidden crevices in their homes and adjacent buildings. Finally the assassin, in an act of bravado, pulls Poncho Diaz's blood covered body out of the car. He drags him into the center of the street, then aims his pistol at the back of Diaz's head. Blam! One shot sounds, echoing much like the gong of a tower bell. The assassin looks around for a few seconds, then waves his pistol and exclaims loudly, "Diaz is dead! Viva La Mexico! Viva La Mexico!"

Both assassins appear boldly on the street, the other assassins still hiding in the buildings disappear into a back street behind the Cantina. Local villagers, men, women, and some children, slowly approach the car, keeping at a distance from Poncho Diaz's body. They all remain silent as they view his bullet ridden body. After more than five minutes of observation the peons turn away, one by one, leaving Diaz's body where it lay.

It is later that afternoon that the Mexican soldiers arrive. Diaz's body, covered with dry blood and dirt, is swarming with flies. The Federale Captain, a smile on his face, yells his orders, "Put the Bastard in a wooden box and cover him. We will take him and the car to Mexico City for public display! Hurry! Hurry!"

Henry is feverishly writing a final draft on proposed legislation in preparation for a meeting on the morning of July 30, 1923. He and John are to meet with the Consulate General of Venezuela, a meeting he has been looking forward to since his arrival more than two years ago. Suddenly a knock on his door breaks his concentration.

"Come in!" exclaims Henry in a firm moderate tone of voice.

Henry's secretary enters and with a sense of urgency displays a telegram. "Señor Washington, excuse me. There is a telegram for you! It is from Mexico. It appears important."

Henry, somewhat anxious and surprised, looks at her seriously as he stands up behind his desk, then comes to meet her. "Thank you, Señora! That will be all."

Henry is anxious as he quickly tears open the telegram and slowly walks back to his chair. As he sits down, his hands tremble slightly in anticipation of its contents. He reads the telegram with deliberation.

"Señor Washington ... it may be of interest ... Poncho Diaz was assassinated ... in the City of Sansio, Mexico, ... morning of July 20th,

... Respectfully yours ... Jesus Salas Barraza"

Henry takes a deep breath as his hands drop to the desk. He first looks at the ceiling, then dropping his head to his arms, he begins to cry. It is a quiet sob, one of both joy and sadness. He feels an emotion which comes with the loss of that which is loved and in the afterthoughts of that which is hated. He unconsciously crumples the telegram with his right fist, sits back in his chair and stares at the office wall. For more than an hour he reviews all the events that have led up to this message. His anger seems unimportant now and the hurt that he has carried for more than three years turns into a sense of guilt and worry. "What purpose has my life carried?" he asks himself in a whisper.

Henry's self-review ends with a knock on the door. Without waiting for an answer John Thompson walks in. Henry's red eyes openly display his emotional state.

"Henry! Are you okay?" inquires John Thompson.

"Yes, John. I'm alright. I've almost got the draft ready."

John, unaware of the telegram, continues in a jovial manner. "You've been working too hard, Henry. Forget the draft for a moment. I've got something else to tell you!"

Henry sits up in a more erect business-like manner. He looks at John Thompson in a confused way. "What's more important than this draft?"

John smiles, "How'd you like to take a trip …. a permanent one?"

Henry isn't in a joking mood and replies quite seriously, "What do you mean, John? A trip? Where?"

"The United States!"

Henry looks at John with skepticism and a squint in his eyes. "The United States? What the hell you talking about? Is this another one of your jokes?"

"No, Henry. Not quite."

"You mean the United States of America?" inquires Henry with a voice inflection.

"That's exactly what I mean! Is there any other?"

John sits down in a chair immediately in front of Henry's desk feeling confident the information he is about to tell Henry will be well received. He is happy for Henry, as he has always held Henry in high regard, both personally and professionally.

Henry is still somewhat stunned and remains quiet as John continues to explain the turn of events.

"I talked with a friend of yours this morning on the new long distant telephone system and your name came up."

Henry, curious and now alert, interrupts. "A friend of mine? Where? In Mexico?"

John hesitates. "No, in the United States," replies John as he quickly wonders why Henry would refer to Mexico, but just as quickly brushes Henry's question off and continues with a pleasant smile. "A Commander of yours … Colonel Novak!"

Henry perks up as he leans over his desk in a quiet state of surprise, acting anxious. "Colonel Novak! Are you serious? What did he say?"

John starts to relate the conversation in a calm, sincere manner. "We both think it's time for you to go back home. He has a position for you in Washington, D.C., as an assistant at the Department of Interior."

Henry encouraged, takes a deep breath, then sighs as he shakes his head. "I don't believe this!"

"It's true, Henry," continues John. "He was appointed Secretary of the Department of the Interior, United States of America ... and he has a position there for you, if you want it."

"Damn!" exclaims Henry in a moment of elation and excitement. "This is too much to take in one day! An opportunity to go back to America and the death of Poncho Diaz."

John Thompson's smile drops from his face at the mention of Poncho Diaz. He looks at Henry with serious concern. "What do you mean ... the death of Poncho Diaz?"

Henry, reacts somewhat reluctantly, and with a certain uneasiness picks up the crumpled telegram. "This!" states Henry in a calm, contrite voice.

John Thompson reads the telegram, then looks at Henry with shock and curiosity, "When did you receive this?"

"About an hour ago," replies Henry.

John Thompson shakes his head and quickly voices his concern. "What happened? Did you have anything ..."

Henry acts with hostility and quickly interrupts, cutting off John's words. "We can talk about that later, John! I want to know more about Colonel Novak. What did he say?"

John looks in silence at the telegram then to Henry, his thoughts concentrating on the meaning of the telegram.

"John! We can talk about the telegram later!" demands Henry. "Tell me about Colonel Novak. How is he?"

John continues to gaze back and forth between Henry and looking at the telegram as he answers. "He requests your answer. The Institute will miss you, but we both think this may be a new calling for you."

Henry relaxes and thinks only for a brief moment as he responds. "I am, John! I'm interested! It's been years since I've been there. God! It's been years. I'm more than ready to return to America!"

John gets up, walks over to Henry and shakes his hand firmly and compassionately. "Let's finish this meeting with the Consulate General and then make the necessary preparations for you to go home."

Just over two months later, on October 2, 1923, Henry's ship floats into the Potomac River outside Washington, D.C. from the Port of New Jersey. At sixty-seven-years of age, Henry looks distinguished in his dark gray suit and neatly trimmed gray hair. His emotions are mixed between anxiety and anticipation. He feels a longing desire to return to the United States, yet has a fearful feeling of dread of what may await him on his return.

At five o'clock in the afternoon the ship pulls in sight of the Potomac Port. Henry feels a sense of faith and trust in his decision to return home and there, on the dock, is Colonel Novak waving. For the first time in more than forty years Henry sees his beloved and respected former Regimental Commander. Henry's heart beats faster as a feeling of delight comes over him. His hopes and desires reconnect a lost sense of pride at the sight of the nation's Capitol and his love for the country he once served.

Henry begins to yell and wave frantically at Colonel Novak, who can't help but notice Henry by his exuberance. Henry is standing by the gang plank as the ship docks, anxiously waiting to see his ex-Commander and now, loyal friend.

As the ship docks and the gang plank falls, Henry rushes toward Colonel Novak. When he reaches a point of within four feet of the Colonel, Henry stops and gives a formal salute. As the old feelings emerge, tears of compassion form at the corners of his eyes. "Colonel Novak, Sir! It's so good to see you again!"

Colonel Novak's respect and affection for Henry are apparent as he quickly returns an informal salute and greets Henry with a smile. "Henry, you son-of-a-gun! Still full of soldier; still saluting. But damn! You look great!"

Henry and Colonel Novak shake hands and embrace. Henry is excited and emotional as he begins the conversation. "It's good to see you again, Sir! And I appreciate this opportunity to work with you."

"Same here, Henry. Now let's get your bags. We still have time to show you your new office and where you'll be working. Then we can have dinner and you can tell me about your experiences in Mexico." Colonel Novak breaks his conversation and talks to Henry in a sympathetic manner. "I was so sorry to hear of your family. It's a tragic loss."

Henry reacts with a calm sense of appreciation at the Colonel's condolence. "Thank you, Sir. It's been a lonely existence without them. There's not a day that goes by without Juanita and Carmen in my thoughts."

Colonel Novak puts his hand on Henry's back and in a moment of empathy changes the subject. "Com'on Henry, let's take a drive."

Henry and Colonel Novak talk enthusiastically about their past experiences as they make their way into the nation's Capitol. The evening sunset enhances the white stone buildings of Washington, D.C.

Henry reminisces as they drive by the Washington Monument and Lincoln's tomb. A renewed sense of pride strikes deep into his soul. "It feels so good to be home! I didn't know I missed the United States so much," comments Henry as he gazes at the sites.

Colonel Novak feels a sense of fulfillment as he watches Henry's passion develop. "Civilian life just doesn't have the same sense of duty and excitement, does it, Henry?"

"It sure doesn't, Sir."

"Henry, do you remember the emblem of the Tenth Cavalry?"

"You bet I do, Colonel."

"Well, I have a surprise for you. I've got one on my office wall and I had one made for your office as well. I think you're going to like what I've lined up for you."

Henry looks at Colonel Novak with a curious glance. "And may I ask you what that is? I'm still not clear as to what my assignment will be, Colonel."

"Tell you what, Henry. When we get into the office I'll give you a quick tour and brief you on your duties."

Henry, anxious to learn more about his new position, acts conservatively excited. "I'd like that, Colonel."

Colonel Novak parks his car in front of the Department of Interior building. Henry anxiously opens the passenger door, gets out and looks around. "I just can't believe I'm here, Colonel. I feel like I've never left!"

"Let's go inside, Henry. We can get down to business there."

Henry continues to look around in child-like awe as he feels a rebirth of emotions. As they approach the large doors to Colonel Novak's office, Henry notices the name plate firmly attached to the door. "Secretary of the Interior," murmurs Henry in a low, but distinct voice. "That's quite an impressive title, Colonel."

"Depends on how you look at it, Henry. Com'on, let's go inside. I think you'll be more impressed with what's there."

Colonel Novak opens the door and motions to Henry to go in. "After you, Lieutenant!"

Henry walks in cautiously. Suddenly there is a gigantic yell. "SURPRISE!" Henry is joyously greeted by seventeen surviving soldiers of the Tenth United States Cavalry, including Sergeant Thomas. Henry is shocked as Sergeant Emanuel Thomas is the first to walk up to him, shake his hand, and give him a compassionate hug.

Sergeant Thomas then salutes and speaks in a military command voice, but with affection. "Welcome home, Suh!"

Henry is full of compassion and emotion, to the point of tears forming in his eyes as he returns a brief salute. Henry tries to respond, but at first chokes. "Sergeant ..." Henry clears his throat. "Sergeant Thomas ... you five-foot-two renegade! I've thought about you often."

Henry and Sergeant Thomas shake hands firmly and smile at one another as the other members of the old H Company quickly gather around Henry to pay their respects and homecoming welcomes. Henry, Colonel Novak, Sergeant Thomas, and the other men of the Tenth, talk and share experiences into the early morning hours. Henry's eyes show a spirit and a twinkle of joy usually reserved for small children at Christmas. Henry is finally home.

For the next three years Henry works as Special Projects Coordinator under the direction of Colonel Novak. He establishes a program of education for disadvantaged children, at first in the Washington, D.C. area, and then on a national level. This includes working with the development of children's organizations, especially orphanages.

After Henry leaves the Service of the United States Government, he continues his private life working for the human rights of all people, especially orphaned children.

It is late Sunday morning in May of 1948. Henry is seated in a chair at the Episcopalian Church in north Washington, D.C.. Ten children are gathered around him, mesmerized by a story Henry has been reading. One of the children raises her hand to ask a question. Henry gives no response. The children look at one another, at first with concern, then fear.

"Johnny, go get Bishop Turner!" screams the girl.

Johnny runs out of the room as the children slowly get up and back near the door.

Bishop Turner rushes into the room, grabs Henry's hand and takes his pulse.

"Is he okay?" inquires one of the children in a low voice.

"You children better leave now," states Bishop Turner in a firm, compassionate tone of voice.

The children back slowly out of the room, their eyes focused on Henry as they leave.

The next day, Bishop Turner is sitting at a table in the Coroner's office as the County Coroner walks in. The Coroner begins to question Bishop Turner on Henry's vital statistics. "Bishop Turner, the name of the deceased is Henry Washington, correct?"

"Yes," answers Bishop Turner.

"And his date of birth?"

"October, 1854."

"Marital status?" inquires the Coroner.

"Married. Wife and daughter deceased."

"Cause of death?

"Don't know, no signs of heart attack. Call it a broken heart," says Bishop Turner.

"His main occupation, Bishop ... Mexican businessman, right?"

"No!" replies Bishop Turner boldly. "Put his occupation as a First Lieutenant, Tenth United States Cavalry, United States Army."

The Coroner looks at Bishop Turner, "I'm confused."

"Don't be," says Bishop Turner.

"Alright. Burial? Arlington National Cemetery I presume since he was an army officer?"

"No, not this officer."

The Coroner acts frustrated by Bishop Turner's answer. "Really! Why not?"

"To be honest, he doesn't qualify. We're taking his body back to his birthplace in Georgia."

"Why doesn't he qualify for Arlington National Cemetery?" inquires the Coroner.

"A long story of questionable justice," answers the Bishop as he signs the Death Certificate.

Henry was buried in a small cemetery ten miles outside of Atlanta, Georgia. The inscription on his small, white tombstone simply reads:

LIEUTENANT HENRY WASHINGTON
TENTH UNITED STATES CAVALRY
1854 – 1948

Below that inscription someone later added an epithet:

"I wonts to be a Union soldier, Ma. I wonts to fight to free you!"

THE END

LaVergne, TN USA
04 December 2009
165965LV00001B/18/A